Contents

The Complete Screech Owls

Volume 2

Roy MacGregor

McCLELLAND & STEWART

Library and Archives Canada Cataloguing in Publication

MacGregor, Roy, 1948–
The complete Screech Owls / written by Roy MacGregor.

Contents: v. 1. Mystery at Lake Placid – The night they stole the Stanley Cup –
The Screech Owls' northern adventure – Murder at hockey camp –
v. 2. Kidnapped in Sweden – Terror in Florida – The Quebec City crisis –
The Screech Owls' home loss.
ISBN 13: 0-7710-5484-6 (v. 1) · ISBN 10: 0-7710-5484-X (v. 1)
ISBN 13: 0-7710-5486-0 (v. 2) · ISBN 10: 0-7710-5486-6 (v. 2)

I. Title.

PS8575.G84C64 2005   jC813'.54   C2005-903880-2

We acknowledge the financial support of the Government of Canada through the
Book Publishing Industry Development Program and that of the Government of
Ontario through the Ontario Media Development Corporation's Ontario Book
Initiative. We further acknowledge the support of the Canada Council for the Arts
and the Ontario Arts Council for our publishing program.

Typeset in Bembo by M&S, Toronto
Printed and bound in Canada
Cover illustration by Sue Todd

This book is printed on acid-free paper that is 100% recycled,
ancient-forest friendly (100% post-consumer recycled).

McClelland & Stewart Ltd.
75 Sherbourne Street
Toronto, Ontario
M5A 2P9
www.mcclelland.com

1 2 3 4 5   10 09 08 07 06

Kidnapped in Sweden

1

"EEE-AWWW-KEEE!"

The moment Travis Lindsay heard the ridiculous yell, he closed his eyes and shook his head. It meant the Screech Owls' big defenceman, Wayne Nishikawa, had come up with a new call.

"EEEE-AWWW-KEEE!"

Nish had certainly been this loud before. He'd screamed worse when he fell through the ice on his snowmobile when the Owls had gone up north, and he'd yelped in real terror that day at summer hockey camp when he'd gone skinny-dipping with the snapping turtle. But the biggest difference was that this time Nish's call was filled with joy rather than horror.

Nish, stripped naked again in the middle of a lake, was having the time of his life.

"EEEE-AWWW-KEEE!"

This time, however, the lake was frozen solid, and Nish *wanted* the world to see him! This time he was fully expected

to have absolutely nothing on, and this time he didn't have to
worry about drowning or an attack from a snapping turtle!

Did they have snapping turtles in Sweden? Travis wondered.

He shivered. He, too, was bare naked, and on a day so cold
he couldn't even breathe through his nose. If they did have
snapping turtles, Travis thought, there was nothing to worry
about today. If one was hiding anywhere around here, it would
be suffering from lockjaw, frozen solid!

Travis couldn't believe how quickly the air could change
from unbearable heat to unbearable cold. A moment ago the
sweat had been pouring off his face so fast it seemed as if Lars
Johanssen, the Owls' nifty little defenceman, had dumped the
bucket of water over Travis's head instead of over the white-
hot rocks of the club sauna. The water had sizzled and steamed
and the temperature had risen so dramatically that Travis had
trouble breathing.

Now, standing outdoors, naked and skinny as the birch trees
that grew down to the edge of this frozen Scandinavian lake, he
had trouble breathing again. Travis's nostrils were frozen shut.
He was breathing through his mouth and the air was coming
out in a fog as thick as the exhaust from his father's car when
they headed out for an early-morning practice back in Canada.

Travis looked around him. Except for Nish and Lars
Johanssen, most of the Screech Owls – Data Ulmar, Willie
Granger, Andy Higgins, Jesse Highboy, Dmitri Yakushev, Gordie
Griffith, Derek Dillinger, Fahd Noorizadeh, Jeremy Weathers,
Wilson Kelly, Mike Romano, the new third-line winger – were
all still huddled next to the sauna building, their hands wrapped
around their naked bodies like too-small blankets.

The Owls looked ridiculous. They were trying to use the building to shield themselves from the wind. Steam was rising from their heads and shoulders the way Travis had once seen it curl up from the team of horses that had drawn the Owls around the maple-sugar bush that belonged to Sarah Cuthbertson's grandparents.

Sarah was here. Well, not *here* – not *now*, with crazy Nish standing bare naked out in the middle of the lake. But she was here in Stockholm.

Sarah would return to her own team after the tournament. Her parents thought the trip would be an excellent opportunity for her to get a feel for the larger Olympic-sized ice surface, where Sarah hoped to play for the Canadian women's team one day.

Sarah and the other girls on the team – Liz Moscovitz, Chantal Larochelle, and Jenny Staples – had all gone off with the Stockholm women's team. For all Travis knew, the girls were going through the same strange ritual.

"Normally," Sarah had said on the bus ride out into the countryside from their hotel near the Globen Arena, "it would be boys and girls together."

"*Naked?*" Nish had asked, his eyes widening.

"Of course, *naked*," Sarah had laughed. "You think they wear full hockey equipment into the sauna?"

"No, but . . ."

"You've got to loosen up, Nishikawa. You're too uptight about everything."

It would be hard to call Nish uptight at the moment, Travis thought. *Crazy*, maybe. Or *insane*.

Nish was standing well out from the shore, a pink hamster in a sea of white. He was using one hand to cover himself and the other to wave at the cars driving by on the far side of the bay. They were, Travis thought, too far away to see him – fortunately!

Lars, who used to live in Sweden, had been the first to break from the pack and go running, barefoot, across the lake and jump straight into the freezing water through the gaping hole in the ice.

Nish, of course, had to be second. One steaming, churning bare-naked butt hurling across the open ice, still waving at the passing cars.

"*It's a breakaway!*" Wilson shouted.

"*Go, Nish! Go!*" they called.

Nish ran towards the open water, where Lars was already splashing about. He leapt and screamed once more before landing, like a pink beluga, in a mammoth splash of black water.

"EEEE–AWWW–KEEE!"

2

Travis felt incredibly alive – which was quite odd, because only a few moments earlier he had been convinced he was dead.

Ever since the sauna and the plunge into the freezing lake, Travis felt as if every pore of his skin had been drilled and flushed and buffed. He sizzled with energy, sparked with new life. Just as Lars had said he would. He felt like he was wearing a brand-new skin, and it was a skin with so much jump in it that, well, he couldn't possibly be the same old Travis Lindsay.

In a way, he figured, he wasn't. The Travis Lindsay who had landed at Stockholm's international airport the day before had come to doubt his own courage, especially when it came to hockey. He had always worried about his own bravery; he still preferred a night light when he was home. But a month ago, in a league game, he had gone down to block a shot from the point and the big shooter had held on too long so that, by the time he shot, it was Travis's face, not his shin pads, that blocked the way to the net. The shot had ripped the cage right off his helmet, and one of the broken screws had cut him just over the eye for two stitches.

Now he was afraid. He flinched whenever anyone took a hard shot in his direction. He was afraid to go down and block the puck. No one – with the possible exception of Muck Munro, the Screech Owls' coach – suspected anything, but Travis knew something was different. And he was secretly delighted that he'd been able to race across that ice bare naked and jump into the open water. At least he still had *some* guts.

Maybe this trip was just what he needed to get right again. So far, it was going perfectly.

Mr. Johanssen had come to the team with the idea. Sweden was hosting the first International Goodwill Pee Wee Tournament, with games in Stockholm, Gothenburg, and Malmö. Mr. Johanssen's lumber manufacturing company was one of the main tournament sponsors, and it had been suggested to him that a team from North America might give the tournament a truly international feel. Almost like a mini–World Cup!

Mr. Johanssen's company agreed to sponsor the Screech Owls, and the head office in Stockholm was able to arrange a special deal with SAS airlines. Before anyone quite realized what was happening, the Owls and most of their parents were all packing for Sweden.

Even Muck was going. The parents went to him with a proposition: if he could arrange the time off, they'd pick up the cost of his flight and accommodation. He couldn't refuse, even though Travis and Nish and some of the other long-time Owls thought he'd like nothing better. He kept grumbling about what his old hockey buddies would say if they found out he was going to Don Cherry's least-favourite hockey country.

No one paid the slightest attention to Muck's protests. Mr. Lindsay booked him on the flight and that was that. There would be no turning back. The team was delighted: no way did they want to play anywhere, not even practise, without Muck as their coach.

Teams were coming from Helsinki and Turku in Finland, and from Oslo in Norway. A German team was entered, a team from the Czech Republic, and, as a last-minute entry, a team was coming all the way from Russia.

Not only that, but the Russian team was from Moscow, and from the same CSKA club that had produced such superstars as Pavel Bure and Alexander Mogilny and Sergei Fedorov. What's more, it would have Dmitri Yakushev's first cousin playing on it. According to Dmitri – and later confirmed by Mr. Johanssen, who checked into it – his cousin, Slava Shadrin, was considered to be the best peewee player in all of Russia. Or, as Dmitri, who rarely, if ever, bragged, put it: "the best peewee player Russia has *ever* produced."

"Hardly," said Travis, who was a great fan of Bure's.

"That's what my uncle says – and he should know."

Dmitri's uncle was Alexander Yakushev, the great scoring star of the 1972 Summit Series between the Soviet Union and Team Canada, so perhaps he would know. But still, Travis found it hard to believe anyone could say something like that about a *kid*.

"How old is he?" Travis had asked Dmitri one practice before they boarded the plane that would fly them to Copenhagen and then on to Stockholm.

"Thirteen, I think."

"Well, how can they say such things about a thirteen-year-old? How can they know?"

"You're Canadian, aren't you?" Dmitri had asked.

Travis was caught off guard. "Yeah, of course. What's that mean?"

"Didn't you ever read any books about Wayne Gretzky or Bobby Orr?"

"Yeah, sure."

"Well, when *they* were thirteen, people knew, didn't they?"

Travis supposed they did. He could hardly wait to see this new Russian sensation. He was half excited at the prospect of seeing someone who must certainly be headed for the NHL, half terrified at the thought of having to play against him. What if he was also a centre? What if Travis had to take the face-offs against him? No . . . Sarah was back. Travis would be moved back to left wing.

The boys were getting ready to head out to the bus when Muck and Mr. Lindsay came in.

"Let's go!" Muck shouted. "You're on in an hour!"

"On the bus?" Fahd asked.

Muck rolled his eyes.

"You're on the bus in five, mister. You're on the ice in an hour."

"*Ice* – where?" Travis couldn't help himself. They hadn't

skated since they got there, and everyone was excited about checking out the big European ice surface.

"Globen rink," Muck said, giving away nothing.

The Screech Owls couldn't believe it. One day in Sweden and they were off to skate in the magnificent Globen Arena.

Where the Maple Leafs' Mats Sundin had played for Djurgårdens.

Where Peter Forsberg's MoDo team from Ornskoldsvik had come to play.

Where the World Championships had been played.

Where the Screech Owls were on in an hour.

3

The Screech Owls were lined up to go on. The ice was glistening in the bright lights of the Globen Arena. Travis looked up through his mask: the building was a perfect circle, the roof high and white and domed, the walls curving down, and bright red seats everywhere. It was the *strangest* hockey rink Travis had ever seen.

"It's like the inside of a golf ball," Sarah said. She was also looking up.

"It's beautiful," said Travis.

And huge. Muck explained to them that the ice surface was only fifteen feet – five adult steps – wider than they were used to, and that there was no difference at all in length. "But it will *feel* longer," he said. "The nets are farther out from the boards, and the corners deeper."

But even Muck's warning had not prepared them for the sensation of the bigger ice surface. Travis hit the fresh ice, did his special stutter step to pick up speed, leaned down to stare at his skates as they marked fresh ice, and felt as if he was skating once again on James Bay, with the ice stretching as far as the eye could see.

He could hear his blades. It was almost as if they were thanking him for the magnificent ice. All he had to do was take a stride and he could feel the blades dig in; all he had to do was push off and he could sense the light snow spraying as his skate dug deeper and flicked.

Travis lifted his head slightly so he could see the traffic ahead of him. Sarah Cuthbertson was skating so effortlessly her blades seemed to sigh while everyone else's sizzled. She floated over the ice surface, somehow capable of picking up speed even when she was gliding.

Travis smiled to himself as he watched her skate. Often, the Owls played teams whose best skaters – always boys, always the team stars – would seethe with such envy they would throw their own games off as they tried to show Sarah up. They would chase her around as if the game were tag, not hockey. And when they couldn't catch her, they would trip her. Sarah was really like two players in one: one to set up the goals for the Screech Owls, and one to draw the penalties from the opposition.

Travis passed Muck, who was skating in his old windbreaker and wearing the old gloves that some of the Owls figured dated from Columbus's discovery of America, or whenever it was that Muck played junior hockey before a broken leg shattered his dreams of playing in the National Hockey League.

Muck was skating with a man Travis had never seen before. He was tall and blond and was wearing a blue-and-yellow track suit with three small golden crowns on the front. He was a big man, and rocked on his skates as he moved, the blades effortlessly tossing a spray of ice on every lift – the sign of a very, very strong skater. He was wearing his hair in a style Travis had never seen before. He could tell it was gelled, for it glistened in the Globen lights, and it stuck up in a series of odd spikes. It was different, Travis thought, and kind of, well, *neat.*

Muck and the blond man skated to centre ice, where Muck blew once on his whistle.

The Owls converged on centre ice.

Muck might as well have been in the arena back home. He had his same old clothes on. Same old gloves and stick and whistle. And, as usual, he had the Owls' full attention.

Muck was unlike any coach Travis had ever known. No shouting "*Listen up!*" No fancy clipboards or plastic ice surfaces and felt-tip pens. Only Muck, talking.

"This here is Borje Salming," he said.

The man smiled. His smile was crooked, his lips and face heavily scarred, as if he'd been carved out of a tree with a chain-saw. But the smile was warm, and the blue eyes danced with friendliness under the gelled hair.

"You want to tell the boys who Mr. Salming is, Lars?"

Lars cleared his throat. Even he had been caught off guard.

"F-former Toronto Maple Leaf and Detroit Red Wing. Defence. First Swedish player named to the Hockey Hall of Fame."

"That's pretty good!" laughed Borje Salming.

Willie Granger, the team's trivia expert, pushed forward and spoke up.

"Six times named to the NHL All-Star team – 150 goals, 637 assists, 787 points."

Salming's eyes widened in surprise. "That's *very* good!"

"Mr. Johanssen's company has arranged for Mr. Salming to spend a practice with each of the teams playing in this tournament," Muck explained. "He and his assistants will be working with you this afternoon."

"ALL-RIGHHHTTTTT!" Willie shouted.

"YES!" shouted Lars.

No one had to turn to see who it was calling loudest from the back.

"EEEE-AWWW-KEEE!"

@

Travis had never thought a practice could be like this. He had been playing now for six years and had been skating since he was three. But today he felt he knew nothing.

There were three other Swedish coaches to help Borje Salming. One of them, an older man with glasses and a beard, had a clipboard that held a book containing the drills they were doing.

They skated for several minutes. None of the counter-clockwise circuits with whistled speed changes that they were used to in Canada, but intricate crossovers and shifts in direction.

Borje Salming blew his whistle at centre ice, and all the Owls skated out to form a circle around him. Nish and Sarah arrived at almost the same time, and stopped at the edge of the circle.

"Nice hair, eh?" Nish giggled.

"I think he's cute," Sarah whispered back.

Nish shook his head in disgust.

Travis noticed that the other coaches were removing the nets from the ice and were bringing out four small, red, box-shaped frames.

Salming scooped up the puck with his stick. He did it the way Travis had seen other NHLers do it. Effortlessly, smoothly, the stick snaked out, snaked back, and, as if by magic, the puck was suddenly lying on the blade and then floating through the air until it landed, perfectly, in the palm of his glove. He didn't seem to be even thinking about it.

Salming held up the puck. "I don't have to tell you that the game is all about this and what you are able to do with it," he said. "But we want to show you how kids learn the game in Sweden."

He reached into his track-suit pocket, removed another puck, and held it up beside the puck he had scooped from the ice. This one was different. It was about half the size.

"We teach Swedish youngsters how to handle small pucks first," he said. "You don't give a full-size basketball to a five-year-old, do you? No matter how tall he is."

"No," Fahd said. Fahd could always be counted on to say the obvious.

"The game in Europe is all about *tempo*," Salming said. "Anyone know what I mean by 'tempo'? Anyone a musician?"

Fahd, of course, raised his hand. "I play piano."

"Well?"

"Tempo tells you how slow or fast to play the piece of music."

Salming smiled, nodding. "Same in hockey. If you can learn to do drills at full speed, then you won't even have to think about what you should be doing during a game. Little kids can't handle NHL regulation pucks the same way they can these little things. And obviously they can't shoot them the same."

He pointed to the four red frames the other coaches had set up. They faced each other in two pairs on each side of the centre red line.

"Little pucks require little nets," he said, indicating the frames. "We teach our skills this way. Young players can handle these little pucks better, and shoot them a lot better. We use the smaller nets to teach accuracy."

Salming divided the Owls into two groups, one for the pair of tiny nets at the far end of the Globen rink, one for the near end. The rules were simple: no offsides, no stoppages, be creative, take chances.

Travis had never heard such talk from a coach — not even Muck, who believed in having fun on the ice and almost always gave them a few minutes of shinny at the end of a practice. But even when they played shinny back in Canada there would be whistles, and play would be stopped, and coaches would explain mistakes. Here there would be nothing. No control. No teaching. No stopping. Nothing.

In all his hockey years, Travis had never experienced anything quite like this. It was *wonderful*! It was exciting. It was fun — more fun, he thought, than he had ever had on an ice surface.

They played in groups of three: Travis, Dmitri, and Sarah against Nish, Data, and big Andy Higgins. Borje Salming and the other coach at their end just threw the puck into the corner and the game was under way. All four coaches then formed a line across centre to stop the little pucks from crossing the centre line.

The pucks felt almost weightless. Travis found he could stickhandle like an NHL pro. And when he shot, it took the slightest flick of his wrist to send a snap shot hard and high off the glass. He couldn't believe it!

And yet there was no point in pounding a shot off the glass just because it sounded great. As he played and sweated and gasped for breath, Travis realized that this explained everything he had ever wondered about European hockey.

Here, on half the ice in the Globen Arena in Stockholm, with a baby puck and a toy net, he could see it all for the first time: the only way that he and Dmitri and Sarah could attack was to keep circling back and dropping the puck to each other, even if they had only half the ice surface to work with. They had to drop the puck and watch for either Nish or Data or Andy to commit themselves, allowing them a quick three-on-two. The puck was so small and light that they could pass it back and forth effortlessly and quickly, and the passing became almost hypnotic as they kept trying out new ideas. They could do anything they wanted – no whistles, no one yelling at them, no score to worry about. They circled and dropped and flicked quick little passes and kept the puck dancing on the ends of their sticks.

Scoring, however, was another matter. The net was so small that with Nish and his big shin pads in the way, it was a bit like threading a needle. If they kept to the usual North American strategy they would lose possession. A shot wasn't always a safe play. Here, a shot for the sake of a shot was a waste. They had to wait, and they had to work at it so one of them would have the ideal angle. No big fancy slapshots. Quick, hard shots exactly placed – nothing else would work.

They played for nearly half an hour, and when Salming finally blew the whistle and the other coaches began to gather up the little pucks and push away the tiny nets, the Owls collapsed on their backs, sweating and puffing and giggling.

"That's *my* kind of hockey," Dmitri said.

"I *love* it!" said Sarah.

Off to the side, Nish was grunting and gasping and trying to laugh sarcastically. "One good bodycheck and you wouldn't be saying that."

Sarah laughed. "You'd have to catch us first, Big Boy."

Nish threw a glove at her. It bounced off her shoulder pads. "We won," he announced.

"Whatdya mean, 'won'?" Travis asked. "Nobody was even keeping score!"

"I *always* keep score –" Nish said.

He had barely finished speaking when his own glove flew back and bounced off his nose.

"So do I," said Sarah, giggling. "And now we're even."

4

The Screech Owls hadn't played a single game, and yet already this was the best tournament ever. After the practice with Borje Salming and the little pucks, the lumber company Lars's father worked for was treating them to a banquet in the restaurant overlooking the ice surface, high up on the seventh floor of the Globen complex. But the Owls kept forgetting that they had come up here to eat. MoDo, one of the Swedish elite teams, was holding a practice below for their upcoming game against Djurgårdens. MoDo was Peter Forsberg's old team.

"They're playing with the little pucks!" Fahd shouted.

"They just *look* little from up here," said Travis, shaking his head at Fahd.

The meal included tiny, delicious boiled potatoes and lots of different kinds of cheese. Lars wanted them all to try the pickled herring, but he couldn't convince them that the herring wasn't a snake all curled up in the dish.

"Let me at it!" shouted Nish from another table.

Ever since the trip to James Bay, Nish fancied himself a new Man of the World. He had eaten beaver, after all – and *moose nostrils!* – so what was the big deal about a little slippery, rubbery fish?

"You eat this, Nish," Lars said, "and you get first dibs on the pudding."

Nish's eyes opened wide. "What pudding?"

"A special Swedish treat. You can go first if you eat this."

"*No prob-lem,*" Nish announced as he sat down and elaborately tucked a napkin under his chin.

He sliced off a bit of the pickled herring, sniffed it, and then began to chew.

"*Mmmmmmm,*" he kept saying. "*Ahhhhhhhhh! Per-fect!*"

Nish chewed and ate as if he'd been brought up on nothing but pickled herring. He loved a show. He loved being the centre of attention.

"You win!" said Lars. "Bring Nish some of the pudding."

Nish put down his knife and fork and dabbed at his chin, waiting, like some ancient king on his throne, for someone to serve him.

A smiling waiter came over with the special dish Lars had promised.

Nish lightly dabbed at his mouth.

"I should have some wine to clean my palate," he announced grandly.

"*You're thirteen years old!*" Fahd scolded.

"There is no drinking age in Sweden," said Nish. "Is there, Lars?"

"Well, you have to be eighteen, actually," Lars said. "But it's pretty well left up to the parents to decide when you're mature enough – which in your case would be roughly the year 2036."

Nish scowled. "*Very* funny."

The waiter placed the pudding down in front of Nish and stood back.

"*Lemme at it!*" Nish practically shouted.

"Go ahead," Lars said. "You've earned it."

Nish didn't even bother to sniff the dish. Like a front-end loader dumping snow into the back of a truck, he spooned up pudding, chewed once with his eyes closed – then stopped, his eyes opening wide!

"W-what *is* this?" he mumbled, some of the dark pudding tumbling out of his mouth.

"The English translation," said Lars, "would be 'blood pudding.' There's beer and syrup and spices mixed together with flour." He paused, grinning. "Oh yes, and the blood of a freshly slaughtered pig. It's a very old, very special Swedish recipe. It dates back hundreds and hundreds of years."

More of the dark pudding rolled out of Nish's open mouth. He turned pale.

"I'MMM GONNNA HU-URLLL!"

They walked out into the brilliant sunshine of a late-winter Swedish day. Outside the Globen Hotel they waited while Nish, still spitting into a napkin, ran into the nearby McDonald's and grabbed a Big Mac to wash away the taste of the dreaded blood pudding. Then they boarded a bus for downtown.

It didn't take Nish long to recover. At the corner they passed a gas station, and Nish pointed at the signs on either side of the pumps.

"'*In*-fart'? '*Ut*-fart'?"

"'Entrance' and 'Exit,'" explained Lars, a trifle impatiently.

"Cars over here *fart* when they get gas?" Nish screamed, holding his nose.

"Very funny," Lars said. He shrugged his shoulders and moved away to the front of the bus.

Once downtown, they were all given a couple of hours to go their separate ways, promising to meet back at the bus at four o'clock.

In the sunshine, and with a light sprinkling of snow on the streets, Stockholm looked like a picture in a fairy tale. Everything seemed so old, and mysterious, and magical.

Travis and Fahd were interested in the history. They were lucky Lars was along. He told them about the canals, the churches, even a bit about the Vikings. But Nish wasn't much interested.

"EEEE-AWWW-KEEE!"

Travis winced. This hardly seemed the place for Nish to try out his new yell. They were passing a church – had he no respect?

"Eeee-awww-keee!"

The second call didn't come from Nish. It was higher pitched and distant, far off down the street.

Nish spun around in his tracks. "What was that?"

"An echo," suggested Lars.

"No way – it sounded like a *girl*!"

Nish held his hands up to his mouth to make a trumpet.

"EEEE-AWWW-KEEE!" he shouted.

"Eeee-awww-keee!" the answer came back, louder now, closer.

"They're answering me!" Nish giggled.

"Maybe they're wolves," suggested Travis.

"EEEE-AWWW-KEEE!" Nish called again.

A throng of kids was coming down the far side of the street.

One of them ran out into the street, held her hands up to her mouth, raised her head, and howled, "EEEE-AWWW-KEEE!"

Nish answered back, "EEEE-AWWW-KEEE!"

The girl waved. Nish turned away, blushing.

"*They're coming over!*" he hissed.

They were Swedish, seven or eight of them in blue jackets and yellow scarves, and three or four others in ski jackets and baseball caps. They seemed like a team, or at least part of a team and their friends. The girl who had been answering Nish's call seemed very much the leader.

"Hi," she said directly to Nish. "I'm Annika. What's your name?"

Nish sputtered, and Travis couldn't blame him. Annika was so cute – perfectly blond, with nice teeth and dimples when she smiled. But the cutest thing about her was the way she talked. When she spoke English, it was almost as if she were singing.

"N-Nish. What's yours?"

Annika giggled. "Annika. Didn't you hear me the first time or is my English no good?"

Nish was flustered. "Y-y-yeah, sure it is. I'm sorry."

"Where are you from?"

With Lars's help, Nish managed to explain all about the team and what they were doing here.

Annika's friends in the blue jackets and yellow scarves were on the Malmö peewee team. They were playing in the tournament and were in Stockholm for a game at the Globen Arena.

"Malmö?" Lars said. "We play twice in Malmö."

"Maybe against us," a tall boy said. "We've got a pretty good team."

"So do we," Nish said. "I'm assistant captain."

Travis waited for Nish to point out that he, Travis, was captain, but Nish said nothing. And Travis couldn't figure out how to say it without sounding full of himself.

"We had a practice with Borje Salming!" Lars told them.

"*No way!*" Annika screeched.

"We did," Nish said, nodding.

"He's my all-time favourite player!" Annika said, her eyes sparking. "I still have a poster of him up in my bedroom."

"When do you go to Malmö?" the tall boy asked Travis.

"We play Russia tomorrow. I think we leave first thing the next morning."

"I'll come and watch you play," Annika said, her amazing eyes studying a blushing Nish.

"I-I'm number 21," he said.

"*Borje Salming's number!*" she yelled.

"Yeah," Nish said. "I know. He's my favourite player, too."

Travis did a double-take. How could he say that? Nish was practically a baby when Salming retired. In all the years they'd been best friends, Travis had never once heard Nish mention Borje Salming. Maybe Bobby Orr. And certainly Brian Leetch. But Salming?

"No kidding?" said Annika.

"Yeah," Nish fibbed. "Sure."

Annika held her hands up to her mouth: "EEEE–AWWW–KEEE!"

5

Next morning they went early to the Globen Arena. Dmitri wanted to see his cousin before the game, and Travis, Lars, and Nish went along with him.

They were already flooding the ice for the Screech Owls–Russia game, but no one was in the stands. Derek's father, Mr. Dillinger, was sharpening the Owls' skates, and he waved at them from the far end of the corridor. Good ol' Mr. Dillinger.

The Russian team, CSKA, was already there, but the dressing-room door was shut tight. A man in a blue suit stood to the side, watching them. He had the sort of glasses that get darker in bright light, and they gave him a shadowed, sinister look. He had a red-and-gold CSKA pin on his jacket, so they knew he was with the team.

He answered in Russian when Dmitri addressed him. He even smiled when he realized Dmitri spoke his language, and he listened carefully, nodding and shaking his head.

Finally the man knocked on the door – two sharp quick knocks, a pause, then a third, more softly – and was admitted.

"What's the big fuss?" Nish wanted to know.

"I'm not sure," Dmitri said. "They don't seem to want anybody talking to the team. I told him I'm Slava's cousin."

"Maybe they're afraid he'll *defect*," Nish said, proud to use such a word.

Dmitri laughed. "Get with the times, Nish. Russians don't run away from home any more."

"Fedorov did. Mogilny did."

"You're talking Soviet Union, Nish. There is no more Soviet Union – or don't you pay attention in history class, either?"

"Well, why are they so nervous, then?"

A few minutes passed and the boys were getting restless. Finally the door opened and the man in the blue suit came out. Then another man, who seemed even more furtive. Then a kid. A skinny kid with slightly buck teeth and unruly blond hair.

"*Slava!*" Dmitri shouted when he saw who was coming out.

"Hey!" the other shouted, smiling.

The two boys hugged each other. Then Dmitri kissed his cousin's cheek, and Slava kissed Dmitri's cheek. Travis was standing close enough to Nish to hear him mumble, "*I'm gonna hurl.*" The cousins hugged again and then separated.

"Slava," Dmitri said. "These are my teammates. Travis, Lars, Nish, I want you to meet Viacheslav Shadrin. 'Slava,' we call him."

"I don't kiss," Nish said.

Even Slava laughed. His big front teeth gave him a wonderful smile when he used it, but he didn't use it often. His English wasn't great, and Dmitri had to do a lot of translating, but the boys were able to talk about the tournament and everything they'd seen and done, including Nish's now-famous Winter Skinny Dip.

Slava nodded a lot and even laughed a couple of times, but he hadn't any stories to tell in return. Lars asked him what he'd seen and Dmitri translated, but the answer didn't amount to much apart from practice and team meetings. He hadn't shopped. He hadn't been to any of the museums.

"Ask Slava if he can come out with us in Malmö," Travis told Dmitri.

Dmitri did, but Slava only shook his head and looked forlorn. He spoke quickly to Dmitri, and he kept checking the two men from CSKA, who were talking off to the side.

"Okay," Dmitri said. "See you later, then, Slava."

Slava quickly shook their hands and turned back towards the dressing room. The man in the blue suit already had the door open. In a moment, all three had vanished inside.

"What was *that* all about?" Travis asked Dmitri.

"*In a minute*," Dmitri whispered. He waited until they had almost reached the Owls' dressing room. Then he gathered the others close.

"The man in the blue suit?" Dmitri began.

"Yeah?" Lars said.

"He's undercover. You know, KGB, Secret Service? He travels with Slava everywhere he goes."

"Even to the bathroom?" Nish had to know.

"Practically – they're worried about the Russian mob."

"Somebody wants to *kill* your cousin?" Travis asked. He couldn't believe it.

"Not *kill* him, stupid – *kidnap* him!"

"*Kidnap* him?" the other three said at once.

"Yeah, hold him for ransom. You know."

"He's that rich?" Nish asked. He was incredulous.

Dmitri shook his head. "Not rich. He's that *good*."

"Explain," Nish demanded.

"The mob has already blackmailed lots of NHL players. They threaten to harm family members back in Russia and the player pays up. It's simple."

"That's crazy!" Lars said.

"Russia's crazy right now," said Dmitri. "They know what everyone is saying about Slava. They say he's the best ever, as good as Larionov, as good as Fedorov, Bure, Yashin."

"But he has no money," pointed out Travis. "He can't even be drafted until he's eighteen."

"Doesn't matter," said Dmitri. "He means everything to Russian hockey right now. He's the proof that there are still great players coming up through the system. The Russian Ice Hockey Federation only exists because of the money they're getting from NHL teams right now. They'd pay whatever ransom was necessary."

"So they send him over here with bodyguards?" Lars said.

"That's it."

"Ridiculous," Lars said, shaking his head.

Travis had to agree. A thirteen-year-old peewee hockey player? How good could he be?

6

lava Shadrin's CSKA team, in uniforms as red as the arena seats, was already on the Globen rink when the Screech Owls came out. It took Travis a while to locate number 13. Slava was certainly an elegant skater, but was he better than Sarah Cuthbertson? Travis looked for Sarah and found her circling about the huge ice surface like milkweed floating on a breeze.

Travis hit the crossbar on his first practice shot and knew he was going to have a good game. As team captain, he lined up the Owls to take practice shots at Jenny Staples and Jeremy Weathers. Jenny was getting the first start in the tournament, and she was nervous. More shots were going in than she was keeping out.

Travis's legs felt good. They had been a bit rubbery after the long flight and then the Swedish-style practice, but now everything was back. He moved without effort, quick, fluid, and smooth. He hoped he looked good to the Russians. He hoped they'd noticed his C for "Captain"; he had already noticed the K for "Kaptain" on number 13.

Muck called them all over to the bench. This was most unusual for Muck, who usually spoke only in the dressing room.

"You're here to *play*, not *watch*," Muck said. "Don't let what you see hypnotize you out there. You want number 13's autograph, you can line up and get it when the game's over."

Travis thought Muck was going too far. Slava didn't seem that special. Sarah could skate as well, and Andy Higgins could shoot a puck as hard as any thirteen-year-old Travis had ever seen. He himself was a pretty good playmaker, wasn't he? And who was faster than Dmitri on a break?

"Sarah, he's your check right through the neutral zone," Muck said. "He crosses our blueline, Nishikawa, and he's all yours. I want you to stick to him like Krazy Glue, both of you. Understand?"

No one said anything. No one had to. Travis hammered his stick on the ice and the others followed suit and then broke from the bench to tap Jenny's pads and get the game under way.

Sarah's line would start. Nish and Data were on defence. Travis felt a little uneasy being back on left wing, but he knew they would play better with Sarah's speed at the middle position. And besides, Sarah had to stick with Slava, who was starting centre for CSKA.

The two teams exchanged gifts – small Canadian flags for the Russians, CSKA pins for the Canadians – and after they had dropped them off into a pillowcase Mr. Dillinger was holding out from the bench, they skated out to start.

Sarah won the face-off cleanly, knocking the puck on her

backhand towards Travis. Travis picked it up, spun back, and dropped the puck to Nish, who looked up and decided to hit Sarah as she broke to split the Russian defence. It was a set play, one they had worked on in practice, and it had gone beautifully before – a quick attack before anyone realized the game had even started.

Nish passed, but the puck slammed straight into a pair of shin pads that seemed to arrive out of nowhere. It was number 13, *Slava*! Two strides and he had left Sarah flying in the other direction – Sarah, who had been supposed to stick to him like Krazy Glue in the neutral zone.

Slava Shadrin split the Owls' defence and flew in on Jenny so fast that the unbelievable happened. Jenny first skated quickly out to cut down the angle, and then, realizing he was simply going to blow by her, she caught and tried to switch instantly into reverse. The move was too sudden and she fell over backwards, flat on her back.

Slava Shadrin went in around the fallen goaltender, spun in a circle, and dropped the puck between his own legs and into the empty net.

CSKA 1, Screech Owls 0.

Sarah's line knew they were going off even though they'd been on for only eight seconds. They skated off, heads down, and Nish and Data followed.

Muck tapped Andy Higgins on the shoulder. "Tell Jenny to come over here," he said.

Travis looked up, puzzled. Was Muck going to pull her?

Andy's line went out and Jenny skated over to the bench. She was crying.

Muck spoke to her. "Sarah missed her check. Nishikawa missed his check. You were the only one in position. So forget it even happened, okay?"

Muck paused a second, and came as close to smiling as he ever did while working the bench.

"And one more thing," he said. "No matter what happens, you're our goaltender today."

Jenny couldn't speak. By now, everyone knew she had been crying, but no one thought it was funny. She nodded, her mask exaggerating the movement, and turned and skated quickly back to her net. Travis could tell from the way Jenny slammed her stick against the posts and set that she was right back in the game.

Sarah's line didn't get another shift until the second half of the first period, and by then Travis had had every opportunity to see why Slava Shadrin was considered so special.

He had never seen anyone – not even Sarah – skate like that. Slava didn't look particularly fast, his legs didn't pump very quickly, but he moved about the ice so cleverly that he always seemed to appear where he shouldn't be. He was as quick going to both sides as ahead, as fast backchecking as attacking.

When Slava was out there, CSKA always seemed to have the puck. He didn't keep it for himself; he could have it just for a moment – a moment in which it seemed every one of the Owls was turning to check him – and then it would be gone. His passes were like darts, quick little flicks that snapped the puck onto his teammates' blades, and they would no sooner have the puck than, instantly, Slava was in a wide-open stretch of ice calling for it.

The Russians were up 3–0 when Sarah's line was given another chance. This time she was ready. Wherever Slava went, she went too. She dived to block passes, she stuck to him like a shadow, and Slava seemed to enjoy it.

Once, Slava came in on Nish and stopped so fast that ice chips flew into his face as if they'd been thrown from a snow-blower. Slava let the puck slip on under its own momentum and right through Nish's skates. One quick turn and he was once again home free. He cut across the net, getting Jenny to follow, and then slipped a pass back to his winger, who knew exactly what to expect.

CSKA 4, Screech Owls 0.

The Owls found themselves a bit in the second. Sarah knocked a pass from Slava out of the air and hit Travis as he broke up the boards. With the Russian defenceman squeezing him out, Travis remembered what Muck always preached: A shot at the net is never a bad decision. The goaltender let a fat rebound come off right onto the stick of Dmitri, who roofed the puck on his backhand.

CSKA nearly scored again when Slava put a pass back through his legs to the point and the biggest Russian defence-man wound up for a mighty slapshot. Travis knew if he dived he might block the shot, or at least tip it up and away, but he couldn't make himself do it. He stuck out his stick warily and the shot screamed right through and clanged off the crossbar. Lucky for Travis.

Next shift, Muck kept Travis on the bench. Muck was letting him know that he had seen him back off. Travis was still afraid of getting hit with a shot.

As he sat out the shift, Travis glanced up into the crowd. Annika and some of the Malmö team were there, singing and waving their club banner, and, every once in a while, shouting "EEEE-AWWW-KEEE!" when Nish had the puck.

A man was standing beside the Owls' bench. There was something about the cut of his suit and the look of him that told Travis he was another Russian. The man was chewing on a toothpick, and when he worked his lips Travis could see the flash of a gold tooth. He looked nasty. But Travis supposed that was how a Russian undercover cop would look.

Late in the game, Sarah scored on a beautiful solo rush when she split the defence, and big Andy Higgins scored on a shot that went in off the toe of one of the CSKA defence. But they couldn't come all the way back.

The horn sounded and the first game of the tournament was over. CSKA had beaten the Screech Owls 6–3, but it could have been much worse. Jenny Staples had made so many great stops after the first disaster that she was named Canadian Player of the Game. Jenny and Slava Shadrin, the obvious Russian Player of the Game, both received tournament banners.

They lined up and shook hands. Travis was in front of Nish, who was still complaining about one of the goals. Nish hadn't had a great game. Travis came to Slava, who had his hand out and was smiling, his big teeth protruding slightly.

"Good game, captain," Slava said.

"You, too," said Travis. He felt a thrill that such a good player would even notice him out there. And he had noticed Travis's C, as well!

Slava passed on to Nish, who had his hand out but without much enthusiasm. Slava took it, pumped it, and made a kissing sound with his lips.

"*Get a life!*" Nish growled.

7

ravis woke with a start. He'd been dreaming about the man with the gold tooth. The man had a gun and was chasing them. They were in a rink, Travis and Nish, and they were in bare feet, and the man was on skates. And he was raising his gun to fire . . .

There was light streaming from the bathroom. Four of them were sleeping in the room, and on his left Travis could see the mound that was Data, and beyond Data, with the sheets kicked off and lying flat on his stomach, was Lars. So it had to be Nish in the bathroom. Travis waited, but there was no sound. No water running. Nothing. He remembered Nish had gone down to the little mall in the evening. He had said he had to get to a drugstore. Maybe he's not feeling well, Travis thought. Maybe I'd better check on him.

He rolled out of bed. The sheets stuck to his back. He'd been sweating. Frightened.

"You okay, Nish?" Travis called lightly.

"Fine," the answer came back, sharply. The door slammed shut.

Travis waited a while longer. Lars was stirring now and starting to get up. They would be leaving for Malmö at nine, so everyone had to get up and pack. They would need the bathroom.

Travis got up and went to the door, Lars — scratching his sides — right behind him.

"Can we come in?" Travis called.

"*In a minute!*"

Lars yawned. "He's in a good mood this morning."

"I don't think he's feeling well."

They waited a moment longer. Travis tapped his knuckles lightly on the door.

"*Okay, okay, okay!*" Nish called from inside.

They could hear him fiddling with the lock. The door opened — and someone they had never seen before was standing in front of them!

All they could see was the hair. Dark hair, standing almost straight up. Hair moulded into shiny, black spikes. Like stalagmites in a dark cavern. Still dripping with something oily.

"*Nish?*" Lars said.

Below the shining, black spikes, a big Nish grin spread across a vaguely familiar face.

"How do you like it? Just like Borje Salming, don't you think? A little mousse, a little Swedish gel — cost me less than thirty krona."

Travis didn't know what to say. His hair was, well, *bizarre*. It was a *bit* like Borje Salming's, but this was also something entirely unique.

"Well?" Nish demanded.

Lars pushed by, giggling. He elbowed Nish out, closed the door, and locked it. He had to use the facilities.

"*Well?*" Nish said again.

Travis still didn't know what to say. He swallowed hard.

"I think you look like an idiot."

"You're just jealous," Nish said, pushing Travis out of the way so he could dress.

Nish's new hair was the highlight of the trip to Malmö. Sarah laughed so hard she had tears rolling down her cheeks. Wilson and Data stood behind his seat holding their noses, for Nish's slicked head had a certain distinctive smell.

"We'll have to drill holes in the top of his helmet," said Muck, shaking his head.

They set off by double-decker tour bus on a cold March morning, but in sunshine so bright it soon heated up the vehicle. Some of the seats were positioned around little card tables with special holders built in for drinks, so the players drank Cokes and played hearts.

They drove south along the coastline and then cut inland, travelling on good, clear highways across the frozen south of Sweden. Travis took off his Screech Owls jacket and stuffed it against his window, then turned and stared out. The bus rolled through countryside with more frozen lakes than Travis had ever seen. On some of the lakes people were ice fishing. There were cars out on the ice, and along the shore Travis saw several saunas – some with smoke rising from them. Once, he could swear he saw a naked man and woman and child rolling in the snow beside one of them, but he didn't say anything.

He didn't want Nish ordering the bus around for a photo opportunity.

"EEEE–AWWW–KEEE!"

Nish was up at the front of the bus even before it passed the Malmö train station on the way to their hotel. They turned left, then right, and finally down a street so narrow it seemed the bus would scrape along both sides until it got stuck. They were at the Master Johan Hotel, their home for the next four nights.

"*Sit down, Nishikawa!*" Muck ordered from his seat just behind the driver.

But it was no use. Nish was already down the stairwell and at the door. Outside, running to catch up, were several Malmö kids, Annika in the lead.

"EEEE–AWWW–KEEE!" Annika shouted.

"*Nish has found his true love!*" Lars called. Everyone laughed.

The Owls spilled off the bus. They were stiff and tired. Sarah and Dmitri were jogging on the spot, trying to loosen up. Nish was high-fiving Annika and her friends and acting as if he were some visiting ambassador.

"*Gillar du hans hår?*" ("How do you like his hair?") Lars asked Annika.

"*Häftigt!*" ("Awesome!")

The Malmö team had already beaten the team from Germany and they were all planning to attend the Screech Owls' game against Finland.

"We're going to cheer for Canada," Annika told Nish.

Canada? Travis hadn't thought of it that way before. To him, they were the Screech Owls. But to these kids, they were Team Canada – just as Kariya and Gretzky and even Paul Henderson had played for Team Canada. They were representing their *country*. Travis felt a tremendous glow of pride come over him. And responsibility.

He was *captain* of the Canadian team.

he Master Johan was perfect. The rooms were huge, with cots thrown in so there could be four or five players per room. It was the fanciest hotel Travis and most of the other Owls had ever stayed at – marble sinks, deep carpets, and a huge courtyard under a glass roof where they served breakfast.

They slept well – no nightmares for Travis this time – and in the morning were given time off to do anything they wanted. Most of the parents were going shopping or to the art museum. A few of the mothers were even going to take the hovercraft across the sound to Copenhagen, in Denmark, for a day of shopping. Heading across the sea to another country seemed no more unusual to the people of Malmö than getting in the van to drive down to the mall.

"There's a castle about five minutes from here," Mr. Johanssen told the kids.

"A castle!" Data screeched.

Mr. Johanssen laughed. "You're in Europe, young man. There are castles everywhere. This one is more than five hundred years old – and it used to be a prison."

"Did they torture people there?"

"I don't know, but some prisoners were executed," Mr. Johanssen said. "But that was a long, long time ago."

"Let's go! Let's go!" shouted Data.

But not everyone wanted to go. Several of the Owls were headed off shopping with their parents. Nish insisted on going to McDonald's with Annika and her friends. In the end about a half-dozen of the Owls went with Mr. Johanssen to see Malmöhus Castle. Data, of course, and Wilson, Andy, Travis, Dmitri, and Lars.

The castle wasn't at all like the one at the entrance to Disney World's Magic Kingdom, but it did have an old moat, and two gun towers were still standing, and it *felt* very old. Travis ran two rolls of film through his camera.

Mr. Johanssen and Lars led them on a tour. What they couldn't see they had to imagine. The castle had also been used as a mint for making coins, as a home for the poor, as a prison – and even as an asylum.

Now it was used for various exhibitions, usually art, but this month featured a special display, "Arms and Armour: Norse and Viking Warriors." They passed through room after room of shiny metal armour, chain mail, shields, swords, spiked flails, mace, and spears.

"Hollywood got it all wrong in the Viking movies," Mr. Johanssen told them. "The basic Viking weapon was the *spear*, not the sword."

But the most fascinating display was the room filled with helmets, some of them real, some of them replicas that they were allowed to touch. There were cone-shaped helmets and helmets that covered all of the head, with only tiny slits to see out through. "Still enough room to stab a sword in," Data pointed out. Travis winced.

"This," said one of the museum guards, picking up a replica of a beautifully curved helmet with stems running down over each ear and another to protect the nose, "is a *spangenhelm*. It's what a Viking warrior would wear."

He turned to Travis, smiling. "You want to try it on?"

"Me?" Travis asked.

"Sure, go ahead."

With the others giggling, Travis reached out and took the huge helmet. It weighed about three times what he expected! "Careful now!" the guard laughed. "Don't drop it!"

With the guard's help, Travis pulled the helmet over his head. He could barely keep his neck straight. He couldn't believe that anyone could even walk with something like this on, let alone head into battle!

"How'd you like to play hockey in something like that?" Mr. Johanssen asked.

"No way!" said Travis.

They helped him off with the helmet, placed it back on the display shelf, and moved into another area with even more weapons.

"Where did they execute the prisoners?" Data asked.

"I can show you," Mr. Johanssen said, smiling, and he led them out to the courtyard.

"I'm going to tell you about something that happened right here at this spot on September 19, 1837," Mr. Johanssen began. Travis tried to imagine how long ago that was.

"The prison governor at the time, Hans Canon, was a hard, cruel man. He used to have his prisoners flogged for the slightest reason."

"What's flogged?" Wilson asked.

"Whipped. Their shirts stripped off and their backs beaten with leather straps until their skin peeled away. Sometimes they bled to death."

"Awesome," said Data.

"You're a mental case," said Travis.

Mr. Johanssen continued. "There were two particularly evil criminals here then. Karlqvist and Wahlgren. The governor hated them both, but particularly Karlqvist, who wore his hair long and was a bit of a loudmouth. One day the governor got so fed up with Karlqvist's behaviour that he came out here and had him dragged inside, and when he had been strapped to a chair, the governor himself cut his hair.

"I guess he did a pretty awful job, because they threw Karlqvist back out here in the courtyard and all the other prisoners laughed at him. But Governor Canon made the mistake of coming out to gloat. Wahlgren and his friend had knives, and the two of them attacked the governor right here where you're standing."

Travis looked down at the rough bricks. The image of the two men stabbing at the governor flashed through his mind. He shivered.

"Was there blood?" Data asked.

Mr. Johanssen laughed – once, and very quickly. "A lot of blood. The governor died of his wounds."

"What happened to the two men?" Andy asked.

"They cut their heads off."

"Here?" Data asked.

"Right here."

"Right off?"

"Right off."

Data looked at the ground as if the bricks still ran red with blood. He stepped away carefully, almost afraid he'd trip on a rolling, bloody head.

"All because of somebody's *hair*?" Data asked.

"All because of somebody's hair," Mr. Johanssen said. "Nish is lucky he's living today and not back then."

9

The Malmö Ice Stadium was much more like a regular Canadian hockey rink than was the strange Globen "golf ball" in Stockholm. At the snack bar, the Owls, who were used to seeing a pop machine at best, couldn't get over the fact that they were selling ice cream and that parents and older players were lining up to buy beer.

The Owls were to face the Finnish team from Tampere. The Finns had already beaten one of the Swedish teams and were said to be almost as good as the Russians. This time, however, it wasn't the way the opposition skated and shot that impressed the Owls during warmup – it was their advertising.

The Tampere team had blue jerseys and socks and red pants, but the blue of their jerseys was almost hidden under the ads for car oil, computers, stereo systems, even a bank.

"They're gonna be slowed down by all the advertising," said Data as he and Travis circled at the blueline, warily watching the Tampere players as they took shots.

Travis laughed. But perhaps Data was right. They didn't seem as swift as the Russians. Certainly, none skated like Slava Shadrin.

The Malmö rink itself was one big commercial. There wasn't a board without advertising. Banners hung from the low ceiling, promoting SAS airlines, Volvo, Burger King . . .

"When we get back home, I'm selling *my* body, too."

Travis turned, surprised. It was Nish.

"Whatdya mean?" Travis asked.

"I'm renting out my uniform. McDonald's, Nintendo, Nike – you name it, I'm going for it."

"They'd never let you."

"What's it to them? Maybe a big 'Coke' painted on the top of my helmet. Whatdya say?"

"You're nuts."

Just as the warmup was about to end, Travis effortlessly deked Jeremy out of the net and backhanded a shot off the crossbar. He could hear his teammates cheer. Funny, he thought. In a game, goals count; in practice and in warmups, crossbars are what matter. He had his crossbar. He was certain to play well.

The Finns had tremendous puck control. They seemed to work the larger ice surface better, especially the defence, but even though the team from Tampere had the puck more, the Owls seemed to know better what to do with it. Andy Higgins scored on a hard shot through a screen, but the Finns tied the game late in the first period after Nish had got caught badly out of position.

At the break, Travis took a look at the crowd as the Owls headed off to their dressing room. He knew Annika was there – she'd been doing that stupid yell every time Nish touched the puck – but he hadn't seen Slava's team come in. The Russians were just taking their seats behind the Owls' bench, all with dull-red team jackets, all sitting down as if they were getting ready for a class. They probably were, Travis thought; they were here to study the opposition.

Sitting just behind Slava were the two men they had seen at the Russian team's dressing room. They seemed strategically placed, watching. The man with the gold tooth wasn't there.

Muck didn't seem particularly pleased with the 1–1 score.

"Nishikawa," he began, "would you mind explaining what 'cycling' is?"

Nish didn't look up. He sat doubled over on the wooden bench with his folded arms pressed between his chest and knees. He stared at the floor as he answered.

"All three forwards work the puck in the same corner. Each one drops the puck back as he circles and then blocks the checker. If there's a clear opening, the player picking up the puck walks out for the shot."

"And did you see that out there today?"

"Yes."

"And did it work?"

"Yes."

"It worked because you fell for the lure. If you don't bite, they can't block you. And if they can't block you, they can't come out."

"I thought I had a play."

"That's the idea, isn't it? You thought you did and you didn't. And they scored on us because you fell for it."

Nish said nothing. He knew.

Muck had only a few words for the rest of them.

"We're here to play hockey, not sightsee. You want to take pictures, you do it out of uniform, okay?"

The second period saw a dramatic change. It was not just the way the game was played, it was also the sound level. Annika's calls for Nish were now all but drowned out by the whistling and shouting, and once even a song, from the Russians sitting behind the Owls' bench.

"How come they're cheering for us?" Travis asked Dmitri when they were off for a shift.

Dmitri smiled. "I thought they were cheering for *me*."

This time Nish let the Finns cycle all they wanted. He maintained his position and simply stepped into any player who dared come out of the corners with the puck to try him one-on-one. If he saw a chance to go for the puck, he took the player and left the puck for the forward coming back. The Finns never got another good scoring chance.

Sarah gave the Owls the lead with a beautiful two-on-one with Dmitri. She let Dmitri break for the net, but, instead of passing to him, she slowed and cut across the slot. The one defenceman who had been in position simply drifted out of the play with Dmitri, and the goalie had to move with Sarah. Once she had him going the wrong way, she slid a hard backhand along the ice that ticked in off the far post.

The Finns pulled their goalie in the final minute. Travis tried to block a shot at the point, but didn't drop down in time.

It didn't matter, as the shot went high and wide, but Travis knew he had hesitated. It had looked as if he'd tried his best, but he hadn't. He'd paused, and even when he did go down he'd kept his eyes closed, afraid of the puck.

Lars ended the tension when he scored in the empty Finnish net with a long shot that barely had enough weight to carry it over the goal line.

The Owls were 1–1 for the tournament.

They still had a chance.

10

The telephone rang in the boys' room at the Master Johan. Nish, who had been trying, once again, to unscramble the television so they could watch free adult movies – "Sweden *invented* sex!" he'd shouted – threw down the loose wires in disgust and rolled across the bed to scoop up the phone.

"*What?*" he demanded. His rewiring was not working out. He was getting frustrated.

Nish held the phone out towards Travis.

"It's for you."

"Who is it?"

"Whatdya think I am, your secretary?"

It was Dmitri. He wanted to meet Travis immediately by the elevator on the fifth floor. He couldn't explain. He wanted Travis to bring Nish and Lars but wouldn't say why.

Nish agreed to go only reluctantly. He was close, he said, to cracking the problem. Travis looked at the back of the television.

Loose wires were everywhere. He only hoped Nish would be able to put it all back together again.

Dmitri was waiting for them at the elevator. "Slava called me," he said. "He wants to go out with us."

"Fine," said Travis. "Where are we going?"

"To McDonald's – he just wants to get away."

"So why the secret meeting?" Nish demanded.

"They won't let him go anywhere. Those two bodyguards watch him like a hawk."

"I thought there were three," said Travis.

Dmitri blinked at Travis. "He says two."

"But I've seen a third," Travis said, thinking of the man with the gold tooth.

"Two, three, whatever. He just wants to hang out. He wants us to bring along Sarah, if we can."

"I've got a date with Annika," Nish said.

"A *date*?" Lars asked.

"Okay, I'm supposed to get together with her."

"Where?"

"Same place – McDonald's. A little later."

"So we'll all be there together," said Dmitri.

"Call Slava," Travis said.

"It's not that simple," Dmitri said. "We have to break him out of here."

"*What?*"

"They won't let him go. He's got no life apart from playing hockey."

"Hockey *is* life," said Nish.

"He just wants to be a kid," said Dmitri. "Lars, you've got

to phone and get one of the bodyguards to go down to the front desk. Slava says he can give the other the slip."

"Won't he get in trouble?" Lars asked.

"Muck would sit one of us out if we did anything like that," Travis said.

Dmitri shook his head. "You don't understand. Slava is the best player in Russia. *He* won't get in any trouble. *They* will."

"Who will?"

"The guys guarding him."

Lars went to one of the house phones and Dmitri dialled the number and handed the receiver over to him. The boys heard a click, then a man's muffled voice. Lars spoke quickly, in Swedish. The man obviously understood. Lars had lowered his voice, and though the boys couldn't understand what he was saying, he sounded very authoritative. The man seemed to be shouting back, angrily. Lars spoke again, very calmly, and hung up.

"Did it work?" Dmitri asked.

"I think so. He should be headed down to the front desk."

"What did you tell him?" Travis asked.

"Nish gave me the idea," Lars smiled. "I told him his players had been fooling with the television sets. I said he was going to be charged 340 krona for the movies they had watched. He got mad and I told him if he wished to discuss the matter he'd have to meet with the manager."

"Brilliant!" Dmitri said, snapping his fingers.

They called Sarah's room next. She was delighted to be asked along. They ran into Data and tried to get him to come, too, but he said he thought he was getting a bad cold and didn't want to go out.

"*Gimme a second!*" Nish shouted at the last moment. He raced up to his room, reappearing a couple of minutes later at the elevator doors. His hair was freshly moussed and gelled and shining, smelling like room refreshener.

They met Sarah in the lobby and all went outside, skirting around to the street behind the Master Johan, where they had arranged to wait for Slava. Several minutes passed, and they had all but lost hope, when the rear door to the hotel opened and a slim young man in a red jacket slipped out, his cap pulled down tight over his eyes.

It was Slava. He ran over, shouting to Dmitri as he reached his new friends.

Dmitri laughed. "He locked the other guy in the washroom by jamming a hockey stick under the handle!"

Slava was now shaking hands with Sarah – very formal for a bunch of kids from North America. Sarah giggled; yet she seemed flattered, charmed by Slava's old-world ways.

"Let's get going!" Nish said.

They headed up towards McDonald's. It was a dull early-spring day, the clouds so low they spread like a thick grey blanket over the city.

At the first corner there were streetlights and a small bridge over a narrow canal which led towards the park where the old castle stood. It was quiet, with little traffic, and they began to relax a bit as they headed over the bridge.

"EEEE–AWWW–KEEE!" Nish shouted. There was no response. Annika wasn't within range.

Travis didn't feel quite right, but the others seemed at ease.

Slava and Sarah were walking together, but saying nothing. Nish was calling out constantly. If he was this bad now, what would he be like when they got to McDonald's?

Travis began to feel something was really wrong. At the far end of the bridge, a car had come to a stop. It must have slid on some ice, for it had swung sideways and was blocking their path. Two men were getting out.

Travis looked back to see if any traffic was coming towards them from the other end of the bridge. A dark van had slid the same way on that side, too! Another man was getting out.

It was the man with the gold tooth!

"*Watch out!*" Travis shouted.

But already it was too late. The others had noticed as well, and were ready to run – but they were trapped. The car blocked one end of the bridge; the van the other.

The quickest way off the bridge was to head back and take their chances with the man with the gold tooth, but as Lars and Travis started to move that way, they saw the man reach into his coat.

He had a gun!

"*Run for it!*" said Dmitri. "*It's them!*"

No one had to explain who. *The Russian mob was making its move!*

The five friends turned, scrambling frantically, not knowing which way to run. Travis caught sight of Nish's face: beet red, terrified.

The other two men were now running towards them.

"*They're after Slava!*" shouted Dmitri. "*We can't let him go!*"

"*Grab onto him!*" shouted Sarah.

She threw her arms around Slava just as the first two men reached them. One of the men roughly grabbed Slava by the arm and yanked – but now Dmitri also had a hold of his cousin and was desperately hanging on. The man yanked again, harder.

Travis had to do something! He was afraid, but he had to act. He dived for Slava's legs and caught him in a perfect tackle.

"HANG ON!" Dmitri screamed.

A boot lashed out and caught Travis on the side of the head. He saw a blinding flash of light, almost as if lightning had struck from inside his head. The pain was incredible, but still he held on. He was not going to chicken out!

Travis felt a huge weight come down on him. Out of his uninjured eye he could see it was Nish. His friend had leapt into action, too, but instead of going for Slava's legs, he had tackled the foot that had kicked Travis! It was the man with the gold tooth! The man went down hard on the roadway of the bridge, his gun spilling away.

KA-BOOOOOOM!

The stunning crack of the gun was followed by instant, eerie silence. Everyone lay still a moment. No one moved.

Travis looked up. The man with the gold tooth had hold of his gun again and was pointing it at them and shaking it. He was very upset.

"Get up!" he barked out in Russian.

"Everybody just get up slowly!" Dmitri translated.

The Owls rose slowly. Travis's head was screaming. He thought he was going to be sick. *Was he going to be shot? Were they going to kill Slava?*

"Move!"

"We're all to get in the van," Dmitri said.

Everybody? Why everybody? Travis wondered. But he also knew this was no time for him to raise his hand to ask a question. This wasn't a classroom.

The men hurried the friends towards the van at the near end of the bridge. Travis listened for police sirens. Someone must have heard the shot.

The men opened the rear doors of the van and roughly shoved their captives inside. Travis struck his head again, this time on Nish's knee.

He felt sick to his stomach. The van smelled of bad cigarettes. He could smell Nish's hair.

Sarah was shoved in on top of him, then Slava and Dmitri. Travis managed to sit up and caught sight of Slava.

He was white as a ghost.

"Move it!" the man with the gold tooth shouted in Russian.

The van wheels spun in the light snow, the rear end fishtailing as it turned on the quiet road and sped away in the opposite direction. The Russians were abandoning the car at the far end of the bridge, where it was still blocking the roadway.

Gold Tooth turned and swatted at them.

"Get down!" he shouted.

"Duck down!" Dmitri translated. He pushed Slava and Sarah down over the other two.

A heavy blanket flew over from the front seat, covering them.

The blinding flashes in Travis's head gave way to darkness.

11

Muck and Mr. Dillinger were waiting for the elevator in the lobby of the Master Johan, but when the doors slid open, they were almost trampled by the CSKA coach and the two bodyguards coming out. The coach looked furious, the bodyguards upset. They didn't even nod hello.

Mr. Dillinger, his eyes wide, turned to Muck.

"What's got into them, I wonder?"

But before Muck could answer, there was more activity. The doors leading from the lobby to the street swung open and Mr. Johanssen hurried in with a concerned look on his face. The sound of a police siren outside filled the lobby momentarily.

"There's been a shot!" Mr. Johanssen called out to the man at the front desk as he walked, fast, towards the elevators.

"*What's going on?*" Mr. Dillinger called to Mr. Johanssen.

"There's been a report of a gun fired behind the hotel."

Muck turned back towards the elevators. "I better check on the team."

@

Travis thought he could hear a dog bark. There were also sirens in the distance. Sirens were different in Sweden — almost as if they were breathing in and out quickly — but they were definitely sirens. Police, he hoped. Someone must have heard the gun go off.

Travis couldn't tell how long they'd been gone. An hour? Two? Muck would be wondering where they were. And the Russians would have panicked once they found out Slava had given them the slip. Even Data would have wondered what was taking so long with his fries.

Travis had no idea where he was. He had been unable to see anything from the back of the van, and the men had kept the blanket over their heads as they pushed and shoved them into wherever they were now. He could smell smoke, something burning. He was lying on his side and could barely see. His right eye was swollen almost shut.

The floor was very hard. Harder even than wood. And cold. There was a smell in the air, almost musty, something like the backyard in spring when the snow melts away and his mother would turn over the garden. The air felt cool, and damp, and cellar-like.

Travis wanted to roll over, but he couldn't. His hands were tied behind his back. He shook off the blanket that had been tossed over him and blinked in the darkness. There was a light somewhere behind him, a light flickering on the wall. He thought he could make out the patterns of stone. A stone wall. He was cold, and shivering.

He painfully sat upright. He could see Sarah sitting the same way, but with her back to the stone wall. Dmitri and Slava were also sitting with their hands tied behind them, and he caught Dmitri's eye. Dmitri was silently urging him to stay quiet; he jerked his head slightly, indicating something behind Travis.

Slowly, Travis twisted around. He saw Nish against the wall. He had his eyes closed and was shaking, but whether he was crying quietly or shivering from the cold, Travis couldn't tell.

He was able to turn his head far enough to see what Dmitri was signalling. Two of their captors – one of them the man with the gold tooth – were in the room with them. They were both smoking, but that wasn't what Travis had smelled. They were huddled close to a small naphtha heater. It was a camping heater, like Travis's father had. It was giving off some warmth, but not nearly enough to take the chill out of the room. The heater was what he had smelled.

The two men were speaking, very low, in Russian. One seemed angry, and also anxious.

Travis was surprised to hear Dmitri whisper, "Keep it low. Those two don't understand English."

Travis turned back. "Do you think they're really the mob?"

"I guess so. We knew they wanted Slava – they just didn't expect to end up with us, too."

Nish was now looking up. His whisper was a hiss, a bit too loud, and filled with fear. "*Where are we?*"

One of the men yelled at him to shut up.

The men were talking very fast now, their anger rising. Dmitri and Slava watched and listened, and Travis watched Dmitri, trying to read his expression. As Dmitri listened he seemed to grow more and more worried.

Travis decided to risk a whisper: "*What are they fighting about?*"

Dmitri blinked: "*Us.*"

"*Whatdya mean?*" Nish hissed.

"*Shhhhhh . . .*"

Gold Tooth stood up from the small heater and kicked angrily at a blanket that caught his foot. He turned and glared at the kids. Travis had never seen such hatred in anyone's eyes. He shivered – and not, this time, from the cold.

Gold Tooth then suddenly stormed out, lifting a solid wooden plank that was blocking the old door, and slamming it as he left.

The second man looked up sharply at the slam and then went back to eating the bread and cheese that he had pulled out of a sack. He also had beer, and when he opened one of the bottles the smell of it drifted across the dank room.

For a long time no one dared say anything. The man ate and grumbled to himself and threw a blanket around his shoulders. He opened another beer, then filled the little heater with naphtha and lighted it again, turning it up high.

Dmitri suddenly spoke up in Russian: "Can you please hang one of these blankets over that window? We're freezing!"

"Shut up!" the man snapped. He fiddled some more with the heater, then looked back at Dmitri with an evil smile. Dmitri had given him an idea.

The man gathered several of the old blankets. One he strung across the window, catching it on a nail on either side.

"Thank God," whispered Sarah.

But the man was thinking only of himself. He pulled his heater over into a corner of the room and assembled a sort of rough tent out of blankets strung across a chair and a stool and an old storage box. He moved the heater inside, then his beer. With one more sly smile at the shivering kids, he ducked down into his private, cosy little shelter.

"*Thanks a lot!*" Nish hissed with great sarcasm.

"I'm freezing!" said Sarah.

"No!" said Travis. "We want this!"

"We *want* to freeze to death?" Nish asked.

Travis hurried to explain. "My dad says never take one of those heaters inside a tent."

"Why not?" Dmitri asked.

"It gives off carbon monoxide gas."

"So?" Nish said.

"So – he'll kill himself, if he doesn't kill us first."

"We're being poisoned?" Sarah asked.

"Not us," said Travis. "There's too much fresh air getting in here through the cracks. But he's blocking himself off."

"What was the big fight over?" Lars asked Dmitri.

Dmitri didn't seem to want to say. "They were just arguing."

"What did they say?"

"Nothing."

Travis knew Dmitri was keeping something from them. "You'd better tell us," he said.

Dmitri swallowed hard and looked at Slava. His cousin couldn't understand much English, but Slava seemed to know what they were discussing anyway. He looked scared.

"The guy who left doesn't want the rest of us around," Dmitri said finally.

Nish brightened up. "They're going to let us go?"

"I'm not sure that's what he had in mind."

Dmitri would say no more, but Travis's imagination filled the rest in: they would be shot, or they would be left here to starve . . .

Travis's head and eye began to throb, badly.

Panic was setting in at the Master Johan. The parents and coaches and the rest of the Screech Owls were gathered in the lobby, but instead of calming each other down, the players were feeding off each other's fears. They were imagining every possible disaster that could befall their missing friends – even murder.

"The police are searching the city," Mr. Johanssen told them after a man in uniform had come in and talked to him. "There's no way anyone could get out of Malmö with all those young-sters and not get caught. They put up roadblocks immediately."

"Has there been a call?" asked Muck.

"One. Just to say they have Slava."

"What about the Screech Owls?"

Mr. Johanssen swallowed hard. "We have to presume," he said, "that they're with Slava."

Muck got up and walked to the window, staring out at a city he didn't know. He had never felt so helpless in his life.

The captives had no idea where Gold Tooth had gone. Probably he was making a call about the ransom.

"I'm so hungry I could eat blood pudding," Nish said.

Travis couldn't help himself: he giggled.

Another empty beer bottle dropped and rolled along the floor, and Travis heard the man burp. His breathing was becoming loud and uneven. The man was falling asleep. All that beer and the carbon monoxide was getting to him.

"*He's passing out!*" Travis whispered to the others.

Sarah strained to see past the hanging blankets, but could hardly move with her hands and feet tied.

"*Shhhhhh,*" she said. "*Wait!*"

They waited. The man's breathing continued to grow ever slower, deeper. Finally he began to snore.

Sarah twisted over onto her side. In the poor light, Travis could see her twisting and pulling at her bonds. He heard her stifle a cry once. It was no use; she was just hurting herself.

"Nish!" Sarah said quickly. "Get over here!"

Nish blinked. "What for?"

"Just do it! Quick – Gold Tooth could come back any minute!"

Nish groaned but did as he was told. He fell over onto his side and then rolled across the room until he was close to Sarah.

"*I feel like a worm!*" he complained.

"You *are* a worm!" Sarah said. "Now twist your stupid head around here so I can get at it!"

"What?"

"Just do as you're told! And hurry!"

As soon as Nish was within reach, Sarah turned her back to him and began rubbing her bound hands back and forth over his hair.

"*You're hurting me!*" Nish complained.

"Just shut up, Nish!" Sarah said. "I need your grease!"

So that was it! Travis watched as Sarah very deliberately rubbed her wrists back and forth over Nish's heavily greased hair, working in the mousse and gel so the ropes would slide. Back and forth, back and forth, back and forth over Nish's magnificent hairdo.

Nish whimpered almost in silence: "*Ow-ow-ow-ow-ow-ow . . .*"

Sarah worked a little longer, then stopped and caught her breath. "I'm going to try it," she said.

She took a deep breath and pulled as hard as she could. Nothing. She took another deep breath and yanked harder – *and her right hand came out!*

"*I'm free!*"

12

The Malmö police had come to the Master Johan with police dogs. They let them sniff some of the Screech Owls' hockey equipment, but the dogs had been unable to pick up any trail as the police worked them around the nearby streets.

Muck was beside himself. It was all his fault, he told anyone who would listen. He should never have let them wander about on their own . . . He should never have let them leave the hotel without informing him . . . He should have known that Dmitri would try to get together with his cousin Slava . . .

Muck clenched his hands into tight fists and chewed fiercely on his lower lip.

"*Muck?*"

The small voice behind him caught Muck off guard. It was Data, and he was trembling.

"I think I might have an idea . . ."

Sarah worked quickly. She untied her own feet, and then moved to untie Travis. He could hear her breathing. It seemed like she was fighting back tears, and in the dim light Travis could see that one of her wrists was bleeding.

No one said a word. They scrambled to untie the others and then all moved quietly towards the tent made of blankets.

When Travis lifted one corner, he could smell the naphtha and feel the heat inside against his face. The Russian was lying on his back, breathing deep and long and very, very slow. His throat rattled with each long-drawn breath.

"He's out cold!" Lars said.

Travis moved to turn off the heater.

"Leave it!" Nish said. "We haven't time!"

"He could die if we don't get some fresh air to him," Travis said. He turned off the heater and ripped down the blankets so the air from outside would get in.

Sarah was already at work, trussing the man's hands and feet with rope. He never even stirred.

Lars tried the door. It gave a bit. He pulled and it creaked loudly.

"*Shhhhhhhhhh!*" Dmitri hissed.

"What should we do?" Travis asked.

"*Run for it!*" said Nish.

"What if Gold Tooth's coming back?" Sarah asked. "He's the one who wants to kill us."

Lars yanked the door the rest of the way open. "I thought so," he said.

"Thought *what?*" said Nish.

"It's the castle!"

Travis looked around. The *castle?* Where they'd come with Lars's father?

"This is the old prison part," Lars said. He seemed very sure of himself, excited. "The courtyard is just across there."

The courtyard: where the two murderers stabbed the warden, and where they lost their heads, for a haircut. Travis couldn't help but think of the dead warden, bleeding to death on the stones.

"There was that armour exhibition," Travis said, not quite so sure. This didn't seem at all the same.

"This is the really old part," said Lars. "The exhibition should be . . . ," he turned in the dark, searching, ". . . up this way."

"Won't they find us?" Sarah asked.

"It's Sunday – I th-think," said Lars, slowly. "It will be closed."

"We've got to head for the courtyard," said Travis.

"You're right," Lars said. "If we get there, we know how to get out."

"*Which way?*" called Nish.

"This way," Lars said, heading down the darkened corridor. "I think."

"*You better be sure,*" said Nish. He sounded scared.

It was dark, but not quite pitch black. There was light leaking in through the occasional window or crack in the walls. Lights from cars passing, perhaps. Or searchlights, Travis hoped. He thought he heard another dog bark. Once, he thought he heard Nish's stupid call.

Then he knew he had heard it: "*Eeee-awww-keee!*" faint and distant.

"*That's Annika!*" Nish hissed.

They stopped and listened. Again the call.

"Hoist me up!" Nish said.

There was a window, with a crack between the sill and frame. Lars and Dmitri and Slava grabbed onto Nish's legs and lifted. He grasped the sill and pulled. When he reached as close as he could, he shouted out.

"EEEE–AWWW–KEEE!"

From the distance, faintly, the call came back. "*Eeee-awww-keee!*"

"I think she heard!" Nish said.

He was about to call again when they heard a mighty creak and clatter of metal from far down the corridor.

"*Shhhhh!*" Lars said. The boys let Nish back down, quickly and quietly.

They could hear footsteps. Heavy shoes. A man, moving quickly.

"*It's Gold Tooth!*" Travis said.

They listened. There were more steps. And then two voices. *Russian* voices. And angry.

"There's *two* of them!" Nish hissed.

"Who's the other?" Sarah gasped.

Dmitri listened to the hurried, angry talk. "It sounds like Gold Tooth's boss. He's really upset. They can't get through to the Russian team. There's police all around the hotel. He's blaming Gold Tooth for involving us in it."

"What do you mean?"

Dmitri paused. "The new guy wants to shoot us and try to get Slava out of here."

"*Why us?*" Nish squealed. "*We're not going to the NHL.*"

"We've *seen* them," Dmitri explained. "We know what they look like."

Nish was silent. He was beginning to realize just how much danger they were in.

"What'll we do?" Sarah asked.

It was Lars who answered. "If they're talking like that, they didn't hear Nish's call. They don't know we're out. We've got surprise on our side."

"*Whatdya mean?*" Nish asked.

Lars seemed very thoughtful, very thorough. "Look, they're going to come through that doorway ahead. Maybe we can latch it shut and cut them off."

"They'll know we did it," cautioned Travis.

"Maybe. Or maybe they'll just think it swung closed. What's it matter anyway? We have to stop them. Gold Tooth's got a gun, remember?"

A sound came out of Nish. Not quite a whimper. More animal than human.

"C'mon!" Lars called to Travis. The two boys hurried ahead to the big door. They pulled together, and with a creak the door gave and swung shut. Travis hoped the men were still talking and wouldn't hear it. Lars set the latch.

"What now?" Sarah asked.

"I don't know," Lars said. He sounded scared. "The door will only block them for a minute."

What could they do? Travis's head was hurting from more than just the blow from Gold Tooth's boot. He was trying to think as fast as he could.

He had an idea! It wasn't like a light bulb going off in his head, but there was almost a flash. He suddenly felt excited. "The display?" he said. "Where is it?"

Lars turned. "Huh?"

"The armour display. How do we get there?"

Lars thought a moment. "I think it's straight back that way."

Travis didn't waste a second. "Nish, come with me?"

"Wh-wh-where?"

"Never mind. C'mon!"

He hurried ahead through the dark, Nish scrambling behind him. They passed by the prison cell where they'd been held and where, they hoped, the Russian was still passed out cold. They came to a modern door. With his heart beating wildly, Travis drove his shoulder hard against the door and almost choked with excitement when it gave slightly. It was enough for two young shoulders to push hard the rest of the way. A cheap latch and padlock ripped out of the wood and dropped harmlessly on the floor.

They were in!

A few lights had been left on for security. Travis hoped they had triggered an alarm at the police station. Whatever brought them here as fast as possible was all right with him. This was no false alarm.

They were not far from the display of Viking spears. "Grab a couple of those!" he commanded Nish.

Nish waded into the display, reaching with shaking hands. The spears jumbled and clattered to the floor like hockey sticks in a dressing room. He scrambled to pick up two.

Travis headed into the next room. He knew exactly what he wanted.

The spangenhelm!

"What *is* that?"

Sarah was looking at Travis in amazement. He had handed her one of the spears. Nish was holding the other. Travis had the big *spangenhelm* on tight over his head. He knew he must look idiotic. He could barely keep his head off his chest it was so heavy. His head was rolling, his neck muscles weakening.

Dmitri and Slava were also armed. Dmitri had a flail, its heavy spiked head dragging on the ground beside him. Slava had a huge iron mace, so heavy he could barely lift the massive club.

"What the heck am I supposed to do with *this*?" Dmitri asked. He seemed very uncertain.

Travis himself was uncertain. He didn't know exactly why he'd collected the armour. But he did know they'd need something – *and fast!*

The Russians had reached the latched door. They could hear the sound of surprise in Gold Tooth's voice when he found that their route to the prison cells had been blocked. There was a rattling of the latch, then banging at the door.

"They're breaking it down," said Sarah.

Travis turned to Dmitri and Slava. "Move ahead and get down in the dark on each side. You guys will have to trip one of them up."

"How?" asked Dmitri.

"Swing your weapons as hard as you can," Travis said.

Dmitri and Slava moved a little closer to the door and ducked down into the shadows.

Travis turned to Nish and Sarah. "They go down, you two have to make sure they stay down," he said.

"Understood," said Sarah.

With a mighty groan and snap, the big door gave. They could hear the Russians cursing and kicking it as they passed. They couldn't tell whether Gold Tooth thought it was an accident or deliberate.

The two men hurried along the corridor towards the young friends, their heavy steps growing closer. Travis peered into the distance. He could see their shadows looming in the darkness as they approached.

The friends kept completely silent, but for the wheeze of Nish's breathing.

Closer . . . Closer . . . Closer . . .

"*Now!*" Travis shouted.

Dmitri and Slava swung their weapons at exactly the same time. Travis and the others could hear the sickly sound of metal against bone, and the screams of the first Russian as he went down.

"EEEEOOOOOOWWWWWW!"

Only one went down! Gold Tooth stumbled, but caught himself on the far wall. He turned, cursing.

Sarah had already moved to set her spear against the neck of the fallen man. Nish was right behind her, his spear shaking.

In the dim light, Travis could see Gold Tooth fumbling in his coat.

He was reaching for his gun!

Travis pulled down the *spangenhelm*, lowered his head, and charged. *Straight for Gold Tooth's gut!*

KAAA-BOOOOOOMMM!!

The gun exploded. The enormous, shocking sound filled the corridor instantly. It filled Travis's head and he felt the helmet jerk, then smash into something soft.

"Ooooooohhh!!"

It was the sound of Gold Tooth's breath being forced from his body as Travis drove his head into his stomach. He felt the man's legs give way, and then Travis hit the floor, the heavy helmet ringing as it struck stone.

He had done it.

Travis rose unsteadily to his feet. Gold Tooth gasped again and sank back. The other man was howling, holding his shin and trying to keep away from the spears.

Suddenly the corridor filled with another loud sound. Not a shot, but a voice – a loudspeaker.

"*Stanna där du är! Rör dig inte!*" ("Stay exactly where you are! Don't move!")

Gold Tooth looked up, still fighting for his breath. There was fury in his eyes. There were dogs barking. And men running.

"*Ingen rör sig!*" ("No one move!") a voice commanded over the speaker.

There were lights now. Flashlights in the corridor; searchlights panning across the walls, spilling in through the small windows.

Two police dogs raced into the room, barking, their handlers right behind them.

One dog leapt for Gold Tooth, grabbing his forearm in his teeth. The man screamed and rolled on the floor, the dog on top of him.

The other dog lunged for Nish, barking and using its paws to pin him against the stone wall.

"*I'm dead!*" Nish screamed. "*I'm dead!*"

The Malmö police quickly handcuffed the two Russians and lifted them to their feet, the boss limping badly and Gold Tooth still gasping for breath. Lars directed the police to the cell where the third mobster was still snoring.

One of the policemen had the *spangenhelm* and was examining it carefully. He whistled, and showed his superior, who said something to Lars.

Lars pointed to a dent on the side of the helmet, "The bullet did that," he said to Travis.

Travis couldn't believe it. *He had blocked a shot.*

It all took a while to sort out. More police came, then Muck and Mr. Dillinger, and then the two Russian bodyguards, looking more relieved than anyone. They raced up to Slava and grabbed him, kissing him on both cheeks.

Nish stared at them and rolled his eyes.

"*I'm gonna hurl!*" he said.

For once, Travis thought he might mean it.

Nish had been terrified by the dog, but when he heard why it had leapt for him, he was delighted. They had been hunting everywhere for the kids, but without luck. It wasn't until Data came up with the solution that the dogs were able to do their work.

Data had suggested the dogs follow the smell of Nish's hair. He had them sniff the mousse and gel that Nish had left in the bathroom, and within fifteen minutes the dogs had found the abandoned van and were headed towards the old castle.

A familiar call came from down the corridor.

"EEEE–AWWW–KEEE!"

It was Annika. She must have sneaked past the police line.

For once, Nish didn't answer. Instead, he turned, ducked down, and began pulling at his hair, trying to make it stand back up.

"*Who's got a comb?*" he hissed.

Lars handed one over. Nish frantically pulled and yanked and teased his hair, trying, without success, to make it stand back up in spikes.

He turned on Sarah, his eyes narrow, his nostrils flaring.

"You *ruined* my hair!" he said.

"Your hair saved our lives!" Sarah answered. "*Twice!*"

13

hey'd decided to continue with the tournament. The men had been arrested and the kids had all been checked out at the Malmö hospital. The swelling was already going down in Travis's eye, and Sarah's wrists had been dressed and wrapped in clean bandages.

Sarah and Travis had sat out the next game against Gothenburg, but Dmitri and Lars and Nish were cleared to play. Nish wouldn't have missed it for anything: a chance to be the hero in front of Annika and her friends.

The Gothenburg team had been excellent. They were all superb skaters, and most could handle the puck. But they weren't very big, especially compared to the bigger Owls like Andy, Wilson, and, of course, Nish. With Annika calling out every time he stepped on the ice, Nish had played like he was the size of Eric Lindros.

By the final period, the Owls had pulled away. Dmitri had scored twice and Nish once, on a shot from the point. After scoring, Nish had even pretended not to hear the yells from

Annika and her friends, skating back out to centre with his stick over his knees and staring up at the clock to wait for the score-board to change. Travis and Sarah had to laugh.

"It's a wonder he doesn't stop and comb his hair," Sarah said.

Nish's goal had proven to be the winner. The Owls' record was two wins and a loss, which left them tied with two other teams for second place. The Owls, however, came out ahead, because they'd scored more goals. They were headed back to Stockholm for the championship. And they'd be playing the club with the best record in the tournament: CSKA, Slava Shadrin's team.

Travis Lindsay stood at the blueline and shook. He had never been so excited in his life. He was playing for the International Goodwill Pee Wee Championship – a *world* championship. As high as he could see in the massive Globen Arena, the red seats were filled with fans. *Thousands* of them! And everyone was standing for the anthems, first the Russian and then "O Canada." Travis shivered up the length of his spine.

He knew why so many people had come. The story was an international sensation. A thirteen-year-old hockey player had been kidnapped by the Russian mob. Other twelve- and thirteen-year-olds from Canada and Sweden had helped him escape. Lars Johanssen was a hero in Sweden. ("Maybe they'll put me on a stamp, like Peter Forsberg!" he joked.)

Sarah was insisting on playing – though her wrists had to be dressed again just before the game and she was obviously still in pain.

The big story, however, was Slava Shadrin. If he was good enough to be kidnapped by ruthless mobsters – *how good was he?* The stands of the Globen Arena were filled with the curious. There were even television cameras!

Nish was in his glory. He had worked on his hair half the afternoon. If Slava had thousands staring his direction, Nish knew that at least one in the crowd was staring only at him.

"Behind the net!" Travis had screamed over the cheers as the anthem ended. He was surprised to see Annika had come all the way from Malmö with some of her friends. They were waving a huge Canadian flag.

"Yeah," Nish said matter-of-factly. "I know."

Travis had never seen Muck look so relaxed before a big game. He was smiling, which was unusual. Muck wanted Sarah's line to start. "Remember," he said. "This is a 'goodwill' tourna-ment – you're here to have fun. You're also representing your country.

"And one more thing," Muck said. He paused, grinning. "Don't even *think* about arguing with this referee."

Travis turned around. Across the ice the referee was stretch-ing, one long leg extended to the side, his back to the Screech Owls' bench. But Travis didn't need to see the face to know who it was. The hair was enough.

Borje Salming!

Salming blew on his whistle to call the teams in for the opening face-off. He raised his hands to check the red lights at both ends. He smiled down on the two centres, Slava Shadrin and Sarah Cuthbertson, then winked at Travis.

Travis was in a state of shock as the puck fell.

Sarah won the face-off with her tricky little sweep move – pulling the puck out of the air just before it struck the ice – and before Travis knew it, it had rattled into his skate blades. He tried to kick the puck up to his stick so he could shoot it back to Nish, but he lost it in his skates and the Russian winger jabbed it loose and away.

Travis gave chase, but he was well behind the play. The winger hit a rushing defenceman, who clipped the puck off the glass so it skipped in behind Nish and, in an instant, was picked up by Slava Shadrin, cutting in like a sudden wind.

But so, too, was Sarah. There would be no quick goal this time. She laid her stick over Slava's and leaned hard, driving him off the puck before he could shoot. Data, racing over to cover up for Nish, picked up the puck and iced it. The linesman blew his whistle.

Sarah skated back to the bench shaking her right wrist. She wanted a change. Andy's line came out and Mr. Dillinger and Muck gathered round Sarah. She just nodded when they asked her if she felt all right. Nodded and stared straight ahead, over the boards. Travis, sitting beside her, wasn't convinced.

Ten minutes into the game, CSKA caught the Owls on a quick shift change. Slava Shadrin came over the boards and picked up a loose puck and beat Jesse Highboy easily. He came in on Wilson, beat him, and got past Jeremy with a high wrist shot that pinged in off the crossbar.

Russia 1, Canada 0.

Muck put a hand on Sarah's shoulder.

"Shadrin will kill us unless you stay with him," Muck said. "Are you up to it?"

"Yes."

"You're on, then."

Slava Shadrin's skates had barely hit the ice when the Russian star discovered he had grown a new shadow.

The opposing centres flew about the ice together like two sparrows in a field, Sarah turning precisely when Slava turned. If Slava picked up a loose puck or a pass, Sarah immediately checked him, using her stick on his and pushing down with all her strength so he could neither stickhandle nor pass. With Sarah on him, all Slava could do was dump the puck.

Travis was amazed. He had never seen anyone work as hard as Sarah. Sweat was pouring from her face. And he could tell from the way she winced and shook her gloves as she sat on the bench that she was in pain.

Travis saw Nish circling for the puck. He saw Nish's head come up for one quick look down the ice. Travis knew he wasn't looking for a place to pass the puck. He was looking for an opening.

Travis curled at the blueline, cutting across ice to his off wing. Dmitri read the play perfectly and moved to Travis's wing. Travis was now on the right, Dmitri on the left, as Nish broke straight up centre, carrying the puck.

Sarah saw what Nish was about to do, and she used her shoulder to ride Slava out of the play.

Slava's coach was leaning over the boards, shouting "Interference!" But no referee, not even Borje Salming, was going to call that. Sarah's pick was just a smart play.

Nish beat the first defence by letting the puck slide ahead and then quickly working his stick back and forth as if stickhandling.

The defenceman fell for it and went for the stick blade, while the puck slid right by him and Nish looped around his side and was free.

It was now a three-on-one. Nish dropped the puck and ran right over the second Russian defenceman. More screams from the Russian bench. Dmitri picked up the loose puck and came in on their goaltender. He faked a shot and slipped the puck to Travis, flying in on his off wing. It was easy.

Canada 1, Russia 1.

It stayed that way until the break before the final period. Neither team could score. Slava couldn't get free of Sarah, and Nish couldn't lug the puck down the ice whenever he wanted any more. Both goaltenders were spectacular.

In the dressing room Travis could see that Sarah was in real pain. Her eyes welled up with tears just in taking off her gloves. The bandages were pink with bloodstains.

Mr. Dillinger had made ice packs with plastic bags. He applied the ice and then carefully dressed the tortured wrists again.

"You okay to play?" Muck asked.

Sarah nodded. "I'm fine," she said. Travis noticed the little catch in her voice.

There was a knock at the door. Mr. Dillinger got it and signalled for Muck.

"The referee wants to talk to you," he said.

14

When the two teams came out for the final period, Muck and the Russian coach were still in deep discussion with Borje Salming. There were also two interpreters standing to the side, so it made for a tight little group in the corridor as the teams passed by. Every player was curious to know what was happening.

Then Salming and the coaches shook hands. All of them were smiling.

Nish, of course, was the one to ask: "What was all that about?"

"None of your business, Nishikawa."

Sarah and Slava lined up for the face-off. Travis could sense the tension. A 1–1 tie, Canada versus Russia, the peewee championship of the world – of the *universe*! – on the line.

Why, then, did Borje Salming seem to be chuckling as he raised his hand, a black glove covering the puck?

Slava and Sarah got set. Travis readied himself to jump into the play if Sarah tied up Slava.

Salming opened his hand and the puck fell.

The *little* puck!

Travis could hear Slava and Sarah gasp. He could hear Nish shout, "*What the –?*"

The puck bounced – and nothing was the same again.

Sarah lunged instinctively for the bouncing black disk and managed to tip it to Travis, who caught it perfectly on his blade.

It felt so comfortable! So tiny and small and light and . . . *alive*! Yes, that was it, *alive*!

Perhaps this was how a young basketball player would feel if his hand could hold a ball from above. Or a pitcher if the mound were moved a dozen steps closer to home plate.

Travis stickhandled quickly, the solid little puck dancing to the rhythm of his stick. He knew the Russian winger on his side was charging, but he knew as well that he had never felt more in control of a puck.

Travis spun, and the winger flew by, missing him. He snapped his stick and the puck flew back to Data, who caught it perfectly and fired it across ice to Nish, who was already in full motion.

Nish cradled the little puck as if it were an egg that would break if anyone so much as touched it as he passed by. He turned past the winger, then slipped the puck between Slava's feet and broke over centre, his head level, his hips square, the puck out in front of him and moving back and forth as if it were tied to the blade of his stick.

Soundless! Nish was stickhandling in utter silence, the puck soft on the stick blade, the ice so smooth from the flood there was only the sizzle and sigh of skates digging in and gliding.

Nish fired the little puck towards the far corner. It seemed to catch the wind, almost like a Frisbee as it hung in the air, and flew effortlessly, the rink suddenly filling with a loud crack as it found the glass and bounced back out, landing flat along the face-off circle.

Nish and Dmitri had played it perfectly. Dmitri had taken off the moment he figured Nish would dump the puck in. Dmitri was so fast he blew by the defence in a blur and was at the circle as the puck landed.

Dmitri was in and free – the shoulder fake, the move to the backhand, and the little puck clicked in smartly off the crossbar.

Canada 2, Russia 1.

"Is this legal?" Nish wanted to know when he had high-fived his way to the bench.

"We're here to have fun," Muck reminded him. "Remember?"

"Yeah, but . . . does it count if we use that little puck?"

"Did it go in?"

"Yeah, but –"

"Then it counts, Nishikawa. Relax."

Travis looked up at Muck and could hardly believe his eyes. Muck was laughing in the final period of a championship game, the Owls up by only one goal. Travis had never seen him so relaxed, so easygoing. And all because of a little puck.

Borje Salming faced the two teams off again, and again he dropped the miniature practice puck. It seemed he was going to finish the game with it. And why not? Travis said to himself. Look at how exciting the game has become.

The Russians tied it on a long shot from the point, the shot taking off so fast Travis couldn't even track it from the bench. Jeremy Weathers's glove shot out, but too late.

Russia 2, Canada 2.

Muck tapped Sarah on the shoulder the next time Slava's line came out. She went over the boards immediately, Dmitri and Travis following.

The face-off was in the Owls' end, to the right of Jeremy. Sarah wanted everyone placed exactly right, and while she was signalling to Nish, Jeremy skated quickly out to Travis.

"*No fair!*" Jeremy shouted.

Travis looked up. Jeremy was in despair. His face was red, flushed, and sweaty.

"Whadya mean?" Travis asked.

"I can't stop a puck I can't even see. You guys should have to use miniature sticks and wear skates that are two sizes too small."

Travis giggled at the thought. "Yeah, right."

The linesman blew quickly on his whistle and pointed to the net. Jeremy wiggled back. Travis looked down at the ice and laughed. He could hardly wait to get his stick on the little puck again. But he realized it wasn't the same for everyone. No doubt the Russian goalie felt the same as Jeremy. The goalies would prefer pucks the size of pizzas.

The puck flew back to the point, where one of the Russian

defencemen gloved it and dropped it down for a perfect slap-shot. Travis was the closest Owl. He knew what he had to do. He dived and twisted his body perfectly, the drive from the point hammering into his pants.

Compared with the danger he had faced this week, block-ing a tiny puck seemed easy.

The two teams played back and forth for most of the period, neither side able to penetrate the other's defence. The miniature puck had such a strange effect on the game. The for-wards were clearly more excited, trying harder, more anxious, and it caused a lot of broken plays. The defence were all more concerned, more wary of the power of a shot, and so they played with greater responsibility, always trying to make sure they kept shooters to the boards or blocked shots from the point. The goaltenders, too, seemed more alert, more worried, more frightened that they would let in a bad shot and be held responsible for a loss.

Travis figured he would have one final shift before the game ended. What would happen if the game was still tied? he asked himself. Overtime? A shootout?

They faced off to the left of Jeremy. Sarah won the puck from Slava and clipped it back to Nish, who immediately spun behind the net. Slava charged him. Nish tried a dangerous little move he had worked on in practice, a back pass against the boards just as the checker arrived, the puck bouncing back to Nish as the checker skated by. It worked perfectly! Nish faked to his right and broke out the left side, gathering speed.

Travis heard the call from behind the glass: "EEEE–AWWW–KEEE!"

Nish faked a pass to Dmitri and flipped a little backhand to Sarah, who was cutting across centre. Sarah carried the puck into the Russian end. She dropped for Dmitri, who tried to hit Travis flying in on the left side, but the defence stuck out his skate and the little puck ticked off and into the boards. Slava Shadrin, racing back, picked it up and turned. He failed, however, to see Nish sliding in to block any pass.

It was a dangerous pinch, but it worked. Nish's shin pads swept the little puck away from Slava, off the boards, and down into the corner, where Sarah was waiting. She shot the puck behind the net to Dmitri. Dmitri pivoted and fired it backhand out to Travis, who was fighting through the two defencemen to get to the front of the net.

Travis's stick blade just caught the little puck. It was so small, so light, that it stayed. He was off balance, falling, but he managed to flick a shot towards the net as he went down.

The tiny puck flew up as if Travis had cracked the hardest slapshot of his life. The goalie's glove shot out, but too late. The shot went hard into the roof of the net, exploding the goaltender's water bottle high into the air.

Travis knew it was in before he hit the ice. He couldn't believe it! He, Travis Lindsay, had just scored the winning goal against Russia in the final minute! He was Paul Henderson!

He felt the ice, hard beneath him, and he felt his teammates, soft but heavy as they piled on, screaming and screeching. The tangle of bodies and sticks and helmets slid towards the corner. The last to join in was a whooping Jeremy Weathers, who had skated the length of the ice to jump into the celebration.

"*Travis!*" they yelled.

"*Way to go, Trav!*"
"*We won!*"
"*We won!*"
"*We won!*"

15

There were thirty-four seconds left on the clock, the same amount of time remaining when Paul Henderson had scored the goal to give Canada a win over the Soviet Union back in 1972. There was singing in the stands. Swedish flags and Canadian flags waving, everyone on their feet for the countdown. Travis could see Annika right against the glass in the Canadian end. She was blowing a kiss to Nish. Nish was pretending he hadn't noticed, leaning over with his stick on his knees and fussing with his skate laces. But Travis could see that, every once in a while, Nish was stealing a peek to check what was going on behind the glass.

Muck wanted Andy's line out for the final seconds. They were stronger defensively, but he also wanted Nish out with Lars, the two strongest Owls defencemen.

Travis drooped his glove over the boards and watched. His heart was still pounding. He was the hero, the Canadian hero, and he still couldn't believe it. He looked up towards the face-off circle, where Borje Salming was just moving in to drop the puck.

The little puck had barely hit the ice when the Russian centre bolted for the bench and Slava Shadrin leapt straight over the boards. One moment he was landing on the ice, the next he was a blur across the blueline. There was no time for Muck to get Sarah out!

Lars was a great skater, the best on the whole team at moving backwards or to the sides, but he was helpless against such speed.

Slava took the pass and looped around Lars. He came in on Jeremy, cutting across the crease. Jeremy lunged for the poke check just as Slava dropped the puck into his skates, then kicked it back up as Jeremy's stick bounced off Slava's shin pads. A quick little backhand and the puck was high in the far corner of the net.

Tie game!

"I can't shoot."

Travis said nothing. He, like everyone else, was listening to Sarah Cuthbertson explain to Muck why she couldn't take the first shot in the shootout. The two teams had played ten minutes of overtime without a goal being scored, and the reason was largely Sarah, who had checked Slava Shadrin so well he had not even managed one good shot on net.

But Sarah had paid a heavy price. Both her gloves were off. Mr. Dillinger had wrapped her wrists in towels, but the blood was seeping through. Sarah was crying. And if Sarah was crying, it had to hurt bad.

"Travis," Muck said. "You're up first."

Travis had half wanted this, half feared it. He was going to have to take the first shot for Canada. There was absolutely no doubt who would be taking the shot for Russia.

He took a deep breath and looked across the ice. Slava was already out, circling, staring down at the ice, gathering himself. Travis wondered how this must look to the huge crowd: Travis Lindsay, skinny, goofy Screech Owl, up against Slava Shadrin, the greatest peewee hockey player in the entire world.

Borje Salming was conferring with the two goaltenders. Travis could tell that Jeremy was talking excitedly. The Russian goalie also seemed worked up. Borje Salming was nodding. Salming skated over to the Russian bench, talked with the coach, then came over and spoke to Muck.

"The goalies want to go back to the regulation puck for the shootout," he explained. "It's only fair."

"No problem," Muck said. He obviously wanted Jeremy to have every chance possible.

They would shoot in turn, starting with Slava and Travis. Then four more shooters for each team would follow. If the teams were still tied after five shots each, they would go into a sudden death shootout, beginning again with the first two, Travis Lindsay for Canada, and Slava Shadrin for Russia.

Slava went first. He flew down the ice so fast Jeremy had trouble moving with him, and when he passed by, he reached back and tapped the puck into the open far side. A goal so seemingly effortless that Jeremy slammed his stick in anger against the crossbar. But all the Owls knew how impossible it had been. It was a great goal.

Borje Salming laid the puck at centre ice and blew the whistle for Travis to begin skating.

Travis felt like he was sneaking up on the puck. And when

he reached it, it seemed the puck had grown to the size of a patio stone. It was as if it weighed more than he did. His arms were weak, his legs rubbery. He felt like he was once again wearing the *spangenhelm* and his neck muscles were giving way. He moved up over the blueline slowly, afraid even to stickhandle for fear he would drop the huge, heavy puck and skate right past it.

Should he deke? Shoot? He didn't know and hadn't any time to decide. He was instantly at the edge of the net, trying to put a backhand through the solid mass of the goalie's pads, not a crack of daylight between the goalie and the post.

The puck dribbled off harmlessly to the side.

The Russian bench went crazy. Half the crowd cheered and whistled and sang. Travis skated, head down, back to his bench. No one looked at him.

The second shooters both failed, and so, too, did the third.

When the fourth Russian shooter failed, Muck chose Lars Johanssen to take the shot for Canada. It was a surprising move – *a defenceman?* – but Travis understood. They couldn't use their best player, Sarah. And Dmitri had already shot and just missed a high corner. Lars had moves. And Lars was in his home country, with his family in the stands.

He came up the ice slowly, almost as if he were sitting in a chair relaxing. He didn't seem afraid of stickhandling the big puck. He slowed up even more, seemed almost to stop, then accelerated quickly, catching the goalie for a second off guard. The goaltender moved with him, and Lars reached back with one hand on his backhand and tapped the puck in.

Tied, again!

The Canadian bench emptied and piled onto Lars. Travis was one of the first to reach him, and they went down together under a crush of bodies.

"*Way to go, Lars!*" Travis screamed.

"*I tried my Peter Forsberg!*" Lars shouted back, ecstatic.

The fifth Russian was stopped by a great butterfly move by Jeremy, leaving one final Canadian chance in the first round of the shootout. But who was going to take it?

"Nishikawa," Muck said.

Nish skated all the way back to the Canadian net and slammed Jeremy on the pads. He took off his helmet and skated to the glass, leaned into it, and left a big smudge of a kiss for Annika. The crowd roared and cheered.

Nish then came flying down the ice and picked up the puck at centre. He hit the Russian blueline – everyone thinking deke – and suddenly wound up and let go the wildest, hardest slapper Travis had ever seen, a shot so hard that the follow-through knocked Nish to the ice.

The shot hit the goalie's glove and kept going, the puck like a live mouse as it scurried up over the edge of the Russian's glove and found the net.

Nish, still sliding along the ice on his back, hit the goalie next, the two of them crashing into the net with the puck.

Borje Salming's whistle was in his mouth, and his cheeks were puffing in and out, but Travis couldn't hear. He could see Salming's hand though, and Salming was pointing into the net.

Goal!

Canada wins!

16

f hockey kept such records, this would have gone down as the greatest pile-on in history. The second the red light went on, the Screech Owls poured onto the ice like a pail of minnows dumped off the end of a dock.

Travis felt as if he had left the ice surface at the blueline and hadn't landed until he was at the crease, his stick and gloves and helmet flying as he soared and slid towards the greatest Canadian hero of the moment: Wayne Nishikawa.

"*Hey!*" Nish screamed as the first Screech Owls hit him. "*Watch the hair!*"

But no one paid him the slightest attention. Dmitri pushed off Nish's helmet, Lars wrapped his arms around him, Sarah – trying to protect her bleeding wrists – fell onto him, laughing.

"*The hair! The hair!*" Nish screamed.

Even Muck piled on. In all the dozens of tournaments the Owls had played, Travis had never seen Muck do much more than smile or nod or, a couple of times, shake the hands of the players as they came off the ice. But Muck was digging down from on top, his big face open wide in a laugh that had no sound.

Muck found what he was looking for: Nish's head. He grabbed it in a hammerlock, then sharply rasped the knuckles of his free hand through Nish's pride and joy.

"*Not my hair! Lemme go!*"

Travis could see Nish's beet-red face from where he lay in the tangle. He could tell the last thing in the world Nish wanted was to be let go. He was the hero of the hour – and he was going to milk it for all it was worth.

Travis felt a body pushing up from beneath him. He thought at first it must be Sarah, trying to protect her wrists, but when he turned he realized it was the little Russian goaltender, still trapped in the Owls' pile-on.

The goalie was crying. Travis could see through the player's mask that his eyes were red and swollen and wet. It must have been horrible for him; not only had he let in the goal that lost the tournament, but then he had been forced to be part of the celebration.

They hugged Nish and roughed up his greasy hair and slapped his shoulders and his back, and finally the knot of legs and arms and heads undid itself and the Owls began collecting their gloves and sticks and helmets for the post-tournament ceremony.

Dmitri's stick was over by Travis's left glove. As they bent down, Travis asked a quick question.

"How do you say, 'Great game'?"

Dmitri looked up. "'Great game.' Just like that."

"No, no, I mean in Russian."

"Oh. . . . Try, '*Horoshosvgeal.*'"

"'*Horse-os . . .*'"

Dmitri shook his head, laughing. "'*Horosh-osv-geal,*'" he repeated carefully.

"'*Horoshosvgeal.*'"

"That's it."

They lined up for the handshake. Jeremy went first, Travis last, then Muck. The Russians were very gracious, some of them smiling. Travis came to the goalie who'd been crying and reached out with his arm and grabbed the goalie's shoulder instead of his hand and brought him to a stop.

"'*Horoshosvgeal,*'" Travis said.

The goalie stopped. He blinked, his eyes still red. Then he smiled.

Travis came to Slava, who hit Travis on the shoulder and smiled when he saw him.

"'*Horoshosvgeal,*'" Travis said.

Slava looked back, then roared with laughter.

"Thank you," he said in English. "And the same to you!"

Slava came to Sarah, who couldn't shake hands because of her wrists. He smiled, and suddenly – much to Sarah's shock – grabbed her in a big bear hug, lifting her off the ice. The rest of the CSKA players rattled their sticks on the ice in recognition. Perhaps better than anyone, they knew the job Sarah had done on Slava.

Some of the crowd was on the ice. Annika and her Swedish friends came running and sliding and cheering over to the Owls. Annika jumped at Nish and wrapped herself around his neck. They hugged, but Travis noticed there was no kiss. Nish obviously felt safer with a half-inch of bulletproof Plexiglas between them.

The tournament organizers had rolled out a red carpet for the final ceremonies.

Two young women followed behind Borje Salming carrying medals on velvet cushions.

One by one Salming placed a medal around the neck of each Screech Owl and shook the player's hand. When Sarah couldn't shake, he leaned over and gave her a gentle kiss on the cheek, which brought a cheer from the crowd.

Borje Salming came to Travis and smiled as he put the medal around his neck. "Good game," he said as he shook Travis's hand.

Travis was speechless.

Nish was standing next to Travis. Salming gave him his medal, shook his hand, and then patted his shoulder.

"Good defenceman," Borje Salming said. "Just like me."

Nish, of course, was never speechless: "We have the same hair," he said.

Borje Salming looked at Nish as if he had lost his mind. Nish just stood there, grinning.

"Hey," Nish said, when Salming had moved along, "I had to say *something*, didn't I?"

Silver medals were awarded to the Russian team and then the bronze to the Djurgårdens peewee team that had come in third. They then announced the Most Valuable Player for each team. Slava Shadrin won for CSKA and the crowd gave a huge cheer as Mr. Johanssen made the presentation. The Russian delegation then came out onto the carpet and the Most Valuable Player for Canada was announced.

"*Wayne Nishikawa!*"

Nish looked startled. He dropped his stick and gloves and began skating over, but suddenly stopped. He was right in front of Sarah.

"This should have been yours," he said.

Sarah smiled. "You scored the winner," she said graciously.

Nish smiled back. "You got us into the shootout."

The Russian leader handed him a wrapped present, and Nish took it and then reached out his hand to shake.

The man shook his head. He leaned over instead and kissed Nish on one cheek. Then he went for the other but missed as a startled Nish jumped back, a look of shock on his face.

The Russian laughed and shook his head.

Nish stopped again as he passed Sarah. He handed her the MVP award. "I wish you'd won it in the first place," he said, trying to wipe his cheek with the sleeve of his Owls sweater.

The Globen Arena burst into wild cheers.

Behind Travis, Annika screeched: "EEEE-AWWW-KEEE!"

They then stood by the thousands in Stockholm's Globen Arena. And at the far end of the rink a red-and-white Canadian flag began its long climb up a guy wire towards the rafters.

Travis was barely aware that the anthem had begun, but soon it seemed as if the music of "O Canada" had filled the huge stadium and was pounding in his heart. Behind the great swell of music, he could hear people singing along. The Canadian parents . . . then more and more of the Swedes.

It was the most beautiful sound he had ever heard.

There was another sound a bit behind him. It was a sort of low drone, but growing louder.

He turned slightly to his left. It was Nish, singing off-key, his eyes staring straight up at the flag.

Nish was crying. Big, fat tears were burning down his cheeks and falling freely onto his sweater. He was singing and crying at the same time, and he didn't seem to care the slightest that he couldn't sing a note.

THE END

Terror in Florida

1

Travis Lindsay had two dreams that kept coming back to him, time and time again. In the first, he was at his grandparents' cottage and something had happened to the water. He would wake in the morning and the lake would be entirely dry but for the odd pool of water and a lot of slippery mud, as if somebody had pulled out a big rubber bathtub plug in the middle of the lake. Instead of snorkelling around the surface with his rubber flippers and mask, he was now able to roam the lake bottom on foot, collecting lost lures and finding out, for once, just how big the trout were.

Travis's second dream was about winter vanishing. In Travis's home town, there came a time every late February or early March, when, suddenly, everyone grew sick and tired of winter – even young hockey players like Travis and the rest of the Screech Owls. You got up one morning and, instead of looking forward to practice or a tournament on the weekend, you started looking forward to spring: the first robin, the first sound of flowing water, the first smell of earth wafting up through the snow, the first day you could run out of the house without a winter jacket and boots.

In the dream where winter went away, it always happened instantly. Travis would wake up – at least he'd *dream* he had woken up – and there would be birds in the trees and the smell of manure being spread in the farm fields at the edge of town, and Wayne Nishikawa, *Nish*, would be firing pebbles at his window and shouting for him to come out and play.

This time, however, Travis's end-of-winter dream was different. It was *really* happening! And not just to Travis, but to Nish – snoring away in the seat beside him – and Data, up a row, and Lars, Jenny, Dmitri, Andy, Gordie, Jesse, Derek, Willie, Jeremy, even Sarah Cuthbertson, two seats back and playing hearts with Wilson and Fahd and the Owls' newest player, Simon Milliken. Simon was the smallest player on the team – smaller even than Travis, who was finally going through a growth spurt – and was a bit puck-shy. Nish had pounced on Simon's weakness, tagging him with a dreadful nickname – "Chicken Milliken" – that had, unfortunately, stuck. Fortunately, Nish was sound asleep; otherwise he might have been hounding poor Simon at this very moment.

The Screech Owls filled a school bus, each player allotted an entire seat to him or herself so they could all stretch out and sleep. Even old Muck was on board, in the front seat, the big coach so deep in a thick book that Travis wondered if he even realized they had left Canada and were almost halfway to Florida. *Halfway to summer! Halfway to Disney World!*

With Mr. Dillinger, the team manager, driving, the Owls

had left for Florida at the beginning of the March school break. And though Travis knew it was still March on the calendar, it sure didn't feel like it. Every few hours it seemed like a whole month had passed. Winter was peeling away. They could now see grass in the fields!

Behind the rented school bus – slow, noisy, and uncomfortable, but cheap, Muck said – there were parents' cars and Mr. and Mrs. Cuthbertson's Winnebago, and the two assistant coaches, Barry and Ty, in the rented van filled to the brim with hockey and camping equipment. Camping, Muck had argued, was another way to save them money.

They were off to the Spring Break Tournament, Peewee Division II, with games in Orlando and Lakeland, Florida, with special three-day passes to Disney World and – if they made it to the finals – a chance to play for the championship in the magnificent Ice Palace, home rink of the NHL's Tampa Bay Lightning.

"*Stupid stop!*" Mr. Dillinger called from the front of the bus. "STUUU–PIDDD STOP!"

All around Travis there was stirring and cheering and even a bit of applause. They'd been waiting for this moment. A trip wasn't a hockey trip unless Mr. Dillinger pulled off for one of his famous "Stupid Stops."

Mr. Dillinger, his bald spot bouncing, hauled on the steering wheel and the bus turned sharply into an exit for something called "South of the Border" – a huge restaurant and shopping stop on Interstate 95.

Mr. Dillinger stood at the door as they got off the bus. He had a huge roll of American money in his hands.

"You know what a *per diem* is?" he asked as the first Owl –
Nish, naturally – stumbled down the steps and out into the
warm air and surprising sun of the parking lot.

"Huh?"

Mr. Dillinger was enjoying himself. "In the NHL," he
announced grandly as the rest of the team emerged, blinking in
the bright light, "every player gets so much money each day –
that's what *per diem* means, Nish, *each day* – when they're on the
road. They can do what they wish with the cash. Whatever
they want."

"How much?" Nish wanted to know.

Mr. Dillinger scowled at him, half kidding. "Fifty-five
dollars," he said.

"*Allll-righhhtttt!*" Nish said, high-fiving Data, who was
standing beside him.

"You're not in the NHL yet, son – but there's a five-dollar bill
here for every player who's made the Screech Owls."

"*Allll-righhhtttt!*" several of the Owls shouted at once.

They lined up and Mr. Dillinger, making a great show of it
all, peeled off a bill for each player in turn.

"We can do anything we want with this – right?" Travis
said, as he reached for the bill Mr. Dillinger was holding toward
him.

"No, you cannot," Mr. Dillinger said, looking shocked.
"You do anything sensible with it – you *save* it, for example, or
put it in a bank, or fail to spend it absolutely foolishly all at once
– and we will send you home for being too *responsible* and *mature*
to be a member of the Screech Owls hockey club.

"Now get in there and throw it away – on something *stupid!*"

It took Nish about thirty seconds to find the joke's centre. He was determined to follow the instructions to the letter. Mr. Dillinger wanted *stupid*, Nish was going to *be stupid*.

He talked Data into spending money on some hot gum. He talked Wilson into buying something called Play Sick, which looked, sort of, as if someone had thrown up and the mess had instantly turned to rubber. But Nish wasn't satisfied; he went off in search of more useless stuff, leaving Data and Wilson to fork out their five dollars for things they would never have purchased if Nish had left them alone.

Travis stood looking at a joke display. A hand buzzer. A letter that snapped like a mousetrap when you pulled it out of the envelope. A Chinese finger-trap. A card trick. He didn't think there was anything he wanted.

Suddenly Nish was at his side, hissing, "*Gimme your five bucks!*"

"What?"

"*I need your stupid money, stupid.*"

"What for?"

Nish just looked at Travis, shaking his head. "*C'mere!*"

With one hand holding Travis's sleeve, Nish led his friend down an aisle toward a shelf at the back, where he reached up and plucked down something that didn't look the least bit interesting.

"You want to buy a pair of *glasses*?" Travis asked. What was wrong with Nish? This was hardly stupid.

"They're not just *glasses*," Nish hissed, holding them out like they were made of diamonds. "They're *X-ray glasses*!"

"What?"

"X-ray. You know, see right through things. See right through things like bathing suits. You get what I mean?"

"You're sick."

"I'm not sick – I'm short five bucks. *Are you in?*"

"You can't be serious."

"Dead serious. Now gimme your fiver!"

Travis reached in his pocket and took out his five-dollar bill. He knew better, but he handed it over anyway. Nish snatched it, giggling, and hurried off to the cash register.

What the heck, Travis told himself. Mr. Dillinger had said don't come back if you don't throw the money away on something absolutely useless and ridiculous.

And who better to show how it's done than Wayne Nishikawa, the King of the Stupid Stop?

2

Nish spent the rest of the trip south hounding poor Simon. At the next washroom stop, he took the opportunity to help himself to a pocketful of paper towels. He waited until Simon dozed off to sleep, and then got busy. He carefully laid out several of the brown paper towels on the seat beside Simon. Then he took a bottle of water and sprinkled the towels and had Wilson pull out his rubber vomit and set it carefully on top of the dampened towels. He then took two more paper towels, soaked them, and laid them partially over the vomit so it appeared as if someone had tried to soak the disgusting mess up.

Then Nish really went to work.

He squirted the bottle of water directly into his face, took a paper towel, wet it, and placed it so it was partly sticking to his chin, partly lying over his shirt front. Then he turned toward Simon, made a horrible, sickly face, and began to moan.

"Ohhhhh . . . ohhhhhhhhh . . . ohhhhhhhhh!"

Simon shifted slightly in his seat, half awakened.

"Oooohhhhhh!...Oooohhhhhhh!...Oooohhhhhhhh!"

Everyone was watching now, and Nish twisted violently and moaned even louder.

"OOOOHHHHHH!...OOOOHHHHHH!...OOOOHHHHHH!"

Simon's eyes blinked open. They turned to Nish. They blinked again. Nish twisted and moaned.

"OOOOHHHHHH!...OOOOHHHHHH!...OOOOHHHHHH!"

Simon jumped. He looked down at the seat between them. He instantly went white.

"*Nish has thrown up!*" he shouted.

Wilson was instantly into the act. "*Oh my God!*" he said, as he looked over from the seat directly behind. "*Has he ever!*"

Simon reached out, frightened almost, and very carefully touched Nish.

"Nish. You okay?"

Nish opened his eyes and groaned. "Ohhhh!" He groaned again, louder. "OHHHHHHHH!"

Nish jerked toward poor Simon, his eyes rolling, his mouth opening as if he was going to throw up on him.

"*HHHELPPPP!*" Simon shouted, and he jumped so fast, so far, that he scrambled clean over the seat in front and landed on Data and Andy, who were crouched there giggling.

Nish was howling with laughter. With the wetted towel still stuck to his shirt, he was on his feet and squawking and flapping his arms like a chicken.

"*Wakkk-cluck-cluck-cluck-cluck-cluck!*"

It seemed everyone was laughing at Simon. Even Travis was kind of half-laughing – it was, after all, pretty funny. But it was also pretty cruel.

Sarah wasn't laughing at all. Nish didn't even notice her, though; he was laughing uproariously, his eyes closed and his mouth wide open.

Sarah reached down and snatched the rubber vomit off the seat and stuffed as much of it into Nish's open mouth as she could – which was more than you might expect.

"*AAARGHHHHH!!*" sputtered Nish as he spat it out.

"*Nish gonna hurl?*" Sarah asked sweetly.

"*Yuck!*" Nish spat, wiping his mouth with one of the towels. "*Whatdya do that for, Sarah? Geez!*"

"A taste of your own medicine," Sarah said.

"We were just having a little laugh," said Nish, sounding like he was the one who'd been hurt.

"Fine," said Sarah, "we'll all remember to laugh the next time someone pulls a mean trick on you."

"*Get a life!*" Nish snapped.

"*Grow up!*" Sarah shot back.

@

The rest of the trip passed uneventfully. Nish sulked. Simon and Sarah played cards. Travis dozed off and on and stared out the bus window as summer came ever closer.

Nish had glanced over at Travis while Sarah was ripping into him. Travis knew that his friend was looking for support, any support, but he had felt powerless to say anything in Nish's defence. Yes, it had been pretty funny. Nish, after all, was a good actor – he really looked like he was going to hurl. But if he was going to play practical jokes, he needed to spread them around, otherwise he was just being mean, not funny. Nish had been picking on Simon since Simon had started coming out with the Owls.

Suddenly, Mr. Dillinger began honking the horn. Once, twice, a third time, long and loud.

"*State line!*" he shouted back. "*We just passed into Florida!*"

"*Yay!*" the bus cheered as one.

"*We're there!*" Data shouted.

"*I wanna meet Goofy!*" Nish shouted. He was bouncing back.

"*Look in a mirror!*" Sarah shouted in reply.

3

T. here was no time to visit Disney World that first day in Florida. In fact, it was getting dark when they finally made it to Kissimmee, the town nearest Disney World. When Mr. Dillinger announced they had just crossed over the Florida state line, none of them realized they were still four hours away from their destination.

Mr. Dillinger and Mr. Cuthbertson had made the arrangements. The Sunshine State Campsite had set off a special area for the Screech Owls and the other families who were camping to save money, the Cuthbertsons in their Winnebago included. Muck and the assistant coaches decided where the tents would go up and who would sleep in each tent. Travis and Nish were together in the Lindsays' big old family tent, sharing with Lars, Data, Andy, and, much to Nish's surprise, Simon.

"Lindsay," Muck said as he read out the list, "you're also captain of the tent. You keep a sharp eye on Nishikawa, understand?"

Travis nodded. How could he avoid keeping an eye on someone who always had to be the centre of attention?

Soon they had set up the old tent, and as they pulled their gear inside and rolled out their air mattresses and sleeping bags, Travis filled his lungs with the lovely, slightly musty smell of summers gone by that rose from the canvas. Next to skating out onto a fresh sheet of ice, Travis loved camping. The smell of rain through canvas, the sound of wind in the trees, the wonder of the life that was in every stream and pool and shoreline his family encountered on their annual summer camping trip.

"*Snake!*" screamed Nish.

"*What?*" Travis shouted. "*Where?*"

"*There! Under Simon's bag!*"

The head of a large snake was just visible under Simon's blue air mattress.

"*Lemme outta here!*" Nish screamed, scrambling for the exit.

Travis instinctively backed away as well. Weren't there poisonous snakes in Florida? Could it be a viper? A rattler?

Simon froze. He had been rolling out his sleeping bag, but now he stood absolutely motionless. Maybe it was a copperhead, thought Travis, his heart pumping fast. Andy was edging along the far side of the tent toward the door. He looked terrified. Lars was already outside.

Travis looked again at the snake. It wasn't moving. It wasn't even flicking its tongue, which Travis knew all snakes did in order to check their surroundings. Impulsively, he reached out and grabbed the snake and threw it, in one motion, out of the tent.

"*Rubber!*" he announced.

He could hear Nish outside, leading the laughter: "*Wakkk-cluck-cluck-cluck-cluck-cluck!*"

Nish was flapping his arms and walking around like a huge chicken, and Andy and Data were tossing the wiggling snake back and forth. It must have been what Andy's five dollars had gone toward at the Stupid Stop.

"Very funny!" Travis said as he came out of the tent.

"I thought so," Nish said defiantly.

Travis shook his head. Nish could be the nicest guy in the world one minute, the biggest jerk the next. He never seemed to know when to let up until he had gone too far.

"No more picking on Simon, okay?" Travis said.

Nish saluted. "*Yes, sirrrr! Mr. Lindsay!*"

Travis felt the morning sun, already hot, as it burned through the thick canvas of the tent. The air felt heavy, stale, and he threw back the flap to breathe in the fresh air and take his first look at a Florida morning.

It was a beautiful day, the dew sparkling on the grass and the pine needles, the campsite already alive with activity. Mr. Cuthbertson was headed down the pathway toward the showers, shorts on over legs the colour of milk, and a towel, nearly as white, slung over his shoulder. Muck, in his old windbreaker despite the warmth of the day, was at the Coleman stove, boiling water for a cup of coffee. Muck caught sight of Travis staring out from the tent and winked. It was just a wink, but it was all

Travis needed to know that the Owls' coach, who hadn't much wanted to come when the Florida trip was first suggested, was now quite content to be here.

"Is it time to get up?" a voice broke from behind.

Travis turned, his eyes adjusting to the darker interior of the tent. It was Simon, and he was blinking through red eyes.

"Are your eyes ever red!" Travis said.

"They are?" Simon said, rubbing fists into both of them. "Allergies, I guess."

Travis guessed not. Unless, of course, Simon was allergic to Nish's taunts.

"Up 'n' at 'em, Lindsay!" Muck called from over by the picnic table. "We're on the ice in an hour!"

4

he following hour had passed quicker than winter had vanished on the way down, and now the Screech Owls were on the ice and everything about it felt wrong.

The Owls had reached their destination only the evening before the tournament was to begin, and so had no time to practise. They were about to play the Ann Arbor Wings, a peewee team from Michigan, but instead of skating out for a warm-up and firing a puck off the crossbar to get ready, Travis was preparing for the match by hanging on to one side of a bedsheet, with Nish holding on to the other. Had there been enough wind in the Lakeland Arena, they would have been *sailing*, not skating down the ice.

"Fog," Muck had announced the moment the Owls got off the school bus and headed into the old rink. When the hot, humid Florida air from outside hit the cold air inside the arena, the result was a thick cloud of fog. It was so bad that Jeremy Weathers, who was to start the first game in goal, couldn't see to centre ice, let alone all the way down to where the Wings' goaltender was busy preparing his crease.

The Zamboni driver came out with an armful of old sheets, handed them out, and Muck and the Ann Arbor coach organized the players to skate about in pairs with the sheets billowing between them, trying to break up the fog.

"We look like ghosts, not hockey players," grumbled Nish.

"It's working, though," Travis answered.

It was, too. As the players skated about, they began to create air currents. From one end of the ice to the other, Travis could see the fog moving in chunks, first sideways, then up, eventually melting away. Players came into view, vanished, and appeared again. Nish was right; they did look like ghosts.

Finally, the referee blew his whistle at centre ice. There were still some cloudy patches, but the players could now see from one end of the ice to the other. They dumped the sheets into the outstretched arms of the arena attendant, and the game was on. No warm-up. Travis didn't feel right at all.

Sarah's line was first out, with Travis on left wing and the speedy Dmitri Yakushev on right. Nish and Data were starting, as usual, on defence.

For a moment, Travis was able to study the Ann Arbor team. They were larger than the Owls, and had beautiful green uniforms with a magnificent white wing on the chest. He checked the winger opposite him: Nike skates, the best money could buy.

Travis shivered, then remembered something Muck had once said to them: "The one thing in hockey you can't buy is skill." Muck hated to see a kid come out with a brand-new pair of gloves – "You may as well dip your hands in wet cement," he'd say – and told them all that top-of-the-line skates were a waste of money for players who were still growing. "What's it matter if you start the season with an extra pair of socks and end it in your bare feet?" he'd ask. "Bobby Orr never wore socks in his skates – and he was the best skater there ever was."

Still, Travis felt a bit embarrassed by his equipment. His skates were not only used – "one season only," the newspaper ad had claimed – but they still had the previous owner's number, 16, painted in white on the heel, whereas Travis's number was 7. He worried sometimes that other players might think the "C" for captain was left over from another player as well. He wasn't the best player on the Owls, after all – certainly not when Sarah was part of the team – and he was almost the smallest. Before Simon had come along, he *was* the smallest.

The puck dropped and, instantly, the cost of equipment meant nothing. Sarah did her trick of plucking the puck out of the air, and Dmitri picked it up and circled back, tapping off to Nish, who was already moving to the side to avoid the first check.

Travis knew the play. He knew Nish would be looking for him. He cut straight across centre ice, one skate on one side of the line, the other skate on the other side. That way, even if Nish shot from within the Owls' own zone, Travis would still be onside.

Nish fired the puck at Travis's head. No problem; they'd talked about this play before, though this was the first time Nish had ever attempted it in a real game.

Travis caught the puck in his glove and dropped it straight down onto his stick. He was free on the right side, Dmitri's side, and Dmitri crossed over onto Travis's wing. Travis knew that

Sarah would have curled and would be directly behind him as
he crossed the blueline. He dropped the puck between his legs
and "accidentally" bumped into the closest defenceman, taking
him out of the play. Sarah wound up for a slapshot, causing the
second Ann Arbor defenceman to flinch, standing up stiffly
with one glove over his face, but instead she snapped a perfect
pass to Dmitri, now on his off wing. Dmitri one-timed the shot
high in behind the goaltender, who had made the mistake of
heading out to take away the angle from Sarah.

Owls 1, Wings 0.

"They're still in a fog," Nish giggled when they went off on
a line change.

He was right. And so, too, was Muck. You can buy fancy
equipment, but you can't buy skill. And skill was winning handily
against the Wings.

By the end of the period, the Owls were up 4–1 on Dmitri's
goal, a long shot by Andy that bounced once before slipping past
the goaltender, a Derek Dillinger tip-in, and a pretty goal by, of
all people, Simon, as he skirted around the Wings' defence and
flicked a quick backhand over the goaltender's shoulder.

Muck had nothing to say to the Owls during the brief break
between periods. They were playing well, but, more to the point,
the opposition wasn't very good. Muck always seemed to worry
more about games like this than he did about close ones. He said
lopsided contests encouraged bad habits. What he meant, of
course, was that the easier it seemed out there, the more Nish
liked to hang onto the puck.

Travis sat and caught his breath. He had never played in such
humidity. It seemed like he was *drinking* air rather than inhaling

it. The others always liked to joke that Travis never broke a sweat, but he was drenched.

"Let's go!" Muck said when he got the signal that the break was over. "And remember, Nishikawa, one superstar rush and you're on the bench. Got it?"

"Got it," Nish answered in a choirboy voice.

The Ann Arbor Wings came out with a little more zip this time and scored a second goal before the Owls took charge. But once they were back in control, the Owls slowly, simply, began to wind the game down. Muck didn't like it when a team – the Owls or anyone else – ran up the score on an outmatched opposition.

Sarah, in particular, was great at what Muck called "ragging the puck." She could hold onto it for ever, circling back and back until it all but drove the other team crazy.

"I'm gonna try a between-the-leg-er," Nish said to Travis as they sat on the bench after another shift in which nothing happened.

All winter long Nish had been trying to score a goal like the one on the Mario Lemieux videotape that had come out after the Pittsburgh Penguins star had retired from the game. The Owls all thought it was the greatest goal they'd ever seen: Lemieux coming in on net with a checker on him and getting an amazing shot away by putting his stick back between his own legs and snapping the puck over the poor goalie.

"Don't even think of it!" Travis warned.

But the next chance he got, Nish picked up a puck behind his own net and came up ice, weaving and bobbing, until he suddenly turned on the speed and split the Wings' defence. He broke through and came in on goal, Sarah hurrying to catch up. She banged her stick on the ice twice, the signal that she wanted the puck.

Nish, however, had other ideas. Letting the puck slide, he turned, stabbed his stick back between his short, chunky legs, and with a neat flick of his wrists managed to trip himself – all alone on a breakaway! Wayne Nishikawa's reach was not the same as Mario Lemieux's.

With the puck sliding harmlessly past the net, Nish, tumbling on one shoulder, flew straight into the boards, where his skates almost stuck in they hit so hard.

The whistle blew and everyone raced to see if he'd been hurt.

Nish lay on the ice, flat on his back, moaning.

"You all right, son?" the referee asked.

Nish opened his eyes, blinked twice. "You calling a penalty shot?" he asked in his choirboy's voice.

This time it was the referee's turn to blink.

"What for?"

"I got dumped on a clear breakaway, didn't I?"

Nish struggled dramatically to his feet. With the small crowd of fans applauding to show they were happy he wasn't hurt, he skated, stiffly and slowly, straight to the bench, where he walked to the very end and sat down, removing his helmet and dropping his gloves.

He wouldn't be getting another shift this game.

5

"You gotta come see this!"

It was Nish, and he was foaming at the mouth. Whatever he'd seen had got him so excited he hadn't even finished brushing his teeth – he'd run straight to the tent, where Travis was just putting on his sandals to start the day.

"*Where the heck are my glasses?*"

"They're on top of your head, dummy," Travis informed him.

Nish ripped his wraparound sunglasses off and tossed them into his sleeping bag.

"*Not these ones – the X-rays!*"

Nish was thrashing about the tent like a bear in a garbage dump, turning bags upside down, rummaging through everything he came across – whether or not it was his.

He emerged from his own corner triumphant. "*Here they are!*" he shouted, holding them up. "*Let's go!*"

"Let's go *where?*"

"Just follow me!"

Travis followed Nish out of the tent and quickly down along the trail leading to the shower and laundry facilities. Nish was breathing heavily as he ran, the sweat already blackening his T-shirt. He hurried ahead, then left the trail abruptly, aiming for a thick bush almost directly in front of the shower building.

When Travis caught up, Nish was already trying to put the cheap X-ray glasses on, but Nish was so sweaty they kept slipping off.

"What are we doing here?" Travis whispered.

"You'll see."

People were coming and going. Travis looked at men carrying shaving kits and women with towels wrapped around their heads to dry their hair – but he could see nothing unusual.

"*There!*" Nish hissed.

Travis didn't have to look twice. From out of the women's shower room came one of the most extraordinarily beautiful women Travis had ever seen. She was tall, like a model, and had wrapped a huge beach towel around herself for the walk back.

"*Damn!*" Nish cursed. His X-ray glasses had slipped right off his sweaty nose and disappeared into the thick brush.

While Nish fumbled for his glasses, Travis watched the woman walk away.

She seemed a little frightened, thought Travis. Not of Nish, who was thrashing around in the bush, but of something.

At the end of the path, two men were waiting for her. They both wore dark sunglasses. One, with his head shaved, wore army-style camouflage pants. The other, his dark hair tied back in a ponytail, wore a Chicago Bulls basketball jersey. They didn't look much like campers.

The man with the ponytail caught the woman by the arm as she passed and hurried her along the path in the opposite direction. The man with the shaved head waited, watching, as if checking to make sure no one was following.

"*Got 'em!*" Nish announced, emerging from his search. There was dirt on his face and all over his prized glasses. He looked absurd.

"*Where'd she go?*" he demanded.

Travis pointed past the guy with the shaved head. "Down that path. I don't think you want to follow, unless you want your stupid glasses broken."

"Whatdya mean?"

"I think that guy's a bodyguard or something."

Nish removed his glasses, blinking to clear away the sweat. A thought seemed to be registering.

"You think maybe she's a movie star or something?"

"In a *campsite*? I don't think so."

"Well, who is she then?"

"I have no idea."

6

"D on't anybody tell him!" whispered Sarah. "Not a word – promise?"

She quickly went around to the rest of the Screech Owls gathered in the shade of the trees as they waited for the most popular ride at Disney–MGM Studios: the Tower of Terror.

The Owls had risen early for their first full day at Walt Disney World. They would do some of the MGM Studios rides in the morning, then head over to the Magic Kingdom, where they would catch the parade down Main Street, U.S.A., before eating on the Boardwalk and waiting for the fireworks display to close out the day.

The Twilight Zone Tower of Terror had been a topic of conversation for much of the trip down to Florida. Data, who had been to Disney World only the year before, had talked about it endlessly.

"The elevator," he said, "drops thirteen floors *in less than two and a half seconds!*"

There was just no doubt, from the moment Mr. Dillinger had turned the full school bus onto the entrance drive to Disney World, that the Tower of Terror was a main attraction. Attached to a huge billboard in the median were larger-than-life dummies suspended from a broken elevator, their faces filled with fright and their hair standing straight up on end.

"Looks like your hair in Sweden!" Lars had called back to Nish.

"Very funny!" Nish had protested, secretly delighted that everyone remembered the new look he'd tried out in Stockholm.

"He won't even go!" Sarah had shouted. "He's afraid of heights, remember?"

"*Am not!*"

"Oh?" Sarah had said. "And what, then, was all that fuss about when we were up the mountain at Lake Placid?"

Almost as if they'd planned it, several of the Owls had turned at once and, in exaggerated Nish voices, shouted out, "I'M GONNA HURL!"

"*No way!*"

"You won't go," Sarah said, sure of herself.

"A dollar?" Nish had challenged, his lower lip pushed out as he dared Sarah to bet on whether he'd go on the ride.

"You're on, Big Boy."

Even though they wouldn't be going on the Tower of Terror until later in the day, the ride – and the bet – were never far from their minds. The sounds, sometimes distant, sometimes close, of gearwheels grinding, cables slipping, and riders screaming had followed the Owls around wherever they went – even all the way to Catastrophe Canyon. To half of the Screech

Owls, the screams were a warning. To the others, an invitation. Travis wasn't quite sure how he heard it: he was half tantalized, half fearful.

The lineup for the big attraction was long. A sign said they were forty-five minutes away from the actual ride. Fortunately, the wait would be out of the sun.

The line, twisting in a gentle curve rising toward the entrance, was shaded by shrubs and trees that were filled with birds. They could buy drinks and ice cream while they waited, and soon the big wait was forgotten as they talked about their day and moved ahead a few steps at a time. Several of the Owls tried to catch one of the speedy little lizards that darted up the walls and around the trunks of the trees. Data had his father's Polaroid camera with him, and desperately wanted a photo-graph of himself with one of the cute little lizards in his hand. But the lizards were too quick to be caught.

The two quietest Owls were Simon and Travis, each trying to calm his growing fears on his own. Nish had already pre-dicted Simon would bail out before they got on the ride, walking around him with his arms flapping and doing that idiotic "*Wakkk-cluck-cluck-cluck-cluck-cluck!*" Travis dearly hoped it would be Nish, not Simon, who chickened out, and he planned to have the entire Screech Owls team do a "*Wakkk-cluck-cluck-cluck-cluck-cluck!*" around Nish when Sarah collected her dollar bet. That would serve him right.

Nish seemed to be gathering himself. The closer they moved toward the entrance, the quieter he became. He stood off to one side of the line, his eyes closed and his arms folded across his chest. He was in another world, dealing with his well-known fear of heights.

Nish didn't even notice when a brilliantly coloured bird landed on a branch directly over him and let go a sloppy white poop that landed directly on top of his head.

"*Scores!*" shouted Lars.

"*Shhhhhh!*" hissed Sarah, jumping directly in front of Nish and turning to the rest of the Owls, most of whom were pointing and laughing at Nish, who stood there with his eyes closed.

"*Don't anybody tell him!*" whispered Sarah. "*Not a word. Promise?*"

The Owls all stifled their giggles. Andy pointed silently to Data's camera, and Data got the message. With Andy and Derek's help, Data stood on the top of the concrete wall and aimed the Polaroid down at Nish's majestic new hair ornament. The camera flashed – Nish never even blinked – and Andy and Derek quickly helped Data back down onto the ground.

Incredibly, no one said anything as the line continued to inch forward. Nish seemed only half awake, moving with the flow. A few tourists noticed, but each time they were stopped from saying anything by the Owls. Data pulled out the film and, when it was time, carefully peeled away the protective cover to reveal a perfect portrait of Nish's bird topping. The Owls managed to hand it around without breaking out into hysterical laughter. After everyone had seen it, Sarah took the photographic proof from Data and stuffed it carefully into the pouch she wore around her waist.

They reached the entrance without Nish catching on, and were directed into what looked like a seedy old, rundown, musty and dusty hotel. There were newspapers tossed on tables, with dates that read 1939 – long before even the parents of any of the Owls had been born! They passed through the lobby and into the library, the sense of dread building.

Once they were in the library, a bolt of lightning seemed to strike, bringing a dusty television to life with an introduction from an old show called "The Twilight Zone," which some of the kids seemed to know. A man with a deep voice made Travis shiver as he recounted the tale of the family that had disappeared forever when another bolt of lightning had struck the old hotel, causing the elevator they had been riding in to shoot out through the top of the building and far, far into outer space – all the way to "The Twilight Zone."

From the library they were ushered into the boiler room, where another snaking line led to the only elevator still working: the service elevator. Travis could almost smell the fear in the crowd. The screams from those actually on the ride were far, far louder now, the sounds of machinery grinding, then snapping, even more alarming. Travis's mouth felt dry; the palms of his hands were wet.

They had barely stepped into the boiler room when Simon broke. He just stood there, shaking for a moment, then suddenly turned on his heel and hurried back through the entrance.

Unfortunately, Nish noticed.

"*Wakkk-cluck-cluck-cluck-cluck-cluck!*" he chanted, with Andy joining in, both of them flapping their arms as Simon dashed through the door and away.

Their taunts made Travis all the more determined to stay — no matter how tough it got.

It was crowded in the boiler room: it seemed the walls were closing in. Travis had trouble swallowing. He knew from here they would be crammed into an elevator, and the idea of being trapped in that small space was as alarming as the thought of the thirteen-floor plunge.

The wait was growing worse. They moved by inches. The people seemed to pack in tighter and tighter. He was losing his ability to breathe. His heart was missing beats, trying to go faster than the heart muscles could pump.

There was a warning sign by the final steps leading up to the actual ride. Travis read the sign quickly: "*Those who experience anxiety in enclosed spaces should not ride.*"

Now he couldn't swallow at all. His shirt was sticking to his back. His heart was pounding. *He knew he had to get out!*

Travis looked around. No one was watching him; Nish and Andy were well ahead. Nish seemed to have somehow conquered his fear, or else he was just so determined to prove Sarah wrong that he had no choice but to follow through with it. Travis couldn't summon the same courage, false or not. He couldn't do it.

All eyes were on the entrance to the ride, all ears on the grinding gears and sliding cables and terrifying, hideous screams that came from above. Travis quickly checked the last sentence on the warning sign: "*Visitors who wish to change their minds may exit to the right.*"

For a moment he was undecided. He looked up toward the "service elevator," where the next trip was being loaded. Some were already screaming. A young woman lunged back towards the doorway, already in tears, but her boyfriend grabbed her and hauled her forward. Those waiting for the next ride laughed.

Travis couldn't take it. When he was sure no one was looking, he bolted for the safety exit. Through a doorway and up a quick, open elevator, and he was out into the Florida sunshine and could breathe again.

He had chickened out.

Travis was miserable. Even if he covered his ears, he could still hear the sounds of the Tower of Terror – the cables slipping, the gears grinding, the trap doors breaking open, the rush of wind as the elevator plummeted again and again, and the endless, chilling screaming.

He waited around for the others by the exit, where he found a handy washroom. There was also a souvenir store, where they sold everything from T-shirts that bragged "I survived the Tower of Terror" to coffee mugs depicting the attraction. The store even had a booth where they sold photos that must have been taken at the very top of the tower, when the riders were at their most terrified. The billboard had been no exaggeration – their hair really was standing on end!

Travis watched as laughing, relieved riders came off the ride and entered the shop. He noticed Simon standing just outside the door.

Travis's first instinct was to call to Simon. His second was to keep quiet. He knew that everyone had seen Simon bail out, but he was fairly sure no one had seen him do it too. And since not all the Owls would fit into the same elevator ride, perhaps no one would ever realize he had chickened out. As long as Simon didn't notice him now, there was still a chance that Travis's secret would be his alone.

Feeling like a fool, like a traitor to his own team, he ducked behind a rack of souvenir coffee cups. Simon couldn't see him here, and his teammates might miss him as they came off the ride.

Travis heard the Owls coming even before he saw them. Loudest, of course, was Nish, and he was in full brag.

"*It was nothin', man! I shoulda bet twenty dollars!*"

They all rounded the corner at once, a laughing, pushing, shoving throng of kids in T-shirts they'd picked up everywhere, from Lake Placid, New York, to Malmö, Sweden. A few had Screech Owls caps on. Nish, of course, had another type of cap on. The bird plop was still there. It had survived the trip!

"*Hey!*" Nish shouted. "*Let's check out the pictures!*"

Travis could see Data wink at Lars. The Owls hurried to see the expression on Nish's face when he saw what was lying on top of his hair. Travis slipped unnoticed into the group.

"Great ride, eh, Trav?" Andy said as Travis edged up beside him.

"Yeah," Travis said. "Great."

"Which one were you on? I didn't see you."

"The other elevator."

Travis winced a bit. Technically, he wasn't lying. It obviously had been a great ride, and he *had* taken the other elevator. But not the next elevator on the ride.

"*Pay up!*" Nish was ordering Sarah up ahead. "I need some cash for the picture of me."

When Sarah held out the dollar Nish had won, he grabbed it and elbowed through to the front of the line.

"WHAT THE – !?" Nish shouted.

The man running the photo booth had just put up the photograph of the Owls' ride. Sarah's long hair was standing straight up, as was Lars's. Nish's hair was sitting flat, most of it trapped under a white mess.

"*This picture didn't come out right!*" Nish practically shouted at the man.

The man merely looked at the top of Nish's head and shrugged, smiling slightly.

"Looks pretty accurate to me," he said.

Nish slipped one hand up to his ear, then carefully onto his hair and up to the top of his head, where he found what he feared.

"*Who did this?*" he demanded, turning on the other Owls.

Willie, the trivia expert, answered: "I believe it was a cardinal."

The Owls all laughed, all except Nish. He yanked a Kleenex out of his pocket and began batting at his hair, disgusted. He looked around, spotted the washroom, and bolted for it.

"Quick!" Sarah said. "We've got to buy this for him. You know how Nish has to have a souvenir of everywhere he goes!"

They collected the money as fast as hands could reach into pockets and haul out change and small bills. Sarah made the purchase, and the man put the photograph into a bag for her to carry it in. The Owls then went outside to wait.

Simon was still out there, looking sheepish. No one said anything to him. Everyone knew what had happened, and Simon *knew* that everyone knew. No one, however, seemed to suspect that Travis had also bolted, not even Simon. Travis felt like a sneak, but he still couldn't let Simon know he wasn't alone.

When Nish finally came out, it looked like he had washed his hair – perhaps he had, leaning into the sink and scrubbing in that awful pink stuff that shoots out the soap tap. His hair was glistening and combed, with not a touch of white to be found anywhere. He did not look in the mood for teasing. He walked up to Sarah and stood directly in front of her, his lips moving furiously before he spoke.

"*Give me it!*" he demanded.

"Give you what?"

"The picture."

"What picture?"

"*The-picture-you-are-carrying-in-that-bag.*"

Sarah looked at her purchase as if she'd just noticed it for the first time.

"Oh," she said. "*This?*"

"*Give it to me!*"

"We were going to give it to you, Nish. It's a gift from all of us so you'll never forget your trip to Florida."

Nish grabbed the package as Sarah held it up to him, yanked out the photograph, and, without even looking at it, ripped it into little pieces. He then walked over to the nearest garbage can and dropped it in.

He turned, slapping his hands together. "There," he smiled sarcastically at Sarah. "Already forgotten."

Nish then turned on his heels and stomped off.

Sarah, far from beaten, merely smiled and waved at Nish behind his back. Then she patted her waist pouch, where Data's Polaroid still lay, well protected from Nish's chubby hands.

"Not entirely forgotten," she whispered, then patted the treasured pouch again.

7

he Screech Owls arrived too early for the parade down Main Street, U.S.A., so they killed some time by poking around the stores. At the Emporium, where Sarah and Data were lining up to get their names stitched on the mouse ears they had purchased, Travis thought he saw the beautiful young woman from the campsite. He told Nish.

"Geez," Nish said. "Why didn't I bring my X-ray glasses?"

Travis shook his head: "They don't even work."

"You have to *believe* in them," answered Nish.

Travis just shook his head again. What was the point in even trying to talk to Nish? How, Travis wondered, did this lunatic ever become his best friend?

Even without the help of his glasses, Nish wanted to check her out. Travis had seen her in the books section, buying a guide to the Magic Kingdom, and they hurried over in order to catch her before they left.

There was indeed a young woman there. She was putting her purchase into a large pram she was pushing, the baby shielded from the sun by a canopy.

"It's not her," said Nish, turning away.

Travis wasn't so sure. But he could have been mistaken. Perhaps the baby had just been sleeping back at the campsite and the man with the shaved head was her husband. Or the guy with the ponytail.

The Owls killed a bit more time by checking out some of the Fantasyland attractions – Mr. Toad's Wild Ride, Legend of the Lion King, It's a Small World – all of which they considered were for "little kids," not anyone who had ridden the Tower of Terror.

This, of course, only opened up more teasing opportunities for Nish. He tried to get Simon to take one of the rides, and for a while he and Andy and Wilson followed Simon around, taunting him in high, childlike voices: "*It's a small world, after all. It's a small world, after all. It's a small world, after all . . . It's a small, small world. . . .*"

Wilson looked very uncomfortable and quit after the first obnoxious verse. Andy quit after the second. Nish didn't know when to quit. He continued singing in a high-pitched voice while walking around behind Simon, until Simon looked as if he wished that he, like the star of Peter Pan's Flight a few steps down the street, could simply make a wish and fly away.

Travis waited until he had an opening. "Knock it off, Nish," he whispered.

"*Yes, sirrrr! Mr. Lindsay!*" Nish barked back. But at least he shut up and stopped singing.

"We better head off for the parade," Sarah said, checking her new Minnie Mouse wristwatch.

They were heading quickly back through Fantasyland and across Liberty Square, just opposite the Hall of Presidents, when Nish, at the head of the line, brought the Screech Owls to a sudden stop.

"*The Goof Man!*" he shouted.

Nish was pointing to the side of the building. The object of his attention, standing in the dark shade of the building, was concealed slightly by a parked maintenance truck.

"*It's Goofy!*" Data shouted, fumbling for his camera.

"*C'mon!*" Nish called back to them. "*I gotta have my picture taken with the Goof Man!*"

The Screech Owls turned like a swarm of bees, heading straight for the Hall of Presidents and the maintenance truck.

"*Hey!*" a uniformed maintenance worker shouted as they rounded the truck. "*This is a restricted work area. You kids can't come in here!*"

"We want to see Goofy!" Nish protested. "We just saw him here!"

The worker angrily checked his watch. "Parade's in fifteen minutes, kids. Catch him there."

Just then the side door to the hall opened and Goofy emerged: big toothy dog's grin, black floppy ears, eyelids half closed, red shirt, yellow vest, and black pants, white three-fingered gloves. Just like in the cartoon the Owls loved about Goofy trying to play hockey on a frozen pond.

"*Goofer!*" Nish shouted.

Goofy turned sharply to see who was calling, then began to move in the opposite direction. He has to get to the parade, Travis figured. He hasn't time for all the photographs and autographs the Screech Owls are going to demand.

Nish shouted after him, "*Goofy! Hey, wait up!*"

With Andy and Data behind him, Nish raced past the truck and brushed right by the outstretched arm of the maintenance worker. Nish barrelled straight on down past the door Goofy had just come out of. He caught Goofy by the arm as he was about to slip away between two buildings.

"C'mon, Goof Man! All I want is a picture to prove I met you!"

Goofy turned, shaking Nish's hand off his arm. When he spoke, the muffled voice from inside the suit sounded irritated.

"There's a picture session at the end of the parade, son."

"We know that, Goof Man! But we'll never get through all the parents and strollers. Just a quick one, okay?"

Goofy shook his head impatiently, but Data already had his Polaroid out and Nish was posing for the camera as if he and Goofy were the greatest friends in the world. Nish had a big *hey-look-at-me!* grin on and had slipped an arm around Goofy's waist.

With no way out, Goofy gave up. He quickly threw an arm around Nish, posed, and Data took the shot.

"Only one!" Goofy said. "I gotta go!"

"No problem, Goof Man. We'll catch ya later." Nish didn't care. He had what he wanted.

Goofy hurried away between the Hall of Presidents and the Liberty Square Riverboat, and the Owls turned to continue toward Cinderella Castle for the parade. At the same time, the maintenance worker pulled away in his truck, veering sharply in front of the Owls. Travis got a glance at his face as he passed by. The worker looked furious. *How did he ever get hired here?* Travis wondered. Everyone else in Disney World was so friendly and helpful, but this guy had treated them as if they had no right to be here and had no right at all to be bothering a busy Disney executive like Mr. Goofy.

The Owls made it to Main Street, U.S.A. just as the parade was starting out, and they pushed as close to the front of the spectators' line as they could manage. It was wonderful, with marching bands and all the Disney songs and brilliantly coloured floats showing scenes from all the best-known Disney movies – *The Lion King, Aladdin, Beauty and the Beast, The Little Mermaid* – and bringing up the rear was a huge float with all the best-known cartoon characters: Mickey and Minnie, Pluto, Snow White, Donald Duck, Dumbo . . . and, of course, Goofy.

The Owls couldn't have been better placed. The parade stopped right in front of them for one of the "magic moments," when the cartoon characters from the final float came and danced with the children in the crowd and shook hands and posed for photographs. Travis shook Mickey Mouse's hand, feeling a little silly as he did so.

And Nish, of course, got a second chance with Goofy – who this time was in a much better mood. He posed for several photographs with Nish, then with Sarah and Jeremy and even Andy, who had been claiming he was far too old for this stuff but looked as pleased as Nish to stand arm-in-arm with Goofy while Data took their picture.

"*The Goof Man!*" Nish shouted, and Goofy turned and high-fived him.

Sarah just stood there, shaking her head in amazement.

"A true meeting of minds," she said. "It's almost enough to make you cry."

8

The Screech Owls awoke next morning to the sound of helicopters flying low over the campsite and then off over the swampy land to the south. They were so close that dust was still swirling on the campground paths when the boys emerged from their tent.

"Army choppers," Data announced.

"What're they doing?" asked Travis.

"Maybe somebody's lost in the swamp!" Data said, his imagination also swirling. "Maybe an alligator grabbed somebody last night!"

Travis didn't think so. Maybe there was an air-force base nearby. Maybe they were on manoeuvres. They probably hadn't been as close as it had seemed in the tent, the canvas shaking and the poles rattling as they passed directly overhead.

The boys saw Muck standing off to one side of their campsite, a big fist locked around a cup of coffee. He was staring after the helicopters.

"What was that all about?" Travis asked his coach.

"I have no idea," Muck said. "First there's searchlights passing through the campsite half the night, now these guys. I didn't sleep a wink."

This was no surprise to the boys. In a dozen long bus rides – including this one to Florida – and a flight to Sweden and back, none of the Owls had ever seen Muck sound asleep. He might doze a bit, but sound asleep? Never.

"Must be someone lost," said Data, now more sure than ever.

"I guess," agreed Muck, sipping his coffee. He had things other than helicopters on his mind. "We're on at eleven against Boston. No morning swim – understand?"

"Yes, sir," Travis said.

Travis knew Muck was worried about the strong Boston entry in the Spring Break Tournament. Muck figured if they could only get by Boston, they stood a good chance of making it into the championship round.

"I want everybody on the bus by 10:00 a.m."

"I'll have them there," Travis answered. He was team captain. It was his job.

"We've got enough time!"

Nish was adamant. For breakfast Mr. Dillinger had prepared his great specialty – pancakes, sausages, hash brown potatoes, toast, and, on top of the pancakes, a scoop of blueberry ice cream – and after cleaning up there was still an hour to go before they had to be on the bus with their hockey equipment.

"No swimming, though!" Travis reminded Nish.

"How much energy does it take to *look*?" Nish almost shouted, shaking his head in disgust.

Travis gave in. "Okay," he said. "Let's get it over with."

Nish gave one of his stupid yells – "*EEEEE-AWWWW-KEEEE!*" – and bolted for the tent to retrieve his ludicrous X-ray glasses. He and Andy had come up with another dumb idea to spy upon the gorgeous young woman staying at the far end of the campground. They'd located her tent the evening before, and today they'd go down early, when everyone was beginning to stir to start the day, and maybe catch her headed off to the showers again.

"This time I won't drop my glasses!" Nish promised.

They set off, with Nish well out in front and Andy closest behind him. Travis, the least enthusiastic, brought up the rear, talking to Lars, who wasn't much interested either. Lars also thought the idea of X-ray glasses was about as silly and immature and childish as anyone could get. But he seemed to get a kick out of watching Nish be immature and childish.

Simon was coming along as well. Nish had been about to go into his chicken act, but a sharp look from Travis had stopped him. Simon just seemed to want to be part of the gang.

The path leading out of the Owls' campsite crossed a dirt road, and they had to wait for a truck to pass. The truck had searchlights on both sides, and even though the lights weren't on, the boys felt like they were being examined. There were two men in the truck, both wearing dark sunglasses, both staring at them as the truck moved slowly by.

They hurried along the network of paths until they came to the far end of the campground. It was empty but for the campsite where the beautiful young woman was staying. There were more bugs there, and more undergrowth. It was a site most people would avoid unless they had no choice, Travis thought, but he supposed these people wanted to be away from everyone else.

"*Shhhhhhhh!*" Nish whispered, turning back and placing his finger to his lips.

The six Owls – Nish, Andy, Data, Lars, Simon, and Travis – all fell silent and ducked into the thick undergrowth by the path, where Nish led them, slowly, toward the campsite.

"*We're almost there!*" Nish whispered, holding up a hand to halt them.

He stopped, fumbled in his pocket, and removed the X-ray glasses. He put them on and pulled them tight to his nose and ears. This time, they wouldn't fall off at the crucial moment.

Nish took a step forward and fell flat on his face, his foot catching on a vine. He stifled a curse and yanked off the glasses. Then he stepped forward again, crouching low. He broke through the foliage – Travis could make out the campsite just over Nish's shoulder – and then repositioned his glasses. Travis could see Nish looking from one side to the other.

"*I can't see anything!*" he whispered back.

"*I told you they wouldn't work,*" Travis said.

Nish turned back, his eyes bulging behind the strange-looking glasses.

"*It's not the glasses, stupid. There's no one here!*"

Andy pushed through and checked the tents, without the help of X-ray glasses. He confirmed Nish's findings. "They're gone."

"Maybe they're at the showers," Wilson suggested.

"Naw," Andy said. "We would have passed them on the way."

"I'll bet they're at the beach," Nish said, his enthusiasm returning.

"We haven't time," Travis warned.

"Quit your whining," Nish snapped. "We've got time. Besides, these things were made for the beach – remember the package?"

"We can make it," said Andy.

"Let's do it!" added Data.

Travis looked at Lars, who simply shrugged to suggest they might as well get it over with.

With Nish and Andy leading the way, the boys began running for the beach. There was a back trail leading from this end of the campground to the lake. Perhaps this was why they had come to this out-of-the-way site, Travis thought. It had its own virtually private access to the beach.

The trail twisted and turned. They crossed a wooden bridge spanning a small creek, climbed over a fallen tree, and then came to a final bend in the path. The lake flickered blue through the opening.

Nish held up his hand to stop everyone.

"*They're here!*" he hissed.

Beyond the trees he could see two men on the beach pushing a rowboat out onto the water. The lovely young woman was also there, in a bathing suit. She was already in the water, holding onto the boat as they pushed it off the beach.

"*This way!*" Nish hissed, heading away from the trail toward a stand of trees near the sand.

For once, Travis agreed with Nish's tactics. It was a public beach, but somehow this morning it felt like the public was not welcome. Travis didn't know how, but these people gave the impression they did not want company, did not even want to be seen.

Nish held up his hand. "*Down!*"

The Owls all ducked down and scurried up to the thick stand of trees. Travis put an arm out and pushed away a branch. He could see very clearly now. The men were getting into the rowboat, which had been loaded with a large bundle of some kind. The woman, still standing in the water, began turning the boat with her hands, pushing it out into deeper water. The man with the shaved head, sitting in the middle, put oars into the oarlocks and began rowing, turning the boat some more. The man with the ponytail seemed to be tying rope around the bundle.

Now the woman was wading back through the water toward the shore.

"*They work!*"

The five other Owls turned at once toward Nish. He had his special X-ray glasses on, and he was leaning as far out from his cover as he dared, staring hard and grinning from ear to ear.

"*Fantastic!*" he said.

"*Lemme see!*" Andy almost shouted.

"*Me too!*" said Data.

"*And me!*" added Lars.

Travis turned, looking at Lars with surprise. Lars shrugged and looked sheepish. "I just want to see if they work," he explained. It didn't sound very convincing.

"Cost you a buck each," Nish announced.

"*What?*" they said as one.

"A buck a look," Nish said.

"No fair," complained Andy.

Nish made no reply. He simply stared, grinned, and kept con-gratulating himself. "*Beautiful . . . fantastic . . . I can't believe it . . .*"

Andy couldn't take it any more. "*All right! I'm in. C'mon, lemme see outta them!*"

"Who else?" Nish had to know first.

"Me," said Data.

"I guess me," added Lars.

"Me," said Simon in a quiet voice.

"Trav?" Nish asked.

Travis couldn't believe what he was hearing. "I already paid for half of them. Remember?"

"Oh, yeah," Nish said. "Sorry." He sounded more sorry for himself than for Travis, however.

"Lemme see," said Andy.

"Everybody's agreed then?" Nish said. "A dollar each."

Everyone except Travis nodded.

Nish smiled and took off the glasses, handing them first to Andy. Andy fumbled with them, dropped them, grabbed them up, cleaned them with his fingers, and pushed them on. He moved a branch away and stared out toward the young woman, who was still standing at the edge of the water, watching the progress of the rowboat.

"*Nothin'!*" Andy protested.

"They work fine for me," said Nish.

"My turn!" said Data.

Andy handed them over. Data put the glasses on and looked through the gap in the branches. He stared a long time before saying anything.

"I . . . *think* I see something," he said, finally.

Data slowly removed the glasses and gave them to Lars, who looked quickly.

"Nothing."

Lars handed the glasses to Travis, who knew even before he looked that he would see nothing. The lenses were ridged, so they gave a fuzzy-edged look to whatever you looked at, almost like a videotape on pause. Whatever the effect was, it wasn't X-ray.

"A rip-off," Travis pronounced. He handed the glasses to Simon, who didn't even bother trying them on.

Nish was still smiling. "I can't help it if they don't work for you. They worked fine for me. And Data."

Data didn't know how to respond. "I . . . guess," he said.

Travis looked back toward the water.

"*Look!*" he said.

"*We have been!*" said Andy.

"*No! In the boat!*"

The X-ray glasses and the beautiful young woman were forgotten as the six boys turned their attention to the rowboat, now well out on the water. The rower was standing up, as if keeping watch, and the man with the ponytail was attaching something to the tied-up bundle. The two men then pulled at the bundle and moved it to one side of the rowboat.

With an enormous effort, the men lifted the bundle, and Travis now saw that attached to it were two heavy concrete blocks. They steadied it on the gunwale for a moment, and then pushed it over. It splashed heavily and sank. The shift of weight caused the rowboat to rock so violently that the man with the ponytail fell back heavily. But the boat didn't tip over completely. The one with the shaved head quickly began rowing back to shore, where the woman waded out into the water once again to catch the boat and haul it up onto the sand so they could jump out.

"What do you think they dumped?" Andy asked.

"*A body?*" Data suggested.

Data – the most naive member of the Screech Owls – had the wildest imagination and came up with the silliest, most ridiculous statements.

But this time no one laughed. And no one had a better idea.

"We've got a bus to catch," Travis said.

The others seemed relieved to be brought back to reality.

"Let's go before they see us," said Nish.

He turned, took one look at the X-ray glasses in his hand, and tossed them into the bush. "What a waste," he said.

9

he X-ray escapade was the talk of the Screech Owls' dressing room as the team prepared to meet the powerful Boston Mini-Bruins. Some of the Owls laughed so hard they had tears in their eyes. Nish, of course, was convinced his tricking the others to pay a dollar each for a look erased the trick the joke store had played on him when he bought the glasses.

"No way anyone's going to make a fool out of Wayne Nishikawa," he announced as he began lacing up his skates.

"Is that right?" Sarah said, fumbling in the side pocket of her equipment bag.

"That is correct," Nish grandly announced.

Sarah pulled out the Polaroid snapshot Data had taken in the lineup for the Tower of Terror.

"What's *this*, then?" she asked no one in particular.

Nish looked up from tightening his left skate. His jaw dropped as he realized what he was looking at: a glorious photograph of the bird poop he had worn on the ride.

"*Where'd you get that?*" he demanded, the smile gone from his gaping mouth.

"Oh," teased Sarah, "let's just say a little birdie gave it to me."

"*You better hand that over!*" Nish said, standing up and falling at the same time, as his untied skates gave way.

Everyone in the dressing room again started howling with laughter. Nish scrambled back to his feet and began advancing across the room toward Sarah, who was quickly stuffing the photograph away.

"You're the big deal-maker," she said. "I'll make a deal with you, okay?"

"I'm not paying anything for that."

"No money," she said. "You take us to the championship, the evidence is yours to destroy."

Nish stopped halfway. He mulled it over a moment, then stared fiercely at Sarah. She had him; Nish couldn't resist a challenge.

"Agreed," he said.

⊚

Too bad they didn't have a few more embarrassing pictures of Nish, Travis thought halfway through the opening period.

The Boston Mini-Bruins had been a force. They had worried the Owls during the warm-up – no fog this time – with their size and shots, and Travis had worried himself when he failed to hit the crossbar on any of his pre-game shots.

The Mini-Bruins had taken an early two-goal lead, scoring first on a fluke breakaway that Jesse Highboy gave them when he tried a drop pass, and then on a point shot that went in between Jenny Staples' pads.

Muck had not been amused. He had warned them about the good teams from the Boston area. He had reminded them that many of the best players in the National Hockey League – Brian Leetch, for instance – were coming out of programs similar to that of the Mini-Bruins. "You'll probably be playing against some future NHLers," Muck had said.

And yet, if someone had walked into the Lakeland arena this hot March morning and been asked to point out the two peewee hockey players most likely to reach the NHL, they would have pointed to the Owls' top centre, Sarah Cuthbertson, and the big kid on defence, Wayne Nishikawa. Sarah's deal with Nish was working wonders. He was playing a magnificent game – blocking shots, completing long breakaway passes to Dmitri and Travis, playing the point perfectly, and carrying the puck, for once, at exactly the right time.

How to figure out Nish? To Travis, Nish was his best friend as well as the silliest kid he knew. He was a lazy hockey player one game, the hardest worker the next. This, fortunately, was one of those good times for Nish. He got the Owls back into the game on a brilliant move when he jumped unexpectedly into the play. Sarah had taken the puck up ice and had curled off toward the right corner. Travis knew this was his signal to rush the net, and he raced in, fully expecting her pass. Instead, Sarah threw a saucer pass out into what seemed like nowhere. The puck flew lightly through the air, over the outstretched stick of her checker, and landed flat, perfectly, in open ice, where Nish, racing up past the Mini-Bruins' backcheckers, gobbled it up on his stick, deked once, and, using a surprised defenceman as a screen, roofed a hard shot the goaltender never even saw. Two minutes later, Nish fed Sarah a perfect breakaway pass that tied the game at two goals apiece.

How, Travis wondered, could Sarah and Nish seem such a natural mix on the ice and so different off the ice? When they weren't playing hockey, they were often at each other's throats, Nish baiting Sarah with his big mouth, Sarah refusing to allow him to get away with any of his nonsense. But watching them play this game, watching the way Nish jumped into Sarah's outstretched arms after she had tied the game, Travis had to wonder if, in fact, Sarah and Nish were actually quite fond of each other.

The game remained tied right into the final minutes, Jenny Staples brilliant in the Owls' goal, the Mini-Bruins' goaltender spectacular in his end, stopping first Dmitri and then Travis on clear breakaways.

With less than a minute to go, Nish broke out of his own end and hit Dmitri with a hard, accurate pass as Dmitri cut across centre, Travis criss-crossing with him so they could change wings.

Travis loved this play. There was nothing he liked better than coming in on his off-wing, a left-hand shot on the right side, perfect for one-timers into the corner, where he turned, looking for a passing play. He saw Travis and fired the puck across, Travis one-timing it perfectly off the crossbar!

A Mini-Bruins defenceman knocked the puck down, turned, and fired it high to get it out of the Mini-Bruins' end. Travis turned fast, just in time to see Nish floating through the air like a basketball player about to dunk a ball, only Nish had his glove held high and had somehow snared the puck just before it made it across the blueline. The linesman signalled the play was onside.

Nish dropped the puck even before his own skates touched the ice again. The defenceman who had shot the puck was down to block it, sliding on his side toward Nish.

Nish poked the puck and hopped again, this time right over the sliding defender, the puck squeezing through under his knees, the only space large enough.

Nish was in alone.

The Mini-Bruins' goaltender charged to cut off the angle. Nish deked once and sent a perfect backhand to Travis, who had an unexpected second chance – except this time the net was empty. He made no mistake, the puck bulging the twine in the centre of the net.

The Owls had won!

"I'll take my picture now," Nish announced after the cheering and back-slapping and high-fiving had died down in the Owls' dressing room. Even Muck had come to shake Nish's hand, while shaking his own head at the same time. Travis figured Muck was as baffled as he was by Nish's erratic bursts of brilliance.

"This just gets us *into* the championship game," Sarah said. "You still have to win it."

"Aw, come on!"

"That was the deal, okay?" Sarah said.

"No fair!" Nish said, slamming his gloves and helmet into his equipment bag. He slumped in his seat, exhausted.

Sarah looked up from her skates, and smiled. "Nice game, though," she said.

10

After the win against Boston, the school bus headed back to the campground. Mr. Dillinger drove slowly, with the windows down for fresh air and Derek handing out cold bottles of Gatorade from a case his father had purchased and put on ice for just this moment. Several of the Owls fell asleep, the game, the warm air, and the rhythm of the rolling bus relaxing them until they could no longer keep their eyes open.

Everyone woke, however, when Mr. Dillinger turned off the turnpike and suddenly braked hard, coming to a stop behind a string of cars. Up ahead, they could see a police roadblock.

There were patrol cars everywhere, several with their lights flashing, and the police and several husky men in suits were stopping the traffic in both directions.

"What's up?" Mr. Dillinger called, as he finally rolled the big bus up to the checkpoint.

The two police said nothing. A man in a light-brown suit —
and with a wire running up from under his coat collar to an ear
plug in his right ear — answered for them.

"FBI," he said.

Mr. Dillinger nodded, smiling, and waited for more information, but he got none. The police walked the length of the
bus, staring up into the windows, and then signalled back that all
was okay. Another police officer waved Mr. Dillinger through.
The man with the ear plug said nothing.

"What did he say?" Jenny called from where she was sitting
with Sarah.

"Federal Bureau of Investigation," Data called back impatiently, as if she should have known.

"What're they looking for?" Wilson asked.

"Drugs maybe," Data answered knowingly. "Murderers,
smugglers, kidnappers, terrorists, extraterrestrial visitors — take
your pick."

Once back at the campsite, the roadblock was all anyone could
talk about. A man who'd had his trunk searched said the police had
a clipboard with photographs of criminals on it. Another man
said it was simply a precautionary sweep of the area before the
President of the United States and his family visited Disney
World the following week. A woman with her hair up in curlers
said she knew for a fact that there were "illegal aliens" in the area.

"*Aliens?*" said Lars. "Like in the movie?"

Data happily corrected him. " 'Illegal aliens' means people
who shouldn't be in the country — not monsters."

"Oh," said Lars, a bit embarrassed.

But clearly, no one really knew the reason for the roadblock. Perhaps it was connected with the helicopters and the trucks searching the campground. But what were they searching for? It had to be more than merely looking for people who had sneaked into the country. Probably, Travis figured, the man who said it was just a routine sweep of the area before the President's visit had been right. Nothing to worry about.

⊚

The next morning the Screech Owls were headed back to Disney World, this time to line up for the popular Space Mountain ride at Tomorrowland and then, later, to take in some of the more athletic attractions like Blizzard Beach, where they would all change into their bathing suits and spend the afternoon flying down the greatest water slides in the world.

When Travis rolled out of his sleeping bag, Data was already up, sitting at the picnic table outside the tent and staring hard at some photographs he had laid out carefully in front of him.

"Have a look here, Travis," Data said, when he turned to see who was coming out through the tent flap.

Travis, blinking in the morning sun, rubbed his eyes as he walked over to the picnic table. All the photographs, he noticed, were of Goofy, several showing Goofy and Nish together.

"Which one's Goofy?" Travis asked, trying to make a joke.

Data didn't respond. He picked out two of the photos.

"Take a look at these two shots and tell me if anything's different."

Travis took the two Polaroid photos and examined them. One showed Nish, with his left arm around Goofy, grinning from ear to ear at the camera. The other showed him on Goofy's other side, again grinning from ear to ear.

"Taken from different sides?" Travis suggested. "I don't know – what?"

"Take a close look at Goofy's clothes."

Travis did as he was told. In the first photo, Goofy was wearing a yellow vest; in the second, the vest was orange.

"Goofy changed his clothes?" Travis suggested.

"He wouldn't have. He was racing off to catch the parade, remember, when this picture was taken." Data tapped a finger-nail on the photo of Nish and Goofy at the Hall of Presidents.

"Maybe it's just the camera," Travis suggested. "Yellow, orange – they're practically the same. Maybe it's just the light-ing. My camera does that all the time."

"Not this one," Data argued. "It doesn't mess up colour."

"Then there are two Goofys," said Travis. "Disney World's a huge place, you know."

"Maybe," said Data, looking unconvinced.

The lineup for Space Mountain was only thirty minutes long, and sooner than they expected the first of the Owls were being moved into little six-passenger rockets and heading off into the universe, shooting stars and meteors included.

The cut-off for loading one of the rockets came right in front of where Travis stood beside Simon. An attendant, holding out an arm, said, "Sorry, boys, next one," and for a moment the two Owls were alone with their thoughts.

"I'm just as glad," said Simon.

"So am I," said Travis.

Simon looked at Travis, wondering, afraid to ask.

Travis smiled, and all of a sudden he heard himself say, "I skipped out on the Tower of Terror, too. But no one saw me."

Simon's eyes went wide. "You did? Honest?"

"Honest. We'll do this one together. And if we can handle this, we'll do the Tower before we head home. Deal?"

Simon looked at him for a moment, blinking. He wet his lips nervously. "Deal," he said, and stuck out his hand. They shook just as the attendant waved his arm for the next six riders to board.

Less than three minutes later, their knees a bit shaky and their hearts still pounding, the two Owls stepped off the Space Mountain rocket and high-fived each other.

To get to Blizzard Beach, the Owls first had to walk back through the Magic Kingdom. Travis again noticed a maintenance truck parked to one side of the Hall of Presidents.

The back doors were open, and a uniformed maintenance worker was rolling electric cable off a drum and cutting it.

The man looked up.

Travis recognized him: it was the same worker they had seen here yesterday, but this time he was without his work cap and Travis could see that his head was shaved. It was the man from the campground who had been rowing the boat!

"Look!" Travis said to Nish and Data. "That's the guy from the beach."

The worker turned quickly and headed into the side door, the cable dangling behind him.

"I think you're right," said Data.

"So he works here," said Nish matter-of-factly.

It didn't seem right to Travis. Why would a worker at Disney World be living in a campsite? He kept worrying about it as they rode the monorail to the main entrance. There was a place just inside the gates labelled "Information," and while the others checked out a souvenir store, he made his way across to the stand.

A man in a Disney World uniform turned and smiled at him. "What can I do for you, son?"

"I just have a question," Travis said in a small voice.

"Shoot."

"Would they have more than one Mickey Mouse here?"

The man chuckled. "There's only one Mickey Mouse, son."

"But I mean for the parades and everything. Would there be two Goofys? Two different people in Goofy costumes, I mean."

The man shook his head. "Not a chance, son. People who come here *believe*. You understand what I mean? What if a little kid saw two Goofys? You can't have two Santa Clauses together, now can you? Same goes for Mickey and Minnie and Goofy. As far as this place is concerned, they're *real* people. We couldn't have two of them any more than your parents could have two of you."

"I see," said Travis. "Thanks."

"No problem," the man said.

But it *was* a problem. And Travis didn't know what to do about it.

11

"There's no other way," said Data. "you're going to have to dive."

Travis felt his heart flutter like the wings of a hummingbird. His breath caught. He felt clammy with sweat. But he also knew he could not show his fear. He may have chickened out of the Tower of Terror, but he couldn't back out of this.

The six boys had held a meeting in their tent. Data – and, to a lesser extent, Nish – was also sure that the maintenance worker outside the Hall of Presidents and the man in the rowboat had been one and the same. Data had photographic evidence that there were two Goofys. And the man at Disney World had said there could *not* have been two Goofys – at least not officially.

Those things the boys all knew for themselves. What they didn't know, perhaps couldn't know, was what the roadblock was all about, why the FBI was checking car trunks, why there were helicopters flying low over the campsite, and why there had been security personnel driving around in trucks with big searchlights.

And what, they kept asking each other, had been thrown from the rowboat?

Data was convinced it was a body. "The FBI solves murder cases," he said with authority. "Probably it's both kidnap and murder."

"Drugs," said Nish. "That's what they were getting rid of. They'll stash them at the bottom of the lake and then dive down and get them again when the heat's off."

"I agree," said Andy. "Drugs."

Travis didn't know. All he *did* know was that they were on their own with their wild suspicions. If they went to Muck or the parents, everyone would say that they were imagining these things just because they'd heard someone say "FBI." The photographs made sense to the boys, but anyone else would just think it was different film or a change in light that had made Goofy look different. Only the kids knew the other things that counted: the suspicious attitude of the first Goofy, the angry maintenance worker, the incident with the rowboat – and no one wanted to tell Muck why they had been spying on the young woman and her two companions. So it was up to them to get to the bottom of it.

And getting to the bottom of it, in Travis's case, meant diving.

"You're the one with the equipment," Andy had said.

He was right. Hoping that they might get out to the Gulf Coast and perhaps see some ocean life around the beaches, Travis had thrown his snorkelling mask and flippers into his backpack and brought them along.

"It's shallow," Lars had added, offering some comfort. "It's not even a real lake. It's man-made – a pond, really."

Travis knew he had no choice. "Okay," he said. "Let's do it."

⊚

They got the rowboat out onto the water with no difficulty. The boys all had bathing suits on. They had a strong rope that Data had found in the back of the bus, and Travis had his Swiss Army knife with him, tucked into the pocket of his bathing suit. Andy would row. Lars had borrowed a diving mask from another kid in the camp and was going to hang over the bow, looking down into the water. Nish and Data would sit in the stern for balance.

"Four's enough," Nish said, looking at the water line. "Besides, there're only four life jackets here."

Simon was odd man out. Travis had his snorkelling gear and would be swimming. But Simon had neither gear nor a seat.

"I'm a good swimmer," Simon said. "I'll support Travis."

Travis was grateful for the company. Together, he and Simon pushed the boat out into deeper water and then held on to the stern, kicking while Andy rowed out to where they remembered the men dumping the mysterious bundle. Once they made it to the general area, Andy began rowing in slow circles while the two with masks stared down through the water.

Travis felt uneasy. The water was clear, but the bottom muddy, with weeds. They could see fish swimming, mainly minnows at all levels, but once in a while a darker, larger shadow near the bottom. Travis presumed they were bass. He knew they couldn't be sharks in a freshwater lake.

"*Th-glub-r-glub!*" Lars shouted, his face in the water, from the front of the boat.

No one understood what he said, but everyone knew what he meant. Andy jammed down hard on the oars, bringing the boat to a stop. Travis and Simon let go and swam to where Lars was leaning over the water, pointing.

Lars lifted his face out of the water and yanked off the mask. It left dark red lines around his eyes and nose.

"*I think I see it!*" he shouted.

The Owls in the boat all glanced over, nearly tipping themselves into the lake.

"*Watch it!*" shouted Nish.

"*I see it!*" called Data. "*We've found it!*"

Travis stared down. He, too, could see the dark bundle. It was deeper here, but less weedy. He could see sunlight dancing on the bottom as little waves played on the surface of the lake.

He blew hard on his snorkel to clear it of water; then he dived.

He dived into instant silence. He felt excited, but also afraid. *What if there were alligators in the water?* No, there couldn't be – the beach was safe for swimming. But what about snapping turtles? Why couldn't the little lake just dry up the way his grandparents' lake always emptied in his dream?

Travis was afraid. He knew it – he admitted it to himself – but he couldn't let fear stop him.

He looked up. Simon had taken the mask from Lars and was floating on the surface, staring down. Simon raised a thumb in support, and Travis felt a little calmer.

His breath was running out. He circled over the object. It was wound up in a dark plastic tarpaulin and held together with bungee cords. Lying to one side, attached to the bundle with rope, were the concrete blocks weighing the object down. He wouldn't be able to lift it himself. They'd have to use the rope.

Travis swam back up, his lungs vacuuming in fresh air the instant he broke the surface. He grabbed onto the boat, caught his breath, and realized there were four faces hanging over the gunwale and one staring at him from the water, all waiting for him to speak.

"That's it!" he gasped. "Hand me the rope."

Andy fed one end of the rope over the side; the other end he tied around a seat. Travis grabbed the rope, took several deep breaths, and dived again.

This time he had to go all the way down. He kicked hard with his flippers and felt the pressure rise. His mask pushed hard against his face. He kicked even deeper. He had good breath and felt strong, but he knew he was shivering.

A large shadow flickered underneath him. Travis could feel his heart slam against his chest, the effect all the more alarming under the pressure of the water.

The shadow moved again, slipping away. *A largemouth bass.*

If Travis had been able, he would have gasped in relief. But he needed every last bit of breath. He kicked again and headed straight down through a long curling mass of weed until he reached the bundle.

He quickly tied the end of the rope around two of the bungee cords binding the object.

His breath was running short again. He opened up the Swiss Army knife and cut away the lines attached to the concrete blocks.

He reached up and tugged hard on the rope, the signal that it was now tied on.

Before kicking to the surface, his lungs almost ready to burst, he took a final look. His tug had loosened the tarpaulin, a corner of which wafted back and forth in the water.

As Travis watched, a hand floated out!

His heart thundered. He almost choked, but he kept his breath, turned his face upward, and began kicking toward the surface.

He was panicking. It was as if all the nightmares of a life-time were chasing him. He felt the hand wrap around his ankle, clenching, holding – tugging – pulling him back.

Travis wanted to scream, but couldn't! He kicked hard.

Then, even more firmly, something caught his wrist!

He looked up. It was Simon, his eyes bulging behind Lars's mask. He must have seen the hand come free, too. But he had still swum toward Travis to help, his bare feet kicking fiercely to get him down deep. Simon yanked hard. Whatever it was that had hold of Travis's ankle slipped.

Travis glanced back. It was just the weed. His foot had caught in the weed.

The hand was still hanging free, seeming to wave at the two Owls as they kicked hard and burst through the surface.

"*It's a body!*" Travis shouted as he broke the surface and spat out the mouthpiece of his snorkel.

"*What?*" Nish shouted, disbelieving.

"*I saw a hand!*"

"*I saw it, too!*" shouted Simon. He was trying to scramble into the boat.

"*Careful!*" Andy yelled. "*You'll tip us!*"

"*I'm not pulling up any dead guy!*" Nish announced.

Lars, fortunately, was in control of himself. "Everybody just calm down," he said. "We came out here to do a job, and we're going to finish it.

"Travis and Simon – you guys swim around to the other side to stabilize the boat, okay? We'll do the lifting from this side."

Simon and Travis quickly swam to the rowboat's far side, reached up, and grabbed onto the gunwales. Andy began working the rope under the seat so they would have some support as they raised the body.

The four in the boat gave a mighty heave, but nothing gave. They tried again, and suddenly the boat rocked violently from side to side.

"*It's coming!*" shouted Andy.

"*I–I'm scared,*" Simon whispered to Travis. Travis could see he was trembling, even though the water was quite warm.

"So am I," Travis said. "We get through this, the Tower of Terror's nothing."

Simon smiled, but his teeth chattered hard.

"*Heave!*" Andy called.

Simon and Travis could hear the rope rubbing and straining on the far gunwale.

"*Heave!*" Andy called again.

They pulled and the boat rocked, but not so violently this time. The rope was groaning with the strain.

"*Heave!*" Andy called, and with an explosion of trapped air the tarp broke the surface.

Travis and Simon held on tight, both of them shaking badly now. Andy reached over and grabbed two of the bungee cords, Lars grabbed another, and with Nish and Data pulling on the rope, they lifted the object up out of the lake – the tarp making a huge sucking sound as it left the water – and into the boat.

"*I'm jumping ship!*" Data screamed.

"*Hang on!*" said Lars. "*Look at it!*"

Travis and Simon, still in the water, had no idea what was going on in the boat. They exchanged startled looks. All they could hear was Nish's response.

"*I don't believe it!*"

"*What is it?*" Simon called.

"Have a look," said Andy. His voice was calm, without fear.

The two boys, with Lars's help, pulled themselves up to look over the gunwale.

The first thing Travis saw was the hand: white, with three fat fingers.

Then the face: grinning, gap-toothed, eyes half open, big black ears.

Goofy!

12

The yellow vest," said Data.

There was no need to explain what he meant. Lying in the bottom of the boat like a drowned cartoon character was the Goofy costume from the first photograph – the one taken outside the Hall of Presidents when they had encountered the maintenance worker who also turned out to be the man in the rowboat.

The other man in the boat must have been the person inside this Goofy costume. It explained why the first Goofy had been so anxious to avoid the Screech Owls. It did not explain, however, what he had been up to at the Hall of Presidents.

"We better talk to Muck," Travis said.

"We'll have to take this back with us," said Andy.

"*L-L-Look there!*"

It was Nish, and there was real fear in his voice. Travis looked up with everyone else and saw that Nish was pointing to the beach. The beautiful young woman was there in a bathing suit.

She must have come down for a swim, but she had turned back and was running toward the path.

"*She saw us!*" said Nish.

"Where's she going?" Data asked.

"To get the others!" Travis said.

"Let's hurry!" warned Lars.

With Andy rowing strongly and Simon and Travis holding onto the rowboat's transom again and kicking as hard as they could, the boys raced to shore. Travis was trying to picture the layout of the camp. The quickest trail back to the Owls' campsite would take them right past the campsite of the Goofy impersonators – they couldn't chance that. But there was another, longer, trail that skirted the campsite and ended up by the showers, which were close to the Owls' site.

"*We'll go back by the shower trail!*" Travis shouted up into the rowboat.

"*Got you!*" Andy called back.

As soon as Travis's flippers touched the bottom, he stopped swimming and pushed. Simon did the same. Andy gave one final dig with the oars and the rowboat ground hard onto the beach. The boys scrambled to get out, Andy grabbing the Goofy head and Lars scooping up the body of the costume for the run back. Travis kicked off his flippers and grabbed them.

"*This way!*" Travis called.

With Travis leading the way, the Owls raced toward the head of the second trail.

"*Hey!*"

The shout came at them like a gunshot. It was a man's voice, deep and angry. None of them had to turn to see who it was. They began to run even faster.

"*Hey! You kids! Wait a minute!*"

Another man's voice, this one with fury in it.

"*Drop that if you know what's good for you!*" the first man yelled.

Travis could hear the men running. They were well behind the Owls, but they were fast and, unlike Travis anyway, weren't tired from all that diving and swimming.

The men were gaining, quickly.

Up ahead, Andy rounded a sharp turn in the trail, hit some mud, and slipped down on his side, the Goofy head spilling into the bush. He got up, scrambling and limping. Nish, empty-handed, reached out and scooped up the head. Lars was well in front with the rest of the Goofy outfit.

Travis's snorkelling equipment was slowing him down. He tossed the flippers and mask and ran as hard as he could. He could feel his chest tighten. He turned his head briefly – just enough to see how far back his pursuers were – and in an instant he knew they were going to catch him.

This was real terror, true terror – not the manufactured terror of a ride. He felt like he was going to burst into tears like a little child. What would they do to him? *Kill him?*

The trail widened. He was almost home, but he knew that he wouldn't make it; one of the men was now so close behind he could hear his breathing. He tried one final burst.

The trail curled around a large sycamore tree, the moss hanging down from the lowest branches like a curtain. Travis recognized the tree. Once beyond it, he would be able to see the showers. There was the smallest chance he'd make it, if he could just dig down a bit more and come up with yet one more burst of energy.

But he had nothing left. He was exhausted, beaten, defeated. The man had him. All he could do was make it to the tree and, perhaps, a few more feet along the trail, and hope that someone would see him being captured.

As he rounded the tree he sensed movement, a quick blur, to his right, then the sound of two heavy objects coming together hard.

"*OOOOFFF!*" came the sound from behind.

Travis turned just in time to see the maintenance worker flying through the air, turning a half somersault before crashing, flat on his back, into the low shrubs and mud to one side of the trail.

Standing between Travis and the fallen man, leaning over slightly with his hip stuck out, was Muck.

The second, smaller man was coming up fast and had seen what Muck had done to his partner. He was tired, his eyes wide in surprise, and he all but ran into Muck as he rounded the tree.

Muck stood his ground, both fists clenched. The second man put his head down and lunged, blindly, to tackle Muck around the waist.

Muck pulled back his right fist, took aim, and with one punch sent the second man into the bushes on top of the first, who was flailing desperately in the mud, gasping for breath.

Travis turned back up the trail. Mr. Cuthbertson and Mr. Dillinger were running toward him. Right behind them was

Lars, who had been well ahead of the pack in the race back to the Screech Owls' camp. He must have run into Muck first and sent him back to rescue Travis.

Travis's chest was killing him. He had no breath. He couldn't even stand. He slipped to his knees, choking and coughing. Muck came up to him, ruffled his wet hair with one big hand and put the other on his shoulder.

"Nearly had you, didn't they?" Muck said with a bit of a chuckle.

Travis tried to answer, but could say nothing. He gasped for air. He put a hand to his forehead and it slid right off. He was wet with sweat.

The man with the shaved head was rolling about on his back, trying to get up. He had got his breath back, but it was too late; Mr. Dillinger stood over him, waiting. Mr. Cuthbertson was watching the second man, who was out cold from Muck's single punch.

The trail was filling with people now. They were running from everywhere: the showers, campsites, other paths. A truck with two men in military uniforms was pulling up as close to the trail as it could come, lights flashing.

The other Owls were first to reach the group. Andy and Nish in the front, Simon and Data right behind them. The rest of the Owls – Sarah and Jesse in the lead – were just coming onto the far end of the path, running hard to see what all the commotion was about.

Sweat was pouring off Nish's face. But he was laughing.

"*Great check!*" he said to Muck.

Muck couldn't help himself: he grinned.

"You said the hip check was a lost art!" Nish said.

"It is," Muck answered.

"Yeah, but you also said there was no place in the game for fighting, didn't you?"

Nish grinned like he thought he had Muck. But he didn't.

"This isn't a game, son."

13

t certainly wasn't a game. The two police officers who had driven up in the truck pulled out
their handguns and held them on the two men,
while another searched and handcuffed them, then shoved them
into the back of a police car that soon arrived on the scene.

Before long there were more authorities swarming over the
campground. They found the young woman and handcuffed
her, too, and took her away. Then they brought in a special
crime-investigation unit to begin studying the campsite and,
most importantly, the Goofy costume the boys had brought up
from the bottom of the lake.

Late in the afternoon, a silver-haired man in a light-brown
suit, calling himself Agent Morris, came to talk to them. He was
most intrigued by Data's photographs of the two Goofys and
asked if the FBI could have them for evidence.

"You'll probably receive a special citation for this, son,"
Agent Morris said. "Good work."

"*I'm* the one who got Goofy to pose for the picture," protested Nish.

"Mr. Ulmar," Agent Morris said in a voice of great authority, "is the one who noticed the discrepancies in the colour of vests, sir."

Nish swallowed hard. "Mr. Ulmar" instead of Data. "Sir" instead of Nish. This was not a person to joke with; but then, this was no laughing matter.

Agent Morris explained it this way. The Federal Bureau of Investigation had received an anonymous tip several weeks ago that an unknown terrorist group would be trying something around the time of the President's planned trip to Disney World. The trip had been no secret; most of America knew he would be going and that he would be taking his family. The FBI, however, had almost no other information to go on. They didn't know the day – whether it might be before, during, or after the visit – they didn't know what terrorist group was involved, and they didn't know how the attack would take place, if it took place at all.

"The only other tips we had was to watch the campgrounds and keep an eye out for suspects working in disguise," Agent Morris said. "We knew our sources were excellent, but the information was far from perfect. That's why we set up the surveillance you encountered."

The helicopters had been to scare off the terrorists, perhaps even to flush them out if they were holed up in any of the many campgrounds near Disney World. The road checks, particularly on cars leaving various campgrounds, had been to look for suspicious characters.

"But since we didn't know what disguises might be used," said Agent Morris, "the road checks were pretty useless. If you boys hadn't figured it out for us, we might never have caught these people."

The FBI agent paused, swallowing hard: "And God only knows what might have happened . . ."

Agent Morris was being a bit too kind to the Owls. They hadn't actually figured it out. But the discovery of the Goofy costume had provided the evidence the FBI had needed to lead them to the terrorists. The man with the ponytail had decided to co-operate with the authorities, Agent Morris told them, and slowly the details of their plot were being pieced together.

The information officer at Disney World had been right when he said they would never have a second Goofy on the site. The terrorists had been able to bring the costume onto the grounds by having the young woman pose as a mother pushing a pram with her baby inside screened off from the sun. She seemed so harmless that no one had wanted to disturb her sleeping child, and she had passed through the gates easily. The man with the ponytail had simply paid to enter as a tourist. They used a diaper-changing room to hand over the costume, and the man had slipped into it in a washroom stall.

As for the man with the shaved head who posed as a maintenance worker, he had made it onto the site with forged identification tags and a perfect replica of one of the special uniforms the various Disney workers wear. Since no workers' uniforms had been reported stolen, there was no one on the alert for a maintenance worker, and this guy had seemed to know what he was doing.

The maintenance worker was able to get into the electrical works of the Hall of Presidents, which the real President was scheduled to visit in order to listen to President Lincoln's famous Gettysburg Address. The terrorists did not know, however, the precise time this would take place – the twenty-minute show played throughout the day – so there was no point in merely planting a bomb with a timer. What the maintenance worker had done was smuggle in three small but powerful homing devices in his toolbox.

Since "Goofy" could pretty much come and go as he pleased in Disney World, his job was to plant the devices in strategic locations. One, of course, had been in the Hall of Presidents. Another had been along the parade route where the President and his family were to watch the daily parade of Disney characters. "Goofy" had planted this one in the bottom of the parade's final float, the float that would be carrying the real Goofy, Mickey and Minnie Mouse, and Donald Duck down Main Street, U.S.A., right past the living, breathing, unsuspecting President of the United States.

"These homing devices could be used for a missile attack," said Agent Morris. "Whether they planned actually to attack or to threaten we do not yet know – but the important thing is that they have been stopped."

He paused again. "If you hadn't stopped them – we might have had a national disaster on our hands."

Agent Morris looked around, smiling, then shook hands

with each of the Owls in turn, then with Muck, who seemed a bit sheepish. Agent Morris said to him, almost privately, "Thanks for being there." Muck only nodded.

"What country are they from?" Data asked.

Agent Morris didn't quite follow. "Excuse me?"

"The terrorists — where are they from?"

Agent Morris blinked, his distaste obvious.

"They're Americans, son."

Mr. Cuthbertson, Mr. Dillinger, and Muck called the Owls and their parents to a team meeting. They sat around a campfire and Mr. Dillinger handed out soft drinks. Then the three men sat on a makeshift bench by the fire and talked about what the team had just gone through.

"I just don't understand how they could be Americans," Data kept saying.

"Anybody can be a terrorist," said Mr. Cuthbertson. "It's happened in Canada. A bit before your time, but your parents will remember. All it takes to be a terrorist is to be willing to do whatever is required to advance your cause."

"It seems so stupid," said Data.

"To the rest of us, it does," said Mr. Cuthbertson. "But an American can hate his or her own government, just like a Canadian. There's a world of difference, however, between disliking a government and voting against it and despising that government and seeking to destroy it."

"But they would have killed innocent people," Sarah said.

"That's why they're called 'terrorists,'" said Mr. Dillinger. "They spread the worst kind of fear. When you never know where they're going to hit, or *who* they're going to hit, it's very difficult to protect yourself against them."

"That's why what you guys did was so important," said Mr. Cuthbertson. "You may have saved a great many lives."

Everyone paused while this sank in.

Travis looked at Muck, sitting by the fire. Perhaps it was just the way the fire flickered, but it seemed to Travis that the big coach's eyes were glistening.

14

The following morning, two representatives from Walt Disney World came to the campsite, thanked the Owls for what they had done, and handed out courtesy passes to the entire team. The Screech Owls would have one last day at Disney World. And that night they would travel to Tampa, to the magnificent Ice Palace, where they would play in the championship game of the Spring Break Tournament.

"*Go easy!*" Muck called to his players as they scrambled off the school bus when they arrived, running and screaming toward the entry gates. "*Save something for tonight!*"

But his warnings went unheeded. And judging by the big smile on Muck's face as he, too, hurried along, his bad leg swinging stiffly, the Owls' big coach was advising caution merely because he knew it was expected of him.

"You on?" Travis said to Simon as he caught up to the smallest Owl.

Simon neither turned his head nor smiled. "I'm on," he said.

The two friends headed for the Disney-MGM Studio lot — where the Twilight Zone Tower of Terror was waiting.

They both had a point to prove.

⊚

Fear sometimes felt like a swarm of insects climbing over Travis's body. He and Simon were in the long, twisting lineup for the Tower of Terror, eating ice cream and laughing. It would have looked like he was relaxed, but inside Travis couldn't shake the sense of dread any more than he could brush off a cobweb into which he had just stumbled.

Simon turned, still licking his cone, and said with a smile, "I'm scared to death."

"I am, too," Travis admitted.

They passed into the lobby of the old hotel, and were soon in the boiler room, approaching the terrifying service elevator. Simon had already gone beyond the point where, last time, he had bailed out.

It was in the boiler room that Travis had jumped out of the line, the words "*Those who experience anxiety in enclosed spaces should not ride*" sending shivers up and down his back as if he had a million spiders crawling on his naked body. Travis tensed, his mind fighting to hold him back.

He felt a tug at his arm and turned, panicking.

It was Simon, smiling. He had taken firm hold of Travis's wrist, as he had when the weed wrapped around Travis's ankle.

"We're next," Simon said. "You okay?"

"Yeah, sure," Travis replied. He wondered if his voice betrayed him.

"I'm not," Simon admitted. "Stick close to me, okay?"

Travis did not understand how Simon could admit he was scared when he could not. But Simon clearly needed Travis, and he wasn't afraid to say so. Travis had to stay.

The doors to the service elevator were open, the bellhop urging them in with an outstretched arm and a wicked smile.

Travis stepped forward, hesitated, realized with surprise that Simon was holding onto his T-shirt, then quickly moved along so that Simon would not see his resolve was crumbling.

Travis was inside. Simon was being shown to his seat, and when he sat down, solid safety bars were lowered across the laps of the riders.

The only empty seat remaining was beside Simon, in the middle of the last row, dead centre and completely exposed. The safety bar didn't stretch all the way across. Instead, a huge seat-belt was folded over the cushion.

"Right there, son," said the bellhop to Travis. "Best seat in the house."

The others on the ride turned and laughed, welcoming a little comic relief from their rising anxiety. All eyes were now on Travis. Everyone was watching. He couldn't break down here.

"Th-th-thanks," said Travis. He started to put on his seat-belt, but his hands were shaking badly. The bellhop grabbed the two ends and fitted them together.

"There's nothing to it, son," he whispered before leaving. The bellhop knew. He probably knew *every* time someone had gone further than he or she intended and was trapped in the ride.

The moment the door closed, Travis felt as if his throat had also been slammed tight. He had no air. He was bursting. He twisted hard against the seatbelt, but the straps held him in. He felt if his body couldn't leave the seat, his heart would leave his body – ripping right through his rib cage.

He felt Simon's hand on his forearm. Simon's palm was soaking wet. He needed Travis.

Travis very deliberately began to suck in a breath. He took it slowly and carefully, and felt the air go deep. His heart settled, at least for the moment.

The elevator rose slowly, then stopped, and the doors opened onto an endless corridor. The family of hotel guests who had disappeared back in 1939 – the parents, a little girl – suddenly appeared as holograms, checking into their rooms, then vanishing into ghostly memory.

Travis felt Simon's fingernails dig into his forearm.

The doors closed, and up again went the elevator. It stopped and then slipped sideways out of the shaft and began moving across the hotel. They were surrounded by stars and blackness. It felt as if they were floating in outer space.

He had gone much too far! There was no last-minute exit here!

Again, Travis's breath refused to come. Again, he felt Simon holding on. Travis had to be brave. He was . . . *Captain.*

With a bump the elevator stopped rolling and began to rise. These were the sounds they had heard from outside, the sounds of cables working, cables snapping, that always preceded the ter- rifying screams from the riders.

"*Oh my God! Oh my God!*" a woman shouted from the front

row. The other riders laughed, but as they did, Travis could hear their own anxiety.

Up, up, up rose the elevator, the cables creaking, the tension rising. The cables groaned, seemed to pause momentarily, and then, *snap,* the elevator plunged like a stone!

"*Heaven help us!*" screamed the woman in the front row. No one laughed this time.

Travis knew he too was screaming. He knew his mouth was open. He could feel his hair lifting in the downward rush. He knew, in that instant, he would give anything in the world to get out of that elevator. He would give up his collection of NHL cards, his posters of Mats Sundin and Paul Kariya and Doug Gilmour. He would give up being Captain, his chance at an NHL career. *Anything* to get out of there!

The elevator came to a sudden halt.

He was still alive!

He turned to Simon. His friend looked like he had just swallowed an alligator. His eyes were bulging, his cheeks puffed. Pure terror was written all over Simon's face, and yet the ride was only just beginning.

Again the cables creaked, again the elevator began to rise, only this time with gathering speed.

As the elevator rose faster and faster, it began to feel as out of control as a free-fall. It seemed as if it would crash through the roof and head off into outer space – just like in the Twilight Zone film they had seen.

Up and up, faster and faster still. Travis grabbed onto Simon, Simon onto Travis. People were screaming. The woman in the front row was screaming and praying. Then suddenly, in a flash, they were outside! The roof gave way, and the elevator, for the briefest moment, seemed to lunge out over the Studio lot!

An explosion of light blinded them! Was it just the sudden sun? Was it a camera flash?

"*OHHHHHH MY GODDDDDD!!!*" the woman in the front row screeched. This was not for effect. She was terrified.

"*We're all gonna die!*" shouted a man.

"*Allllll Riggghhhhhtttttt!!!*" screamed another, excited voice.

Travis turned quickly in shock. *It was Simon who had screamed!* He was smiling from ear to ear!

The elevator was plunging. Down thirteen floors in less than three seconds. Travis had never felt such pressure against him – G-force, they called it. It pushed against his face, his arms, his back. It was more powerful than anything he had ever felt diving, more powerful than anything he had ever felt in an airplane. It was pure terror – a force so wild and uncontrollable he was completely helpless. Travis could not have moved even if he'd wanted to. He could not fight it. He had to go with it.

He was on this ride to the end.

"*Fantastic!*" Simon shouted as they left the elevator, their legs a bit rubbery and their eyes blinking fast, unaccustomed to the light.

Travis couldn't stop giggling. He had done it. He had mastered his fear and stayed to the end – not that he had much choice once the bellhop had strapped him in. But far more important than merely lasting, he had *enjoyed* it. There was something about the thrill of utter helplessness.

"*Great!*" he said.

Three times they had risen and plunged. On the third ride up, there was no longer terror in the riders' screams; on the third plunge, the screaming had become a celebration. Had it been put to a vote, they would have gone for a fourth, easily.

"I have to go to the washroom," said Simon.

"I'll wait in here for you," said Travis, heading into the souvenir shop.

Travis didn't think Simon knew about the photographs. He would buy him one for proof – proof, if he ever needed it again, that he hadn't been afraid.

The man at the photo booth was just putting up the photograph of their ride. Travis was amazed that his hair could stand so straight up, stunned that he could look so terrified and moments later be laughing about it. Simon, sitting beside him in the picture, looked like one of the dummies advertising the ride on the way into Disney World.

He quickly paid for the photograph and tucked it in under his shirt.

Simon was just coming out of the washroom when Travis got back. "Anything good?" he asked.

"Naw," Travis said. "Let's go."

15

nce again Travis had trouble catching his breath. Once again he felt clammy all over with nervous sweat, his heart pounding out of control. But there was nothing closed-in about this space.

They were in the Ice Palace, a huge hockey rink that could hold more than twenty thousand people. He could barely see to the rafters. Even the Screech Owls' dressing room was bigger than any he'd ever been in.

He looked up and saw hundreds, if not thousands, of fans. All the parents were there, and all the relatives of the team they would be playing.

Their championship game against the State Selects – an all-star team made up of the very best players from all over the state of Florida – was even going to be broadcast. And in two languages – but not French and English, as would happen back in Canada, but in English and *Spanish*. The radio station that carried the Florida Panthers' games in Spanish – the first hockey games ever broadcast in that language – had decided to come up to Tampa once the Selects had made it to the final, and now half the kids on the Owls' team were shouting out, "*Se metio-ooooo!*" – the Spanish equivalent of, "*He shoots! He scores!*"

Muck had told the Owls to "save something" for tonight, and if they lacked anything in energy, they more than made up for it in enthusiasm. The size, the lights, the *professionalism* of the Ice Palace had them fired up. So, too, had the fans. Their own relatives were there, yes, but there was also a group from Disney World, and even Agent Morris and his family.

"This is a serious team," Muck had told them before the Owls came out onto the ice. "Hockey has taken off in Florida the past few years, so don't think you're up against a bunch of surfers and beach bums. They're a good, fast, big team, and they're very well coached. I should know: Deke Larose, their coach, played with me once. He knows his hockey."

Travis could tell during the warm-up that Muck had been right. The Selects were very well organized. The goaltender looked great and, obviously, had a great glove hand.

"Sarah's line starts," Muck had said just before the Owls left the big dressing room. "Jenny's our goalie tonight."

"*Let's go, Jenny!*" Sarah had yelled.

"*Jen-ny!*"

"*Jen-ny!*"

Not long after, Travis understood why Muck had named Jenny to start, and not Jeremy, who usually played the big games. They were all turned toward the Canadian flag for "O Canada," when the Selects' goaltender yanked off her helmet. The Selects also had a girl in net. Muck must have figured the challenge would inspire Jenny.

Sarah took the face-off – *and lost it!* Travis was shocked. Sarah rarely lost a face-off. But this one she lost clean, the big Selects' centre backhanding the puck to his left defenceman.

Dmitri moved quickly to check the defender, catching the youngster off guard with his extraordinary speed. Panicking, the defender tried to fire the puck back to his centre, but the puck bounced straight up ice into Dmitri's shin pads.

In an instant Dmitri was around the falling defenceman and racing in alone. Travis hurried in case there was a rebound, but he didn't expect one. He had seen Dmitri do this too many times. In hard, a shoulder fake, then onto the backhand and a high roofer to the short side.

Dmitri faked, pulled the puck onto his backhand, and, just as Travis had anticipated, rifled the puck high and hard into the open side of the net.

Only it never got there! A white glove flashed, and the puck disappeared! Dmitri curled away, looking back in surprise. The referee's whistle blew. The Selects' goaltender flipped the puck out and caught it again on the webbing of her glove, then presented it to the referee as casually as if he were at a garden party and she was serving little munchies on a platter.

"*Did you see that catch?*" Nish asked, when he and Travis came off at the end of the first shift.

"Great glove hand!" Travis agreed.

The Selects were indeed well coached. Unlike so many other all-star teams the Owls had played, this one truly was a *team*. There was no hot-dogging, no heroics, no end-to-end rushes. The players had a system, and each knew exactly where he or she fit into the system. They always sent one player in to forecheck, hoping to force a pass while the others clogged up the middle.

"*They're trapping us,*" Muck said behind the bench.

"I can't believe it," said Mr. Dillinger.

Wilson got caught circling his own net and tried a pass to Simon, standing up along the blueline, but the waiting Selects forward pounced on it. Simon might have made a diving check, but chose instead to chase.

The Selects forward passed to his opposite winger in the corner, who then passed quickly to the centre driving in toward the slot. Simon, hurrying back, tried to play the puck, not the man, and the big centre merely stepped around him and drove a hard shot over Jenny's shoulder.

Selects 1, Owls 0.

"We gotta do something about that trap," Muck said, as he sent Sarah's line out again.

"Nishikawa – come back here."

Nish skated back to the bench and conferred with Muck. The referee blew his whistle to get the Owls moving, and Muck slapped Nish's back and sent him into the play.

Nish detoured past Travis as they lined up for the face-off.

"I get the puck," Nish whispered to him. "You head for centre ice."

Sarah won this draw. She pivoted with it, avoided one check, and then dropped it back to Nish, who skated hard for the back of the net, stopping in a spray with the puck and waiting while the Selects sent in their single forechecker.

Nish faked going to the far side and, immediately, the fore-checker moved to force him tight, counting on another cross-ice pass that they could then intercept. But Nish dug in hard and turned the other way.

Travis was already breaking for centre ice. Nish rounded the net and lifted the puck so high it almost struck the clock, floating high and falling just beyond centre ice, where Travis, barely on side, picked it up and was in free.

He knew he had to keep it away from the goalie's glove hand. He came in, his mind spinning with far too many questions. Should he shoot? Deke? Backhand? Forehand? He looked up. No openings. He looked down; the puck was beginning to skid off the blade of his stick. He lost it, regained it, and shot without looking.

Again the white blur! Again the puck vanished!

"You should have gone stick side," Nish said when they got back to the bench.

"Five hole," said Dmitri.

"Just rip it!" said Sarah.

Everybody had a suggestion; no one had an answer.

Then the Selects got a power play when Andy took a penalty for tripping, and a hard shot from the point went in off Nish's toe.

Selects 2, Owls 0.

"My fault," Andy said to Jenny when the Owls went to console her.

"I should have had it," Jenny said.

Travis looked hard at Jenny. At first he thought she was near tears, but then he realized she was just angry. Muck had offered her this challenge, and the Selects' goaltender was beating her.

The Owls barely held off the Selects for the remainder of the period. If it hadn't been for Sarah's checking and a great shot block by Andy, the Selects would have run away with the game. As it was, the Owls were barely hanging on.

Muck waited until they had caught their breath before he entered the dressing room. Nish, as usual, had his head down almost between his legs. Sarah and Travis were sagging, their backs against the lockers, their gloves and helmets off. Sweat was dripping freely from Sarah's face. Travis, too, was sweating heavily for once.

Muck was smiling. He didn't seem the slightest bit concerned.

"Jenny just forgot to turn on her equipment," he said. "Those guys aren't going to get another shot past her – guaranteed."

Jenny didn't look up. She hadn't even removed her mask. She just sat, staring straight ahead, ready to go on a moment's notice.

"Nishikawa," Muck said.

Nish looked up, expecting a blast.

"I like what I see out there. Let's see a bit more of it, though."

Nish looked down, the colour rising in his face.

"Higgins," Muck said, turning on big Andy, who'd played well, apart from the penalty.

Andy looked up, waiting.

"I want to try something: you on a line with Simon and Jesse. I think you're due, Simon."

Simon looked bewildered. He hadn't played particularly well. He'd lost the puck that led to the Selects' first goal.

Muck walked out the door, leaving them to their thoughts.

"You should have had that guy," Nish said across the dressing room to Simon. "He was your check."

Simon twisted defensively: "Don't think I don't know that."

"You can't be afraid of the puck," Nish said in a quiet voice, but one that everyone heard.

"I'm not," Simon said.

"Prove it, then," Nish said.

"Cut it out," Sarah interrupted. "You're not in a position to ask for proof."

"What's that supposed to mean?" Nish demanded.

Sarah answered by pulling an envelope from the side pocket of her equipment bag. She opened the envelope and took out the Polaroid of Nish wearing his bird dropping.

"You're supposed to give me that!" Nish whined, angry at the sight of the reminder.

"We're down 2–0, Bird Poo," said Sarah.

Nish buried his head again in his knees. Simon starting tapping his stick on the ends of his skates.

Travis was captain. He knew he had to stay something.

"Don't forget we're a team," he said. "Don't forget what got us here."

"*Let's go!*" Dmitri shouted from the far side of the room.

"*Let's do it!*" shouted Jesse.

"*We're the Screech Owls!*" shouted Sarah.

"*Owls!*"

"*Owls!*"

"*Owls!*"

16

Nish was again a driven player in the second period. He blocked shots, cut off rushes, and twice tried the sneak pass over centre, but the first time the Selects were waiting on it and beat Dmitri to the puck.

The second time it worked. Andy stepped in front of one Selects defenceman, "accidentally" blocking his route, and little Simon squirted out of the pack to take the lead in the rush for the puck Nish had sent flying over centre.

"*Go, Simon!*" Sarah screamed from the bench.

Simon was so nervous he almost lost his footing as he picked up the wobbling puck. He came in over the blueline, wound up for a slapshot, faked it, and moved to the far side of the net before sliding the puck in between the goaltender's outstretched legs.

Selects 2, Owls 1.

"*Five hole!*" shouted Dmitri. "*Told you so!*"

The Owls' bench went wild. Even Muck and Mr. Dillinger high-fived each other.

Nish, hurrying up behind Simon, caught him in a bear hold as he stepped off the ice and almost twisted his helmet off.

Simon's goal gave the Owls new life. They played far better in the second period, not once letting the Selects trap them on a breakout play. Their opponents were getting frustrated, particularly with Sarah's close checking, which was keeping the Selects' big centre under control.

With less than a minute to go in the second, Data picked up a loose puck in the Owls' corner and clipped it off the boards to Travis, who saw Nish shooting up into the play. Nish took the puck and charged over centre, the backchecking Selects winger unable to stay with him.

Nish flipped the puck again. Not high toward the clock this time, but a gentle little flick that sent the puck between the two defencemen who were beginning to squeeze toward him. Both defence decided to play the man and went for Nish, but Nish jumped high, right between them. He was home free, until he lost his grip and fell.

Nish spun toward the corner, the puck still on his stick. Flat on his stomach, he managed to look up and see Sarah coming in along the near side. He swept the puck to her just before crashing into the boards, and Sarah fired a pass hard across the crease to Dmitri, who had the whole open side of the net to tap the puck into.

Selects 2, Owls 2.

When the second period was up, the Owls skated off to a huge ovation for their comeback. Even Agent Morris of the FBI was on his feet. And all the Disney people.

"Delay Nish for a bit," Sarah said to Travis.

Travis nodded. He waited at the boards, slapping each teammate as the player left the ice, and then grabbed Nish as he was coming off.

"Spanish radio wants to interview you," Travis told him.

Nish stopped dead in his tracks. "*I can't speak Spanish!*" he said.

"Doesn't matter – they'll translate."

"Where do I go?" Nish asked. He didn't seem surprised that they would want to interview him.

"You just wait here," Travis said. "They'll come down to you."

Travis hurried into the dressing room, giggling at his own trick. Sarah was already at work. She had taken the scissors Mr. Dillinger used to cut away tape and was chopping up the Polaroid of Nish into dozens of little pieces, which she then piled carefully on his locker seat.

"Is he coming?" she asked.

"He thinks he's about to be interviewed on Spanish radio," Travis said.

The rest of the Owls looked up, realized the trick that had been played, and roared with laughter.

The door banged open and Nish roared in, furious, throwing his stick and turning on Travis.

"*There was no one there to interview me!*"

Nish was beet red, his face contorted with anger. Travis knew he'd have to do some fancy talking to save this one.

"I guess I got the periods wrong," Travis said. "They must have meant the end of the game. The guy didn't speak English that well."

Nish considered this to make great sense.

"Okay," he said. "But don't waste my time like that again."

Nish wandered over to his seat, dropping his gloves and helmet.

"*What's this?*" he asked.

He brushed away the pieces of the incriminating photograph. "Thank you, thank you, thank you," he said to no one in particular.

"You're playing great hockey," said a familiar voice from the back of the room.

It was Muck.

"Thank you," said Nish again. He thought Muck was speaking directly to him.

"All of you," said Muck. "I have nothing more to tell you."

And with that, Muck walked out of the dressing room, smiling.

17

hether Jenny had "turned her equipment on" or not didn't matter. She was spectacular in the third period, on one occasion stopping the big centre on a clear breakaway.

But Jenny had some help. She got it from Nish (who seemed to block as many shots as she did), and she got it from Data (who kept clearing the puck) and Sarah (who backchecked with ferocious energy). At the other end, Travis and Dmitri kept up a solid forecheck, causing turnover after turnover. The brilliant glove hand of the Selects' goalie took away a sure goal from Andy, and an excellent poke check stopped Travis on what looked like an easy tap-in.

Regulation time came to an end with the teams still tied. Muck spoke to them before the five-minute overtime.

"They're starting to send in two forecheckers," said Muck. "I know Deke's style. He figures to panic our defence. Nishikawa?"

"Yes, sir."

"You like to carry the puck, don't you?"

"Sometimes."

"If you get a chance, go for it. We cut off their two men in deep, we might be able to make something of this. Data, you stay back and do what you have to do."

"Yes, sir."

The chance came a couple of minutes later. Data had the puck hard against the boards in the Owls' end, and both fore-checkers converged on him, convinced they could cause a turnover. Instead of panicking, however, Data used the boards to send a long curling pass around to Nish, who picked up the puck in full stride.

As the two forecheckers peeled away from Data, he "slipped" and fell, spinning into one of them and slipping his stick under the other forward's skate. The skate skittered on the stick and the forward slipped to one knee, losing a valuable second.

Nish was already free and flying. He had the puck on the end of his stick and was cutting across centre on the diagonal, looking for the pass to Dmitri. But Dmitri had headed for the bench, and Simon had already leapt over the boards.

Nish saw Simon coming into the play. He faked a forward pass to Sarah, causing the one Selects defenceman to cross over, then dumped a little backhand pass to Simon just as he hit the blueline. With the defenceman already committed to Sarah, he couldn't turn back in time, and Simon was in, alone.

Simon tried the same play – five hole – again, but this time the goaltender was expecting it. She kicked out the rebound hard.

It slid straight into Travis's feet. He turned his right skate and trapped the puck, kicking it ahead onto his stick blade. As he did so, he turned, realizing the crease was suddenly filling up with bodies. There was only one passing option open to him. *Nish.*

The big Owls defenceman was charging the net. Thanks to Data's "accident," there was still no one on Nish. Travis's pass hit Nish perfectly.

The two defencemen tried to converge on Nish, but suddenly Simon spurted through an opening and brushed against the right one so he spun off to the side. By looking back and appearing to be expecting another pass, Simon had made it look accidental. It might have been.

The other defence tackled Nish. He knew he might take a penalty but, given the time in the game and the score, it was his only play. He leapt at Nish, draping himself over him as Nish tried to bull the puck in toward the Selects' net.

Nish wouldn't go down. The Selects defender wrestled him, but Nish broke one hand free as the puck slid between his checker's skates. He shook off the checker, but was in so close he couldn't quite get his stick past the sliding goaltender and the defenceman's back skate.

Nish had no option. Off balance, on the verge of falling into the net, unable even to see exactly what he was doing, he put the stick between his own legs, tried a blind shot, and fell.

The puck rose without enough force to reach the crossbar. It clipped off the goalie's right shoulder, then rolled up and over – and in!

Nish had scored!

And he had scored on the Mario Lemieux between-the-legs shot!
Final score: Owls 3, Selects 2.

The Owls' bench burst open and they flew onto the ice. In the Selects' end, they piled onto Nish, who was yelling and screaming as if he were still on the Tower of Terror ride. Sarah had both arms around Nish. Nish had an arm around Simon, twisting his helmet again. Data piled in, and then came the players from the bench as the cheers poured down on them from the seats of the Ice Palace.

"*We won!*"

"*We won!*"

"*We won!*"

"*You did it, Nish!*" Simon called from the pack. "*You scored on the Lemieux shot!*"

Nish grinned. "Thanks to you, pal."

"How'd you even see it?" Travis asked.

Nish grinned again.

"X-ray vision," hc said.

The teams and coaches lined up to shake hands – Muck and his old friend Deke Larose hugging each other – and then they stood for the Canadian anthem.

Travis stood staring up at the Maple Leaf and the American Stars and Stripes. He thought about everything that had happened to the Owls this week. He thought about what might have happened if Data hadn't wondered why the two Goofy costumes were different. He thought about what he would do when he got to the dressing room. He would present Simon with the photograph of him on the ride that had terrified him.

After tonight's game, no one would ever again be calling him "Chicken Milliken." Not after what he had done to set up Nish's spectacular goal.

The anthem ended, and a man with dark hair hurried out onto the ice, reaching for Nish, who was trying to get his hands on the trophy. The man pulled Nish aside, and Travis could see him speaking fast to Nish. Nish was nodding, smiling.

The man and Nish began leaving the ice, passing right in front of Travis as they left.

"It's Spanish radio," said Nish. "You were right. They wanted me at the end of the game!"

THE END

The Quebec City Crisis

ci!"

"Travis — une pour moi!"

"Moi, s'il vous plaît!"

"Moi!"

It was cold enough to see their breath, yet Travis Lindsay was sweating as he stumbled and stuttered and tried to answer the shouts of the crowd gathered around him. How he wished he'd paid more attention in French class. If only they'd speak slower. If only he were standing closer to Sarah Cuthbertson, who was in French immersion, and who was yakking away happily as she signed her name, again and again and again.

Travis was helpless. He could do nothing but nod and smile and sign his name to the hockey cards they kept shoving into his hand.

He wished he understood better. He did not, however, wish that any of this would stop. As far as he was concerned — as far as any of the Screech Owls was concerned — this moment could go on forever.

"*Travis! Ici!*"

"*Moi!*"

This was what he had dreamed about all those long winter evenings when he'd sat at the kitchen table practising his signature. This was why he'd worked on that fancy, swirling loop on the *L* of "Lindsay," very carefully putting "#7" inside the loop to indicate his sweater number, just like the real NHLers did. He knew that his mother and father had been smiling to each other as they watched him work on signing his name, and he wished they could see him now. Travis Lindsay – Number 7, with a loop – signing autograph after autograph outside the renowned Quebec Colisée.

There was no end to the surprises on this trip to Quebec City. The Owls had come for the special fortieth anniversary of the Quebec International Peewee Tournament, the biggest and most special peewee hockey tournament on Earth. The Screech Owls were just one of nearly 150 teams entered, and Travis just one of 2,500 players, but every single player felt as if the Quebec Peewee could be *his* or *her* tournament, the moment where he or she would make their mark and be noted by all who saw them play.

Like everyone else here, Travis knew the history of the Quebec Peewee. He knew that it was here that Guy Lafleur and Wayne Gretzky and Mario Lemieux had all come to national attention.

More than fourteen thousand fans showed up in the Colisée to cheer the great Lafleur the night he scored seven goals in a single game. The following day, they sewed seven velvet pucks onto his sweater and his photograph was splashed across the country's sports pages – a national superstar at the age of twelve!

Wayne Gretzky's team had come here from Brantford two years after Gretzky scored an amazing 378 goals in a single season. Mario Lemieux had first demonstrated his amazing puck-handling here. Brett Hull, Steve Yzerman, Denis Savard, Pat LaFontaine, they had all starred here. And so had a young peewee goaltender named Patrick Roy, who was stopping pucks with a strange new style they were calling "the butterfly."

In the forty-year history of the Quebec City tournament, nearly five hundred of the young players who had come here had gone on to NHL careers – a record unmatched by any other minor-hockey gathering in the entire world.

The time might even come when people would talk about this tournament as the one where young Travis Lindsay served notice that he was NHL-bound. They might say this was where Sarah Cuthbertson, captain of the Olympic gold-medal-winning Canadian women's hockey team, first came to national attention. Or that this was where the scouts first began talking about Wayne Nishikawa, the best defenceman in the entire National Hockey League. Travis or Sarah or Nish – or Jeremy, Jesse, Derek, Dmitri, Jenny, Lars, Simon, Andy, Fahd, Wilson, Liz – the Screech Owls were all here, each one with his or her own special dream for Quebec City.

They already had their own hockey cards. And their own fans. Just like in the NHL.

Sure, the autograph collectors were kids, almost all of them younger than the Owls themselves, but the cards were real.

Upper Deck, the best card manufacturer there was, had contacted every team headed for the Quebec Peewee, and team managers, like Mr. Dillinger, had handed out forms for the players to fill out, telling how tall they were and how much they weighed, what position they played, and how many goals and assists they had last season. There was even a question about which NHL player they modelled their play after, and another about what they enjoyed off the ice. Upper Deck had also asked for action shots of each player, and Data's father had taken photos of all of them in turn: Travis stopping in a spray of snow, Sarah stickhandling the puck, Jeremy making a stretch glove save, Nish taking a slapper from the point.

As each team arrived in Quebec City, someone from Upper Deck had met them with a large box of hockey cards for their team manager to hand out. The players were overwhelmed. The cards were of the best stock, complete with a glossy photograph of each player on the front, and a head shot, showing just his or her face, on the back. Each player's statistics and personal information were printed in fine gold lettering, and the team captains – like Travis – skated over a small hologram of the tournament logo.

Upper Deck also distributed the cards – by the thousands, it seemed – among the young fans of Quebec City. The free cards almost caused a riot outside the Colisée, where some of the teams, including the Owls, were lucky enough to book their first practice. The young fans seemed to know what the cards might one day mean. If they somehow had a card signed by Guy Lafleur the night he scored his seven goals, or by Wayne Gretzky when he played here, what would it be worth today?

Everyone wanted the captains' signatures. Travis knew it was because the captains' cards had the beautiful hologram, and he was trapped by eager autograph-seekers as he tried to plough his way through to the team bus after practice.

"*Travis!*"

"*Moi!*"

"*Une carte seule, s'il vous plaît!*"

He felt like a fool, unable to speak to them properly. He signed, and muttered stupidly: "*Merci . . . Oui . . . Merci . . . Bonjour . . . Oui . . . Merci . . .*" He knew they could tell he understood about as much French as a kindergarten student. Why couldn't he be like Sarah, who was talking as much as she was signing? Why couldn't he be like . . . like *Nish*, standing over there in a huge circle of young fans, signing his name as if he was greeting his adoring public outside Maple Leaf Gardens on a Saturday night.

Travis looked over, puzzled, as he signed another card. Why was his best friend drawing such a big crowd?

By the time he finally made it to the old school bus, and Mr. Dillinger had closed the door on the remaining fans who were still holding up cards and calling out their names, Travis was certain that they were calling out "*Nishikawa!*" far more than "*Lindsay!*" He decided to investigate.

Travis finally found Nish, last seat on the bus, flat on his back and holding his right wrist up as if he'd just been slashed.

"I've got writer's cramp, man," Nish moaned when he saw Travis. "Real bad – I don't know whether I can play or not."

"Very funny," Travis said. "Where's your card?"

Nish suddenly blinked, surprised. "You want my autograph?"

"I just want to see it."

Nish made a big thing out of checking his jacket pockets. There was nothing wrong with his wrist now. He patted and probed and seemed happy to come up empty.

"Sorry, pal – all out. Can't keep up with the public demand, it seems."

Lars turned to help. "I traded him for one," Lars said to Travis, reaching back with a card. "Here you go."

"Thanks," Travis said. He caught Lars's eye. There was a message in the look Lars was giving him. He wanted Travis to see something.

Travis returned to his seat and compared Nish's card with his own. Data's father had taken a wonderful shot of Nish firing the puck from the point, and the head shot on the back was fine, but those were the only similarities. Travis had listed his statistics from last year – 37 goals, 39 assists, 14 minutes in penalties – and had said he tries to play like NHL superstar Paul Kariya. He had added that he played baseball and soccer and lacrosse in the off-season and liked any movie with Jim Carrey in it. Nish's card had his statistics right – 14 goals, 53 assists, 42 minutes in penalties – but there truth came to an abrupt end.

Nish had said he'd already been scouted by the Toronto Maple Leafs and the Mighty Ducks of Anaheim.

He had said Brian Leetch, Norris Trophy winner as the NHL's best defenceman, played a lot like him – not that *he* tried to play like Brian Leetch.

He had said Paul Kariya was his cousin.

Nish had his eyes closed when Travis made his way back to the last seat. Travis slapped Nish's knee, causing the choirboy eyes to flutter open. Nish obviously knew what was coming.

"*You can't do this!*" Travis said, holding out Nish's card.

"Can't do what?" Nish asked, blinking innocently.

"*This!*" Travis almost shouted. "How can you say you've already been scouted?"

"Because I have. And you have, too, or don't you remember Lake Placid?"

Travis shook his head. "That was nothing. They weren't NHL scouts."

"They were scouts, weren't they? And everything ends up in the NHL eventually, doesn't it?"

"But they had nothing to do with the Leafs or the Ducks."

"Well, I like to think they did. Those are the teams I'd want to have scouting me, okay?"

"And what do you mean you're Paul Kariya's cousin?"

Nish shrugged. "Don't get your shorts in a knot. He's part Japanese, isn't he?"

"So?"

"So, what do you think 'Nishikawa' is? *French?*"

"And *that* makes you cousins?"

"Sort of."

"'*Sort of*'? You can't say that."

"I just filled it out as a joke," Nish said. "How was I supposed to know what they were going to use those forms for? No one said anything about hockey cards that I remember."

"You can't lie like that," Travis insisted.

Nish took a deep breath, gathering his thoughts. "I just exaggerated, that's all. No one gets hurt by an exaggeration. Paul Kariya? He doesn't even know, and he won't know."

Travis stared out the window all the way back to the drop-off point where the Screech Owls were to meet the families they would be staying with for the tournament. Soon the bus began its slow, twisting climb up into the narrow streets of the Old City. They passed horse-drawn carriages, statues, old churches, and drew up to a hotel that looked more like a palace standing over the frozen river. Sarah and Jenny were at the windows taking pictures of it all, but Travis hardly even noticed.

What if Nish was right? What if there was no harm in a little exaggeration? Maybe Nish did just mean it as a joke and Travis was letting his job as captain spoil his sense of humour.

Or perhaps he was jealous that Nish's card was attracting so much attention.

2

ravis was secretly glad they wouldn't be staying in this fancy hotel. He had never been inside a lobby quite so lovely as the one in the Château Frontenac, but he also felt that to feel comfortable here he'd need to be a member of royalty, not the captain of a peewee hockey team. It was too fancy, too special. Even the doorman intimidated the Owls, shooing them away from the entrance, where they had stopped to watch the hotel guests come and go in everything from stretch limousines to horse-drawn *calèches*.

The Owls gathered in a large ballroom with two other teams. The players were all given pins and a warm welcome by one of the organizers, who told them they were very lucky this year, because their time in Quebec City would overlap with the Quebec Winter Carnival.

They then met their billets. Travis, Nish, and Lars would all be guests of the Duponts, a family in which the parents spoke no English at all, but the children – Jean-Paul, a bantam player more than a year older than the three Owls, and Nicole, who was their age – were perfectly bilingual.

"You can call me J-P," Jean-Paul said as he shook Travis's hand.

"Thanks," Travis said.

"*Bienvenue à Québec, Travis*," Nicole said to Travis, smiling and reaching out to shake his hand.

"*Merci*," he said, and felt a fool. He could say nothing else. Partly it was his lack of French. Partly it was Nicole. She was slim and pretty, with dark, shiny hair that fell over one cheek and had to be tossed back every so often.

Nicole offered the same greeting to Nish, who blushed, and then to Lars, who bowed elegantly, causing Nicole to giggle.

"*Merci bien*," said Lars in a near-perfect French accent. "*C'est une très belle ville, mademoiselle.*"

When Nicole had moved on, Nish and Travis pressed close to Lars.

"Where did you learn to speak French?" Nish hissed.

"I don't know," Lars answered, looking surprised at his friends' reaction. "School when I was still in Sweden, I guess. It's no big deal."

"How many languages do you speak, anyway?" Travis demanded.

Lars laughed. "I never counted. But let me see: Swedish, German, a little Danish, a little Norwegian, English, of course, a bit of French . . ."

"*Et-gay a-ay ife-lay*," Nish said.

Lars looked at him, dumbfounded. "What's *that*?" he asked.

"Pig Latin," Nish said, triumphantly.

"What's it mean?"

"*Get a life!*" Nish almost shouted.

Travis couldn't stop giggling. He hadn't heard anyone use Pig Latin since grade school, but, if anyone would remember, it would be Nish.

Travis was still laughing when Mr. Dillinger took his arm and pulled him aside.

"Travis," Mr. Dillinger said in a quiet voice. "The organizers are asking some of the team captains to keep a short daily diary for one of the newspapers. Muck and I thought you might do a good job. What do you say?"

Travis didn't know what to say. A diary?

"In French?" Travis asked, feeling relief all of a sudden that his French was so weak.

"No," Mr. Dillinger said. "It's an English paper from Montreal. Look, the reporter who's putting the whole thing together is here. You meet with him, you can decide for yourself. Whatdya say?"

"Yeah," Travis said. "Sure."

But he didn't feel sure. He knew it was the responsible Screech Owls captain answering Mr. Dillinger, not Travis Lindsay, who had never even written a letter in his entire life.

"I'm Bart Lundrigan, Travis. *Great* to meet you."

Much to his surprise, Travis felt instantly at ease with the reporter. Bart Lundrigan was young, and he had a shock of dark curly hair that danced down into his eyes. He was wearing jeans and looked more like a movie star than a reporter.

"I'm with the *Montreal Inquirer*, Travis. We're not a very big paper, but we're owned by one of the big chains, which means the stories I write could, conceivably, appear right across Canada.

"The idea is this: a half-dozen of the team captains – players like yourself – are going to record their impressions each day in one of these pocket diaries" – the reporter held up a small red booklet – "and that is going to give fans a real insight into what it's like to play in this tournament.

"I want to know about the games, but I also want you to talk about coming here to Quebec to play. You know, what it's like to play where Lafleur and Gretzky once played. What's it mean to you? What do you think about the city? The people? Your billets? What kinds of things you do at the Carnival? You get the idea."

"Yeah, kind of."

"Good. Are you game, then?"

Travis was still wary. "How much do I have to write?"

The reporter laughed. "Not much. A page a day, if you can. I'll drop around every now and then and read through whatever you've done. Deal?"

Travis couldn't resist the smile, couldn't avoid the hand reaching out to shake his.

"Deal," he said.

"Super," Bart Lundrigan said. "I was sure hoping I'd get you; the Owls are one of the favourites in the C division, did you know that?"

"No, I didn't."

"Well, that's what they're saying, anyway. Lot of excitement about this Wayne Nishikawa kid – Paul Kariya's cousin, eh?"

Travis swallowed hard. He didn't know what to say. Was the reporter suspicious about Nish, or was he only making small talk?

"Nish is a good defenceman," Travis said, avoiding the actual question.

The reporter nodded. He seemed satisfied.

They talked a while longer. The reporter explained how he'd split up the diaries so everyone was represented: the West, Quebec, the Maritimes, an American team.

They talked hockey as well. Bart Lundrigan's dream was to cover an NHL team, preferably the Montreal Canadiens. He was, he said, not much different from Travis himself: both of them dreaming of the NHL, one to play and one to report. They had lots in common, even if the reporter was a good ten years older than Travis.

"I think this is going to be a great, great experience for you," Lundrigan said.

"I do, too," said Travis.

Travis was surprised he said this. But it was true. Fifteen minutes earlier, he had been dreading the idea of keeping a diary for everyone to read. Now he was looking forward to it.

In a small way, he was going to be a reporter, too.

3

T. he Duponts lived in a large bungalow well out of the Old City, on a street running down toward the ice-covered St. Lawrence River. The snowbanks were higher in this part of the city, much higher, and most of the houses had temporary canvas-and-aluminum "garages" to keep the snow off the cars, but apart from this nothing seemed out of the ordinary to the three boys in the back seat of the Duponts' minivan. Travis had no idea what he had expected of his billets, but he was pleasantly surprised to walk into a home where he could smell cinnamon buns in the oven and "The Simpsons" had just come on the television.

The difference was that Bart Simpson was speaking French – "I thought Bart was supposed to be a dummy!" Nish joked – but other than that, they could just as easily have been in a home down the street in their own town. The Duponts had a yappy black mutt they called Puck, frozen burritos for the microwave, and fights over the TV remote control.

No one, however, had much interest in watching TV, for

beyond the downstairs patio doors lay the finest backyard skating rink Travis had ever seen. There were spotlights off both ends of the house and, under the eaves, stereo speakers wired back into the house. The snowbanks were higher even than the boards at the Colisée, but it was the ice that most impressed the boys, so smooth it seemed to have been spread with a knife, not flooded each night with a green garden hose.

"*Je suis un artiste de la glace – le plus grand de tout le Québec,*" Monsieur Dupont told them as he showed off his rink. He was grinning from ear to ear, his chest puffing out the bulky parka he wore as they all stepped outside.

Travis turned to Nicole, who was rolling her eyes at her father's bragging.

"He says he's Quebec's greatest ice-making artist," said Nicole. "It's not even the best rink in the neighbourhood, for heaven's sake."

The three boys all laughed. Monsieur Dupont stood waiting, wondering what his daughter had said to make their visitors laugh. "*Quoi?*" he asked her, and Nicole quickly said something reassuring to her father. Travis thought they had a nice relationship, father and daughter. He assumed Nicole had just told her father a slight fib, but where was the harm in that? He might have been upset if she had repeated exactly what she had said about his rink.

There was a big difference, Travis thought, between holding back something that might be taken the wrong way and throwing something out that would for certain be taken the wrong way, like Nish and his "cousin," Paul Kariya.

"We'll skate after we eat," suggested Nicole.

Travis felt a slight tremor go up his back. He had hoped for a chance to show how well he skated. He skated much better than he talked.

They ate a wonderful meal, with fresh cinnamon buns for dessert. J-P and Nicole had a brief squabble about what music to skate to, and then they went down into the basement to get ready.

Travis was first out the patio doors, and stopped dead in his tracks when he saw what was awaiting him. The rink, it seemed, had become a painting, a frozen island of colour surrounded by the pitch black of night. The ice sparkled and shone; there was even a red line painted across the middle of the rink for centre ice!

He stepped out, glided on his left foot and pumped twice with his right, the little jump he always did when stepping onto fresh ice. He felt instantly at home. What a strange, wonderful country Canada was, he thought. People who can't even talk to each other have a game that does it for them. From coast to coast they skate and play hockey, from the time they learn to walk until they're older than Travis's own father.

Travis loved real ice. He loved the way his skates dug a little bit deeper than they ever did on artificial ice. He loved how, on a sharp turn, ice chips sometimes flew; on an indoor rink there would only be a slight spray of snow. He liked the way air felt outdoors: fresh and sharp on his face, more *alive* than anywhere else.

Lars and Nish were also out now – Nish trying his fancy backwards skating around the nets at both ends, Lars just looping around slowly, taking it all in. He had a huge smile on his face.

J-P was on the ice, and instantly there was a new sound in

the air: the sizzle of weight. J-P was just big enough to have a big-league sound to his cornering, and when he came out of the corners, chips and spray flew behind him. The perfectly smooth surface, Monsieur Dupont's magnificent creation, was being destroyed, but Travis knew it was with his blessing.

There was another sound on the ice. Quick, sharp – the sound of Dmitri skating, Travis thought, although Dmitri wasn't with them. He turned fast on his skates to move backwards so he could see. It was Nicole! She had on hockey skates, and she was whipping around so fast that Travis stumbled slightly as he shifted again to skate forward as she flew past. He hoped she hadn't seen him nearly trip.

They played a quick game of shinny: Anglos versus Francos. The two Duponts, with J-P's size and Nicole's speed, more than held their own against the three Owls – but then, Travis thought, this was their rink, they knew it as well as the inside of their house.

Travis had the puck behind his net. He looked up and knew at once why he loved backyard shinny. No one cares. No one yells. No one corrects. Everyone was out of position. Everyone was simply *playing*.

He began moving up ice just as J-P came in on him, the older boy skating fast to panic Travis. Travis saw Nish off to his right, waiting. He had only one play, *the back pass*. It was Travis's favourite move in street hockey, and even though he'd often tried it in practice, he'd never dared it in a real game. It was too risky, too much a hot-dog play. Muck hated it, and blew the whistle every time Travis tried it in practice.

But there were no whistles here. Travis moved to his left, then placed the puck on his backhand and whipped it, across ice, to Nish, who picked it up before J-P, whooping with surprise, was able to turn towards him. Nish instantly sent the puck back to Travis, who was free. He dug in deep, aware that J-P was chasing him. He could hear the growl of J-P's skates, gaining ice on him.

Nish was hammering the ice with his stick for a pass. Travis skated up to centre, faked the pass and laughed as Nicole fell for it, sliding on her knees between him and Nish, who was still tapping hard even though Travis was now home free. Travis ignored him, skated in on the empty net, and ripped a snapshot in off the crossbar.

"*C'est bon!*" J-P shouted as he caught up to Travis. "Nice shot, Travis."

Far behind, Nicole slapped her stick on the ice in acknowledgement. It had been a nice shot, and it had gone in exactly as Travis had hoped.

He felt something big brush past him. A shoulder knocked him slightly. It was Nish.

"Puck hog!" Nish hissed as he skated by. It was a whisper, but one that shouted with anger.

Travis smiled to himself. Of course: *Nish* had wanted to be the hero. He had wanted to roof the shot that won the admiration of the Duponts.

"*Let's whip!*" Nicole shouted.

Nicole and J-P were stabbing their sticks into the snow nearest the patio doors. Then they cleared the nets off the ice, stacking them together at the far end. Travis and Nish and Lars stabbed their sticks into the snow too.

Nicole skated up to Travis and took his hand in her mitten. She got Lars to hold on to Travis's other hand, and J-P then took Lars's free hand and reached for Nish.

Around and around they skated, with Nicole leading the way. At every turn she built up speed until, finally, she all but stopped at centre ice and, holding on tightly to Travis, spun the line around her in an ever-faster circle, Nish at the far end gliding with the force of the spin.

"*Now!*" Nicole shouted.

J-P let go on his sister's signal and Nish took off, flying.

"AAAAAAAAAAYYYYYYYYYYYYYYEEEEEEEE!"

The force of the "whip" sent him barrelling down the ice towards the largest snowbank, where he hit head first – and stuck!

"HELLLLLLLPPPPPPPPPP!" came the muffled shout.

Laughing wildly, the other four raced to pull Nish free. His face was covered in snow, and Travis could tell he was on the verge of blowing up, but Nicole took off her mittens and, very gently, brushed the snow out of his eyes.

The snow on Nish's face was melting fast, and Travis knew why; his friend's cheeks were burning red. Not from anger. Not from embarrassment. From Nicole's touch.

Suddenly Travis understood why he had been called a puck hog. He knew Nish too well not to see he was smitten with Nicole.

But then it hit Travis that so, too, was he.

"*Travis's turn!*" Nish announced.

Travis was delighted to be next. They whipped him the same way, burying him to his shoulders, and Nicole also helped him with the snow, much to his delight.

Travis couldn't stop smiling.

I have something to write about, he thought.

4

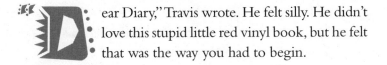

ear Diary," Travis wrote. He felt silly. He didn't love this stupid little red vinyl book, but he felt that was the way you had to begin.

Dear Diary,

The Screech Owls are here in Quebec City for the most exciting tournament of our lives! We have already held one practice at the Colisée, which is the same rink where Wayne Gretzky and Mario Lemieux played when they were peewees just like us!

We were told the story of how Guy Lafleur scored seven goals and they sewed seven velvet pucks on to his sweater for the next game. I'd love that to happen to me!

Two neat things have already happened and we haven't even played a game yet. The first was the hockey cards made for us by

Upper Deck. They are just like the real NHL cards. I must have signed fifty of them today. The next was getting to stay with the Dupont family and skate on their outdoor rink, which is the best one any of us have ever seen. We played shinny and then played "whip," which was a lot of fun.

Our billets, Mr. and Mrs. Dupont, don't speak English, but it doesn't seem to matter. Their children, Jean-Paul and Nicole, speak perfect English and translate everything for us.

Nicole played a little trick on her dad when she made a good joke in English about his rink and he didn't understand her. She then told him something completely different in French so his feelings wouldn't be hurt.

Lars Johanssen is on my team and he's billeted with Wayne Nishikawa and me at the Duponts. Lars is from Sweden but speaks pretty good French, which sure surprised Nish and me. (We call Wayne "Nish.")

Nish is more like me. He doesn't speak French at all. He made a great joke on Lars by telling him to "Get a life!" in Pig Latin, which Lars had never heard of. I think he thinks Nish is pretty smart and speaks a real foreign language like Pig Latin!

I did really poorly in French this year and don't think I'll be taking it again. I won't speak French to anyone – I guess because I'm too embarrassed – and I find it hard to understand when they speak to me. They talk way too fast. It sure is a lot easier when they speak English, like J-P and Nicole do for us.

I'm really excited about the first game against Halifax. We're supposed to be the favourites (or so they say), but Muck, our coach, says that Halifax is the "sleeper" team in the tournament. That

*means that they're going to do much better than anyone expects.
Anyone but Muck, that is, I guess.*

Your friend,
Travis Lindsay

The Halifax Hurricanes were indeed much better than most
people expected. One shift into the game, and it was Halifax 1,
Screech Owls 0. The "sleepers" had jumped on a poor pass
between Data and Nish when a diving Hurricane punched the
puck ahead with his stick and the big Halifax centre picked it
up and beat Jeremy in goal with a delayed backhand.

"*Wake up out there!*" Muck said when they skated back to the
bench.

Muck was talking about more than the bad pass. The Owls
had skated out on the ice to be greeted by more than six thousand fans. The noise had been incredible. Youngsters were hanging over the boards and waiting in the corridors for autographs.
Nish – now known widely as "Paul Kariya's cousin" – was by
far the most popular player, and Muck had to stop him from
signing everyone's card during the warm-up.

The Halifax team had one superb line, and Sarah's line, with
Travis on left and Dmitri on right, was assigned to check them.
Muck kept changing Sarah, Dmitri, and Travis on the fly to
keep his matchups the way he wanted, and it meant that Sarah's
line couldn't concentrate on offence as much as they might have

liked. Fortunately, little Simon Milliken got the Owls back in the game with a nifty backhander.

Sarah played brilliantly. She stayed with the big centre without letting up, and every time he got a pass she was there to intercept it or lift his stick just enough for him to miss the puck.

"You're getting under his skin," Muck whispered to Sarah as she came off for a rest. "Next shift, I want to see him go off."

Travis could see Sarah smile as Muck said this. He knew she got as big a kick out of checking players as she did out of scoring goals. Most players with Sarah's ability to skate and shoot thought of nothing else but scoring and being a hero, but Sarah was different.

The Halifax coach tried to sneak his big centre back out by changing the line immediately after the face-off. Muck slapped Sarah's shoulder pads and called for Jesse, who was closest to the bench, to get off the ice while Sarah leapt the boards and gave chase.

The Halifax centre picked up the puck at his own blueline. He hit his right winger and then burst up through centre, rapping his stick on the ice for the return feed, which came almost instantly. Sarah, however, was already there, deftly lifting the centre's stick as he looked for the pass, and using her skate to tip the sliding puck back behind him so she would have it free.

She was already past him, the puck hers. She took one quick stride and went hurtling, face first, towards the Halifax blueline, the referee's whistle screaming as she fell.

The big centre didn't even pretend to be innocent. He slammed his stick on the ice and skated angrily to the penalty box.

"Stay out there," Muck said when Sarah, still smiling, tried to come off. "Travis, Dmitri, Nish, Data."

The first power-play line hurried out, and though Sarah was still gasping for air, she took, and won, the face-off. She fired the puck back to Nish, who skated behind the Owls' net and waited. Travis skated past and pretended to pick up the puck, taking one of the forecheckers with him and leaving the puck for Dmitri, who was coming in from the other side.

Dmitri hit Sarah at the blueline, and Sarah tapped a little return pass between the defenceman's feet, leaving the puck alone for a moment until Dmitri, with his exceptional speed, caught up to it and started in, two-on-one, with Travis.

Dmitri would usually shoot in this situation – "You can never go wrong with a shot," Muck always said – but this time he came in and turned in a spinnerama, dishing off the puck to Travis as the defenceman played the body.

Travis was home free. A quick deke, a pause, and he snapped the puck high, his heart singing as it rang in off the crossbar.

Owls 2, Hurricanes 1.

After the Owls took the lead, the game was all Sarah's. She so frustrated the Halifax team, particularly their top player, they took penalty after penalty. The game ended 5–1 on a second goal by Travis, who merely tapped in a puck that Sarah left for him at the side of the crease as she drew the poor Halifax goaltender completely out of the net.

"Room service," she joked as they skated off.

"Thanks," said Travis.

"That one was too easy," Muck told them as they sagged in the dressing room. "Next one's going to be twice as hard for you, so don't get any fancy notions into your head."

He stood at the centre of the room, scowling at them, his eyes slowly moving over each and every player. Nish, as usual, had his head down, almost between his legs.

"Good game," Muck added, then walked out.

Outside, J-P and Nicole were waiting. Nicole hugged Travis, who'd been named Best Player of the Game for the Owls, even though he knew, and everyone else seemed to know, that Sarah Cuthbertson had been the best player by far.

"*Bon match, Travis!*" Nicole shouted. "*Très bon!*"

"*Merci*" was all Travis could say. All he could ever say.

"I scored, too," said Nish. He was practically between them.

"I know, I know," she said. "Nice goal, too."

Nish smiled, happy to be noticed.

"Who's number 9?" J-P asked.

"Sarah Cuthbertson," Travis answered. "She's good, eh?"

"She's *fantastique!*" J-P said. "*Incroyable!*"

"*Hey! Travis!*" a voice called from down the corridor.

Travis turned. The reporter, Bart Lundrigan was coming at him, his face one huge smile.

"Great, *great* game, Trav!" the reporter said.

"Thanks," said Travis.

"You bring the diary?" the reporter asked.

"Yeah, I did."

"Great! *Super!* Can I get it off you now?"

"Yeah . . . sure," Travis said. "It's in my bag."

"Great," the reporter said. "*Super!*"

5

he Screech Owls had a practice scheduled for noon the following day at a small rink in Levis, the town directly across the St. Lawrence River from Quebec. Before they headed over on the old school bus, however, Mr. Dillinger and Muck took the Owls on a walking tour of the Old City.

They parked near the Quebec legislature, an imposing grey building that was almost dwarfed by, of all things, the largest snow fort any Owl had ever seen. The "fort" was actually the Ice Palace, where Bonhomme, the mascot of the Winter Carnival, lives during the festivities. Some of the Owls – including Nish, of course – got their pictures taken with the jolly mascot, who was kind of a cross between a snowman and a fur-trading *voyageur*, with his white costume topped by a long red tuque and with a red-and-blue sash around his middle. Then they set off in a large group. They walked through a stone gateway and down Rue Petit Champlain, which Muck claimed was the oldest street in all of North America. They toured a church that was more than 350 years old and then twisted down so many narrow streets that eventually the Owls gave up trying to keep track of where they were.

Muck, oddly enough, always seemed to know. He would stand a moment, consider his options, then point in a certain direction, and always they would come out onto a main street where the *calèches* were clomping and jangling by, steam rising from the backs of the horses. There were crowds watching jugglers and clowns and men on enormous stilts. And everywhere there were young hockey players with team jackets or caps or tuques on – players from Canada and the United States and Sweden and Finland.

Muck led them behind the towering Château Frontenac and onto Dufferin Terrace, a massive boardwalk that had been shovelled off and sanded for walking. The boardwalk overlooked the St. Lawrence River, which was choked in a treacherous jumble of broken ice floes.

Muck pointed out a place in the distance where the Iroquois people had set up fishing camps hundreds, thousands, of years ago, long before anyone else came along to "discover" this land and claim it for any king or queen that lived in France or England.

"Right on!" shouted Jesse Highboy.

Muck told them where Samuel de Champlain had set up his first fur-trading post in 1603, and how the French explorers had all but starved to death the first couple of winters here. If it hadn't been for the natives, Muck said, they would never have made it.

With his big arms sweeping up and down the river, Muck showed them how the English ships had come down under cover of dark back in 1759. He walked them to the steep cliffs where the English had somehow climbed up from the river for a twenty-minute battle with the French that had decided Canada's future for the next 250 years, and was, according to Muck, still being fought by the politicians.

He told them that the old part of the city down below the Château had been virtually turned to dust by the English bombardment.

"Forty thousand cannon balls," said Muck. "Forty thousand cannon balls and ten thousand fire bombs – you think you could stop all that, Jeremy?" he said, turning to the young goalie.

Jeremy giggled. "No."

Muck took them out onto the Plains of Abraham, where Quebecers in rainbow-coloured outfits were cross-country skiing, and he showed them where the British invader, General James Wolfe, was shot and lay down to die in the grass as the battle raged around him, and then where the French general, Marquis de Montcalm, was hit by a musket bullet and lay mortally wounded.

"Did he die?" Fahd asked, breathlessly.

"That's what 'mortally wounded' means, son – but he didn't die here."

The Owls looked around, expecting a marker. "Where, then?" Andy asked.

Muck considered a moment. "The French carried their leader back into the Old City," the coach told them, "but the battle for Quebec was already lost. They took him to the Ursuline chapel, thinking he'd be safe in the care of the nuns, but he died there a couple of days later, and they buried him in the crypt. The British had already taken possession of the city."

"There's a *crypt* around here?" Data, the horror-movie buff, asked.

Muck smiled. "There are lots of crypts around here. That's where they used to bury people."

Data went silent, obviously disappointed.

"They kept his skull, though," Muck added, almost as an afterthought.

"*What?*" several Owls shouted at once.

Muck seemed shocked at such interest. "His skull," he repeated. "They dug Montcalm up about a hundred years later, and the Ursuline Sisters took his skull away. It's on display up in the Old City."

"You've *seen* it?" Data practically screamed.

"Sure," Muck said.

"*Can we?*" Andy pressed.

"You want to see an old skull?" Muck asked, pretending to be surprised.

"*Sure!*" the Owls shouted at once.

"Well, good," Muck said. "I didn't know this team had so many history buffs."

Travis giggled silently to himself. "History" had nothing to do with it. They just wanted to see a human skull, and if it had a hole in it where a bullet had gone through, so much the better!

"I'll make a deal with you," Muck said to Data.

"*Anything!*" Data screeched.

"You get a point the next match, we'll all go pay the Marquis a visit."

"*Alll righhhttt!*" the Owls shouted.

They headed back along a short cut that returned them to the Ice Palace and the parking area where Mr. Dillinger had left the bus.

Travis found himself dropping back.

"Muck?" Travis asked tentatively.

The big coach turned his eyes on his young captain.

"Yes?"

"Where'd you pick up all the history? That was neat."

Muck smiled. "There's more to life than hockey, Mr. Lindsay. Surely you know that by now."

"Yeah, but . . . well, how come you know all that stuff?"

"That 'stuff' is who we are. I'm a Canadian. I want to know what makes us the way we are."

"Oh," said Travis. "I see."

But he really didn't see at all.

6

now was falling when they came out of practice at the Levis ice rink. Travis looked across the river, but he could no longer make out the towering Château. He turned his face upward, and the sky seemed neither to begin nor end, just to fade away into grey as millions of fat, fluffy snowflakes came drifting straight down upon him. Nish was also looking up, his mouth open as the large flakes landed, and melted instantly, on his cheeks and nose and outstretched tongue.

"*They're big enough to eat!*" he shouted.

Soon all the Owls were dancing around in the muffled silence of a heavy snowfall, their open mouths turned towards the sky. The snow gathering on the players' shoulders and tuques was fast changing the entire team from a variety of bright colours to the soft white of fresh snow. The Owls were vanishing before each other's eyes.

Mr. Dillinger was sitting in the driver's seat as the Owls boarded, but for once there were no high-fives or friendly shoulder punches. Mr. Dillinger had a newspaper spread over the steering wheel, and he was staring at it as if it were some broken piece of equipment he couldn't for the life of him figure out how to fix.

When Mr. Dillinger saw Muck approaching the bus, he folded up the paper and jumped down the steps, intercepting the coach before he could board. The two men hurried back towards the rink doors, where they huddled together under an overhang in the roof as Mr. Dillinger showed Muck something on the front page. Mr. Dillinger made his way back onto the bus, scanning the seats for someone in particular.

He caught Travis's eyes.

"Travis," Mr. Dillinger said in a very serious voice. "Could you come out here a moment?"

Travis got up, painfully aware that the other Owls were staring at him. There must be a problem, but what was so important that Travis had to be dragged off the bus for a conference with Muck and Mr. Dillinger?

Muck had finished reading whatever it was that Mr. Dillinger had showed him. His eyes looked partly sad, partly angry.

"You'd better have a look at this," Muck said, tapping a front-page headline.

Travis read the headline quickly, his heart beginning to pound: "PIG LATIN AS GOOD AS FRENCH, YOUNG ANGLO HOCKEY PLAYER SAYS."

Travis didn't understand. He read the byline: "By Bart Lundrigan, Staff Writer." He looked at the top of the page: *The Montreal Inquirer.*

"It's apparently run all over the country," Mr. Dillinger said. "I called home. It's in the Toronto papers. Vancouver. Calgary. They all picked it up."

Travis was still reading:

QUEBEC CITY − As far as some young anglophone hockey players at the Quebec International Peewee Tournament are concerned, the French language is no better than school-yard "Pig Latin."

This is only one of many revelations to come from a series of young players' diary excerpts obtained by *The Inquirer.*

The "Two Solitudes" that first did bloody battle here back in 1759 are still going at it, it appears, nearly two and a half centuries after French and English forces met on the Plains of Abraham.

Take, for example, a diary excerpt from Travis Lindsay, a tousle-haired, sweet-smiling 12-year-old, who brags, "I won't speak French to anyone."

Lindsay, who admits to having studied French in school, shows nothing but disdain for Canada's other official language.

"They talk way too fast," he complains in his diary. "It's sure a lot easier when they speak English."

Young Lindsay compares this Canadian "foreign language" to the game of "Pig Latin" played in schoolyards, where children make up a silly language by slightly changing each English word.

Apparently members of Lindsay's team, the Screech

Owls, have been making fun of French by choosing to speak Pig Latin instead.

Lindsay's billets, André and Giselle Dupont – who are putting Lindsay and two teammates up for free – speak only French. But talking with them directly is not worth the effort, according to the young peewee player, because the Dupont children "speak perfect English and translate everything for us."

Lindsay tells approvingly of how Nicole Dupont pours scorn on her unsuspecting father in English.

Another young peewee player, 13-year-old Brent Sutton, captain of the Camrose Wildcats, a team from Alberta, writes in his diary that he doesn't like the food and that, "There should be a law that all the signs are in English as well.". . .

Travis had read enough. He folded the paper and handed it back to Muck.

"Those your words?" Muck asked.

Travis didn't know what to say, he was in a state of shock. The words were kind of what he had written down, but he had never meant them to say what the paper was saying.

"I–I didn't say it that way."

Muck stared at his young captain, measuring him up.

"You got that diary with you?" Muck asked.

"Right here," said Travis, pulling it out of his pocket.

Muck read through Travis's first entry. He seemed satisfied with what he read. He didn't even bother to read the paragraph Travis had written last night before he went to bed.

"He's twisted everything," Muck said.

"That dirty son of a –!" said Mr. Dillinger through clenched teeth. "I'm sorry, Travis – I thought it would be pretty harmless. This is all my fault –"

Muck cut off Mr. Dillinger, who seemed near tears. "You want to keep on doing this?" he asked Travis.

"Not if it turns out like that," Travis said.

"Fine," Muck said. He stuffed the diary hard inside his jacket. "I'll be the one keeping the diary now, okay?"

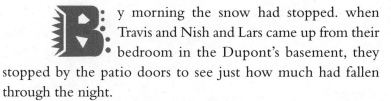

7

By morning the snow had stopped. when Travis and Nish and Lars came up from their bedroom in the Dupont's basement, they stopped by the patio doors to see just how much had fallen through the night.

Travis hadn't slept well. He kept going over the contents of that awful newspaper article, comparing it to his recollection of what he had written in the diary. None of it seemed to fit quite together. There were links, but all the strings connecting them had ugly knots in them.

All Nish and Lars could talk about was the snow. The world was whiter than any of them had ever seen, the snow piled so high on every surface, large and small – branches, fences, rooftops, telephone wires – that it seemed to have been squeezed on, like thick layers of toothpaste. Every now and then a pile on a branch would topple over, the snow spraying into powder as it fell, the sun dancing off the flakes and causing the Owls to wince as they stared out.

Monsieur Dupont was already up and making himself busy outside. At least Travis presumed it was Monsieur Dupont: a tall man covered head to foot, his face in a black ski mask that had two small slits for the eyes.

"*It's a bank robbery!*" Nish shouted.

"It's Mister Dupont," said Lars. "He's just clearing off the rink."

Sure enough, Monsieur Dupont was standing in front of a large red snowblower, brushed clean of snow. He yanked its starter cord once, twice, and instantly the silence of the morning was lost. The snowblower roared and coughed into action, and Monsieur Dupont adjusted the chute and put it in gear. The chains and tires caught and the machine jumped into action, the clear winter air between the boys and Monsieur Dupont filling once again with heavy snow. Only this time it was going up, not falling down.

The radio was on in the kitchen. It was in French, but the boys caught enough of the talk – ". . . *Travis Lindsay . . . the Screech Owls . . . Anglais . . .*" – to know that the commentators were discussing the newspaper article Bart Lundrigan had written.

"You're in big trouble, my friend," Nish whispered as he poured himself a second bowl of Honey Nut Cheerios.

Travis snapped a quick look back at Nish, one that told him to sit on it and keep quiet. Travis didn't want to discuss the matter. J-P and Nicole were also in the kitchen now, and neither of them had said a word about the newspaper article.

The telephone rang. Travis thought he was going to hit the ceiling he jumped so high.

Madame Dupont answered. She spoke a few words of French and then turned to the table, looking first at Travis — hurt written all over her face — and then holding the receiver out towards Nicole.

"*Oui*," she answered. "*Oui* . . . Nicole Dupont . . . *oui, c'est vrai* . . . *non* . . . Yes, I speak English."

There was a long pause while Nicole listened. She turned to the table, twisting the telephone cord in her fingers and rolling her eyes to indicate boredom.

"No. He's already left for the rink," she said. "Sorry . . . Yes, I will . . . Fine . . . Yes . . . Yes, goodbye."

Nicole hung up the receiver and came back to the table. J-P and the three Owls were all staring at her, waiting.

"It was the local CBC," she said. "They wanted to talk to Travis about the article. I said you weren't here, okay?"

Travis felt immense relief. "Yeah," he said. "Thanks."

She had lied for him. No, fibbed for him. A white lie. A harmless lie. Instead of anyone getting hurt, Travis told himself, someone got saved: himself.

He knew that "Thanks" was not enough. The Duponts deserved more.

Travis cleared his throat. He felt awkward, embarrassed. "That article," he began.

"Don't even bother," Nicole said. "We know you didn't say those things."

Travis closed his eyes. Thank heavens; they believed him without him having to prove it.

"But I did *kind of* say those things," he said. It was spilling out of him. "Nish was kidding Lars in Pig Latin, but no one ever said it was the same thing as French. Nish just can't speak French either. And I said it was easier to speak English, because I'm so bad at French and so embarrassed that I don't speak it better."

"You shouldn't have written that thing about my father," Nicole said. Travis looked down, ashamed. But then she smiled; her point had been made and, as far as she was concerned, the matter was closed.

But Travis was near tears. "I know," he said. "I didn't know what that reporter was going to do with what I'd written. He took what I said and twisted it."

J-P looked up, grinning. "A better story for him, I guess."

"But it's not fair," said Nish.

Nicole smiled. "You get used to this stuff in Quebec," she said. "We just ignore it."

The side door opened with a waft of cold air that died the moment the door was slammed shut again. Monsieur Dupont was in the hallway. They could hear him stomping his boots and brushing the snow off his shoulders. They could hear him unzipping the heavy snowmobile suit he wore while working the snowblower. Travis noticed that the two Dupont children had stopped eating. They were waiting to see if their father already knew what had happened.

Monsieur Dupont came into the kitchen. His hair stood out all over at odd angles, uncombed since he had yanked off his ski mask. Travis could sense Nish was on the verge of a giggle, and knocked his knee against his leg to shut him up. There was a new tension in the air.

Monsieur Dupont came into the kitchen, stopped, and

stared once, hard, at Travis. Travis swallowed uncomfortably. No one said a word.

Monsieur Dupont seemed sad rather than upset. He moved his mouth as if to speak, but then decided not to say anything. He moved instead to the sink, took a cup out of the cupboard above it, then turned to fill it from the coffeepot.

Nicole leaned over her cereal towards Travis, glancing meaningfully at her father and then back to Travis.

"I'll explain to him," she said. "Don't worry."

"Thanks," Travis smiled. But he was deeply worried all the same.

The team was to meet, again, at the parking area near the Ice Palace. From there, the team would travel, by bus, to the Colisée. Madame Dupont could drop the Owls and their equipment off on her way to her job at the provincial tourism office, just down the street from the Château. She seemed fine, smiling and laughing. But Travis noticed that when she got into the minivan the radio was on, and that she'd quickly turned it off before starting out.

There was a commotion around the school bus when they arrived at the parking lot. Nish was first to spot the activity out the minivan window.

"*Television cameras!*" he called, excitedly.

Travis felt a sinking feeling inside. No one would normally be interested in a peewee hockey team heading out for a tournament game.

"*There's more over here!*" said Lars from the front seat.

The Owls got out, and someone shouted, "*It's him!*"

Pandemonium struck as the boys tried to get their gear clear of Madame Dupont's vehicle. Three or four television crews and several people with tape recorders and microphones with little station logos on them descended on Travis, Nish, and Lars as they sorted out their bags and sticks.

"*Which one of you is Travis Lindsay?*" shouted a hatless man with a hard helmet of sprayed hair.

"*Not me!*" said Nish, hustling to get out of the way with his equipment.

Travis was surrounded. He knew he looked frightened; he *was* frightened. The cameras were rolling. The reporters were all shouting at him.

"*What do you think of French, Travis?*"

"*Parlez-vous français?*"

"*Can you explain what 'Pig Latin' is, please?*"

"*Are you having any trouble with the signs?*"

"*Do you think Quebec has the right to separate from Canada?*"

"*How do you get along with your billets, Mr. Lindsay?*"

"*How do you feel about playing a Quebec team today?*"

The questions were flying at him, too many, too fast. Travis cringed against the back of the Duponts' minivan. Other reporters were at the driver's side of the van, trying to get a comment from Madame Dupont, who was hurriedly rolling up her window. She shook her head and put the vehicle in gear, forcing it through the throng. Travis watched as it slipped away from him until he was all alone in the centre of the parking lot, the camera operators and reporters circling him like wolves moving in for the kill.

"*Just a minute!*" a loud voice commanded. "*Un moment, s'il vous plaît!*"

It was Muck's voice. Muck speaking French – something Travis had never even imagined.

The circle broke as Muck barged his way through and took Travis by the elbow. Travis was almost overcome with relief. He felt like he had just been shaken awake from the worst nightmare of his life. He knew, even before it was over, that it was going to be all right. Because it was Muck.

"*Are you the coach?*"

"*Vous parlez français?*"

"*What do you have to say about your captain's anti-French remarks, sir?*"

Muck was already pulling Travis away from the throng. He paused, looked back, and caught the eye of the woman who had called out the last question.

"Just this . . . ," Muck said. The cameras and microphones instantly pressed closer. "There is no story here for you. Sorry to disappoint you – but there's no story."

"*How do you explain the diary entries then?*"

"You'd better ask Mr. Lundrigan about that," Muck said. "He's the one who made up the stories, is he not?"

The questions now came even faster.

"*Are you accusing the reporter of making up quotes?*"

"*Travis – are you denying you said those things?*"

"*Why are you running from us?*"

Muck had no more to say. He still had a firm hold on Travis's elbow and was half pulling, half leading him toward the bus. Travis wasn't sure his feet were even touching the ground, but he tried to hurry anyway. He could feel Muck's huge strength in his grip. His elbow hurt, but he wasn't about to say anything.

The reporters and cameras were following right behind, videotaping it all. But Muck never looked back. With Travis in tow, he rounded the bus and came to an abrupt stop on the far side by the door.

Mr. Dillinger was frantically at work with a rag and cleanser. He was wiping as hard as he could, but to little effect. Someone had spray-painted the side of the Screech Owls' bus. In large, crudely formed red letters was the message: "ANGLAIS PIGS GO HOME!"

Travis looked up at Muck, who had forgotten to let go of his elbow. The coach had shut his eyes, as if wishing everything would somehow go away. When he opened them again, he directed a helpless look at Mr. Dillinger, who was still wiping hard. But Mr. Dillinger shot back an equally helpless look: the paint wasn't coming off.

The reporters had seen it now. In near panic, they scrambled over each other to get their shots – some pushing and pulling, some yelling and shoving as they fought for position.

Travis felt, rather than heard, the breath go out of Muck.

"They got a story now," the coach said. "They've got their story now."

There were more cameras waiting at the Colisée. The bus pulled up and the rush was on, camera operators rushing and pushing and sliding and slipping and pulling and shouting as they hurried toward the bus, desperate to angle the shot so they would get both the team as it left the bus and the painted message on the vehicle's side.

Muck stood up in his seat at the front of the bus and turned to face his team.

"You walk out like you're here to play a hockey game, nothing else – understand!"

Each Owl murmured that he or she understood. No one – not even Nish – was making light of this.

"Don't talk to anyone. Don't even look at anyone. Collect your equipment, and go directly to the dressing room."

The players started moving. Travis felt as if he was going to throw up. There was a terrible pain in the pit of his stomach. He felt like crying.

"I'll walk with you."

Travis looked up. It was Sarah.

"Thanks," he said.

With Sarah by his side, Travis collected his equipment and sticks and began heading towards the door.

"*Voilà!*" a man outside called, pointing.

Sarah descended the steps first and turned to wait for Travis. He tried to concentrate on her smile instead of the cameras, and jumped down quickly to stand beside her. She fell in beside him, their shoulders touching as they pushed through the gathering horde.

"*Excusez*," Sarah said to one camera operator, smiling.

"*Pardon*," Sarah said to another as she began to push through.

"*Est-ce que vous pouvez reculer un peu, s'il vous plaît?*" Sarah said, very politely. "*Bonjour, madame, c'est une belle journée, n'est-ce pas?*"

Travis's first thought was that Sarah should shut up. Hadn't Muck told them not to talk? But then he realized what she was doing; what effect her French, and her lovely accent, were having on the media. They were moving. They were confused: if Travis was the anti-French Englishman, then who was this sweet French-speaking young woman who obviously cared for him?

"*Mademoiselle!*" one of them called. "*Une interview? C'est possible?*"

"*Non, merci*," Sarah responded with a lovely smile. "*Il faut que nous jouons le match du hockey maintenant – peut-être après le match.*"

Travis almost giggled. He wasn't exactly sure what Sarah was saying to them, but he was sure enough they had no idea what to make of her.

So much for the French-despising Screech Owls.

⊚

"*Stop!*" hissed Travis.

He and Sarah had just entered the corridor leading from the Colisée ice surface to the dressing room when Travis turned back and caught a glimpse of a familiar head of curly hair.

Bart Lundrigan, the reporter.

Lundrigan was standing in the seats. He was facing a camera set up on a tripod. Behind the camera were lights shining in his face. Another man was down on one knee, working the dials on a machine.

Travis and Sarah dropped their equipment and crept along the Zamboni exit closer to where Lundrigan was standing. The reporter seemed to be listening to someone who wasn't there, and then they noticed an earplug in his ear. He was nodding and smiling. He seemed very pleased with himself. Travis noted he now had a suit on, and a tie.

"That's correct, Peter," Lundrigan was saying. His speaking voice had changed. It seemed so practised now, so filled with confidence. "You wouldn't expect to find such incidents here at an event like this, but there you go. It tells us something about our country, does it not?"

"*Cut!*" the man working the machine called. "We just lost the line to Toronto."

Lundrigan turned, obviously annoyed. He was adjusting his earplug and fiddling with his hair when he caught Travis and Sarah out of the corner of his eye.

"*Travis!*" he called. "*Hey, wait there a minute!*"

The reporter yanked the earplug out and came running down the steps, two and three at a time. Travis and Sarah were trapped.

"*I'm so glad you're here!*" Lundrigan shouted as he hurried toward them. "*I've got to talk to you!*"

Travis didn't know how to respond. Sarah pulled his arm, but he stood his ground, still not willing to believe completely that this friendly, smiling man had done something so evil.

Lundrigan was smiling ear to ear. His *eyes* were smiling. He still looked like the nicest person Travis could have wanted to meet.

"You've seen the story?" the reporter asked.

"The coach showed it to me," Travis said. He did not return the smile.

"I'm far more upset than you could ever be," Lundrigan said. "Honest to God, I don't know what happened. What they ran was not the story I filed. They reworked it on the desk, I guess. That happens in our business, but they're supposed to clear any changes with us. They never called me."

"You mean you didn't write that?" Sarah asked, sceptical.

"Honestly, kids. I wrote a nice piece and included all the diary quotes. They took what they wanted, I guess, and made something wild out of it. I don't write the headlines, either."

"Can't you get them to fix it?" Travis asked. He felt relieved. He hadn't been wrong about Bart Lundrigan.

Lundrigan shrugged. He smiled sheepishly. "I can *try*," he said. "But I can't guarantee anything."

Another voice filled the corridor.

"Don't you think you owe this young man an apology?"

All three turned, surprised. It was Muck. He was walking toward Lundrigan, his hands down at his sides, but clenched tightly.

Travis could sense Lundrigan cringing. "I just did," Lundrigan said.

"I mean a *written* apology," Muck said. "Front page – same as your story."

"Who're you anyway?" the reporter asked.

"I'm the coach of this team, and I'm very upset with what you have done to this young man."

Lundrigan was almost like a puppy confronted by a large dog.

"I just explained a minute ago to the kids," he said. "It had nothing to do with me. They rejigged the piece and put that headline on it. I don't write the headlines."

"But you could write an apology," Muck said.

"I will," Lundrigan said. He was sweating, breathing hard. "I swear. But I can't guarantee they'll run it, okay?"

"You work for this paper but you wash your hands of what they do to your work?" Muck asked.

Again the sheepish grin: "Well, not usually – but sometimes they mess things up."

"You ever play hockey?" Muck asked.

Lundrigan blinked, unsure what this had to do with what they were discussing here.

"A bit," he answered finally, "but what's that got to do with it?"

"Travis makes a mistake," Muck said, "Sarah, here, doesn't blame him. Same if she makes a mistake. We take responsibility for each other on our team, mister."

"Yeah, well, that's all well and fine, but there's a big difference between a game and reporting –"

"*Is there, now?*" Muck asked. And with that he turned both Travis and Sarah around and marched them back to the dressing room.

9

ravis had never believed there would come a time when he wished he wore another number. He had worn number 7 since his very first practice, when his father sent him out with a Detroit Red Wings sweater with the 7 sewn on the back and above it the name *Lindsay*. They were the same number and the same team sweater that his father's older cousin, "Terrible Ted" Lindsay, had worn back in the 1950s.

Now he'd take any other number – even one too large to fit into the loop at the end of the *L* in his autograph. Besides, no one was asking for his signature any more. They were still chasing "Paul Kariya's cousin," Nish, and there was huge interest in Sarah, who had played so brilliantly in the opening game, but the team captain of the Screech Owls, despite the magnificent hologram at the bottom of his card, was a bust. No one but the reporters wanted anything to do with him.

Well, that wasn't quite accurate. Most of the crowd seemed to know who was wearing number 7. There were a few boos during the warm-up, and shouts of "Shame!" from different sections in the stands.

"Pay no attention," Muck told him. "Remember, you're here to play hockey. It's what happens on the ice that counts."

The Owls were up against the other pre-tournament favourite in their division, the Beauport Nordiques. Beauport was just outside Quebec City, so the stands were packed with Beauport fans. The team also wore the *fleur-de-lys* pattern of the old NHL Quebec Nordiques, which apparently made for good television, because during the warm-up every camera that had been chasing Travis over the past few hours was down by the glass to get close-ups of Travis gliding past the opposition sweaters.

Nicole and J-P had explained it to Travis. The old Nordiques, with their sweaters so similar to the provincial flag, had come to symbolize the fight for an independent Quebec. Whenever the Nordiques played the Montreal Canadiens, the event was hailed and promoted as a rematch of the "Battle of Quebec," the same battle the French and English had fought on the Plains of Abraham back in 1759. And when the Nordiques won, it was a victory that reversed the outcome of the original battle. A victory for Quebec's independence, a victory for the French language and culture.

Travis couldn't follow all of this. But he got enough of an idea to see what was being played out here between the Beauport Nordiques and the Screech Owls. No wonder the cameras were here.

The Beauport team was big and fast and slick. Travis could tell from the warm-up that they were a superb hockey team. He knew Muck was concerned, too; why else would the Owls' coach have bribed them with a trip to see Montcalm's skull if they won? And Travis knew he would find it hard to play his best. He couldn't shut out the noise. The boos hurt him. And he had missed the crossbar every shot he had taken during warm-up.

Muck tried to change things around by starting Andy's line. He said it was to open up a bit of ice for Sarah and Dmitri and Travis by keeping them away from the Nordiques' top combination, but Travis knew it was to take him out of the picture. Muck didn't need the entire Colisée coming down on Travis's head just before the puck dropped.

The teams were well matched. The Nordiques were as good as Travis had guessed. They carried the puck well, but the Owls checked better, particularly Andy and Sarah, who were brilliant at centre. Jeremy was in goal again, Muck taking advantage of Jeremy's "hot hand," and Nish was his usual force on defence.

The moment Travis stepped on the ice for his first shift, there were more boos. He heard them as he chased a shot down the ice, and heard them, louder, when he first touched the puck. The first time he had the puck long enough to try a play – a simple give-and-go with Sarah – he stumbled and fell going for the return pass. The Colisée exploded with cheers.

Travis skated off almost in tears. He had blown the play. He had let the crowd get to him. He wished he never had to take another shift.

"You can answer them," Muck told him as he leaned over from behind, his big hand working the tense muscles in Travis's neck.

"H–how?" Travis asked. He knew his voice was breaking. He didn't even try to say more.

"You play your game. The people here know their hockey better than any crowd in Canada. You show them what you can do, they'll respect your abilities. And you don't have to say a word."

Travis tried to gather himself. He felt ashamed that he had ever thought he wouldn't want to wear the number of "Terrible Ted" Lindsay. By playing badly, he was not only letting his team down, he was letting his family down.

Next shift, Travis went in to forecheck, the boos seeming to chase him up and down the ice. He came in on the defence, faked going to one side and stuck his far leg out just as the defence passed cross-ice. The puck slammed into Travis's shin pad and bounced into the corner. He was on it instantly, the boos rising in waves around the rink. He stickhandled as the defender who had given up the puck came in on him, slipped the puck between the player's legs and danced out the far side of the corner with it, free for a play.

Nish was thundering in over the blueline. Travis hit Nish perfectly, tape to tape, and Nish wound up to shoot but, instead, faked the shot and passed off to Sarah, who one-timed the puck perfectly.

Owls 1, Nordiques 0.

"Think of the boos as cheers in another language," Muck said as he slapped Travis's shoulder and draped a towel around his neck.

The Nordiques tied the score in the second period on a splendid end-to-end rush by the same defenceman Travis had checked, and then went ahead 2–1 on a lucky shot from the corner that was supposed to be a pass but clipped in off the back of Nish's skate and in behind Jeremy.

Muck sent Sarah's line out with only two minutes left. The Owls were trailing by a goal, in a game they had to win, or at least tie, if they were to have any hope of reaching the finals – and, just as important, in Data's case, anyway, if they were going to get a look at a real skull.

They lined up for what might be the final face-off in the Owls' end, Travis up hard against the Nordiques' right winger, who was determined to rush the net as soon as the puck dropped.

Their shoulders touched. They pushed. The Nordiques' winger slashed Travis quickly across the ankle. The referee either didn't see or didn't *want* to see. Travis looked up into the player's mask as their shoulders met again.

"*Maudit Anglais!*" the player said, spitting out the words.

Travis was confused. He couldn't ask for a translation. He knew he didn't need to. He couldn't pull out his diary and show the player where his words had been twisted by the newspaper reporter.

"You've got it all wrong," Travis said quickly. He looked again at the eyes. It was obvious the player did not understand what he had said. Travis cursed himself again for being so bad at French. Why can't I tell him? he thought. Why can't I even try?

He had to try.

"*Je . . .* ," he began, tapping his Owls crest with his glove. "*J'aime vous . . .*"

The player blinked in what looked to Travis like shock, then laughed.

What did I say? Travis wondered, panicking. I just wanted to tell him that he had it all wrong, that I liked him. But it's not "*J'aime vous,*" for heaven's sake. It's "*Je t'aime . . .*" But wait a second, that's not it either. Oh no, oh no, oh no – I think I just told him, "I love you!"

Travis could feel the colour rising in his face. Mercifully, the puck dropped. Sarah took out her man and Data moved in quickly, plucking the puck free and taking it back behind his own net, where he quickly played it off the boards to Dmitri, on the far side.

Travis knew his play was to head for the middle. He broke hard, looking at Dmitri for the pass, only to find he was flying into the boards instead, crushed by the right winger's shoulder.

The arena was cheering wildly. They were singing, "*Na-na-na-na, na-na-na-na, hey, hey, hey, goo-ood bye . . .*"

The big Nordiques winger was leaning down, smiling at him. "*Je t'aime,*" he said in a sarcastic, sing-songy voice.

Coming out of nowhere, Nish's glove hit the player's shoulder, spinning him around. But before the two could do anything, Sarah had taken a stranglehold on Nish and was wrestling him away.

It was the smart move. The referee's hand was up; the winger who had charged Travis was getting a penalty. And the Owls desperately needed the advantage. With a power play and less than two minutes left in the game, they still had a chance for the tie.

"You okay?" Muck called as Travis skated slowly to the bench, the boos following him all the way.

"I'm fine," Travis said. In fact, he could hardly catch his breath. His chest hurt. He had slammed hard into the boards.

"Good," said Muck. "You're right back out there."

Travis turned back towards the face-off, the boos growing louder still, as if someone had grabbed the volume control and cranked it as high as it would go. Travis had never heard such noise. And it was all because of him. If only it had been cheers instead.

Sarah won the face-off and sent the puck to Data, who fired it around the boards to Dmitri. Travis, grimacing with the pain, broke for the blueline and Dmitri hit him perfectly. Travis used the boards to chip the puck past the first defenceman, broke around him, and picked it up again just outside the Nordiques' zone.

There was one player back. Travis came in, ready to shoot, but then looked for Sarah, who was flying up over centre and had beaten her own check with her wonderful speed. Travis knew he had to try it. It had worked in practice. It had worked in the street. It had worked in the Duponts' backyard rink.

The back pass!

He knew what Muck thought of it. "This isn't *lacrosse*, mister," he'd say in practice. But if ever the situation was perfect . . .

He could hear the boos, still just as loud. If he could pull this off, Travis thought, he might silence them.

Travis reached forward and put the blade of his stick in front of the puck. He had to be careful now; with the puck on his backhand he was working against the curve of the blade. He pulled the puck back until it was behind his skates and hidden from the defender.

Instead of bringing the puck ahead of him again on his fore-hand, he continued the backward sweep until his stick was directly behind him, the puck still on the wrong side of the curve, and he slipped a pass, backwards, to where Sarah was skating.

Sarah picked up the pass in full flight. The defender couldn't turn right, having already committed to Travis, and she blew past him, coming in on net and turning the goaltender inside out and down with two quick stickhandles and a shoulder fake.

She slipped the puck easily in on the backhand.

Tie game, 2–2. With the clock running out.

"No more back passes," Muck said as the Owls left the ice to a chorus of boos.

"It worked," Travis said, grinning.

"No more back passes," Muck repeated.

Travis said nothing. He was privately delighted with the back pass. But his heart sank as he turned the corner: the way to the Owls' dressing room was blocked by cameras and reporters.

"*Will you be issuing an apology?*" a woman shouted.

Travis said nothing.

"*We're told you will be making a statement – is that correct?*" a man called out.

Through the crush, Travis caught a glimpse of familiar curly hair. It was Bart Lundrigan, and he was being interviewed by another man. They were both seated and surrounded by lights and cameras. Lundrigan was talking, and the man interviewing him was nodding. Bart Lundrigan seemed to be enjoying himself.

Travis realized that the reporter had chosen the location and time of his interview very carefully. The Owls – Travis, Nish, Mr. Dillinger, Muck – were all a dramatic background for his television appearance.

"Inside," Muck said.

"*Mr. Lindsay!*" someone called.

"*Coach – can you give us a few minutes?*"

"*Travis!*"

And then they were through the door and had slammed it behind them, the warmth of the Owls' dressing room, the smiles of familiar faces, the cheers of his teammates, rising over Travis like a warm blanket at the end of a terrible nightmare.

10

Muck was true to his word. The Screech Owls had managed a tie, a single point, against the powerful Beauport Nordiques, and so they were off to see Montcalm's skull.

They parked at the Château Frontenac, and before continuing, Muck led the Owls inside and met with an older man who seemed to know him from a long time ago. They talked a while about old hockey games and then moved off to a corner. The man had a notebook and took down some of the things that Muck said. Most of the Owls investigated the hotel souvenir shop while they waited, but Travis couldn't fight his curiosity. He guessed that whatever it was that Muck and the man were discussing, it involved him. He thought at one point that he saw Muck hand the man a small book with a red vinyl cover. The diary?

Muck said nothing to Travis about the meeting. When Muck had finished, he and Mr. Dillinger paraded the Owls away from the hotel and turned into a series of older, smaller streets until they came to one called Donnacona, which was so narrow it looked more like a side alley than a real street. They came to small sign, "MUSÉE," and Muck turned in, with the rest of them following.

It was a small chapel. Apart from a few nuns, most of them old and all clad in the same grey habit, the Owls were the only visitors. Attached to the chapel was a small museum filled with period clothes and religious items, most of which meant nothing to the Owls. In a small room on the ground floor, however, there was a glass case on a desk against the far wall, and inside the case was what they had come to see.

Montcalm's skull.

"*Awesome*," said Data.

Travis would have used another word. *Repulsive*, perhaps, or *frightening*. There was nothing here that brought to mind the passions of the Battle of Quebec. There was no magnificent blue waistcoat or brilliantly white shirt, nothing heroic in the eyes as the Marquis lay mortally wounded, his men about to carry him off to the chapel where they hoped he might recover in time to save the city. There were not even eyes – only empty sockets.

There was nothing here to suggest anything but death, and the mystery of what becomes of you when the spark of life is gone. The skull seemed so small to Travis – too small, surely, to have ever been a man. He could not see the face of the Marquis in it, only bone yellowed with age, the grinning jaws containing just a few remaining stained and broken teeth.

"Can we take it out of the case?" Data asked.

"Don't be foolish," Muck said. "Show a little respect for the dead, if you don't mind."

Travis noted that Muck was practically whispering in reply to Data's near shout. Data saw everything from the point of view of someone who watches too much television. To him, the skull was a prop, just a toy. To Muck, the skull was the past, a real man who had suffered a real and painful death after a real battle.

Travis tried, desperately, to see Montcalm the man in the hollowed-out, yellow eye sockets. *What was the last thing he had seen?* he wondered. *Did he know that Wolfe had won? Did he know that his men were beaten and that he was going to die?*

Travis pictured the French general lying there, blood staining his white tunic and beautiful blue waistcoat. *If he had felt such pain just hitting the boards, how much pain had Montcalm felt? Was he frightened?*

He felt a current of air on his neck. Was it the heat coming out of a ceiling vent? The breath of someone behind him? Or Montcalm's presence?

He shook it off and turned his attention from the curious skull to the typewritten notes beneath it. There were two: one in French and one in English. He read the English.

It was a strange note. Instead of explaining the Marquis's life, it attacked the king of France for abandoning Montcalm in death. When the French and English settled their differences and put an end to their war in 1763, the king of France was given the chance to keep any piece of land he chose from the New World. Though the king knew his faithful general had given his life defending this land where Travis now stood, he passed on Quebec and selected, instead, three tiny Caribbean islands.

Whichever of the elderly nuns had typed this curious note,

she had ended it with an even more curious line: "He let the Canadians down."

Travis shivered. *He did feel the Marquis's presence!*

Perhaps it wasn't Travis's fault, but that was just the way he felt, too — that he had somehow let Canadians down. *All* Canadians.

If only he'd never agreed to do that damned diary. If only he spoke better French. If only they hadn't booed . . .

11

"That's more like it," said Muck.

He was sitting up front in the Owls' old school bus as Mr. Dillinger made his morning rounds to pick up the players from their billets. Muck was holding *Le Soleil*, the Quebec City newspaper, on his lap, and Sarah, with another copy of the paper, was sitting in the seat across the aisle and translating a story into English for him.

Travis's original diary entry had been printed in full. The story in *Le Soleil*, written by the man Muck had met with at the Château the day before, was a scathing attack on the tactics of reporter Bart Lundrigan of the *Montreal Inquirer*. Lundrigan had been interviewed for the story and had come out looking very bad. He claimed that the quotes he had run in the paper were actually a combination of diary entries and interviews with the kids, but all of the players denied that they had been interviewed.

"He's been completely discredited," said Mr. Dillinger. "Serves him right."

"Why would he have done it?" Data asked.

"He wanted a good story," Muck said. "He couldn't find one on his own, so he manufactured one."

"That's dishonest," said Wilson.

"There are good reporters and bad reporters," Muck said. "Just as there are good players and bad players." In other words, case closed.

The story in *Le Soleil* had an immediate effect that morning, and was first noted in the Dupont home where, at breakfast, Madame Dupont had greeted Travis with big kiss on both cheeks and a hug, much to his embarrassment. Monsieur Dupont was also pleased, and smacked Travis's back as he came for his second cup of coffee. Nicole and J-P had just smiled.

Nicole and J-P joined the bus with Travis, Nish, and Lars when Mr. Dillinger swung by the Duponts' house. The players were free until the game that night, the Owls' third, against a good team from Burlington, Vermont, and Mr. Dillinger was taking them all to the Ice Palace, where he would pick them all up later.

"*Ish-nay ee-fray!*" Nish shouted as they got off the bus. *Nish is free!*

"Cut it with the Pig Latin, if you don't mind," said Travis. "I'd just as soon never hear it again."

Nish giggled. "*O-nay oblem-pray, avis-Tray!*"

What's the use? Travis thought. Nish would never change.

Travis forgot about his problems and fell in with the running, shouting gang of Screech Owls and their new friends. He felt a mitten in his glove, and saw that Nicole had grabbed his hand. She was smiling.

"I have to stick close to you," she said. "Sarah says we're going to work together on your French!"

Great! thought Travis. If French classes were always like this, he'd soon be fluent!

They raced along the boardwalk to the top of the toboggan run, where they lined up to go down. Data waited at the bottom with his special wristwatch switched to run as a stopwatch. Nish was a good two seconds faster than anyone else.

"*Ish-Nay ampion-chay!*" he shouted in Travis's face. Travis didn't care. He was having fun. And Nicole's mitten was still in his hand.

Nish tried to buy one of the bright-red hollow plastic canes so many of the adults were carrying about – and drinking from – but no one would sell him one. It was still morning, yet some of them were stopping every few minutes and taking enormous swigs, the liquid splashing down their cheeks and off their chins as they laughed and yelled while at the same time trying to drink.

"I don't think it's Gatorade," said Nish.

"Neither do I," said Travis.

He finally found one sticking out of the snow beside a bench and carried it with him as if he were one of the grown-ups, but he threw it away after twisting off the cap and smelling the contents.

"Here, Trav," he said, handing the cane over to Travis. "Give this to your buddy, *Barf* Lundrigan – might help him write a little clearer."

They walked back towards the Château, Nicole pointing to everything, from the river to the benches, and having Travis repeat the French word for each. They then headed down the little side street where the artists worked, and Nish and Data and Wilson all posed for a caricature that showed them playing hockey, Nish with his stick broken and with his front teeth out and a big black eye as he sat in the penalty box.

They went down the side streets and stairs to Lower Town and the harbour area.

"Let's take the funicular back up when we're done," suggested Nicole. "It's only a dollar each."

Travis had never seen a funicular before. It was a sort of *outside* elevator enclosed in glass. It ran straight up the side of the cliff from Lower Town and stopped just outside the Château. Everyone agreed that it would be a terrific ride up.

After they had seen Lower Town, the Owls lined up for the funicular. It would take them all in three separate runs. Travis and Nicole, her mitten still securely in his hand, were in the first car, and everyone squeezed in tight for the doors to close and the climb to begin.

Travis and Nicole stood with their faces pressed to the glass. There was a jolt, and then the older part of the city began to fall away from them. They could soon see over the rooftops, and then all the way over to Levis. Up and up the cliff they went, higher and higher.

"I THINK I'M GONNA HURL!" shouted a voice from the back. Nish, of course, the fearless defenceman who couldn't stand heights.

"Bet you can't say that in Pig Latin," said Travis, and everyone laughed.

Travis felt so good about things. The article in *Le Soleil* that had changed everything. The backwards pass that had tied the game against Beauport. The little joke he had just made with Nish. The soft, warm mitten curled within his fingers.

The gears wound to a stop and, with a chug, the big doors opened at the top.

"*What the –!*"

It was Nish's voice again. He was at the back, and first off. There was alarm again in his voice – only this time he wasn't kidding.

Travis and Nicole pushed through to see what it was that Nish had seen.

There were cameras waiting!

Travis cringed, but then he saw that the cameras weren't pointed at him, for once. They were jostling for position around a wall to one side of the funicular.

The Owls all pushed out. There was a crowd gathered. People looked upset.

It took a minute for them to struggle far enough through the crowd to see what the cameras were filming. Then they wished they had gone as fast as possible in the opposite direction.

Someone had spray-painted the wall, in large, dripping, red letters.

"QUEBEC SUCKS! . . . FRENCH = PIG LATIN!"

"*Oh, no!*" said Nicole in a near whisper. Travis could feel her hand clench.

"*Regardez!*" shouted a man with a camera, backing away from the wall. "*C'est lui!*"

He was pointing straight at Travis. Others looked up and scrambled to move their cameras around. A reporter came running over.

"*You're Travis Lindsay, aren't you?*"

"*Leave him alone!*" Nicole shouted angrily. "*This has nothing to do with him!*"

"*Any idea who might have done this, then?*" a woman reporter asked.

Travis had none.

"*Get him out of here!*" J-P called to the rest of the Owls.

With Nish behind him, pushing, the Owls rushed Travis through the wall of cameras and reporters forming around him. Travis knew this would look like they were running away, but what else could they do? He didn't want to talk to them, and he had no answers anyway. He had no idea who might have done this.

Travis could feel that awful pain in the pit of his stomach coming back again.

12

The alarming work at the top of the funicular was not the only display of hate graffiti. Nor was it all anti-French. Freshly scrawled over billboards and along the wooden walls around construction sites, and even on the sides of the Colisée, were the slogans "GO HOME ANGLAIS" and "UGLY ENGLISH" and "MAUDIT ANGLAIS." The New Battle of Quebec was being waged with spray-paint cans, not muskets.

"Who can be doing this?" Travis kept asking as the Owls gathered in their dressing room at the Colisée for game three of the peewee tournament.

"It's probably lots of different people," said Data. "Obviously at least two, because there's two different points of view."

"What are they trying to prove?"

"*Prove?*" said Data. "I doubt they're trying to prove anything. They're just spreading hate."

"What's the point?" Travis asked.

"To show that it's impossible for English and French to get along, I guess."

"Why don't they come to the Duponts'? They'd see we get along just fine."

Muck came into the dressing room, and all the players looked up. The coach looked concerned, but it wasn't about the spray-painting.

"I don't like doing this," he said when he was satisfied he had their attention, "but Mr. Dillinger has done some calculations. The tie with Beauport has put us in a tough position. We have to win by at least five goals tonight, according to Mr. Dillinger's mathematics, if we're to have any chance of making the finals. If we win, and Beauport wins tomorrow morning, it's going to make three teams tied at the top in points: us, the Beauport Nordiques, and a team we never even got to play – the Saskatoon Wheaties.

"Saskatoon's already finished their three games. They've got a tie, too, but altogether they've scored four more goals than we have and three more than Beauport. If we want to make sure we play in the final, we'd better win by five."

"We'll win by ten," Nish predicted.

Muck didn't even smile. "Five will be adequate, Nishikawa," he said, and abruptly left the room.

"Geez," said Nish. "What's got into him?"

"Nothing," said Travis. "He just doesn't like it when teams run up scores, that's all."

"*Ig-bay eal-day*," Nish said, shaking his head and bending down to tighten his skates.

The team from Burlington, Vermont, had yet to win a game – but they weren't that bad. They had size and they had heart. Travis had rarely seen a team work so hard. But as Muck always said, "You can't teach talent." And the Burlington Bears had precious little talent to spare, apart from a quick little centre and one defenceman who was every bit as good in both ends as Nish. Overall, the Owls were faster, smarter, and much better coached. If one of the two Bears' stars didn't do it for their team, it basically didn't get done.

Just before the opening face-off, Sarah had skated away from centre ice and, bending over, with her stick resting on her knees, had drifted by Travis for a quick, quiet consultation.

"It's up to us to get Muck's five," she said.

"We'll do it," Travis replied.

In fact, Sarah would do it by herself. Because he had to have the goals, Muck started double-shifting her towards the middle of the first period. She would take a shift with Travis and Dmitri, catch her breath while Andy's line was out, and then be thrown back out by Muck on a makeshift line with Derek Dillinger on one wing and little Simon Milliken on the other.

She played magnificently. Even though the Bears' coach was smart enough to have his good defenceman stay on her every time she was on the ice, Sarah could not be stopped. She scored twice in the first period and three times in the second – and with only five minutes to go in the game, and with the Owls leading 7–2, Nish pointed out something that Travis had been afraid to say out loud.

"*You can go for the record!*" Nish called down to Sarah from the defence end of the Owls' bench.

Sarah was bent over, gasping to catch her breath, and only nodded. She knew, just as Travis knew. She had five goals; young Guy Lafleur had scored seven the night before they sewed the velvet pucks onto his sweater.

"We're . . . already up . . . by five," she finally gasped.

"C'mon," Nish prodded. "Give it a shot!"

The Bears were giving up. If the defenceman or the little centre didn't carry the puck, no one else seemed to want it. They just wanted the clock to run out, and were dumping the puck from their own end, causing an endless series of icings.

Nish hated icing, and would do whatever he could to prevent one. Travis had rarely seen Nish skate *forward* as fast as he was flying backwards next shift to snare a dump-in before it crossed the icing line. He reached it just before the linesman could blow his whistle. The linesman waved off the icing, and Nish circled his net, still gathering speed.

Travis headed for centre. Nish fired the high, hard one – a play they rarely attempted – and it worked perfectly. Travis caught the puck in his glove, and simply let it drop down onto his stick as he crossed centre. *What a perfect pass!*

Travis was in with only the Bears' good defenceman back, and Sarah was moving up fast. He was on the left side, with a shot at a bad angle, but Sarah might be able to get the rebound. He didn't think he could get around the defenceman going one on one.

But there was still the back pass! Sarah was uncovered – the rest of the Bears not even bothering to come back with the game so clearly lost – and she was dead centre, just at the blue-line and headed for the slot.

Travis slipped the puck onto his backhand, checked once on Sarah, and then pulled the puck back and around.

As soon as he let the pass go, he knew he'd blown it. The defenceman had read the play perfectly and, with the game already out of reach, had decided to gamble. He leapt past Travis, giving him a clear run to the net, but since Travis had already committed himself to the high-risk pass, he was doomed.

The defenceman picked up the puck in full stride. Travis was off-balance and turned, badly, into the boards. Sarah had been going full-speed towards the Bears' net and couldn't turn in time. Dmitri was on the far side, racing for a rebound, and he, too, was out of the play.

The defenceman was at the red line when the little centre turned and broke for the Owls' blueline, directly between Nish and Data, who were back-pedalling fast and trying to squeeze him off.

The defenceman's pass was perfect, a floater that the little centre knocked down with the shaft of his stick as he jumped through the opening between Nish and Data. Nish turned, flailing, willing to trip and take the penalty, but the little centre's skates were off the ice and Nish's desperate sweep met nothing but air.

The centre was in, alone, on Jenny. He faked once to his backhand, kept it on his forehand, and merely waited for Jenny to go down. Just before he lost the angle, he fired the puck high, ticking it in off the far post.

Owls 7, Bears 3.

Travis skated back to the bench with his head bowed. He could feel Muck's eyes boring right through his helmet, the heat of his coach's stare unbearable. He knew what Muck had said about the back pass. He knew he had blown it.

With neither coach nor captain saying a word, Travis made his way down the length of the bench and plunked himself down beside Jeremy Weathers, who was back-up goalie this game. Even Jeremy wouldn't look at him.

Travis sat, staring down between his legs, disgusted with himself. He felt a towel fall around his neck. Good old Mr. Dillinger. But then, he thought, the towel was also a sure sign he wouldn't be going back out.

"We have to have five," Muck said.

Travis could tell from the tone of Muck's voice that the coach didn't like saying this. More goals from the Owls at this stage of the game would look like they were just running up the score. Muck couldn't turn to the sparse crowd – none of them booing Travis this night – and explain to them why he had to have a five-goal victory. He just had to hope he got it, and could get out of this awkward game as fast as possible.

"Sarah," Muck said, "you're centring Dmitri and Lars."

Travis looked up. *Lars?* But Lars was a defenceman! He was being replaced by a defenceman?

Five Owls lined up for the face-off at centre. Sarah, Dmitri, Lars, Nish, and Data. Travis checked the clock. Less than three minutes to go. They *had* to have a goal.

Muck's hunch paid off almost immediately. Lars was so quick, so smart with the puck, he was able to pluck it out of the face-off scrum when Sarah got tied up with the little centre.

Lars circled at centre and dumped the puck back to Nish, who immediately tried his long floater play. He lifted the puck as high as he could, the puck flipping through the air as it rose over the Owls' blueline and centre ice.

The Bears' star defenceman had read the play correctly, and leapt to snare the puck with his glove, but it was just a touch too high for him. It clicked off a finger of his glove and fell behind him.

Sarah was already moving. She picked up the puck, moved over the Bears' blueline, and fired a quick slapshot that surprised the Bears' goaltender, who completely whiffed on the glove save. The puck bulged the net, the red light came on, and the Owls' bench, Muck included, went wild.

Owls 8, Bears 3. The five-goal lead was back in place!

Muck sent Andy's line out to check the Bears, and when Andy's line tired, he put back the same five who had scored the big goal.

With less than fifteen seconds left, Lars, with his uncanny ability to knock pucks out of the air, caught a long pass at centre ice. He moved in fast, completely fooling the only defenceman back by moving with a great burst of speed to go to the side, and then slipping the puck back into the slot area, where he was able to dodge around the defenceman and go in clear.

It was one on one, Lars on the goaltender. He shifted. He faked. He stickhandled so fast the Bears' goaltender went down on his back, lying there helplessly. All Lars had to do was flick the puck over the goalie.

But he instead skated to the side of the net and turned, looking behind him. The Bears' star defenceman was coming in fast, racing straight for Lars.

Lars waited until the final possible moment, then flipped a

saucer pass over the stick of the defenceman and hit Sarah perfectly for a tap-in goal, the net as good as empty as the goaltender turned on his back and stared helplessly while Sarah scored her seventh goal of the game.

"*You did it!*" Nish shouted as he joined the pile-on. "*You tied the record!*"

"Lars shouldn't have done that," Sarah laughed. "That was embarrassing."

"*It doesn't matter!*" Nish shouted. "*You got your seventh — same as Lafleur!*"

Nish wasn't the only one who had noticed. Tournament organizers rushed from the stands to congratulate her. The Bears, led by the quick little centre and the good defenceman, lined up to shake her hand. Reporters and photographers were milling onto the ice to get shots of her holding seven pucks.

How nice, thought Travis. They're no longer chasing me.

He still felt foolish about the back pass, but then, if he hadn't blown it, Sarah wouldn't have had to score a sixth goal and would never have been on the ice with Lars, who gave her the seventh.

Travis dressed quietly. Apart from one sharp look from Muck, who shook all the players' hands, nothing more was said about the messed-up glory play. There was no need.

When they left the rink, a light snow was beginning to fall. Nothing had been painted on the bus this time, Travis noted with some gratitude. Perhaps the whole thing was just going to fade away.

"*Travis!*" someone called.

He turned, nervous, instantly on guard – but this was no reporter. It was a young voice, though in the dark of the parking lot and the light snowfall, Travis couldn't quite make out its source.

"*Travis!*" called a couple of voices this time, and three figures came racing up, puffing and wiping melting snow from their eyes.

They were kids, all younger than Travis.

"*S'il vous plaît!*"

They were holding out hockey cards. Travis Lindsay hockey cards. They wanted his autograph.

Travis took the offered pen and the cards. He signed each one carefully, a big loop on the *L*, and the number 7 inside each loop.

"*Merci*," he said as he handed each one back. "*Merci.*"

Travis's world felt right again.

13

The Owls had signed autographs after the big win against the Bears – Nish still the biggest draw – and then boarded the school bus. Instead of delivering them to the usual pick-up spot where they would meet their billets, Mr. Dillinger took them out on the main road towards the university, then turned down the Duponts' street and parked opposite their driveway, where Nicole and J-P and several of their friends from the neighbourhood were waiting.

"Now you skate for fun!" Mr. Dillinger announced as he turned off the engine and yanked on the emergency brake.

It was a wonderful surprise, arranged almost entirely by Nicole and J-P. Monsieur Dupont was just putting away the snowblower. The ice glistened, the perfect result of a careful flood. There were patio lanterns strung on poles around the rink. Madame Dupont had hot chocolate for everyone, and homemade cookies and tarts and tiny chocolate *bonbons* that she had made herself.

The Owls all had their skates. They put them on while sitting on benches in the tent garage, then stepped carefully along a path made by Monsieur Dupont's snowblower, then onto the ice. J-P had set up the sound system so it would first play a song in English that everyone knew, then a French song, then an English song again. All the Quebec kids knew the French songs by heart, and the others, like Sarah and Travis, wondered why they had never heard them before, for the music was wonderful.

They skated in circles to the music. They played "whip" until Nish was so exhausted he lay on his back like a beached whale on top of the far snowbank, tossing mittfuls of snow onto his own face, where it melted and cooled him. They drank hot chocolate and ate candies and regretted that soon Muck's curfew would be in force and Mr. Dillinger would have to deliver them all back to their billets.

"Let's go for a walk," Nicole said to Travis. "Sometimes from the end of the street you can see the northern lights."

They slipped away down the path, tiptoeing on their skates until they reached the tent garage, and then quickly changed into their boots.

Travis's feet always felt odd when he first put on his boots after skating, but particularly so after skating on an open-air rink. They felt slightly unsteady, like he had rubber bands connecting his joints instead of muscles.

He pretended to stumble and reached out and took Nicole's hand. She giggled softly. He could feel the colour rising in his face. He knew his move must have looked pretty dumb – faking a fall so he had to grab something to hold him up. But Nicole didn't seem to mind. She tightened her grip on Travis's hand. He felt his face turn even hotter.

They were away from the lights now. The street was dark but for a few streetlights. Travis looked up; the stars were thick and plentiful. He recognized Orion by the belt, the Big Dipper by its handle. He wondered if he should point them out to Nicole. She might be impressed. But he knew only two constellations. If she asked about any others, he wouldn't have a clue.

"There," she said. "You can see them rippling."

Travis knew Nicole was referring to the northern lights, but he wasn't looking up any more.

A dark shape was moving by the school bus!

Something was there, but he didn't know what. A big dog? A person? He had seen a shadow, and the shadow had jumped as if it was hiding.

"*Shhhhhhh*," he said.

Nicole turned, surprised, and saw that Travis was pointing toward the bus. They ducked into the nearest driveway, using the high snowbanks as cover. They peeked out from behind, waiting.

"What's going on?" Nicole whispered.

"I don't know."

"Is it one of your team?"

"I don't think so."

They watched for a moment. It was definitely a person. Whoever it was, he was wearing a bulky parka, with the hood drawn up. The hood had a thick fringe of fur, so his face was hidden.

The figure rounded the side of the bus. A big glove came off, and a hand went into a side pocket and came out with a can of something.

"Spray-paint," whispered Nicole.

"What'll we do?"

"I'd better get my father!" Nicole said.

The two of them cut through the deep snow of a neighbour's backyard. They scrambled over the Dupont's back fence and ploughed through the heavy snow until, with difficulty, they climbed the snowbank at the far end of the rink, rising over it just as Nish, still lying on his back and eating snow, caught sight of them.

"*Ohhhhhhhh – where–have–you–two–been?*" Nish sang in his most irritating voice.

Nicole and Travis were bounding down the side of the snowbank.

"Where's Muck?" Travis called.

Nish pointed towards the patio doors.

Nicole was already at the back of the house. She yanked the patio doors open and ran in, her mother shouting at her – probably about getting snow all over the carpet, Travis figured.

By the time Travis got inside, Nicole was calling to her father, who was already up and moving.

"*There's someone painting the bus!*" Travis shouted at Muck and Mr. Dillinger, who had been sitting over a cup of coffee with Monsieur Dupont. There was a cribbage board and cards on the table and a hockey game on TV. Montreal Canadiens versus the Mighty Ducks of Anaheim, Travis noted. Strange, he'd been so caught up in this tournament, he'd almost forgotten about the NHL. He tried never to miss "Hockey Night in Canada" when Paul Kariya was on.

Muck was pulling on his big snow boots, reaching for his coat. Monsieur Dupont was already at the door. Mr. Dillinger was struggling to tuck in his shirt.

"*Vite!*" Monsieur Dupont called to his wife. "*La police!*"

Madame Dupont moved quickly towards the downstairs telephone.

Muck and Monsieur Dupont were out the door, doing up buttons and zippers as they ran.

Through the glass of the patio door, Travis could see the kids all standing on the ice, watching with puzzled faces. Everyone knew something was up.

Travis and Nicole fell in behind the men. As the only two already out of their skates, they were the only ones who could follow.

Travis had barely reached the end of the Duponts' driveway when he saw Muck in full flight down the street toward the bus.

The spray-painter in the hooded parka saw him and bolted. Whoever it was, he was very fast.

Muck turned and yelled at Monsieur Dupont, who had fallen in behind him.

"*La voiture!*" Muck shouted.

Monsieur Dupont spun on his heels and ran back to his car, started it up, and backed out with the heavy winter tires spinning a sudden spray of snow. He switched to a forward gear and sped away, the car fishtailing down the street as he joined in the chase.

"*C'mon!*" shouted Nicole. "*We can cut him off this way!*"

To Travis, they seemed to be running in the wrong direction. But Nicole knew how the streets ran. She and Travis dashed up one block, across another street, then turned right.

Down the street Travis could see the hooded spray-painter, running straight towards them. Muck was still in pursuit, but had fallen behind.

He was coming closer! Travis had no idea what to do.

What if he had a gun?

What if he had a knife?

"*We have to turn him!*" Nicole shouted.

There was just one side street between them and the hooded figure. She jumped in the air and shouted.

"*Yahhhhhhhh!*"

Travis didn't know what to do. He jumped up and shouted, too.

"*Yaaaahhhhhhhhhh!*"

He hoped their winter clothes made them look bigger than they were. It didn't matter, though, as Nicole was already racing towards the spray-painter. Travis joined her, praying that the dark figure would turn away from them into the side street.

He did!

His face still hidden deep inside his hood, he took one look up at Nicole and Travis, then one look back at Muck, who was grimly churning up the street towards him. Mr. Dillinger was now in view farther back, still trying to tuck in his shirt as he ran, jacketless, after the man who'd dared deface his bus.

Just as the hooded figure turned, a pair of extremely bright headlights snapped on, catching him in their harsh light and bringing him to a stop as suddenly as if he'd just run into a wall.

It was Monsieur Dupont. He had been lying in wait in his car, his headlights off.

That moment's hesitation was all Muck needed. He dropped his shoulder and charged straight at the spray-painter. The man's knees buckled, spilling him onto the road with Muck hanging on tight.

Monsieur Dupont shot the car forward, then jammed on the brakes, causing the car to slide halfway up a snowbank, where it hung helplessly, the snow frying in the heat of the exhaust system and steam rising from under the rear wheels.

Mr. Dillinger, his shirt flapping loose, went down on one knee, spinning into Muck and the hooded figure as they lay on the icy road. He grabbed the man by both shoulders and slammed him hard down on the ice.

A siren howled!

Travis and Nicole turned quickly to see where the awful sound was coming from. Three police cruisers, their lights flashing, were turning towards them off the Duponts' street, the cars swaying dangerously on the ice.

Monsieur Dupont roughly grabbed the can of spray-paint and tossed it angrily into the nearest snowbank.

Muck was up on his knees now. He seized the hood of the parka and yanked hard.

Travis gasped. He couldn't believe what he saw as the hood came down.

Brown, curly hair.

It was Bart Lundrigan — the reporter from the *Montreal Inquirer*.

14

e wasn't content with just *reporting* the news — it seems he had to *create* it, too."

The man speaking was the editor of the *Montreal Inquirer*, a big man, with a face as round and red as a face-off circle. He had come up to Quebec City to meet with police and apologize to the people of Quebec City for all the trouble Bart Lundrigan had created.

He met separately with the Owls and those parents who had come along on the trip, and he both apologized profusely to the team and handed over a cheque for one thousand dollars to Mr. Dillinger, who said that it would go towards cleaning up the old school bus and that the remainder would be put into the local minor-hockey program once the Owls got back home.

The newspaper editor's explanation for his reporter's behaviour confirmed what everyone had guessed. Bart Lundrigan had simply been too ambitious. He dreamed of getting to the NHL as a reporter, and he must have figured that breaking a major story involving minor hockey would get him there faster.

The editor said that his newspaper hadn't changed a single word of Lundrigan's original story, despite the reporter's claim that this whole affair only got started when someone at the *Inquirer* meddled with his work.

Lundrigan must have figured that all the interviews he would get because of his sensational story were going to get him closer to his dream of a bigger and better job. And after the article in *Le Soleil* had thrown his reputation into doubt, he had taken matters into his own hands to prove he really did have a story. It had been Lundrigan who had spray-painted all those hate-filled messages over the city – both the anti-French and anti-English. There never were two warring sides. One man with a single can of spray-paint had created something that the rest of the media was treating as a huge crisis.

Lundrigan had been charged by the police with public mischief and with defacing public property. He had been fired by the *Inquirer*, and his career as a reporter was over, because he could no longer be trusted. He had made much more out of things than was really there, had taken something true and twisted it into a lie.

Among the many victims of Bart Lundrigan's lies were the people of Quebec City. They felt terrible about Travis Lindsay, the little peewee player who had borne the brunt of their anger.

Travis, once again, became the focus of the media. But now the cameras seemed to be smiling at him. It was a strange experience, like landing on two different planets, and yet he had not changed. Just the way they saw him was different.

Travis was asked to go on a French television program called "Le Point" with Muck and Monsieur Dupont, but said he couldn't do it. The woman who had approached him with the idea put his refusal down to the nerves of a quiet-spoken, shy young boy. She hadn't asked if he spoke any French. Perhaps they had been planning to translate whatever he said. But Travis couldn't do it. He was ashamed that he hadn't the nerve even to try speaking French.

©

"*You* are coming with us," Nicole Dupont said, as she took Travis by the arm and pulled him away from the rest of the Owls. Travis was surprised by the sneak attack, but delighted that it was his new friend, Nicole. Right behind Nicole, also smiling, was Sarah Cuthbertson.

"Where are we going?" Travis giggled as Sarah took his other arm, marching him towards the door.

"School," she said. Nothing else.

15

Et le numero sept, number seven, le capitaine des Screech Owls, the Screech Owls' captain, Traaaa-vis Liiiinnnnnndddddd-say!"

A moment ago, Travis had been standing at the gate leading onto the Colisée ice. He had been surrounded by black, the lights down low in the packed arena. Now, as the Colisée announcer called his number, and his name rumbled and echoed about the building, spotlights and lasers exploded from the rafters.

Travis skated out, but he had no sense of his skates ever touching the ice. He felt as if he were floating on air. His Screech Owls uniform shone brilliantly under the spotlights, and those lights and the roar of the crowd had tracked him all the way to the blueline, where his skates somehow managed on their own to bring him to a graceful stop. He stood, unsteadily, beside Nish and Data and Jenny and Jeremy, who had already been introduced and were standing there waiting, skittering back and forth on their skates.

Nish turned and slammed his stick into Travis's shinpads. He had a big, wide smile on his face. He knew what was going on.

The rise continued to grow. It built and built from the moment Travis's name was announced until it seemed it would go on forever, the Colisée filling with the roar of thousands upon thousands of voices. It was a noise so utterly different from the fierce roar of the crowd the last time Travis and the Owls had played Beauport.

Travis turned on his skates. He looked down modestly at his laces. But still the roar built. They wouldn't quit. He looked toward the doorway. Sarah was standing there, waiting, a big smile on her face as she looked out at Travis, who was shifting more and more uncomfortably on the blueline, the roar holding fast, deafening.

Nish's stick slammed again into his shinpads. Travis could hear him shouting, only it was muffled, as if there were three walls between them, not three feet. He had to lean into Nish to make out what he was saying.

"*Acknowledge them!*" Nish was screaming. "*They're waiting for you to do something!*"

Travis, in his shyness, hadn't understood. Nish, of course, understood perfectly the rules and regulations of being the centre of attention.

Travis skated out in a small loop. He raised his stick like a sword and saluted the crowd.

The roar nearly split his eardrums! It built to an impossible pitch, then at last died suddenly away. The fans sat, as one, back into their seats, and the announcer began to introduce Sarah, which caused the roaring to begin all over again.

Everyone knew about the girl who had tied Guy Lafleur's record of seven goals. It seemed that even the souvenir hunters knew about Sarah's great achievement, for as the team had dressed for the final game, Sarah was unable to find her Screech Owls sweater. Someone had taken her jersey with her lucky number. Mr. Dillinger had been forced to go to the equipment bag and find a replacement, and instead of wearing her usual number 9, Sarah now had to skate out with the number 28 on her back. She didn't seem too pleased about it.

Sarah saluted the crowd, and then, one by one, the rest of the Owls came out to loud applause and cheers: Dmitri, Simon, Jesse, Lars . . .

The Owls assembled on the blueline until the coach, Muck Munro, was introduced and the roar exploded one more time. Muck gave an embarrassed little wave as he walked, unsteadily, around the boards towards the Owls' bench.

After the Owls had all been introduced, the announcer turned to the Beauport Nordiques, the other team to reach the championship game in the Quebec International Peewee Tournament. The Saskatoon Wheaties, despite the same over-all record, had been eliminated from the final because they hadn't scored as many goals as the other two teams. The significance of Sarah's seven goals was now known to everyone and appreciated by all.

The Nordiques were still the local favourites. Each player received an enormous roar from the friendly crowd, though none, it seemed, got as loud a reception as Travis. But then, none of them had been through what Travis had been through this week.

The introductions done, the players began to head for the bench, the starting lineups remaining on the ice to wait for the anthem. Travis was nervous, but ready. He had hit the crossbar twice in the warm-up. He had felt the warmth of the crowd. He wanted the puck to drop.

A man in a blue blazer was moving towards centre ice. He was carrying a microphone. He spoke first in French, then in English, about a special guest and a special presentation that was going to take place before the anthem.

The crowd was already rising for a better view. Some had recognized who it was that had just moved towards the entrance to the ice surface. The crowd was mumbling, the noise growing, and some fans were pointing and cheering.

Was it Guy Lafleur? Travis wondered. Obviously the crowd recognized whomever it was. It *had* to be a hockey star.

The man in the blue blazer was still introducing the special guest: "*He has come here following last night's game in Montreal to show his continuing support for Canadian minor hockey . . .*"

It couldn't be Lafleur. It had to be a current NHL star!

The crowd was all up now, the cheering rising to a roar as loud as the one that greeted Travis. A handsome, dark-haired young man in a suit was moving through the crowd of tournament officials and about to step onto the ice.

"*. . . captain of the Mighty Ducks of Anaheim . . . Paul Kariya!*"

Despite the roar, Travis heard a voice beside him.

"*I'm dead meat!*"

Travis turned and looked at Nish. His friend had turned the colour of the fresh-flooded ice. Nish closed his eyes as if he wished he could make the great Paul Kariya vanish.

The Mighty Ducks' captain was about to find out that according to some kid's hockey card he had a long-lost "cousin."

A man was coming out onto the ice behind Paul Kariya. He was carrying something over his right arm. It looked like a hockey sweater, with the same colours as were worn by the Screech Owls. Paul Kariya took the sweater, and the man in the blue blazer began talking again in French and English, switching back and forth between the two languages. With the noise of the crowd and the echoes of the Colisée, Travis caught only pieces of what he was saying.

"... *les sept buts de Guy Lafleur ... a record that has stood for nearly four decades ... un effort incroyable ... so it is with great pleasure that the organizing committee of the fortieth Quebec International Peewee Tournament honours Sarah Cuthbertson!*"

Once more the Colisée burst into a tremendous roar. How, Travis wondered, could the fans keep it up? A stunned Sarah skated towards centre ice, where Paul Kariya congratulated her and then held up the hockey sweater.

It was Sarah's "stolen" sweater! Number 9, with seven velvet pucks sewn on the front – *just like Guy Lafleur's!*

The Colisée crowd seemed to blow like a volcano when they saw it. Some of the Owls on the ice dropped their sticks and gloves and held their hands over their ears, but even their hands and helmets could not keep out the roar.

With Paul Kariya's help, Sarah pulled off the replacement sweater and pulled on the new one. Photographers skidded along the ice to capture the moment, and then Sarah and Paul Kariya, both of them smiling, posed for a picture together while the crowd continued to cheer.

From just behind Travis came Nish's voice again.

"She'd better not tell him about my card!"

16

The moment the puck left the referee's hand, Travis knew he had never been in a hockey game quite like this one. It was as if an electrical cord ran from every player and had been connected to the same charge. There was the proud history of the tournament. There was the great size of the rink. There were the peewee ghosts of Guy Lafleur, Wayne Gretzky, Mario Lemieux, Patrick Roy. There was Paul Kariya, the NHL's newest star, watching from the stands. There were television cameras. There were the more than ten thousand fans, the noise like an explosion every time something happened on the ice. And there were the Beauport Nordiques, the crowd favourites, up against the Screech Owls for the divisional championship trophy.

The crowd no longer intimidated Travis. He seemed to take energy from the roar. He still tingled with the surprise of his greeting, still thrilled at the memory of tilting his stick in salute. And he had hit the crossbar during the warm-up.

Sarah seemed inspired by her seven velvet pucks. She played as if possessed by the spirit of Lafleur. She was all over the ice, checking, attacking, never out of position, never selfish with the puck. Twice she fed Dmitri with breakaway passes, only to have the marvellous Beauport goaltender turn Dmitri away. Once she fed the puck to Travis, coming in fast on left wing, and he ripped a shot that just hit the wrong side of the crossbar. Had it struck the underside, the Owls would be leading. But it struck the top and flew into the crowd, a throng of excited kids scrambling for the souvenir.

But the story today was Nish. Travis had no idea what it was – Paul Kariya's presence, envy over Sarah's velvet pucks, the chance to win the Quebec Peewee – but whatever it was, it was bringing out the best in Nish's game.

Twice in the first period alone, Nish saved goals on plays that already had Jeremy beaten. Once he fell, sliding, and swept away a puck one of the Beauport forwards was about to slip into the open side of the Owls' net. Once he went down on his knees behind Jeremy, who was out of the play, and took a hard, point-blank shot from a Beauport defender straight in the chest, then batted the rebound away with a baseball swing of his stick before the puck could land back in the Owls' crease.

On the ice, Travis had no time to think. The game was so fast, so unpredictable, the action end-to-end and furious. The crowd roared with each rush, cheered each good defensive play. Travis felt wonderful, as if he were part of a huge, well-oiled machine that was demonstrating hockey as it should be played. He was honoured to be part of this game, pleased that he could be out there with these wonderful peewee players and fit right in. Not only that, he was *captain* of one of the teams.

On the bench, Travis could watch – and think. He was inspired by how hard the other Owls were working: Andy all over the ice, little Simon leading rush after rush, Jeremy Weathers leaping to cover rebounds, Jesse Highboy throwing himself in front of shots, Lars ragging the puck until he could see his pass, Data always back, always dependable.

The Nordiques scored first again. Travis was on the ice, and a pass from Nish came too high along the boards for him to handle. The Nordiques' defenceman cradled the puck in his skates, kicked it up to his stick, and sent it fast across the ice to the far winger, waiting just to the side of the goal. Jeremy stopped the one-timer, but Beauport's big centre swiped the rebound out of the air and sent it high into the net.

"My fault," Travis said as he skated back to the bench.

"No," said Nish. "Mine. Bad pass."

The next shift out, Nish made up for it. He intercepted a Beauport pass just beyond centre and stepped around his check before rapping a hard pass off the boards that Dmitri took in full flight.

Dmitri led his defenceman off into the corner and used the boards to drop the puck back to Sarah. He knew she'd be coming in behind. She picked up the puck, moved toward the slot, and hit Travis perfectly on the tape as he broke for the net. He shot as soon as he felt the weight of the puck. The puck flew high – too high, Travis thought at first – and then clicked in off the underside of the crossbar.

Owls 1, Nordiques 1.

"*Un bon but.* Good goal," the winger opposite said as they lined up for the face-off at centre.

Travis looked up. It was the same winger who'd dumped him last game, the one who'd sarcastically said, "*Je t'aime.*" But this time there was no sarcasm.

"Thanks," Travis said. Then, as an afterthought: "*Merci.*"

The game remained tied 1–1 until there were only ten minutes to go. The crowd was still screaming. The game remained as fast-paced and intense as it had been on that first shift.

Nish again made the key play when he executed a give-and-go with Sarah coming out of the Owls' end. He stickhandled behind his own net, then hit Sarah as she came back over the blueline and cut to the right. The moment Nish passed, he took off, heading straight up ice, and Sarah returned the puck to him on her backhand, the play catching the Beauport forwards by surprise.

Nish put his head down, his skates sizzling even on the chewed-up ice. Travis dug in hard, double-stepping on his right skate before completing his turn and pushing hard on his left skate, his leg fully extended and a flick of his ankle giving him one final surge along the ice.

Nish looked up and saw him. He shifted slightly to pass, Travis hurrying to get a step on the defenceman, who was reading the play. Travis had just enough on him to be free.

Nish tossed the puck ahead of Travis, who was able to scoop it off the boards in full flight.

The defenceman had turned and was giving chase. Travis thought he had the angle, but didn't quite. The defenceman was on him by the blueline, and even with him as he crossed.

He had only the back pass left! Travis knew what Muck had told him. He knew what had happened last game. *But there was no other play!*

He knew Nish. Travis knew he would still be coming hard. He could hear Nish's stick pounding the ice: the signal that he wanted the puck.

Travis just had time to slip the puck onto his backhand. The defenceman was on him, reaching, ready to bowl him over if necessary. Travis waited, waited, and just as the defenceman completely committed to checking him, he dumped the pass blind behind his back. He spun round as he and the defenceman fell.

Nish had the puck! It had hit his stick perfectly. Travis couldn't have sent a better pass if he had drawn it with a pencil and ruler.

Nish was in, the last Beauport defender racing to cover him. He waited, then did the spinnerama move he usually only dared in practice, spinning right around with his back to the defenceman and carrying the puck past.

The defenceman turned, catching Nish just as he tossed the puck off to Dmitri, who was in all alone.

The crowd roared, and like a thousand jack-in-the-boxes they sprang up in their seats.

Dmitri faked once and drilled a hard shot for the high far side.

Travis was already moving his stick into the air to cheer when the Beauport goalie's blocker flashed high and knocked the puck away.

Nish, still barrelling in past the last defender, picked up the rebound. He turned, moving the puck to his backhand, and was actually skating backwards as he reached around the falling goalie and slipped the puck, barely, into the far side.

Owls 2, Nordiques 1.

Nish hit the boards and crumpled – not hurt, but very happy. He lay there grinning and pumping his fists, waiting for the pile-on.

"*A great goal!*" Travis shouted. "*A video highlighter!*"

"*You did it, Nish!*" shouted Dmitri. "*You did it!*"

Nish had done it – but there were still ten minutes left.

"*No more fancy stuff!*" Muck shouted, as he sent them back out for the face-off.

Travis felt he was speaking directly to him. No more behind-the-back passes, that was for sure. But it *had* worked!

Muck wanted defensive hockey, and that is what he got. With Sarah killing time by hanging on to the puck and circling ever backwards, the Owls waited until the frustrated Nordiques charged and then dumped – trying at least to cross centre ice first so they wouldn't cause an icing.

When the Beauport team charged, Nish was there. Diving, sliding, and throwing himself across the ice, he broke up play after play, until after one whistle he lay on the ice, completely exhausted. It was the strangest thing Travis had ever seen in a hockey rink. Nish lay there, gasping, and some of the fans began clapping.

The applause rose until everyone in the rink was clapping.

Then, as Nish picked himself up off the ice, they rose, and delivered the most incredible standing ovation Travis had ever seen. Even under his helmet, he could feel the hair on the back of his head standing up.

As Nish made his way to the bench, his head hanging down, his stick dragging, the Beauport team decided to pull its goaltender for the extra attacker.

Muck called the one time out he was allowed, and the Owls skated over to hear what he had to say. But Muck said nothing; he stood behind the bench, Mr. Dillinger at his shoulder, and stared at Nish, gasping on the end of the bench, waiting for him to catch his breath.

Finally, with the referee signalling the end to the time out, Nish looked up and caught Muck's eye.

"Can you go?" Muck asked.

Nish couldn't even speak. He nodded once and jumped the boards, the rink again exploding into cheers.

What fantastic hockey fans, Travis thought. When Muck said they knew their hockey better than any fans in the world, he wasn't kidding. They came wanting Beauport to win, but they knew that they had seen the most extraordinary effort imaginable from both teams, particularly the heavyset, red-faced defenceman for the Owls, and they were bound to give the Screech Owls and Nish their due.

With their extra attacker, the Nordiques charged relentlessly. Even with Sarah out for the entire final shift, the Owls couldn't gain control of the puck. They couldn't score on the empty net. They couldn't even get an icing.

If it hadn't been for Nish, all would have been lost.

He dived head first to knock a sure goal away from the big Beauport centre. He threw himself into the net three times to block scramble shots that Jeremy couldn't hold. He took the puck off the big centre and faked a rush outside, sending the Nordiques players over the blueline, then circling back into his own end and, with the centre giving chase, heading as fast towards his own goal as he might have rushed the Nordiques' net.

Nish whipped around the net, the big centre right behind him, and dropped the puck onto the backhand so it hit the boards and bounced out again, nestling against the back of the net.

Nish turned instantly and grabbed the puck he had left behind as the big Beauport centre flew out of the play. He stick-handled patiently, then lifted the puck high towards the clock. It slapped back down on the ice just as the horn sounded to end the greatest championship game the Owls had ever played.

They had won the Quebec Peewee!

17

ravis Lindsay thought he knew what a great roar was. But he had no idea. What he had heard during his introduction, what he had heard during the presentation of Sarah's sweater, was nothing compared to the roar that went up when they announced the Most Valuable Player for the C division of the Quebec International Peewee Tournament.

". . . WAYNE NISHHHHHHI-KAAWWAAAAAA!"

Players on both sides began banging their sticks on the ice in tribute. The fans, every single one of them, were already on their feet, cheering, screaming, yelling. The noise was deafening.

"*Oh no!*" Nish said, as he spun in a frantic circle beside Travis.

"*What?*" Travis asked.

Then he saw.

The MVP award was to be presented by Paul Kariya. The NHL star had a large silver trophy in his arms, and he was smiling in Nish's direction.

"*I can't go!*" Nish said.

"*Get over there!*" Travis shouted, hoping he could be heard above the cheering.

Reluctantly, red-faced, Nish laid his stick down at his feet and then his gloves. He took off his helmet, the cheers rising, and handed it to Travis, then skated slowly over to where Paul Kariya was waiting with the trophy.

Nish was beet red by the time he got there.

Paul Kariya reached out, shook his hand, and gave him the trophy. Then he grabbed Nish and hugged him, the crowd erupting with an even greater cheer.

Travis could see Paul Kariya whispering something in Nish's ear. Perhaps he was shouting. He would have to shout to be heard above this.

Nish came back, redder still, but smiling. He raised the MVP trophy as a tribute to the crowd, then to the Beauport team, which made the cheering fans go wild.

"What'd he say to you?" Travis said as Nish gathered his gloves back up.

"Who?" Nish asked.

Travis couldn't believe it. "*Paul Kariya! What did he say?*"

"Oh, that," Nish said nonchalantly. "Just, 'Nice game, cousin.' That's all."

Travis looked at him in shock. Nish was grinning from ear to ear, both arms around his trophy.

They had brought the championship trophy out on the ice. A swarm of officials had gathered, and the man in the blue blazer with the microphone was moving towards the shining silver cup.

Travis could hear his name being called. He could hear the crowd cheering him as he skated.

But he wasn't thinking at all about being captain, or about the cheers. He wasn't even thinking about how, so many years ago, "Terrible Ted" Lindsay of the Detroit Red Wings had hoisted the Stanley Cup high above his head and thus established a grand tradition for victorious team captains ever since.

Travis would do all that. And he would then hand it off, first to Sarah, and then Nish. He knew he would be bringing Monsieur and Madame Dupont, his billets, out on the ice so they could hold it too. He knew that he would ask for a photograph of him and Nicole with it, something to have that would forever remind him of this wonderful, miraculous moment.

But before any of that he had something else to do. He tried to clear his mind and think only of what Sarah and Nicole had taught him since that moment they dragged him off to "school."

He had shaken the officials' hands. He had the championship trophy in his arms. But now he reached for the microphone.

The man in the blue blazer seemed a little surprised, but he smiled and handed it over.

Travis cleared his throat. He knew the roaring was dying down, the cheers were stopping. They were quieting down to hear what he had to say.

His hand was shaking as he brought the microphone up to his face.

"*Merci beaucoup, mes amis,*" he began.

"*C'est pour moi et les autres Screech Owls le plus grand honneur des nos vies de hockey . . .*"

He continued without hesitation, his mind remembering perfectly the words and pronunciations that Nicole and Sarah had drilled into him.

He thanked the fans.

He thanked *"le magnifique"* team standing opposite, the Beauport Nordiques.

He thanked the Quebec Peewee Tournament organizers.

He thanked the City of Quebec.

He could have gone on. But no one – not any of the players on the ice, not Muck or any of the coaches, not one of the ten thousand fans – would have heard a word Travis Lindsay was saying over the enormous roar that went up.

The loudest roar of a most extraordinary day.

THE END

The Screech Owls' Home Loss

1

"*L*ook outside!"

It seemed such an absurd order; Travis Lindsay could not yet see *inside*, let alone look out. His eyes were still sticky with sleep, his mind in another world. His own voice seemed like it belonged to some dim-witted creature, not even human, as he tried to speak into the cordless phone.

"*Whuh?*"

"*Look outside!*" Nish shouted again at the other end, loud enough this time that Travis's mother, still standing by the bed after handing her son the telephone, heard and answered for him.

"*He's awake, Nish!*" she called out towards the receiver. Travis blinked upwards. His mother was laughing at him as he struggled to surface from a deep, deep sleep.

"Nish is right," Mrs. Lindsay said to Travis. "Get up and have a look."

Travis rubbed his eyes. He checked the clock radio: 7:03 a.m. Too early even for school. And it was *Saturday*, wasn't it? *What was Nish up to?*

"*He's moving, Nish!*" Mrs. Lindsay called towards the receiver.

Travis set the phone down on his pillow and pushed back his covers. He instantly wished he could dive straight back under them, burrowing into their warmth and slipping back into the magnificent sleep that had just been stolen from him. He fought off the urge and struggled to his feet, stretching and yawning hard as his mother, still laughing, stepped back to let him pass. Behind her, Travis could see his father standing in the doorway with a cup of coffee in his hand. He was trying to blow onto the steaming cup, but he couldn't purse his lips properly. He was laughing too. *What on earth could be so funny about looking outside?*

Travis scratched his side and chewed on the stale taste of sleep as he all but staggered towards the window. His mother reached out in front of him, yanking the heavy curtains back.

Travis reacted as if he'd just been blindsided by a hard check. The window seemed to explode with light, like a million flash-bulbs firing at once.

He stepped back, his hands over his eyes. In the background he could hear Nish's voice squeaking like a mouse as he continued to shout over the telephone, which lay, completely ignored, on Travis's pillow.

Travis rubbed his eyes hard, the light still flashing red and yellow and orange in the front of his brain. He rubbed and waited, peeking first through his fingers as he approached the window again. It was still too bright, the light like blinding needles, but slowly his eyes adjusted. Still squinting, he moved closer to the window, the glass quickly fogging with his breath, then clearing as he stood back slightly.

The world had turned to glass!

Travis looked out over the backyard, out past Sarah Cuthbertson's big house on the hill, and off towards the river and the lookout that sat high over the town of Tamarack. *Glass!* Glass everywhere: shining, sparkling, silver down along the river, golden along the tip of Lookout Hill where the sun was just cresting, hard steel along the streets of the town that lay still shaded for the moment by the hills to the east.

The window was fogging up again. Travis pressed a fist against the cold glass, circling to clear the window. The condensation clung to his skin, cold and wet and tickling.

He blinked again. The sight reminded Travis of a counter at the jewellery store owned by Fahd's uncle, diamonds shimmering under bright lights, expensive crystal glittering on glass displays.

A town truck was moving down River Street, heading for the road up towards the lookout. The truck was spreading a shower of sand, the silver road turning brown as the truck crept slowly along. But at the turn for the bridge and the hill, the truck kept sliding down River Street, the wheels spinning uselessly, the big vehicle turning, slowly, like a large boat, until eventually it crunched sideways into an ice-covered snowbank.

Travis could see children outside a home on King Street. They were stepping as if they were walking on a tightrope rather than a wide street. One went down, smack on his back, and slid helplessly. The other youngster leapt after the first one, spinning wildly.

There was an urgent squeak at Travis's ear.

"*Ya see it?*"

Travis turned quickly, almost jumping. His mother was holding the phone out for him. He had forgotten all about Nish!

Travis took the phone. "*Neat!*"

"*Whatdya mean, 'neat'?*" Nish's voice now barked clearly over the telephone. "*It's awesome! It's amazing! It's unbelievable! C'mon – we gotta get out on it. Grab your skates!*"

Nish didn't even wait for an answer. He slammed his own phone down so hard Travis winced.

Grab your skates? It looked more like Travis should be grabbing a rope and a bucket of sand – perhaps even his father's spike-soled golf shoes – to walk on that. But he saw Nish's point: Tamarack had turned into the world's largest skating rink.

"It's called *verglas*," said Mr. Lindsay after Travis had handed his mother back the cordless phone. "At least that's what my friend Doug's grandfather called it. He was an old Scot, and he said he'd seen it only three times in his life. This is the second time for me."

"What is it?" Travis asked. He was back at the window, clearing a porthole with the side of his fist.

"You have to have a deep thaw followed immediately by a deep freeze – and no snow in between. It's a freak of nature. Beautiful – but dangerous."

Travis looked out and thought about the last week. Tamarack had seen record snowfalls through January – the snow was piled so high along the streets that pedestrians stumbling along the sidewalks couldn't see the cars passing alongside them. But then, on the first of February, a south wind came in, bringing record-high temperatures. Nish had even turned up for hockey practice in shorts and sunglasses.

Then it had rained. Not enough to melt the snow, but enough to turn the streets to ponds. And just last night the winds had suddenly shifted, and a bitter cold front had moved in from the north. The thermometer outside the kitchen window had fallen so fast it seemed to have sprung a leak. The cold was so deep that twice during the evening the Lindsays had gone to the window when maple trees in the backyard had cracked like rifle fire.

"That's what Old Man Gibson called it," said Mr. Lindsay. "*Verglas.* It don't know what it means. Gaelic for something to do with 'glass,' I suppose. You can see why."

"How long did it last?" asked Mrs. Lindsay.

"Only a couple of days. But if I had to pick two winter days out of my childhood I'd never want to forget, I'd probably take those two. Maybe because they closed the schools down and no one could even get to work."

"They closed the schools?" asked Travis.

"It's Saturday," said Travis's mother, crushing his hopes.

Mr. Lindsay went on, lost in his own memories: "They put chains over their car tires back then. That was before they sanded the roads. The chains would bite into the ice so they could get a grip. We used to grab onto the back bumpers of the cars and they'd drag us on our rubber boots up and down the streets."

"*Charles!*" Mrs. Lindsay said abruptly.

But Mr. Lindsay was laughing, enjoying a sweet memory. "We called it 'hitching.' It was kind of like waterskiing, except it was winter, and we were being pulled around by cars, not motorboats."

"You're lucky you weren't killed," said Mrs. Lindsay.

"I guess," Mr. Lindsay answered slowly. "But cars went a lot slower back then, and there weren't as many on the road."

"*Still!*" she said.

"You're right. I wouldn't recommend it now. But you kids should get out there and skate on it. It's a once-in-a-lifetime experience."

"You've seen it twice," Travis corrected.

"Yes," his father said. "But I was only young once."

Mr. Lindsay went to the window. He was smiling, but it seemed to Travis a sad smile. Then his father turned, slapping his hands together to break the spell.

"You'd better get dressed, young man."

Travis looked out in the direction his father had been gazing. A thick-set young man in a blue Screech Owls jacket and cap was churning full force around the corner, his skates digging deep where normally there would have been pavement.

The young skater kicked out suddenly and flew through the air – like a wrestler going for the throat – until he slammed, side down and laughing, onto the slope of the road. The ice offered no resistance, and followed by his stick, gloves, and hat, the youngster came spinning and sliding like a fat hockey puck straight towards the Lindsay driveway.

It was Nish, coming to call.

2

ne by one, the Screech Owls found each other. It was as if centre ice had become the intersection of River and Cedar and Muck had blown his whistle for them all to assemble. Sarah was out – her long, graceful stride as powerful and elegant down River Street as it had ever been at the Tamarack Memorial Arena. Lars Johanssen, with two sticks over his shoulder, came kicking a puck between his skates along Cedar Street. Jeremy Weathers, stiff and unsure in his goalie skates, came with Dmitri Yakushev from the apartments down by the frozen river. Data, Fahd Noorizadeh, Gordie Griffith, Jesse Highboy, Andy Higgins, little Simon Milliken, Liz Moscovitz, Chantal Larochelle, Jenny Staples in her goalie skates and thick street-hockey pads, carrying a bent and torn street-hockey net over her shoulder. From the other direction, pushing an equally bent and torn net ahead of him as he skated towards the gathering of Owls, came Derek Dillinger.

"*Not here!*" shouted Nish, whose face was already beet red and covered in sweat.

"Where, then?" Jenny shouted, dropping the net with a clatter.

"*The creek!*"

Of course, the creek. Behind Derek Dillinger's house was a large field belonging to Derek's uncle, who grew corn and oats and raised beef on the edge of town. A creek ran from the woods and twisted down through the fields, past the school and the rink, and emptied into the river.

A few times in other winters they had gone out with shovels and cleared off an area for a game of shinny. It was hard work, though, and the ice was often bumpy, with cracks that could catch a skate blade and twist an ankle. Today's ice, however, was as smooth as marble.

"*Let's go!*" Derek shouted.

They skated down the streets and across the lawns. They dug in to go up hills and leaned back to go down them. They skated to the end of King Street, crossed the glassed-over highway, then slid down the embankment and under the barbed-wire fence — now rendered harmless by thick sleeves of crystal-clear ice — to where the frozen creek spread across the open field.

Nish had chosen well. At first they were content just to skate around the field, laughing as they danced through the corn stubble on the far side, and then barrelling together through a stand of bulrushes that snapped and shattered like fine glass as they passed, the sparkling shards ringing on the ice as they spun away.

"*Let's play!*" Travis shouted. He was captain. He was taking charge.

Travis threw his stick down, and the others followed suit. Travis then waded into the pile, randomly grabbing up and tossing the sticks, half of them towards Nish, half towards Data.

"You two are the captains," he said.

Travis finished dividing the sticks and stood back. "Pick up your sticks and stay with your captain," he said. The Owls chased after their sticks, picked them up, and began looking around to see who was playing with whom. Sarah reached out and gently slapped Dmitri's tuque; the two linemates were still together.

"No fair!" said Nish. "They got all the speed."

"Don't worry about it," Travis said. "We'll make them play into the wind."

"Yeah," Nish said, looking up with a sly grin. "Good idea."

Travis told Jeremy to take one of the nets and start skating until he reached the gate at the far end of the field. Jenny was to take her net and head towards the fence by the road. The distance between the nets would be, approximately, four hockey rinks. The fences on either side of the field would form the "boards."

"What're the rules?" asked Fahd, who always had to know the rules.

"There are none," said Nish, with a fake snarl.

"No body contact," said Travis. "No hoists on goal. No slapshots. Everything else goes."

And everything did. With no offsides, Nish, with his good wrist shot, could make a pass that almost took the puck out of sight before Travis, bolting across the field at top speed, caught up with it and came down, coasting, onto the flat ice of the creek and in on Jenny, who was backing up fast and kicking out her foam-rubber pads in anticipation.

Travis came in and stopped hard, the good sharp of his skates sending up a swirl of snow that temporarily blinded them both as it flashed like fireworks in the sun. Jenny instinctively turned from the spray, and Travis, laughing, tucked the puck behind her on an easy backhand.

"*Cheater!*" Jenny shouted. But she, too, was laughing.

Sarah and Dmitri got the goal back quickly on a European-style, circling, end-to-end "rush" that took almost five minutes and left the two of them, and every other Screech Owl, flat on their backs and gasping for air.

"In Russia," Dmitri said, panting, "we call this *bandy*."

"In Canada," growled Nish, also short of breath and flat on his back, "we call it 'hog.'"

"No," said Dmitri, "really – *bandy* is a game. Curved sticks, a ball, a huge ice surface like this, and lots and lots of players. Hockey developed from it."

"Russia *invented* hockey?" said Nish with enormous suspicion. "Is that what you're saying?"

"As much as anyone else did, I guess."

Nish howled with laughter. "And what else did you invent? Big Macs? Nintendo? *The wheel?*"

"Who do *you* think invented it?"

"We did, of course. The Stanley Cup is *Canadian*, not *Russian* – or perhaps you didn't notice."

"There are paintings," countered Dmitri, "that show kids

playing something that looks a lot like hockey in Holland more than five hundred years ago."

"Paintings aren't photographs," said Nish.

"*What?*" said Sarah, sitting up, a look of astonishment on her face.

"You can paint anything you want. I want proof."

"They didn't *have* cameras five hundred years ago!" Sarah shouted.

"That's just my point," he said, smiling smugly. "Then there's no real proof, is there."

"You're impossible!" said Sarah, scrambling to her feet.

"You're nuts!" said Dmitri, also getting up.

"I'm right," said Nish. "And you all know it."

Travis lay on the ice, shaking his head in amazement at the ridiculous way Nish's brain could sometimes work. He'd seen it in school a few times, and he'd seen teachers stare at Nish as if he'd just been dropped in on the classroom from another planet.

"*Will you look at that!*" Sarah shouted as she bent to pick up her stick.

Everyone turned to see. At the far end of the field, four large figures were standing at the fence, trying to figure out how to get over. Then one climbed up, leapt over the top, and landed on his skates, sliding and shouting. It was Ty, the Owls' assistant coach. And right behind Ty, also leaping over the iced-over barbed wire, was Barry, the other assistant, also in skates. And behind Barry, tossing over a pile of hockey sticks, was Mr. Dillinger, his bald head covered only with earmuffs, which seemed hopelessly inadequate.

And right behind Mr. Dillinger was *Muck!*

Mr. Dillinger's brother, the farmer who owned these fields, must have telephoned him, and Mr. Dillinger – who could never turn down a chance to be a kid again – must have called the two assistant coaches, who also loved to play shinny.

But Muck?

Muck Munro wasn't one for playing around. The coach often suggested to the Owls that a game of street hockey or a round of pond shinny was twice as good as a practice, but for him to come out and play as well was very, very unusual. He had that bad leg, after all, and sometimes it seemed he was having difficulty just getting through a hard practice.

But Muck was up the fence and over, his bad leg wiggling uncertainly for a moment as his skates hit the hard ice on the other side. The four figures came across the field to the rousing cheers of the Screech Owls, all of whom were now back on their feet and collecting their sticks.

Ty and Barry, both fine skaters who, as junior players, had for many years been coached by Muck Munro, were flying over the ice. Muck was coming slowly, businesslike. Mr. Dillinger, with his ankles bending terribly, was struggling, but even in the distance they could hear his high-pitched, uncontrolled laughter. Good old Mr. Dillinger. Game for anything. Any time.

Muck came up to the circle of Owls and stopped. He had his whistle around his neck. He blew it.

"Okay," he said. "You're loosened up. Let's work on a few drills."

"*Not a practice!*" Nish howled.

"And why not, Nishikawa?" Muck asked, looking sternly on his favourite target.

"They said on the radio that the rink was closed, everything cancelled."

Muck looked around, as if for the first time. "Rink looks fine to me, Nishikawa."

He blew his whistle again. "Okay, we have a big game against Orillia next Friday. I want to see some breakouts and sharp passing, understand?"

Travis could hear Nish sigh behind him: "Geez."

"Old crocks against young hotshots," Muck said, smiling now. "But we get Sarah's line and Jenny in net, okay?"

It took a moment for the announcement to sink in. Muck wanted to play! They had come to join in the shinny game! Travis felt a shiver go up his back. He had never seen Muck play before, only heard about him: the brilliant junior career, the shattered leg in the pile-up, the operation that didn't quite work, the end of Muck Munro's great dream of one day playing in the National Hockey League.

"ALLL-RIGHTTTT!" Nish screamed right into Travis's ear. Travis winced, but began shouting himself.

Travis and Sarah and Dmitri were lined up at centre, waiting for Data to flip the puck in the air between Sarah and Andy for the opening face-off. Behind Travis, waiting with his stick perfectly poised on the ice like some old 1950s hockey card, was Muck. To Muck's side was Ty, then Barry, with Mr. Dillinger barely holding his balance behind them, and far behind them all, Jenny was kicking out her foam-rubber pads, ready.

Never had skating felt so sweet and fun. With no boards to consider, Travis could let his feet go where they wished. He could turn at will, skating backwards or forwards whenever he felt like it. Sarah picked up the puck, circled twice, and dropped it back to Muck, who took the pass perfectly and hit Travis with a single stride and a long, hard pass that sent him straight up the creek and free.

Muck's pass had felt different on Travis's stick. Strong, sure, accurate, it hit the blade so hard it nearly knocked the stick out of his hand.

An NHL pass. That was the phrase Muck always used when he talked to them about the importance of making sure passes got through, how accuracy and speed won hockey games, not soft passes that people had to slow for or reach for. Travis hadn't varied his speed a moment for the pass to arrive perfectly.

Travis came in on Nish, his friend backing up wildly, laughing and pointing the blade of his stick at Travis's face, taunting him. Travis could hear skates sizzling up alongside him, then breaking away. Heavy skates – Ty in full flight. He flipped the puck, hoping Ty would catch it on the far side of Nish, and it worked perfectly. Ty was in alone, but without looking, he passed hard straight back down the ice, and the puck cracked hard and sure on another stick: Muck was coming straight through centre.

Nish turned back, still laughing, and lunged at the oncoming coach. Muck very casually slipped the puck through Nish's feet, and then, as he passed by, reached with his stick and dumped Nish flat on his back, sending him crashing into a stand of bulrushes.

Muck, a huge grin on his face now, snapped a wicked pass

that shot under Travis's stick, past Ty, and hit Sarah coming in on the fly. The pass was so perfect it shot like a laser in a science-fiction movie. Sarah faked once, slid the puck across to Dmitri, and Dmitri tipped the puck into the side of the open net.

"*No fair!*" Nish was screaming. "*No fair! It doesn't count! I got dumped!*"

"What are you talking about?" Muck said as he tapped Sarah for her play.

"*You dumped me!*" Nish wailed.

"You fell over your own big feet, Nishikawa. Everyone saw what happened."

"*No way! You dumped me! Didn't he, Trav.*"

"Not that I saw," said Travis.

"Anybody see it?" asked Muck.

"Not me," said Ty.

"He fell," said Barry.

"Fell," said Data, who was on Nish's team.

Nish was spinning around, his face twisting in fury. He looked like he was going to explode. He screwed his eyes shut, then stared hard at Muck for a moment.

"I'll get you back for that," he vowed.

For another hour they played, until the sweat was rolling down their spines and their shirts and jackets and pants were damp. Mr. Dillinger's horseshoe of thin hair was soaking wet and there was sweat dripping off Muck's chin.

But no one – no one – was as wet as Nish, who played like he was possessed, carrying the puck, passing the puck, driving the net, trying always, without success, to dump Muck Munro whenever he came close.

"He can play this game when he wants to," Muck said after Nish made one magnificent rush that resulted in a pretty goal by Jesse Highboy.

Travis knew what Muck meant. You had to fire Nish up – bug him a little – to find the hockey player that was hidden inside. And nobody was better at firing him up than their coach, Muck Munro.

Muck blew his whistle, serious this time.

"I don't want anybody catching cold," he said. "Everyone head home now and change into something dry."

The Owls all groaned. No one wanted to quit. But everyone knew that Muck was right. It was time.

"This is the way the game was meant to be played," Muck said. "Good workout, all of you – even you, Nishikawa."

Travis looked at Nish, who was beaming through his sweat. Nish clearly knew he had put on a great performance, and he probably also knew how Muck had inspired it.

3

n the evening it began to snow. It snowed hard, all through the night, and when Travis woke on Sunday morning, his bedroom window was covered with frost on the inside, and half covered with soft, pillowy snow piled up on the sill outside. The frost was beautiful. It looked like intricately painted white feathers.

With the back of his hand, Travis wiped away the icy feathers and looked out on the town. It seemed a world removed from the strange and beautiful landscape of the day before. Where yesterday had been hard as glass, today was soft and familiar as a quilt comforter: Tamarack under snow, the morning after a heavy fall.

And yet this day was just as different as the day before. Usually a big snowfall meant snowploughs and sanders and salt trucks working through the night, but today the streets were blocked. The heavy snowfall was like a throw rug over a newly waxed, slippery hardwood floor, dangerous to the step, nearly impossibly to plough.

Travis, yawning and scratching his sides, wandered into the kitchen. The radio was on low in the background, an announcer reading a long list of cancellations due to weather.

"There's a pot of porridge on," his mother said. "Cream of wheat – help yourself."

Travis began spooning the thick, sticky porridge into a bowl. His father was at the kitchen window. He was leaning over, craning to see past the bird feeder and into the sky.

"It's clouding over," he said. "I think we're in for more of it."

@

Nish telephoned in the early afternoon. Some of the other Owls were heading out to the hill over by the school, and Nish wanted Travis to bring some cardboard for them to slide on.

It turned out they hardly needed the hill. Travis, hanging onto two large sides cut from a cardboard box, virtually glided down River Street to Cedar, where Nish was waiting for him.

There were two perfect channels in the snow where Nish had slid across the intersection and landed, flat on his back, in the snowbank on the far side. He lay there, calmly picking up mittfuls of snow and dropping them into his open mouth as if they were juicy grapes.

"No school tomorrow," Nish announced as Travis came, slipping and sliding, to an uneasy stop beside him.

"How do you know?"

"No way they're going to get the streets cleared in time. My dad says they can't even get the trucks out onto the road."

"I liked it better yesterday," said Travis.

"So did I," agreed Nish. "Best winter's day in history."

Travis didn't bother to argue. Christmas was usually pretty good, and so was Travis's birthday, March 18. But he knew Nish's way of talking only too well. Everything was either the best thing that had ever happened, or the worst thing that had ever happened. In between didn't exist for Nish. In between, Travis smiled to himself, was where the rest of the world – the real world – lived.

They set off for the hill by the schoolyard, dragging their cardboard behind them. Data and Andy were already there and had their own supply of cardboard, which flattened the fresh snow against the ice below and made a slick, quick run that took them flying down the hill and right out across the schoolyard where, eventually, they came to a halt. Nish, with his extra weight – and, Andy claimed, a little bit of cheating – set a "New World Record" for distance, reaching the far side of the playground on one great run.

Slowly, the Owls gathered. Sarah and Jenny showed up together, followed by Liz. Jesse Highboy came wearing a pair of mukluks from James Bay, soft rabbit-skin boots that let him slide so easily the rest of the Owls were able to stand in a circle in the schoolyard and send him skidding and bouncing back and forth like a pinball. Dmitri came, and Lars, Derek, Wilson, Jeremy, Simon – one by one they arrived until virtually the entire Screech Owls team was assembled at the schoolyard, the very place that next day most of them were hoping to avoid.

"A *new* New World Record!" Nish announced grandly from the top of the hill. "Guaranteed!"

Everyone stood back and watched him preparing to leap, like a belly-flopper, off the crest of the hill and onto the cardboard slide.

A car horn honked loudly.

"Thank you," Nish waved toward the car. "Thank you very much. Thank you."

The horn blew again.

"He's not honking at you!" Andy shouted. "He's stuck!"

Nish paid no attention. Presuming, as always, that the entire world was watching him, cheering him on, he leapt out into the air and landed, with a puff of light snow, on the top of the run.

The car horn honked again, longer this time.

"Let's see if we can push him out!" Jesse called to the rest of the Owls.

"C'mon!" called Jeremy.

"He shouldn't even be out," said Sarah as she caught up to Travis.

"I can't make out who it is," said Travis.

The car was almost completely covered in snow. The driver had dug a round hole through the snow on the windshield, but otherwise there was no way of seeing in or out. The back window was buried. The side windows were caked with snow.

"That's dangerous," said Sarah.

"Dangerous just to try driving in this," said Travis.

The driver's door opened, and the snow just above it on the roof broke off in a silent, white explosion, covering the red coat and hat attempting to emerge.

It was Mrs. Vanderhoof, an elderly woman from the apartments near the church. In a moment she was brushing away the

snow from her coat and face and seemed, somehow, both frightened and excited at the same time.

"Well," she said in a grand, theatrical voice, "*that* was quite
a ride!"

She was giggling and shaking at the same time.

"They haven't sanded the roads," said Sarah. "Cars can't get
anywhere."

"I can see that, my dear," Mrs. Vanderhoof said indulgently.
"I think I shall simply return home and wait for them to fix the
streets properly. This wouldn't have happened, young lady, if my
father were still the mayor of this poor town."

Mrs. Vanderhoof began getting back into her car. Sarah
winked at Travis and went to work trying to clear off a better
view for the old woman. She used her arms to sweep the windows clear, and some of the other Owls moved in to help.

Travis was amused by the way older people so often talked
about *the way things used to be.* It seemed nothing was ever as
good as the way things used to be. If he believed everything his
parents and grandparents – and people like Mrs. Vanderhoof –
told him, then surely the past had to be a world where the sun
always shone, where no one ever had any money but everyone
was far happier without it, where everyone was honest, where
the cuts of meat were always better, where a pop cost a nickel,
where people helped each other out, and, it seemed, where the
moment a snowflake struck the ground, a sander was standing
by to make sure no one slipped on it.

The automatic window on the driver's side groaned, then
gave, and as it lowered, the snow it was supporting dropped away,
sending a cloud of sparkling white in over Mrs. Vanderhoof's

shoulder and face. She practically spit through the snow as she
barked out her orders.

"You're going to have to push me out of here!" she commanded.

The Screech Owls crowded around the rear of the car
where the wheels had caught in the heavier snow. Some of the
kids pulled snow away with their arms. Others kicked it away
with their boots.

"*New World Record! New World Record!*"

None of them even turned as Nish, red and sweating, came
scrambling up the incline to where Mrs. Vanderhoof's car was
marooned.

"I beat – my old – record by twenty – feet!" he puffed.

"Who cares?" Sarah said. "Get back there and push!"

Nish looked shocked at her lack of interest, but he hurried
back to the rear of the car anyway, where the others were starting to push.

"I got a new world . . ." Nish began again.

But no one was listening.

"If we rock it enough," Andy was saying, "it'll come free."

"*Now!*" Data called. "*Now!*"

With Mrs. Vanderhoof gunning the engine, and the car
wheels screaming as they spun and found nothing but ice, the
Owls worked steadily, as a team. Finally, on one of Data's
mighty yells, the car lifted free and slid out onto the road again,
Mrs. Vanderhoof hauling the wheel the wrong way so the car
almost spun right around.

"*One-eighty!*" Simon shouted. "*Go for it, Mrs. Vanderhoof!*"

"Go easy on the gas," Sarah told her through the open window. "Take it easy and we'll push."

Mrs. Vanderhoof nodded and gripped the wheel as if she were a fighter pilot about to drop down through the clouds. Sarah turned so she wouldn't laugh and hurried to rejoin the rest of the Owls preparing to push once more.

"*Easy, now!*" Sarah shouted ahead to Mrs. Vanderhoof.

Mrs. Vanderhoof listened. She eased off on the gas, and, with the Owls pushing hard, the tires found some grip on the ice and the car began moving, slowly, back up the street.

They pushed until the road flattened out near Mrs. Vanderhoof's apartment building. Travis was working hard, his eyes closed. When he opened them, he realized that Mrs. Vanderhoof's was the only vehicle out on the road. The way back to her apartment was absolutely clear but for her own winding tracks through the snow; no one else had been foolish enough to try the roads before they were ploughed and sanded.

This must have been the way it was in the days before they salted and sanded the roads, thought Travis. This must have been what roads were like when they used chains on the tires. He remembered his father laughing when he talked about "hitching" in the good old days.

Why not? Travis thought. *Why not?*

4

he car was moving on its own, now. Most of the Owls had already let go as Mrs. Vanderhoof began gathering speed, the tires holding fairly well on the flat stretch.

"*Go!*" Nish called as he gave one last mighty push.

Travis was the last of them still hanging onto the car. He knew he, too, should push off. But he had to see what "hitching" felt like. He dropped down into a crouch, and grasped the bumper firmly.

He felt the ground rush under his feet; he was sliding along behind the car as if on air.

No wonder his father had compared it to waterskiing! Travis giggled as he felt the ice cobble of the road tickling the bottoms of his feet through his boot-soles. He was slipping along faster, now, the ground moving under him quickly and smoothly.

"TRAAA-VISSS! WHAT'RE YOU DOING?"

Travis giggled at the challenge in Nish's voice, the near anger. For once, Travis was the one misbehaving and Nish was acting sensibly.

He let go again with his right hand and waved.

Mrs. Vanderhoof slowed for the turn into her parking lot, and Travis dug hard, using the edges of his winter boots against the ice. The moment he felt them bite, he let go and flew on down the street, while Mrs. Vanderhoof, completely unaware that she had had a "hitcher," headed back into the safety of her parking lot.

Travis slid and slid, turning gracefully in his crouch as he travelled towards a waiting snowbank. He could hear the rest of the Owls, shouting and screaming as they chased after him.

"*Traaaaa-visssss!*"

"*YAY, TRAA-VISS!*"

There was no disapproval in Data's voice, or Andy's, or Jesse's, or even Sarah's. He could hear them all, running after him, as thrilled as he was by his father's old game of "hitching."

Nish was one of the first to reach Travis. Unlike the others, he seemed almost angry.

"*What're you doing?*"

"Hitching."

"*What?*"

"Hitching," Travis repeated.

"*What's that?*"

"My dad used to do it in the days before they salted and sanded the streets. He and his friends used to travel all over town that way."

"*They did?*" squealed Jenny. "*Neat!*"

"Awesome," said Simon.

"Some people do it on the country roads in Sweden," said Lars. "But it's against the law."

"It probably is here, too," said Travis. "Besides, you can't do it once the streets are salted. Your feet would catch and you'd go down face first."

"Sounds dangerous," said Sarah.

"Sounds *fun*," said Andy.

"Sounds *stupid*," said Nish.

"You're just jealous 'cause you weren't first," said Data, matter-of-factly.

No one else said anything. They all knew Data was right.

"*Let's go hitching!*" shouted Wilson.

"*Yeah!*"

"There's no other cars out," said Nish in a voice that would dampen spirits at a birthday party.

"Yes there is!" said Andy. "There goes one!"

There was indeed another car out, crawling slowly along the next street. It, too, had just a small spyhole cleared through the snow on the windshield, and another small hole on the window of the driver's side. Apart from that, the driver might as well have been in an army tank.

Before Travis could stop them, half of the Owls had broken away in a slipping, sliding run for the nearest intersection, where they waited for the car to ease down into a half stop and then "walk" through the turn onto River Street.

Andy was first to chase after the car and dip down to hitch onto the back bumper. Nish was second. The driver, his wing mirror caked in snow, his rear window buried, had no idea that they were there. They held tight, and the car swooshed them away over the frozen road.

The car turned again at Cedar Street, and both Andy and Nish

let go, yelling and screaming as they used the turn to launch themselves off in a long, spinning freestyle ride farther down River
Street. The others chased along, thrilled with their new game.

Travis felt a sudden burst of guilt. What if his father saw
them? What if something happened?

But what could happen? The roads were smooth with ice,
the banks were soft, enough snow had fallen to pad any falls, and
the cars were barely creeping along.

They played past dark. They set up a system where a couple of
Owls would struggle up the sliding hill by the school and spot
cars daring to chance the slippery streets. A call that one was
coming along Cedar would send a pack of Owls to the intersection, where they could hide until the driver – keeping his
eyes fixed warily on the road ahead – had almost passed. Then
they would scurry out, grab the bumper, and away. A call that a
car was coming up River would send them in another direction.

"*Cedar!*" Andy called out from the hill.

Andy was doing hill duty with Travis, and in the sweep of
headlights as the car turned onto Cedar and headed for the
intersection, Travis could see Owls scurrying. Data with his
head down, Nish jumping and rolling behind cover.

Nish wasn't complaining now, Travis thought. Of course by
now, Nish would believe he had invented the game. Soon he'd
be claiming a "New World Record" for hanging on to bumpers.

The car slowed, and Nish and Data slipped out, grabbed the
bumper, and were away down the street.

Travis was looking ahead of them up River. Headlights
were approaching, bouncing from one bank to the other.

Another car was coming. *And this one was out of control!*

"*River!*" he shouted.

Andy immediately saw the danger.

"*They better ditch!*" Andy shouted.

"DITCH!" Travis yelled.

"BAIL OUT! BAIL OUT!" Andy called, cupping his hands around his mouth.

But it was no use; they couldn't hear.

The car was coming too fast! It slipped from side to side, the headlights running up the nearest snowbank and splashing out for a moment over the schoolyard and up the hill to Travis and Andy.

Travis began running down the hill, slipping and calling at the same time.

"NISHHHHHH!" he called. "DITCH!"

The driver pulling the two "hitchers" swung to avoid the fishtailing vehicle, and his quick yank of the steering wheel sent the rear of his car sliding out over the centre of the road.

With the sudden movement Data lost his grip. He flew out across the road, rolling, with Nish hurtling right behind him.

"DAAAA-TA!" Travis called.

Travis and Andy watched helplessly as a terrible scene unfolded below them. Both cars jammed on their brakes, the wheels locking and sliding, hopelessly, on the ice. Data and Nish seemed to float at first, still unaware of the danger they were flying into. And then Data raised his arms to cover his face.

There was no *crash*, no screaming, no crunching of metal or glass or, for that matter, bones.

Just a *whumphhhh!* The sound of a pillow swung against a wall.

Not even a cry.

And a second later, another soft thud, the sound of Nish hitting next, farther down the side.

Then the sound of one car going up on the bank, the snow and ice crunching it to a halt. The sound of the other car finally catching, the wheels coming to a halt.

And the sound of Travis's own voice, screaming, "NNNN-OOOOOOOOOOOO!!"

5

ravis was first over the snowbank and down onto the road. The driver who had, without knowing it, been towing the two boys was already out of his car, the door wide open and the interior light casting an eerie glow onto the scene.

Nish was lying flat on his back, moaning, holding his arm.

Data was lying to the side, halfway up the bank, his head pushed down against his shoulder. He was silent, as if sleeping.

"What the hell's going on here?" the first driver shouted. There was anger in his voice, mixed with concern.

The door of the other car popped open, and the pale light inside revealed a large figure, huddled over the steering wheel, in a thick woollen tuque pulled down low.

The second driver made an uncertain move to get out, his galoshes catching on something and kicking it free so that it jumped out the door and fell, ringing, on the icy road.

Travis and Andy had to skirt the second car to reach their friends. Travis was so close he could feel the heat rising from the open door. And he could smell something. Something strong.

Alcohol!

"*Nish!*" Travis called. "*Data!*"

Nish was moaning, twisting his body so he could cradle his arm. He was starting to cry. If Nish was crying, he had to be hurt.

But still Data was silent, not even moving.

Travis headed for Nish; Andy for Data. Andy dropped down onto his knees, almost spinning into their injured friend.

"DON'T TOUCH HIM!"

It was Sarah, screaming at the top of her lungs.

"ANDY, DON'T TOUCH HIM!"

Andy backed off as if Data were suddenly too hot to touch. Sarah's scream had such urgency to it, such sureness, that he scrambled out of the way as Sarah and Jenny and several of the other Owls arrived at the scene.

"*He mustn't be moved!*" Sarah shouted. "*Somebody call an ambulance!*"

The driver of the second car, the one that had hit the boys, was half out of his car. Travis looked up from where he was crouched beside Nish, who was starting to cry louder from the pain. Travis couldn't make out a face; all he saw was someone large and unsteady. Then suddenly the bulky figure dropped back into the car and slammed the door.

"I've got a cellphone," the first driver said. He hurried to his open door and reached in towards the passenger seat.

The engine of the second car roared. There was a loud clunk as the transmission was forced into gear. The car jumped slightly, and then the tires caught.

"*Look out!*" Andy called. "*He's moving!*"

Travis had to push Nish farther to the side, raising a terrible, blood-curdling shriek from Nish, who was in no condition to move.

"STOP! STOP!" Sarah screamed at the driver, half crying. "CAN'T YOU SEE THERE ARE PEOPLE HURT HERE?!"

But he would not stop. The car lurched, shuddered, slid again. The wheels sang hideously on the ice, and the car jerked away, the Screech Owls scattering in its path.

"*We need the police here, too!*" the first driver shouted into his cellphone. "*And hurry, please!*"

There was such desperation in the man's voice that Travis shuddered.

"STOP! . . . STOP! . . . PLEASE STOP, BEFORE YOU HURT SOMEONE ELSE!" Sarah screamed after the departing car. But it was useless. Sobbing now, Sarah sank to her knees in the snow-covered street.

Travis pulled her up, and as Sarah regained her feet, still sobbing, he helped brush off the snow.

"How's Nish?" she asked.

"His arm might be broken," Travis told her. "Are you okay?"

"I'm fine!" she said, starting to run back. "Come on, we've got to make sure no one moves Data! He's hurt bad." She sobbed again. "Really bad."

They turned together, holding on to each other. Travis could feel Sarah shaking through her heavy winter clothes. Car headlights danced over her face, showing not only tears, but also a fury Travis had never imagined possible in one so kind and mild as Sarah.

There were more headlights approaching.
And sirens.
The ambulance was here.
And right behind the ambulance, the police.

6

Travis's mother and father sat up late with him that night. He'd tried to sleep, but couldn't.

He lay in his bed and tried to turn his thoughts away from everything that had happened, but each time he was about to drop off to sleep, the day's events would swarm back into his head.

His father was on the telephone. Mr. Lindsay had called the police, the hospital, Muck, Mr. Cuthbertson, Nish's parents, Data's parents, the police again.

"It seems no one got the licence-plate number," he said at the end of this final call. His voice sounded tired, discouraged.

Travis was drinking hot chocolate. It seemed to lessen the sting in his throat, but he still didn't think he could talk without starting to cry.

"What about the car?" Mrs. Lindsay asked.

Mr. Lindsay shook his head. "No identification. There was so much snow over it, none of the kids could even tell what kind it was, let alone what colour."

"The man who stopped, didn't he see anything?"

Mr. Lindsay shook his head sadly. "It was Art Desmond. The real-estate guy. He was using his cellphone when the other guy drove off. He didn't even get a look."

The police wanted to come around and talk to Travis in the morning. He wouldn't, after all, be going to school, but this was hardly the day off he and Nish and Data and the rest had imagined. Travis had no idea what he could tell them. He hadn't seen the driver's face. It was too dark, and his tuque had been pulled down too low.

Nish's parents telephoned from the hospital. Nish had a broken wrist, but apparently it had set easily. He'd have to wear a cast for four to six weeks.

"Then he'll be as good as ever," Mr. Lindsay explained.

Good as ever? Travis wondered. *Nish?* He was tempted to make a little joke, but the impulse quickly died.

The news about Data wasn't as promising.

"He's still in surgery," Mr. Lindsay said.

Two police officers came to the house to interview Travis. One was a young woman, who was very concerned about how he felt. The other was an older man, who acted almost as if the Owls were the real criminals here. Twice he told Travis they could be arrested for "hitching." Twice Travis told him they'd never do it again. He wished the policeman would believe him; he had never been more serious about anything.

They went over the facts again, but they didn't add up to much. Travis couldn't think of anything to help in their search for the missing driver.

"There was a bottle found at the scene," said the woman officer.

"What sort of bottle?" Mr. Lindsay asked.

"Seagram's V.O. rye whisky, thirteen-ounce – commonly known as a mickey," the policewoman answered. "Empty."

"I think I heard something fall out of the car," said Travis.

"You're certain of that, son," the older officer said sternly.

"Yes," Travis said.

"There must be fingerprints on the bottle," Mrs. Lindsay suggested.

The older officer looked at her quickly. "Fingerprints only mean something if you have someone you can match them to, ma'am," he said. "Besides, he was probably wearing gloves. It was cold that day."

"We can't even be absolutely certain it was his bottle," said the younger officer with a sad look.

"I think I smelled it," said Travis.

Both police officers turned back to Travis, keenly interested.

"Smelled what?" the older officer demanded.

"When he opened the door," Travis said, "this strong smell came out. I thought it was alcohol."

"You know what alcohol smells like?" the older officer asked.

"I think so."

"*Think so* isn't good enough," the officer said. "Would you be confident enough to tell a judge and a full courtroom that you smelled alcohol?"

"Before we get to court," Mr. Lindsay cut in, "you're going to have to come up with a suspect, aren't you?"

The older officer looked up, as if challenged. "That's fairly obvious, sir."

"And have you?"

"Have we what, sir?"

"Have you come up with a suspect."

"Not so far. No."

Around noon they got word about Data. One of the bones at the base of Data's neck had been broken in the accident, but the surgery had gone well. He had been fitted with a thick wire "halo" around his head to keep his neck absolutely still. It was attached by screws that had been planted into his skull, and rested on his shoulders.

Travis shuddered when he heard this. A "halo" suggested good behaviour, but they had been doing something terribly foolish – and it had all been started by Travis.

Travis was feeling desperately sorry for himself when the telephone rang again.

"It's for you, son," his father said, handing the receiver across the table.

"Hello?" Travis said uncertainly.

"It's Muck," a deep voice announced.

"You're our team captain, Travis," Muck said. "I want you to make the calls. I want the whole team at the hospital at five o'clock. Understand?"

"Y-yes," Travis said, uneasily.

"We're going to see Data," Muck said.

"Is it all right?" Travis asked.

"Yes, it's all right. He's asked for the whole team," said Muck. "Are you okay?"

Travis knew he wasn't. "I guess," he said.

"Be there," Muck said. "And be captain, okay?"

Travis knew what Muck meant. He wanted Travis to make sure the visit went right. Muck would expect the same if they were down two goals in an important game: no matter how they might feel inside, the Owls had to believe things would work out, that in the end they would succeed together as a team.

"Okay," Travis said.

7

The Owls gathered on the third floor of the hospital. Most of them had brought gifts. Sarah was going to give Data the old teddy bear she usually kept hidden away in a pocket of her hockey bag. Andy had a copy of *The Hockey News*. Jesse had a beautiful dream catcher that he wanted to hang from Data's window to keep away the bad dreams and let in the good ones. Dmitri had a hockey cap from Moscow Dynamo that his cousin, Slava, had given him.

Even Nish was there, holding out his cast as if it were some kind of medal for bravery.

"It's not plaster," he said. "It's some new kind of plastic they developed for space missions. I might even be able to play with it on."

Nish's eyes were both black from hitting head first into the side of the car the drunk had been driving.

"You look like you were in a fight with Tie Domi," Sarah teased.

"I was," Nish shot back. "And if you think I look bad, you should see him. They got him in a room down the hall. He can't walk or talk yet."

It would take more than a couple of black eyes and a broken wrist to shut up Nish.

"Here come Data's parents!" Jenny whispered urgently.

The Owls fell silent. Mr. and Mrs. Ulmar and their daughter, Julie, came down the hall and turned into the reception area. They looked drained and beaten. But Mrs. Ulmar managed a smile. As soon as she saw them, she walked up and gave Nish a hug. Nish hugged back, using one hand, and turned beet red.

"Larry's glad you came," she said. "He's waiting for you."

"You – look – like – a – raccoon," Data said when he saw Nish.

"You look like an angel," Nish shot back.

"Not – yet," Data said, a weak smile forming. "Not – for – a – long – time . . . I – hope."

They gathered in a group around the bed. Data lay on his back, completely still, the halo preventing any motion of his head and neck. It was as if they were staring down at a stranger, not their friend. Travis felt nervous; he didn't know how to act. Everyone had noticed the way Data spoke, each word like a sentence on its own.

Sarah took charge. She walked to the head of the bed, then kissed her fingertips and gently placed the kiss on her friend's cheek.

"I brought you someone to keep you company," she said, holding up the bear.

Data couldn't turn his head to look, but his eyes moved down so he could see.

"Thanks," he said.

One by one, the others went up with their gifts and their hellos, and Data seemed pleased each one of them had come.

"Do the screws hurt?" Fahd asked when it was his turn.

"Only – when – I – do – somersaults," said Data.

Everyone laughed, and it felt, to Travis, like a magic remedy had just taken away the sick feeling in the pit of his stomach. It was still Data, good old Data.

"What can you feel?" Nish asked.

Travis winced. Like Fahd's question about the screws, this was something everyone wanted to know but no one else had dared to ask.

"Not – much," said Data. "The – doctor – can't – tell – how – much – feeling – will – come – back."

"Will you be able to play again this year?" Fahd asked. The answer to that one was obvious, and as Fahd's question hung in the air, they all wished he hadn't asked it.

Data shut his eyes. He couldn't shake his head to say no. He had to say it out loud.

"I – I guess – not," he finally said.

8

O n Friday night, the Screech Owls played at home against Orillia. Mr. Lindsay drove Travis down to the rink, as usual, but for once neither father nor son said a word. Travis had never felt less like playing a hockey game in his life.

When he reached the dressing-room door, he thought, at first, he must be early. Normally, as soon as the door was open just a crack, he would be greeted by the squeals and shouts of the Owls getting dressed for a game. But this time, as he shifted his bag and sticks off his shoulder and backed in through the dressing-room door, there was no sound from inside.

And yet the dressing room was half full. Sarah was there, already dressed but for her skates and sweater. Fahd was there. And Lars, sitting quietly with his Owls sweater hanging above him. Mr. Dillinger was busy at the back of the room, sharpening Sarah's skates.

Travis came in and set his bag quietly on the floor. He rested his sticks against the wall and moved to his own seat. Still, no one had said a word. He looked over at Sarah, who was biting her lip. She pointed back at her sweater. She wanted him to see something.

Travis looked at his own sweater, number 7, hanging at the back of his stall. There was a new little crest sewn on it over the heart, just to the side of his *C*. It was a small four-leafed clover, with the number 6 in the centre.

Data's number.

Travis looked back at Sarah, who jerked her thumb towards Mr. Dillinger, busy as ever at his sharpening machine. Of course, Mr. Dillinger would have had the crests made, would have stitched them on himself and hung the sweaters up without a word. Good old Mr. Dillinger.

Soon the team was all there, each player entering in silence, then sitting in silence. Some even with their helmets pulled on. There were two sweaters still hanging up untouched. Data's number 6, of course, but also number 3: Nish.

Still no one had said a word.

The door opened and Muck came in. And right behind Muck – with his arm in a sling poking out through the opened zipper of his Screech Owls jacket – was Nish. Nish's cast had a green four-leafed clover painted on it, with a number 6 in the middle.

"We have a new assistant coach, tonight," Muck announced.

Nish beamed from ear to ear and took a ridiculous bow in Sarah's direction. Sarah rolled her eyes.

"And we have another one who can't be with us," Muck added.

He said nothing else, just turned and walked out, staring straight ahead. For once, Fahd didn't have to ask the obvious:

who? It was Data – tonight the Screech Owls were playing for Data.

"*Let's go!*" Sarah suddenly shouted, jumping up and pumping a gloved fist in the air. She grabbed her stick from the wall and slammed it, hard, into Jenny's big goalie pads.

"*Stone 'em, Jen!*" Sarah shouted.

"*Let's do it for Data!*" Andy called.

"*For Data!*" Lars yelled.

"*Data!*"

"*Data!*"

"*And Nish!*" someone called.

Travis turned to look. It was Nish calling for himself.

Nish shrugged sheepishly, and Travis smiled. He swung his sticks back as he plucked them from the wall, and tapped his good friend lightly on the shins.

"For Data *and* Nish," he said.

What was it about this game of hockey, Travis wondered, that sometimes everything could feel wrong – even the way your feet fit into the skates – and a day later everything could feel exactly right? He felt this Friday night as if skating had somehow become the natural way of human movement. He felt as if the ice were at his mercy; he was in no danger of slippery corners or too great a distance. If he reached for the puck, it seemed to reach back for him, puck and stick blade seemingly magnetized. He put his first two warm-up shots off the crossbar.

Muck and Nish and Barry worked the bench. Ty was out of town, so Nish pretty much handled the defence on his own, taking signals from Muck and using his good arm to tap the backs of sweaters to indicate line changes.

When Sarah's line was out, Muck wanted Sarah to go in hard with one winger on the forecheck and try to stop the good Orillia defence before they could get out of their own end with the puck. The other winger was to lie back around the blueline, hoping to intercept any pass that Sarah and the other winger might force.

Travis was first in on the top Orillia defenceman, and he came in hard, skating as well as, if not better than, he'd ever skated before. Was it because of their day of shinny in the open creek? Was it because of Data? He didn't know; all he knew was that as soon as he saw where he needed to be, he was there. He flew into the Orillia end, racing towards the other team's best puckhandler. He had no idea how he knew, just that he knew. He came in hard and then dragged his right skate just as the defender tried to slip the puck between Travis's feet. The puck caught, and Travis, instantly, came free with it on the other side.

He kicked the puck up onto his stick, dug hard to turn towards the net, and then deked back again to the near side of the net, forcing the Orillia goalie to shift tight to his post. A quick little pass across the crease and Sarah had buried the puck with a quick snap of a shot.

First shift, and the Owls had already scored.

The Owls on the ice mobbed Sarah but she shook them free. She hurried to where the linesman was digging the puck out and held out her glove for it. He handed it over with a smile. Perhaps he thought it was her first-ever goal.

"For Data," Sarah said when she got back to the bench.

She handed the puck to Nish to hold for her. Nish took the puck in his good hand and jammed it into his pocket.

"*Ouch!*" Nish yelped, and yanked his hand out, fast. His thumb had caught on something. It was already beading blood.

Mr. Dillinger quickly grabbed a towel to press against the cut. He dabbed quickly and looked carefully at the damage.

"Not deep," he said. "I'll get a bandage."

Travis's line was back out for another shift. When they got back, Mr. Dillinger was just finishing up. With the scissors he carried on his belt, he snipped off the last wrap of bandage.

"Great!" Nish said. "Now I've got *no* hands!"

If they thought the game against Orillia would be easy, they were wrong. The Owls had scored first, but the Orillia goalie had no intention of letting in any more goals after Sarah's.

Travis had rarely worked harder in a game. He skated well and had plenty of good chances, but it was as if a huge plywood board had been nailed over the other team's net. He was robbed twice on glove saves. Dmitri failed on two breakaways.

Something was wrong with Owls. They were giving fine individual efforts, but they weren't working like a team. Travis thought it was as though they were missing something – and then he shut his eyes and shook his head hard.

They *were* missing something: *Data*.

Inspired by their goaltender, the Orillia players slowly mounted their comeback. Playing magnificently – everyone working together – they tied the game in the second period and went ahead, to stay, early in the third. Muck pulled Jenny in the final minute, but even with an extra attacker the Owls could not get past the splendid Orillia goalie.

The game over, the Screech Owls headed for their dressing room in silence, heads down. Travis felt he had failed Data even more than he had failed the team. They had wanted to take him a win, but instead they had lost, and Orillia were now the top team in their division.

But at least they had the puck from Sarah's one goal. It wasn't much, but it was something to take to Data.

Sarah asked for Data's puck, and Mr. Dillinger had to reach into Nish's jacket pocket to get it.

"Watch your hand," Nish warned, holding out his bandaged thumb as proof of the danger.

"Okay," Mr. Dillinger said, "I got it."

Mr. Dillinger carefully pulled out the prized puck and flipped it to Sarah, who caught it easily.

But Mr. Dillinger wanted to find out what it was that had cut Nish's fingers.

"You've got something caught in here, son," he called.

Carefully, Mr. Dillinger pulled a sliver of shiny metal out of Nish's pocket.

"That's what I cut my hand on!" Nish shouted.

Mr. Dillinger blinked at the piece of chrome, turning it over and over. He handed it to Muck, who took it and carefully looked himself.

"Looks like a piece of trim," Muck said.

"Off a car," Mr. Dillinger said.

Nish shot a surprised and excited look at Travis.

A clue.

9

t took two days for the police laboratory in Toronto to report back on the piece of metal that had turned up in Nish's pocket. It was side stripping from a car, all right. The car would have been a Chevrolet, but there were two different models it might have come from, and those models had been in production for three years. In other words, there were tens of thousands of cars the piece of metal could have come from. Dozens around Tamarack alone.

"They say the car might not even have come from here," Mr. Lindsay told Travis and Nish.

Travis sighed deeply. "What are they going to do?" he asked.

"They'll check similar cars in the area," Mr. Lindsay said, "see if one of them's missing some stripping from up around the front left side – but don't get your hopes up too high, boys. Travis's grandfather drives a Chevrolet. So does Mr. Dillinger. It's almost too common a model to do us any good."

Travis and Nish tried to play video games to pass the rest of the day, but Nish claimed he couldn't play up to his usual high standards with a cast on, and after a while they simply paused the game and talked.

"It can't be from out of town," Travis said.

"How do you know?" asked Nish. "It could have been driven here from anywhere. It's a *car*, after all."

"Yeah, but don't forget the day. It was so slippery, cars couldn't get anywhere. No one would drive any distance that day."

Nish was only half listening. "Maybe."

"And don't forget where he was. The back streets. No one would drive up here from Orillia or someplace like that and be driving around our back streets drunk, would they?"

"Probably not – but who knows what a drunk will do?"

"And that's significant, too," Travis almost shouted. He was excited; his brain was really working.

"What's significant?"

"He was drunk."

"Obviously."

"But he had to *get* drunk first."

"Obviously again."

"So, think of the direction he was headed."

Nish thought for a moment. "Towards Main Street, I guess."

"*Exactly!* Which means he was coming from . . . ?"

Nish looked at Travis, bewildered. "I don't know. There's nothing much up Cedar beyond the curling rink and the baseball diamonds . . . Mr. Turley's farm . . . a few houses on the other side of the road . . ."

"An out-of-towner wouldn't come along that way. But somebody who lives up here would. Or maybe somebody who was at the curling rink, drinking."

"There was a bottle that fell out, remember. He didn't have to go to the curling rink to get drunk."

"Yeah, you're right. But maybe it was an old bottle, already empty. Or maybe he was already drunk and then continued drinking in his car. There's a good chance he was either someone from around here, maybe even up Cedar Street, or someone who'd been at the curling rink."

"That's not much to go on," said Nish, unimpressed.

"But we have something else," Travis protested.

"What's that?"

"The Chevrolet. We can find out who drives one who also lives out that way. Maybe even who has one and belongs to the curling club."

"Didn't you listen to your father?" Nish said, absentmindedly. "He said there were dozens of them."

"There are," said Travis, grinning with satisfaction. "But only one is missing a strip of metal."

Nish looked back at Travis, finally prepared to admit Travis might be right. "Let's get some help," he said.

They raised whatever Owls could be located quickly by telephone calls and knocking on doors. Sarah was there. And Jenny, Lars, Andy, Fahd, Dmitri, and Liz. Travis outlined what it was they were looking for: a mid-sized Chevrolet at least three years old but no more than six years old, colour uncertain.

"I can't tell one car from another," said Sarah.

"Don't worry," said Travis, "we can wipe off the snow until

we see if it's a Chevrolet or not. And if it is, it'll just take a second to check the driver's side near the front for missing stripping. That should be simple enough."

They marked out an area of approximately six blocks, plus the curling rink, plus the new houses across from Turley's farm. Then, setting out in pairs, they arranged to meet back at the curling rink in an hour.

Travis and Nish found two Chevrolets that fit the description, but one was Travis's own grandfather's – and Harold Lindsay had never touched a drop of drink in his life – and the other was in perfect shape, its stripping as good as new. Sarah and Liz found three. One of them had a bashed-in side, but the damage was on the passenger side. The other two were in perfect shape, trim intact. Andy and Dmitri found only one, but it belonged to Mr. Dickens, who owned the Shell station at the corner of River and Main and who had coached most of the Screech Owls in atom. Like Travis's grandfather, he was one of the most respected men in town, and anyway, there was no damage on his car. Jenny and Fahd found none.

Six cars, and no suspects. But they still had the curling-rink parking lot to do.

"What if someone catches us?" asked Fahd, who was always worried about something.

"We'll pretend we're having a snowball fight," suggested Sarah. "Get your snow off the backs of the cars – that way you can check the make out."

"No fair!" complained Nish. "I can't pack."

Sarah rolled her eyes. "It is not a *real* snowball fight, Nishikawa. We are *pre-tend-ing*."

Sarah's idea worked brilliantly. They packed snowballs and checked for Chevrolets. They ducked down and, while they were hidden between cars, checked for missing metal stripping. One man even came out of the curling rink, saw them, and started laughing at their game. Little did he know he had just walked into the middle of a criminal investigation.

Finally the Owls had worked their way through all the rows and all the cars. They were snow-covered and exhausted.

"Four Chevrolets," said Travis, summing up, after they had all reported.

"And nothing missing," said Andy, dejected.

"Well . . . ," mumbled Fahd, seeming to search for the right words.

"You found something?" Travis asked.

"Not really, but –"

"But what?" Nish said impatiently.

"I think we need to look at one of them again," said Fahd.

He led the seven other Owls along one of the rows of cars, dipped between two of them, and in the next row found the one he wanted.

Andy checked carefully along the driver's side.

"It's in perfect shape," he announced.

"But," said Fahd, swallowing, "that's the point."

"*What*'s the point?" Nish asked in a challenging voice.

"It . . . it's *too* perfect," Fahd mumbled. "This is not a new car."

They all leaned closer around Andy. Travis took his glove off and rubbed it along the side of the car. Andy knocked the snow off further along. He wiped the metal clean, so it shone.

"This guy's had bodywork done," said Andy.

"And recently, too," said Travis.

"We've got something," said Sarah.

A second clue.

10

All eight Screech Owls scrambled up and over the high snowbank at the end of the lot. They lay on their stomachs, watched, and waited.

"I gotta be in by nine," Fahd warned.

"I'm good till nine-thirty," said Sarah.

"Nine."

"Nine-thirty."

"Nine."

"Nine."

"Nine."

"Midnight."

Travis turned to his side and looked crossly at Nish, who was beaming from ear to ear. Nish, the Man About Town, who would tell them he and his uncle sometimes enjoyed a good cigar after dinner. Who once maintained he'd driven the car around the block. Who in his imagination would stay up all night long, drinking and smoking and partying, but who would wake up in his Toronto Maple Leafs pyjamas in the morning and expect his mother to bring him in a bowlful of Fruit Loops while he watched the Saturday-morning cartoons.

"In your dreams," Sarah said.

How late they could all stay mattered. What if this really was the car they were looking for, and what if the driver was going to be curling and drinking until midnight? Would Nish still be on watch for him? Whoever it was who drove this Chevrolet with the new bodywork, he had to come out before the Owls went to bed.

They waited and talked. About the loss to Orillia. About the team. About Data. Strangely, though they couldn't help thinking about Data, none of them wanted to talk about him for long. Someone would say something about how well he was doing – how he could sit in a wheelchair now and was learning to drive it with his right hand, which he could move a little – but then, just as quickly, someone else would change the subject.

"I signed up for the Mock Disaster," announced Fahd.

"You *are* a disaster," said Nish.

"What is it?" asked Travis.

Fahd told them that Mrs. Wheeler's class had volunteered to work on an emergency drill the fire department and the hospital were putting on. It was basic training for the ambulance drivers and emergency-room hospital staff. They were going to simulate a bus accident, and some of the kids from school were going to be made up to look like they'd been injured in the wreck.

"I'm doing fake blood and broken bones," said Fahd. "It's fantastic!"

"Only *you* would think so," said Sarah, clearly relieved she wasn't in Mrs. Wheeler's class.

"*Look!*"

It was Lars's voice, low and urgent. The Owls shut up immediately and turned flat on their stomachs to peer over the bank. There was a large man moving out among the parked cars, headed in the general direction of the Chevrolet.

"*It's Booker!*" hissed Nish.

Booker? It took several moments before the name registered on Travis. Of course, Mr. Booker had once come out to help Muck with the early-season assessments, but he had been so foul-mouthed on the ice Muck had ordered him off and told him to go home. This was minor hockey, Muck told him, not the military.

The hockey association kept Mr. Booker away from coaching, but thought he'd do no harm as a team manager. They'd been wrong. Even in house league he'd been thrown out of games for abusing the referees, and finally he was banned altogether after he grabbed an opposing player by the scruff of the neck and pinned him to the arena wall when the two teams had left the ice. The player had tripped one of Mr. Booker's players during the game, but as Mr. Lindsay had explained to Travis later that night, tripping is a penalty, holding a kid by his throat against a wall is assault. Mr. Booker's career in hockey was over.

"*He's heading for it!*" hissed Andy.

They watched as Mr. Booker twisted his way through the cars towards the Chevrolet. He was fumbling in his pocket. He dropped something – keys, probably – and swore loudly as he bent to pick them up.

"Charming," said Sarah.

"He's drunk," said Lars.

Mr. Booker came up with the keys and fumbled with them at the door. Soon the interior light of the car came on as the door cracked open and they could see him getting in. He closed the door, started the car, and let the windshield wipers shake off the light dusting of snow that had fallen since he'd arrived. He sat a moment, letting the engine warm the windshield. Then his headlights came on, and they could hear the crunch of tires on the snow as he moved slowly out of the parking lot.

"Where does he live?" said Fahd.

"I don't have a clue," said Travis.

"I do," said Liz. "My mom and Mrs. Booker are friends."

"Where, then?" said Nish.

"Across from the farm. At the very end of Cedar."

"*Yes!*" Travis said.

The quickest route from the curling rink to the end of Cedar Street passed through the intersection where Data had been struck.

Booker would have been going home! Just like this, drunk, from the curling rink!

They had a third clue.

11

n Sunday, the Screech Owls practised at noon – Nish skating, but unable to shoot – and afterwards Muck asked the team to assemble again at the hospital in an hour. They were going to visit Data.

When the Owls got there, they found Data's doorway almost blocked with other patients trying to look inside. There were even a couple of doctors on tiptoe trying to get a peek over the crowd. The fact that the doctors weren't pushing their way through to get to Data and were smiling told Travis there was nothing to worry about.

Everyone made room to let the Owls pass through, single file. There were more people in the room, doctors and nurses, and a man in a blue suit leaning over Data's bed. The man had dark curly hair that was turning grey. *Who was it?*

Whoever he was, he looked up when Muck came in and shook his hand warmly. Muck looked sheepish, but the man seemed delighted, as if running into an old friend he'd been missing. Travis was no closer to guessing who the man was, but he did look oddly familiar.

Muck turned to the small crowd around Data's bed, and everyone went even quieter than they had been.

"This, here, is Paul Henderson," he said.

Paul Henderson! *Of course!* Travis had a special coin at home with Paul Henderson on it. He had a sheet of stamps with Paul Henderson on them that he had put away. Paul Henderson, hero of the 1972 Summit Series, the man who had scored the winning goal for Canada against the Soviets with thirty-four seconds left in the final game. The most famous goal in hockey history.

"How ya doing, boys?" Paul Henderson said, then caught himself, seeing Sarah and Liz off to one side, Jenny and Chantal on the other. "And girls? Good, good, the Screech Owls are a truly modern team, I see."

"Mr. Henderson has something to announce," Muck said.

"Well, actually it's something Larry — sorry, *Data* — and I would both like to announce," said Paul Henderson. He turned, smiling, towards Data.

"We're going to play a game!" Data said from his bed. His voice sounded surprisingly strong.

"I proposed to Data that I bring a team of NHL old-timers up to Tamarack for a match. Muck's lined up the Flying Fathers to play against us. They're a bunch of priests who happen to play hockey — some of them pretty darn good — and they put on a great show. So — whatdya say to that?"

"Go for it!" shouted Nish.

"Yes!" shouted Andy.

"*Shhhhh*," cautioned Sarah, reminding them where they were.

"Data, here, is going to need a few things," said Paul Henderson. "We want him to have the best wheelchair money can buy. And we want to get him a special computer so he can get back to school. And his parents are going to need a special van so they can get him to hockey games and the like."

Travis glanced quickly at Sarah, who smiled back. Travis wondered if Paul Henderson should even be talking about such things. But then, Data was already making unbelievable progress. The halo was gone, the small wounds where the screws had been tightened right into his skull were healing well. Best of all, he was getting some feeling and movement back in his shoulders, and he could move his right arm, though he had trouble gripping with his hand.

There was still nothing, however – no feeling at all – from Data's chest on down. The doctors said it likely wouldn't come back, and unless science one day figured out how to repair spinal cords, Data was never going to walk again.

"How did you find out about Data?" Fahd asked Paul Henderson. They were all wondering the same thing, but no one but Fahd would dare ask.

Paul Henderson smiled at Muck, who was standing in the far corner of the room, trying to avoid any attention.

"From my old friend, Muck. My old *winger*, I guess I should say."

Winger? As in *hockey* winger? Muck seemed to be blushing.

"Muck played with *you*?" Fahd asked.

"*I* played with Muck," Paul Henderson laughed. "We were on the same line in Kitchener."

Every face in the room, including Data's, was now turned towards Muck, who seemed to wish he could vanish into the wall. Every one of them was looking at Muck as if they'd never seen him before. He *played* with Paul Henderson?

"Was he any good?" Fahd asked.

"*A lot better than me!*" Paul Henderson laughed. "Maybe if you hadn't busted that leg so bad, Muck, you'd have scored that goal in Moscow."

"I'd've missed the net," Muck muttered.

Then Muck cleared his throat, changing the subject. "Let's clear this room so Data can get some rest now, okay?"

o much had happened. The Larry Ulmar Fundraising Game was scheduled for the first Sunday afternoon of the new month. The Flying Fathers were coming, complete with their hockey-playing *horse*. Paul Henderson had lined up some of the greatest names that ever played for the Toronto Maple Leafs, including Eddie Shack, Darryl Sittler, Lanny McDonald, and Frank Mahovlich. And right after the big game, the Screech Owls themselves were going to play, a return match against Orillia – another chance to get the win they'd so desperately wanted for Data.

The *Toronto Star* and the *Sun* and the *Globe and Mail* were all sending reporters and photographers. The Sports Network was coming to do a documentary on the charity work of the Flying Fathers. And Nish was getting a new cast.

"It's plastic and has a zipper," he told Travis. "I can take it off and put it on. Once the doctor says I can start playing again, I

can use it just for games until the wrist heals completely. I'll be
back sooner than anybody thinks."

Everything seemed to be going well – except the investigation.

The police were getting nowhere.

⊚

"Garbage night," Travis said to Nish.

"Huh?"

"Tonight's garbage night."

"Don't look at me – I can't lift a thing with this wrist!"

Travis shook his head. "I'm thinking about what *other* people
put out."

"Whatdya mean?"

"We know what the guy who hit Data drinks, don't we?
Seagram's V.O. whisky."

"Yeah. So?"

"So we check out Booker's recycling bin. See if that's what
he drinks."

Nish thought about it a while. Finally he looked at Travis
and smiled. "Good idea. Let's check it out."

Travis told his parents he was taking his geography notes over
to Nish, which was true enough – only Nish told his parents he
was headed over to Travis's to borrow the same notes. They met
at the corner of Cedar and River, where Travis handed over the
notes. Nish stuffed them into his backpack, and they set off for
the neighbourhood where Mr. Booker lived.

It was a beautiful clear evening, already dark and very cold. Some houses already had their garbage out, in green plastic bags and blue recycling boxes for bottles and cans.

"Evening, boys!" a voice called across the road.

Travis and Nish turned to see Mr. Dickens, the old coach, set down two heavy garbage bags. He was clapping his bare hands together and rubbing them as he walked towards the boys.

"Hi, Mr. Dickens," said Travis.

"How's it going?" said Nish, who always talked the same, no matter whether he was speaking to a toddler or someone's grandmother.

Mr. Dickens stomped his feet and stabbed his hands deep into his pockets. "What do you young men hear from the hospital?" he asked.

"Data's doing pretty good," Nish said.

"He's moving around in a chair," said Travis.

Mr. Dickens seemed disappointed. "Then it's true what we hear: he won't walk again?"

"I guess not," said Nish. "Muck says it'd take a miracle."

"*Damn it!*" Mr. Dickens said, swallowing. He smiled. "Sorry, boys – I can't help it."

"Everybody's upset," said Travis. "Data's handling it better than anyone, to tell you the truth. You should go see him."

"Yeah," added Nish. "You used to coach Data, didn't you?"

Mr. Dickens tried to speak, choked slightly, then cleared his throat. When he spoke, his voice was thin, breaking. "I'll pay him a visit, boys, I will. You tell him his old coach was asking after him, okay?"

"Sure, Mr. Dickens," said Travis.

Mr. Dickens looked at them. Travis could tell how much the old coach was bothered. It could have been the cold, but his eyes were damp, and he looked so sad, so upset. Like them, he was helpless to do anything about what had happened.

"Thanks, boys," he said.

Mr. Dickens turned and headed back, his boots slipping on the hard, slick snow cover. He nearly went down, caught himself, and walked back towards his garage to bring out the rest of his garbage.

"Need any help?" Travis asked.

"*No!*" Mr. Dickens said sharply. "No thanks."

He didn't look back.

Travis was pretty sure he knew why. Mr. Dickens didn't want them to see how upset he was about poor Data.

Booker lived a few blocks farther north, down a dead-end street called Poplar. There was a streetlight at the corner, but no other lights apart from the houses. This was both good and bad. Good, because the dark gave them cover; bad, because they could barely see.

"I wish the moon was full," whispered Nish.

They were trying to walk quietly, taking soft steps so their boots wouldn't crunch in the snow.

"That's it – up there!" Travis whispered.

He pointed – despite being unable even to see his own hand – up towards a small one-storey wood-frame house with two dim lights attached to the side. One cast a dull glow over the front door; the other was at the near corner of the little house, barely illuminating the driveway.

"Good," said Travis. "He's already put his garbage out."

It was dark, but in the poor light from the house they could make out the dark shapes of two green garbage bags at the end of the driveway. Beside the bags was a single dark box.

The two moved towards the snowbank closest to Booker's driveway.

"No car!" Travis whispered.

"Maybe he's at the curling rink," said Nish, hopefully.

"Maybe."

"Let's do it fast," said Nish.

Travis moved to the edge of the driveway, peeking around the high shovelled bank. He could see the recycling box. He could see the thin glow of the house lights dancing on glass.

There were bottles in it – lots of bottles!

"*Go!*" Nish hissed from behind him.

Travis took a deep breath. He hunched down, then darted across the front of the driveway, from one bank to the next. He stopped to gather his breath. His heart was pounding. He was sweating. Travis Lindsay, who hardly ever sweated during a game, was sweating now in the freezing cold of a black winter's night.

One deep breath and Travis darted into Booker's driveway. Crouching down, he hurried over to the recycling box.

He'd been right; it was full of bottles.

As he reached down into the box, his glove brushed one of the bottles on top, which slid down from the pile and clinked hard against more glass below.

"*Hurry!*" Nish hissed from the distance.

Travis reached into the bin and pulled a bottle out by the

neck. He couldn't read the label, but he knew from the smell it was liquor.

Nish's voice cut through the still night air.

"CAR!"

No! Travis thought. *Not a car! Not now!*

He ducked down instinctively, just as the car's headlights swept over the tops of the banks and washed along the side of Booker's house.

But Nish must have panicked. Instead of sticking fast to the bank where he was hiding, he tried to come around it into the shelter of the driveway, where Travis was crouched out of sight.

His timing couldn't have been worse. As the car began to turn into Booker's driveway, Nish ran out into the glare of its headlights, and like a frightened deer stopped dead, petrified.

They could hear the whirr of an automatic window as the car came to a stop.

"*Run!*" shouted Travis.

"HEY! WHAT'RE YOU KIDS UP TO?"

It was Booker, all right. The same insulting, angry voice that used to burst out in the arena whenever a linesman missed a call.

The car door opened.

"*Wha' the hell 'r' you doin' here?*" Booker growled. He was drunk, judging by the way his words were running together.

There was no choice. They would have to run directly at the car and then break to the left, putting the vehicle between themselves and Booker.

Travis bolted first. He could hear Nish yelp behind him – the sound Nish's dog made when his tail got shut in the sliding door.

"*Hurry!*" Nish shouted.

"YOU LITTLE . . . !" Booker roared as he lunged across the hood of the Chevrolet, reaching for Nish and catching the hood of his jacket.

"NOOOOOOOO!!!!!" Nish howled. He jerked ahead with all his might, the hood tearing away slightly from his jacket, but ripping free of Booker's hand at the same time.

"*Move your butt!*" Nish screamed at Travis.

Travis was racing as fast as he could. The two Owls ran out under the brighter streetlights of Sugar Maple Drive, and turned hard to head back down towards Cedar and safety. Behind them, Travis could hear Booker's car door slamming and the engine race as the tires whined in reverse.

"*He's coming after us!*" Nish warned.

He was, too. Even in the brighter lights of Sugar Maple they could see the headlights playing in the trees as Booker reversed and turned and pulled out behind them.

The bottle! Travis knew he could run better if he wasn't cradling the empty bottle in his jacket. But he needed it for evidence.

He could hide it! And get it later . . . after they'd escaped.

Travis ran quickly to the side of the nearest snowbank and screwed the bottle down under the soft snow at the top.

Nish was now ahead of him. Travis could almost feel the headlights on his back; Booker was flicking his lights, from high beam to low, and he was gathering speed on the slippery street.

We don't want another accident! Travis thought. He was sure Booker was drunk, and he knew the alcohol would slow his reflexes. They had to deke him just as if they were playing a hockey game.

"*Next – corner!*" Travis shouted through his puffs. "*Turn – sharp – on – him!*"

With the car now roaring right behind them, they came to the next side street, and just as they seemed to be bolting straight through the intersection, both boys turned hard to the right.

Travis could hear Booker's car horn blast as the Chevrolet's weight carried it right past the turn and down the street, the brakes on full and the tires sliding helplessly.

"He'll come back!" said Nish.

"I think so, too," said Travis.

"Where next, then?" Nish asked. It was a good question. This street was another dead end.

"*Head for Mr. Dickens's!*" Travis shouted. "We'll duck in there till he goes."

Nish was already headed towards Mr. Dickens's driveway on the corner. The boys raced past the garbage and stopped at the side door, where a light burned brightly.

"What'll we tell him?" Travis asked.

"Nothing," said Nish. "He's a good guy – he won't even ask."

Nish pushed the buzzer. Pushed it again just as headlights swept down the empty street. There was a shadow at the door window, peering out.

It was Mr. Dickens. They were safe!

The door popped open.

"What're you boys up to?" Mr. Dickens asked. He was smiling, but seemed nervous, almost blushing.

"*There's a guy in a car chasing us!*" Nish said. Good old Nish
— always right to the point.

Mr. Dickens stuck his head out the door. He was quite red
in the face now. *Anger?* Travis wondered. *The cold?*

"I don't see anybody," Mr. Dickens said.

"He just went by again," said Travis.

"Can you give us a ride home?" Nish asked, again to the
point.

Mr. Dickens looked stricken. *Was he afraid of Booker, too? . . .
No, how could he be? He didn't know who was chasing them.*

"Can't," Mr. Dickens said, shaking his head vigorously. "No
can do — car's not running right."

Travis couldn't shake the feeling that Mr. Dickens was
hoping they'd just go away. *Did he not believe them?*

"Who's chasing you, anyway?" Mr. Dickens asked. He still
hadn't asked them in.

"Some guy who thought we were firing snowballs at him,"
Nish invented.

Mr. Dickens turned and stared hard at Nish. "Were you?"

"No, sir. We didn't throw anything at anybody."

Mr. Dickens looked once more down the street. "Well," he
said. "Whoever he was, he's gone now."

It was clear to Travis that they weren't going to get invited
in, and he was almost glad. The warm air from inside the house
smelled sickly sweet, and of smoke. Not clean and fresh like his
own home, or Nish's home. And there was something not right
about Mr. Dickens. He seemed to have a bad cold. Maybe that
was why he'd been so reluctant to help them out.

Mr. Dickens closed the door on them, shutting off the flow of warm air and unpleasant smells.

Nish turned, his face puzzled. "What got into him?"

"I don't know."

"Maybe he's sick," said Nish.

"Maybe."

They were still standing on Mr. Dickens's porch. They scanned both directions.

"I don't see the lights any more," said Travis.

"It's all clear," said Nish. "Let's get out of here."

"We've got to go back for the bottle," Travis said.

They hurried down the driveway and back up the street until they came to the spot where Travis had hidden the bottle. It took them a minute to find it in the powdered snow. Travis held the bottle up towards the streetlight, turning it carefully.

"What's wrong?" asked Nish.

"This isn't a whisky bottle," said Travis, turning the label towards Nish. "It's rum – Captain Morgan's rum."

13

T. *hey had the wrong bottle!*

"Maybe Booker drinks rum, too," suggested Nish.

"Maybe," Travis said. But something didn't feel right.

Booker could be someone who drank a bit of everything, of course. And besides, finding a Seagram's bottle at Booker's house wouldn't really have proven anything anyway, apart from the fact that Booker and the hit-and-run driver bought the same drink. But at least it would have been a clue, one that was linked to the scene of the accident and their only other clue: the piece of metal from an unknown Chevrolet.

Nish took the bottle and twisted off the cap. He sniffed the opening quickly, and jerked his head back. "Yuck! Makes you want to throw up without even drinking!"

Nish pushed the opened bottle towards Travis, who instinctively turned away. But then Travis turned back, sniffing hard.

"Let me see that."

Nish handed over the bottle with a puzzled look, and Travis took it, sniffed again, wrinkled his nose, sniffed yet again.

"You're supposed to drink it," Nish said, "not *inhale* it."

"This isn't anything like what I smelled when Data got hit," Travis said.

"We know that. This is a rum bottle, not whisky, remember?"

"But it isn't even *close* to what whisky smells like."

"The accident was weeks ago – how can you even remember?"

"Because I just smelled it again a few minutes ago."

Nish blinked, waiting.

"At Mr. Dickens's."

It took a moment for it all to register. The eerily familiar, sweet smell of whisky coming out the front door, the red face of Mr. Dickens, his strange, unwelcoming behaviour.

Of course, thought Travis, *that's what was wrong with him. He wasn't sick. He didn't have a cold. Mr. Dickens was drunk! And maybe that's why he wouldn't drive them home; he was afraid to drive after what had happened before . . .*

"We have to go back," Travis said.

"Not again!" said Nish. "He'll be watching for us this time!"

"Not to Booker's – to Mr. Dickens's. I want to check his garbage."

This time they crept up warily on Mr. Dickens's house, crouching low. The lights were still on, but there was no movement. Travis crouched even lower and scooted across the driveway to where Mr. Dickens had put out the garbage. On the other side of the bags was the blue recycling box.

It was full of cans. Only cans. Bean cans, corn cans, chopped-fruit cans, tomato-sauce cans, spaghetti cans . . . No bottles at all!

Travis desperately searched for a telltale glint of glass. But there was nothing. It was hard to believe someone could get through so many cans in a week; they almost seemed to have been arranged there on purpose.

Too perfect, he thought. He dug deeper, removing one can after another.

Glass glinted below!

Travis reached down and pulled a bottle free. He spun the cap off and sniffed, once.

The same sickeningly sweet smell.

He spun the bottle towards the best light.

Seagram's V.O. rye whisky.

@

Travis now had the clue he and Nish had been looking for — even if it had shown up in an unexpected place — but he also knew that it didn't really prove anything.

Finding the right kind of whisky bottle was no better than finding the right make of car. It seemed half the people in town drove Chevrolets, and the whisky was probably the most popular brand on the market.

Mr. Dickens was also one of the best-liked people in town. He was well-known and well-respected. His garage had an excellent reputation for good work and honesty. But still, Travis couldn't shake a gut feeling. Mr. Dickens had behaved so strangely when they'd come to his door seeking safety.

The garage! Of course, Travis thought. Mr. Dickens's garage! Where no one would ever need to know what work had been done. Not if you owned the garage. Not if you did the work yourself!

Travis felt sick. Sick because suddenly he felt certain it *had* been Mr. Dickens that night. Sick because someone like Mr. Dickens had lied and then tried to hide what had happened. And sick because, while he had two real clues – the Chevrolet and the empty whisky bottle – everything else added up to pure speculation.

All Travis really had was a gut feeling. And gut feelings didn't count for anything with the police.

Travis shook his head in despair, and when he thought of what Mr. Dickens had done to Data, he wanted to cry.

14

The next day, the Screech Owls practised after school. The big day of the charity game, and the Owls' rematch against Orillia, was less than a week away, and Muck had a lot of "little things" he wanted them to work on.

Muck skated the Owls hard. Nish called these skates "no-brainers," and it was as good a description as any, Travis thought. The last thing in the world you wanted to do out there was think about what you were doing: skating hard in both directions, stops and starts, turning backwards on one whistle, forward on two whistles. If you thought about it, it seemed to hurt more. If you thought about nothing – treated it as a no-brainer – it seemed to go faster and, somehow, hurt less.

But this day Travis couldn't command a no-brainer. He tried to think about what it would be like to see all those wonderful heroes of hockey history: Henderson, Sittler, McDonald, Shack, Mahovlich . . . He tried to think about the comedy tricks the Flying Fathers would pull. Was it really true they had a *horse* that could play hockey?

But nothing worked: all he could think about was Data and what had happened since he had suggested they try "hitching."

The whistle blew loud and long: Muck's signal to pack it in and head for centre ice.

Travis and Sarah flew around the far net, sweaters rippling in the wind. Sarah let out a whoop of appreciation. The no-brainer was over!

Nish had anticipated Muck's whistle and broken away early. He'd ignored the last net they were supposed to circle and had cut fast to centre, stopping before Muck in a fine spray and immediately bowing down on his knees, breathing hard and deep, the sweat dripping from his face as if he'd just sprayed it with the Gatorade bottle.

Travis and Sarah skated up laughing. Nish hadn't fooled anyone. Muck would have seen him skating around in the rear and then cutting out early, hoping to fool the coach into thinking he, not Sarah, had been leading the hard skate.

"Okay, you've earned it," Muck said. "Black against white."

Everyone whooped this time. Sarah and Travis and Lars slammed their sticks hard against the ice. *Black against white.* They were going to scrimmage.

Practice was never better than when they finished up with a good scrimmage. Scrimmage was the best kind of hockey, Travis thought. They could try out the plays they'd been day-dreaming about. There weren't even any parents in the stands to watch. That was one good effect of the no-brainer: the parents had all gone off in search of fresh coffee or newspapers. Anything to avoid watching.

"Black against white" meant dark sweaters against light – Sarah's line against Andy's, Lars's defence against Nish's, the other players all divided up evenly.

Muck tossed the puck to Ty, his assistant, and carefully pulled the whistle off over his head and placed it on the bench in the penalty box. He then adjusted the small shin pads he wore, punched his gloves tight and skated back to defence, where he tapped Nish on the pads.

Nish understood immediately. Even if it was only a scrimmage, he shouldn't play with his broken wrist. Nish shook his head, pretending to be outraged, and skated off happily.

Ty reached out and let the puck fall, and Travis felt a chill run up his spine. Nothing to do with the cold. Nothing to do with how much he'd been sweating. *Everything* to do with seeing Muck there, his stick ready, back arched, just the way Data would wait.

Sarah plucked the puck out of the air and cuffed a quick backhand over to Travis, who circled back, lifting his head to see if he had a play. Sarah was pounding her stick as she jumped through centre, racing towards the other blueline.

Travis sent a saucer pass over Jesse's stick that was perfectly timed. But for *Muck*, not Sarah! Laughing, Muck knocked the puck out of the air with the blade of his stick. He moved quickly, as fast as his bad leg would allow, up across centre, where Lars was racing back to check him.

Muck simply shifted his big body to block Lars from the puck. Then, still laughing, he came in along the far side of the boards.

Jenny moved out from the net in anticipation – her catching glove snapping like a lobster claw, her pads wiggling as she moved forward.

Muck wound up for a slapshot. Jenny readied herself. Muck looked up, then ripped a hard pass across the ice to where Jesse Highboy, flying in from the blueline, merely had to tip the puck into an empty net.

Muck and the "whites" high-fived and screamed in the corner. Muck came skating out, slammed his stick on the ice and teased Travis.

"Thanks for the pass."

Travis smiled sheepishly. He'd been so proud of his little saucer pass to Sarah. It had led to a perfect goal – but by Muck and the "whites," not Travis's "black" team.

They played for almost twenty minutes. Travis wondered why Muck was letting them play so long. But then, as time went on, he came to realize the scrimmage wasn't just for them.

Muck was having as much fun as anyone.

15

"Travis, you've gotta come and see what we're doing," Fahd said the next day as school was getting out.

"I'm supposed to go over to my grandparents'," Travis said. "My dad's picking me up there."

"It'll just take a minute," said Fahd.

"Okay, but make it fast."

Fahd led Travis down to Mrs. Wheeler's room, where they were deep in preparations for the mock disaster that would take place the week after Data's big night.

The windows of Mrs. Wheeler's room were covered up with paper to prevent the rest of the school from standing around gawking. Inside, they were preparing "bodies" for the practice disaster. They were making crash victims and burn victims and even what Fahd called "a bloody axe murder," though to Travis it looked more like a store dummy that had been cut up by a chainsaw and coated with spaghetti sauce.

"Gruesome, eh?" said Fahd. "*I love it.*"

Some of it was gruesome, some of it was stupid, thought Travis. But when he saw some dummies being prepared to stage an automobile crash, he shuddered. These ones were spooky.

Fahd opened the door that led into the art room.

"This," said Fahd, "is where we work on *real* bodies."

Inside, there were student volunteers in white coats and other students lying on tables.

"We have to have 'real' victims, too," said Fahd. "I'm being trained in disaster makeup. These are living survivors we'll be taking to the emergency ward by ambulance. The doctors and nurses have to treat them like they are really hurt. The kids even have to answer questions about their injuries – except, of course, for those who'll come in 'unconscious.'"

Travis stared around the room, open-mouthed. He recognized some of the students on the tables, but now they looked exactly like crash victims and burn victims, bloodied and bandaged, some with their skulls shattered, eyes destroyed, arms and legs broken. Only instead of screaming in pain, they were talking – even laughing.

"Neat, eh?" said Fahd.

"Yeah," said Travis, "neat. But I gotta get going."

"Okay," said Fahd. "Hope you don't have trouble getting to sleep tonight."

Travis didn't need to wait until bedtime to have a nightmare. All the way to his grandparents' place he thought of nothing but car accidents and broken bodies and what on earth he was going to do about finding the person who had hit Data.

But *what* could he do? He was going over the clues and what, if anything, he could tell the police. He needed proof – not guesswork. But by the time he reached his grandparents' house, he was still only guessing.

Travis's grandmother was a character. She had a great, huge laugh and was about as far removed from anyone's idea of an old woman as Travis could imagine. She worked out almost every day. She wore a track suit more often than a dress. She listened to the "Golden Oldies" radio station, usually singing along. And she was never so happy as when she was at the cottage, curled up in her hammock beneath the pines, sipping a cold beer straight from the bottle while reading a mystery novel.

Of course, Travis thought, mystery novels. If anyone would know how to help him, his grandmother Lindsay would. The bookcases at their house were full of mysteries. And every week she watched British mysteries on Public Television. Her favourite character was Miss Marple, a crime solver who looked exactly the way Travis thought a grandmother was supposed to look. You'd never catch Miss Marple drinking beer straight from the bottle.

Travis's grandmother put out some oatmeal cookies and made Travis some hot chocolate and, before he knew it, Travis was telling her everything he knew about what had happened since the night of the accident.

"So you know who did it," she said when Travis was finished, "but there's no proof."

"We *think* we know," said Travis. "But that's not enough. The police would just laugh at us."

"You should read more mystery novels," Travis's grandmother smiled. "The police are *always* the last to clue in."

"But we're just kids," said Travis. "No one listens to us, anyway."

"*I'm* listening, young man."

His grandmother sat for a while, staring at Travis as he munched on his cookie.

"A guilty party," she said finally, more to herself than to Travis, "but no clue strong enough to stand up." She had one finger pressed tight to her lips, thinking.

Suddenly she stood up, a look of determination on her face, and walked towards the doorway.

"Where are you going?" Travis asked.

"I'll be right back," she said over her shoulder.

Travis could hear her poking around in her bookcases.

"*Aha!*" he heard her exclaim.

She came back into the kitchen, thumping the book on her hand. "I knew Miss Marple would have been through that," she said, setting the book down so Travis could read the cover. It was *The Moving Finger*, by Agatha Christie.

"This is about a drunk driver?" Travis asked.

"No," his grandmother smiled. "But it *is* about catching a murderer when there is absolutely no evidence and the criminal is considered one of the most upstanding citizens in town."

Travis grabbed at the book, turning the pages, fast. "How do they catch him?" he asked.

"Miss Marple," said his grandmother, "sets a brilliant trap."

Travis finished the book in three nights, reading until his mother called for him to turn out his lights. He was fascinated, and frightened.

Miss Marple had indeed encountered a similar situation. A body turns up, and no one – no one but Miss Marple – suspects foul play. There is no evidence. There is only her own suspicion that one of the village's best-known and most-respected citizens is hiding something. She sets an ingenious trap, and it works perfectly.

There was a passage in the final chapter of *The Moving Finger* that Travis read twice. A man is criticizing Miss Marple for having put them all in danger:

> "My dear young man," Miss Marple had answered. "*Something* had to be done. There was no evidence against this very clever and unscrupulous man. I needed someone to help me, someone of high courage and good brains. I found the person I needed."
>
> "It was very dangerous for her."
>
> "Yes, it was dangerous, but we are not put into this world . . . to avoid danger when an innocent person's life is at stake. You understand me?"

Travis understood. Now he needed "someone of high courage and good brains."

And he knew just the person to turn to.

16

"**N**o way!"

Travis had expected this response from Nish. He knew his plan was the stuff of books, not real life, but they had no choice.

"Maybe we can get him to confess," argued Travis. "It works in books."

"Books are stupid," said Nish.

"You're stupid," replied Travis. He couldn't help thinking that maybe he should have gone somewhere else to find "someone of high courage and good brains."

"Tell me how it could possibly work, then," Nish said, "if you're so smart."

Travis half made the plan up as he went along, hoping that once it was all said, it might somehow make sense.

If the trap was going to have any chance, Dickens would have to be in his car and he would have to be drunk again.

But Nish's questions were only beginning. How would they know Mr. Dickens was drunk again and driving?

Well, they'd have to be lucky on that part, Travis admitted, but he felt there was a good chance.

How would they get him to stop?

Well, they'd have to trick him. Maybe get him to think he'd hit someone again.

How would he *think* he'd hit someone?

"Well . . . Fahd," said Travis.

"*What?*" said Nish.

"Fahd," Travis repeated. He'd had an idea. A sudden, flashing idea. Perhaps even a brilliant one. "Fahd can help us."

"*Absolutely no way!*" Nish shouted this time.

But no one was listening to Nish. The others – Fahd, Sarah, Andy, and Lars – had embraced Travis's idea immediately. Sarah came up with the idea of setting the trap along Cedar and River, exactly where the original accident had happened. Andy thought of the snowball. Lars was already trying to calculate the timing and wanted to do a few dry runs first. Fahd thought about how to set things up for the best effect.

Travis kept his doubts to himself. If he was wrong, if Mr. Dickens hadn't done it, it was going to be a huge waste of time. But they had to try.

Nish, on the other hand, had no problem expressing his doubts.

"*No way!*" he repeated.

"Oh, come on, Nish," said Sarah. "Only you can pull it off. You're the best moaner I ever heard."

Travis knew that Nish would never really turn down the starring role. Everything, in the end, would depend on him.

Nish closed his eyes tight, opened them, blinked, and chewed his lip. Finally he spoke.

"Okay, let's do it."

It took three evenings before the conditions were right for the Owls' daring plan.

Mr. Dickens's car had been found parked behind the bar down by River Street. It had snowed hard earlier in the day, and some of the streets had still not been ploughed. Most of the cars were snow-covered, and, just like the last time, some were being driven with "portholes" dug through the snow on the windshield, with no view at all through the rear window.

Lars had a large flashlight in his coat pocket. He and Sarah would stand watch and be able to signal from the far corner when Dickens turned onto Cedar on his way home. Andy and Travis were responsible for making the huge snowballs. Lars had timed a couple of trial runs, and now one was packed and ready at the top of the hill at the edge of the schoolyard. If they pushed off just as a car passed by the church, it would smack right into its side as it passed below the hill.

Fahd's job was toughest of all. He had to make Nish look like he'd just been hit by a car.

Fahd's mock-disaster training was key. He had become an expert on gory, slimy, bloody entrails and broken bones and missing eyes and caved-in skulls. For nearly a month, every day had been like Hallowe'en to Fahd. But his big test wouldn't be the mock disaster. It would be tonight.

"*He's ready!*" Fahd called up the hill.

Travis and Andy watched as Fahd attended to Nish, whose leg seemed set at a weird angle. It was bent all wrong, and he seemed to be shuffling along on his other leg. But then they realized: Nish had put both feet through one pant leg, the other, shattered one was phony.

They could barely make Nish out in the streetlight. But then, he hardly had a face any more. He had one eye knocked clear of its socket. It was hanging down his face, suspended by stringy flesh and bouncing off his cheek. He had a huge, black wound on his forehead. His mouth was bleeding, the teeth hanging out one side through a hole where his cheek should have been.

"You look awful!" Travis shouted down.

"I do?" Nish answered, pretending to be surprised. "Funny, I feel *great*."

"Hurry up!" snapped Fahd. "We can't have him see us."

"*The light!*" Andy shouted. Lars was flashing the signal.

"*Hurry!*" Fahd hissed. He grabbed Nish's "broken" leg and pulled him along by it, forcing Nish to hop to stay upright. They ducked into the nearest driveway, their heads down.

Travis and Andy got behind the giant snowball. They were well out of sight, and could look around to see what was coming.

A snow-covered car was weaving down Cedar. Only half the windshield had been cleaned, and the car was drifting from side to side. From behind, the flashlight signalled again – confirmation from Lars that it was Mr. Dickens, for sure.

"I hope this works," said Andy as he leaned against the huge snowball.

"*It has to!*" said Travis.

Travis watched, his heart pounding. The car passed by the last of the houses, the church manse, the church itself, the church drive . . .

"*Now!*"

The two boys heaved with all their might. The huge snowball groaned, and began to move.

"*Push!*" Travis called. Andy grunted loudly, and the ball rolled. It was off, gaining speed.

Travis's heart skipped a beat. The car fishtailed slightly, then straightened. The snowball rolled down and up slightly at the bank, then flew out into the air.

He has to see it! Travis said to himself.

It's going to miss! was his next thought.

But Travis's imagination was also airborne, moving faster than the giant snowball. It seemed as if the ball was hanging in midair. It seemed as if the car was stopped. The ball hanging, the car frozen – and nothing but his own hammering heart to mark the passage of time.

"*Perfect!*" Andy whispered.

And it was, too. With an enormous *whomp!* the snowball hit squarely against the passenger door.

The car lurched violently to the side. Whether it was the force of the snowball or Mr. Dickens's frightened reaction, Travis couldn't tell, but the big Chevrolet swung against the far bank and came to a stop in deep snow.

"*C'mon, Nish! Move it!*"

The voice was Fahd's. Travis could hear the fear it contained; Fahd was nearly hysterical.

From the near driveway, two small figures hurried out, the one in front straining ahead, the one behind hopping madly.

"*Hold your horses!*" Nish hissed. "*I don't want my makeup to run!*"

Travis couldn't help himself. He started to giggle. He felt Andy grab his elbow, pulling him down out of sight.

Travis could see Fahd, the perfectionist, laying Nish out in exactly the position he wanted. It seemed almost comic – if it weren't so dangerous! He wondered if they'd make it in time.

A door opened on the Chevrolet. Greenish light spilled out onto the street. It was the passenger door, as the driver's door was now hard against the far bank. A large figure was struggling to get out of the car. He was wearing a dark coat. And a tuque.

Travis shivered. He had seen that same figure before, and in this very spot.

"*Damn it all t' hell!*" a voice was cursing.

Fahd was already away, scrambling back up the near driveway. Travis looked up the street. He thought he saw two small figures crouching down as they hurried along. It would be Sarah and Lars.

Now it was all up to Nish.

Travis shut his eyes: *For Data, Nish, for Data . . .*

The moaning began soft and low.

"Ohhhhhhhhhhhhhhhhhhhhhhhhhhh . . .

"OHHHHHHH . . . Owwwwww.

"*H-h-h-help me! Help . . . mmeee!*

"OWWWWWWWW!"

The figure was out of the car now and standing on the hard-packed snow of the street.

"*Wha' the hell!*" he muttered.

He took a couple of steps forward, slipped and went down on one knee. He cursed angrily.

Nish moaned again, softly: "Ohhhhhh . . . Ohhhhhhhh . . ."

The man regained his footing and stepped forward, uneasily.

"*H-h-h-help me! Help . . . mmeee!*" wailed Nish.

"*Oh, goodness, no . . . no . . . no!*" the man said. He came closer, close enough to see the twisted leg, close enough, perhaps, to see the smashed head of poor Nish, dying in the street.

"*Oh, Lord, no – this can't be happening! Why me?*"

Why me? Travis thought. This man is standing there feeling sorry for *himself* while he's already put one kid in hospital and another is bleeding to death in front of his very eyes.

The man came even closer, close enough to lean down and touch Nish, if he wanted.

Nish was silent. *Dead* silent!

The driver seemed to stand, staring, for the longest time. He didn't reach out for Nish. He didn't lean down.

Good! thought Travis. If he gets too close, he might see it's a trick. And if he finds out it's a trick, Nish might just as well be dead.

The man seemed to lean forward a little, perhaps about to bend down and help, but then he stepped back, stumbled, and appeared to stare in new horror at poor Nish, lying broken and bloody in the snow.

Nish picked his moment well: "*H-h-h-help me! Help . . . mmeee!*"

But the man couldn't do it. The urge to save himself was stronger than the urge to help. He turned, slipping again to one knee, and with another curse got up and bolted for his car.

"*What do we do now?*" hissed Andy.

"*I don't know.*"

The man slipped and slid and cursed his way to the passenger door of the Chevrolet, ripped the door open, and jumped back in. The engine was still running.

He put the car in gear and slammed down on the gas. The car bucked, then sank into the snowbank some more.

He put it in reverse and hit the gas again. The car jumped but only settled in deeper.

He rammed the transmission from reverse to forward, to reverse again, back and forth, the car bucking like a horse but unable to spring free of the deep snow.

The door flew open again, and the man spilled out, swearing. "*Damn it all to hell! . . . Damn it . . . damn it . . . damn it! Why me?*"

"*Drunk as a skunk!*" Andy said, almost under his breath.

The man had no intention of going back to help Nish. He slammed the door and began to stumble down the street, slipping and sliding, lurching his way home, trying to run away from what he had done – for the second time.

"*He's getting away!*" Fahd cried as he came out from behind his snowbank.

Nish was sitting up, watching him go.

"It doesn't matter," Travis said as he and Andy scrambled down towards them.

"Whatdya mean it doesn't matter?" Nish asked, trying to yank off his "broken" leg. "The guy who did this to me should go to jail!"

"It doesn't matter," said Travis, "because we have his car."

17

"I see," said Mr. Lindsay into the telephone. "Thank you very much, then . . . Yes, I will . . . Goodbye."

Travis's father hung up the phone. He took a sip from his coffee and stared out the window towards the bird feeder, which was alive with chickadees fighting over sunflower seeds.

"*Well?*" Mrs. Lindsay said, waiting.

Mr. Lindsay turned quickly, almost as if he were snapping back into reality.

"That was the police," he said slowly. "There's been a development in the hit-and-run incident."

"What?"

It seemed Mr. Lindsay didn't even want to say at first. He shook his head. "It was Tony Dickens."

"Tony *Dickens* was the one who hit Data?"

"Apparently. Funny, I always thought he was a first-class person."

"Would you like a list of the 'respectable' people who have been caught drinking and driving?" said Mrs. Lindsay. "Let alone a list of those who *haven't* been caught?"

"I know, I know. It's just that he was always so good with kids. I backed him for the presidency of the hockey association one year, you know."

"You can never tell what people are really like," Mrs. Lindsay said. "How did they catch him, anyway?"

"The police found his car ditched along Cedar. Called in at his house and he was sitting in his kitchen, crying. Confessed it all right there and then, without their even saying a word to him."

"A guilty conscience, I guess."

"Guilty's hardly the word for it," said Mr. Lindsay. "Kept claiming he'd hit *two* kids, not one."

Mrs. Lindsay went back to her magazine. "Well, hard drink will do that to you, won't it?"

Mr. Lindsay was again looking out the window. The chickadees fluttered wildly as a squirrel dropped down onto the feeder.

"I guess."

Travis Lindsay, sitting quietly over a bowl of Cheerios, could barely conceal his smile as he bit into another spoonful.

18

Travis had never felt such electricity in the Tamarack Arena. There must have been two thousand fans jammed into the stands this Sunday afternoon, and the cheering had started the moment the first of the Maple Leafs Legends had stepped out onto the ice.

"*Lanny McDonald!*" Fahd had called.

It was indeed – hair a bit thinner than in his picture on the hockey card, but his moustache still red and thick as a broom.

"*Frank Mahovlich!*" Jesse shouted.

And after Mahovlich, Darryl Sittler . . . Eddie Shack . . . Paul Henderson . . .

"Where's Muck?" Travis asked, straining to see.

"There," said Sarah, pointing.

But Muck didn't look like Muck. He was wearing full equipment, and a beautiful Maple Leafs Legends sweater. Travis noticed the number first – 6, same as Data – and then the name sewn over the number: Munro.

Out on the ice surface, Muck looked smaller than some of

the other players, but his passes were the same as the rest of the Legends': crisp, hard, and perfectly tape to tape.

The Flying Fathers were hilarious. Perhaps this was *called* a hockey game, but it didn't always seem like one. When Lanny McDonald scored the first goal of the game, the Flying Fathers held a ceremony at centre ice where they made Lanny kneel, and then "blessed" him with a cream pie straight in the face.

The crowd loved it. The best of the Flying Fathers, perhaps the best skater on the ice, pulled a trick that had Travis laughing so hard his stomach hurt. At the face-off the referee only faked dropping the puck, and instead the Father dropped his own puck, which he'd hidden in his glove. It looked exactly like a normal face-off, except that this puck was attached by fishing line to the player's stick.

He took off up the ice, stickhandling so wildly it seemed the puck would shoot off into the stands. But each time it came back, perfectly, to the blade of his stick. He went around every laughing, staggering NHLer, Muck included, and then tossed his stick – puck included – into the NHL net. The red light came on. Tie game.

The Legends protested, but it was useless. The Fathers played with illegal sticks and even brought out illegal players – including, at one point, their horse! With one of the Fathers holding onto its tail, it galloped down the ice, clearing the track, and the Father simply threw the puck into the net.

In the final period, however, they all settled down to a real game of hockey.

Perhaps it was a little slower than an NHL game, but the skill shone through: the passes, the quick, hard, accurate shots, the fine little plays that would instantly leave a man open, with only the goaltender between him and the net.

Halfway through the third, the Owls started up a chant.

"*Muck . . . Muck . . . Muck . . . MUCK!*"

Soon much of the crowd had joined in.

"*Muck . . . Muck . . . Muck . . . MUCK!*"

There was no doubt the Screech Owls' coach heard, but no way was he going to show he had heard. He was on Paul Henderson's line, just as they had been as teenagers so many years before, and while Henderson could still fly down the ice, it was apparent to all who were watching that Muck's bad leg was holding him back.

When Henderson's line was off for a shift, Mr. Dillinger made his way over to Muck and unlaced the coach's skate and removed his pads. Mr. Dillinger had an aerosol can in his hand.

All the Owls could see what was happening. They'd seen it before in NHL games. Mr. Dillinger aimed the can and sprayed up and down Muck's bad leg, "freezing" it to reduce the pain. Muck was gritting his teeth and holding his bare leg out so Mr. Dillinger could cover it entirely.

Two shifts later, Henderson's line came back out, with Muck testing his leg cautiously on the ice. Travis could see that Muck was in real pain.

Partway through the shift, Paul Henderson darted back after a loose puck. No sooner had he picked it up than Muck was rapping his stick hard on the ice on the far side. Henderson passed hard and right on target, the puck cracking solidly onto Muck's blade and sticking.

Muck dug in, his gait slightly off as he gathered speed. He

neatly stepped around the first checker and then shifted into centre ice and bore down. He was over the Fathers' line, with two defencemen back, both back-pedalling and tightening the knot on Muck.

Muck slipped the puck ahead and jumped – *jumped* – clean through the gap between the two defenders, both of whom were laughing as they crashed together, nothing between them but air.

Muck wobbled slightly as he landed, but kept his footing. He still had the puck.

He wound up and snapped a shot, high and hard.

The goalie's glove hand whipped out, but like the defenders found nothing but air.

The puck rang off the crossbar – *and in!*

As the red light flashed on, the arena seemed to explode.

"ALLL RIGHHHT, MUCK!" Sarah screamed, leaping to her feet.

It turned out to be the winning goal, as if anyone really cared. The crowd was already on its feet, screaming and cheering as the final seconds wound down and the horn sounded. Even before the referee blew his final whistle, the Flying Fathers and the Maple Leafs Legends were shaking hands and hugging each other.

Travis watched Muck. The Owls' coach was grinning from ear to ear. They were slapping him on the back.

Muck seemed concerned about something else, though. He was looking for Paul Henderson. And when he found him talking to the Flying Fathers' goaltender, Muck skated over and held his own stick out towards his old friend.

Paul Henderson laughed and happily exchanged sticks with Muck.

So, Travis thought to himself, there was a little bit of the kid in Muck Munro. He was after a souvenir.

"Let's go," Sarah said, yanking on Travis's jacket sleeve.

Travis turned, about to ask, "Where?"

"We're on next," Sarah said. "We should already be dressed."

19

can go."

The Screech Owls had dressed without Muck, who was still changing with the Legends. The dressing room was silent but for the determined voice of Wayne Nishikawa, injured defenceman.

"*I can go*," he repeated.

No one else spoke. Mr. Dillinger had gone off to fill his water bottles.

Travis figured, as captain, it was his duty to take control of the situation.

"You can't," Travis said gently. "Your wrist."

But Nish was already almost dressed.

"I've got my new cast," he said.

"What if you get hit?" Sarah asked. There was genuine concern in her voice.

Nish looked up, smiled. "I've got a secret weapon."

No one asked what.

Nish dug into a side pocket of his equipment bag and pulled out a spray can — the same can Mr. Dillinger had sprayed on Muck's bad leg.

Freezing.

"You *can't!*" Sarah said.

"Mind your own business," Nish said. "I've already sprayed my arm once. I'll do it again between periods."

"Where'd you get that?" Travis asked.

"It was on the Legends' bench at the end of the game. Nobody was around, so I . . . borrowed it. I'll put it back after our game."

"You shouldn't," Sarah warned.

"Maybe not," Nish smiled. "But I already did — so let's get out there."

Travis knew there was no use arguing.

Travis led the Owls out onto the fresh ice surface, stunned, as he stepped onto the ice, to realize that the huge crowd that had turned out for the big game had stayed! For an ordinary peewee regular-season game!

He checked the crowd as he waited for his turn to shoot. He could see his parents and grandparents. His grandmother gave him the thumbs-up. He wondered if she had guessed about the trap they had set for Mr. Dickens.

He scanned the seats on the other side and saw that a section had been set aside for some older men, some of them vaguely familiar. And then he realized:

That moustache could only belong to Lanny McDonald!

And there was Paul Henderson! And the rest of the Maple Leafs Legends! And the Flying Fathers!

They had all stayed to see the Owls play!

The puck came out to Travis and he kicked it easily up onto his stick blade. Suddenly, there was no noise, just the flick of his skates. He saw Jenny come out, her catching glove yapping at him, her pads skittering as she moved.

He deked once, moved to the outside, and shot high and hard.

Crossbar!

Travis turned and looked up into the crowd. Lanny McDonald pumped a fist at him. *He knew!* Lanny knew! An NHLer knew that there was nothing so sweet as the sound of a puck on the crossbar — so long as it wasn't in a game!

The public-address system crackled. There would be a ceremonial face-off. Travis wondered who it would be to drop the puck. Maybe Paul Henderson himself. That was probably why all the hockey heroes had stayed. He stood by Sarah, waiting for a name.

But there was none. The public-address system was silent.

Then all around him the crowd began to rise. All through the arena there was the sound of people getting to their feet. And with it came the sound of applause. A few began clapping at first, and then dozens, then hundreds — the sound growing as loud as thunder.

Travis followed the direction of the crowd's stares.

The Zamboni entrance was open. Muck was there, and Muck's big hands were on a wheelchair.

And in the chair was Data!

The clapping became a roar as the crowd realized what was going on.

Muck pushed out and the chair rolled onto the ice. Data slowly raised the one arm he could move. He had his Screech Owls jacket on. He was smiling.

Travis turned to look at his teammates. Sarah was bawling, her glove uselessly wiping at the huge tears dropping off her cheek.

Muck rolled Data along the blueline, passing by each Owl, and Data reached out to tap the gloves of each player. Muck stopped, and stared hard at Nish before moving ahead down the line, shaking his head.

When they got to Travis, Data held his hand up for Muck to stop again.

Data looked up and smiled a bit crookedly. "I know what you did," he said. "Thanks."

Travis tried to speak, but he couldn't. What could he say? It was his fault, after all, wasn't it? It was his idea to go "hitching." If he'd never done that, Data would be standing on the blueline instead of sitting in a wheelchair.

Muck pushed Data ahead, but not before taking one quick look at his captain. Muck's eyes seemed to be begging an explanation. But he would never get one.

Sarah and the Orillia captain took the ceremonial face-off. Sarah picked up the puck and presented it to Data with a kiss on the cheek and a long hug. Travis could see that she was still crying. And she didn't seem to care who knew.

20

I f the Owls had ever played a greater game, Travis couldn't remember when. Every player seemed at the top of his or her game.

Data had been given a special place between Muck and Mr. Dillinger behind the bench and he cheered as loudly as he could. Muck never said a word. Not to Nish about his arm. Not to Travis about what Data had said. But Travis wondered how much Muck knew.

Sarah sent Dmitri in on a breakaway halfway through the first period for the first goal, then scored herself on a beautiful backhand deke. Travis got the third, and Wilson the fourth.

Late in the final period, with the Owls up 4–1, Travis noticed Nish wincing.

"You okay?"

"I'm fine."

But Travis knew the freezing was wearing off. Nish could barely hold his stick, but he wouldn't quit.

Sarah won the face-off and dropped the puck to Wilson, who spun back and bounced a pass off the backboards onto Nish's stick.

Nish started to rush. He moved out slowly at first, then jumped across the blueline, picking up speed.

Sarah was straight up centre, expecting the pass. But Nish held on. He carried in over the Orillia blueline and circled. He faked a pass to Travis, stepped into the slot, drew back his stick, and pounded the puck as hard as he could.

It almost went through the back of the net! Travis, circling at the side of the net, watched the twine spring and then shoot the puck back out as fast as it had come in.

The whistle blew; the referee was signalling a goal.

Nish was already halfway to the bench, crouching over to cradle his arm.

"Get – me – the – puck," he said to Travis, grunting with the effort.

Travis skated to the linesman, who was coming back with the puck. "Don't blame him," the linesman said as he handed it over. "Hardest shot I ever saw in peewee."

Travis skated back to the bench. He held the puck out towards Nish, who was bent double, holding his arm. Nish looked up, shook his head.

"For – Data," he said. "Give – it – to – him."

Travis skated further down the bench and handed it to Data. Data took the puck in his good hand as if it were an Olympic gold medal.

Muck shook his head. "Nishikawa can play this game when he wants to," he said.

"Too bad we can't freeze his brain, too," Sarah said under her breath.

The Screech Owls had won their rematch. When the final horn blew, the Orillia team lined up and shook hands, and then, in a move Travis had to admire, they skated to the Screech Owls' bench, where they took turns tapping their gloves against Data's outstretched hand.

As Travis watched he realized Data was still holding on to Nish's puck. He had never let go.

There was still one small matter of unfinished business. Before the Zamboni came out, the doors nearest the stands opened and all the Maple Leafs Legends and Flying Fathers came down onto the ice to an enormous cheer from the crowd.

Paul Henderson and Frank Mahovlich were carrying a huge rectangle of cardboard, but none of the peewee players on the ice could see what was on it. Muck and Mr. Dillinger were wheeling Data out of the home bench and onto the ice, where the photographers were waiting.

Mr. Dillinger pushed Data up to centre ice, where, with a grand flourish, Paul Henderson and Frank Mahovlich turned the big cardboard rectangle around for everyone to see.

It was a giant cheque, made out to something called The Larry Ulmar Foundation.

The amount was for thirty thousand dollars.

Again the crowd roared its approval.

Travis looked back towards the bench and saw that Muck was leaning over and pulling a stick free. It was the one he'd traded with Paul Henderson.

Muck walked cautiously back over the ice, clearly trying not to limp too badly. He went over to Data and laid the stick across his lap. Data looked down at it, carefully turning the stick over and over with his one good hand.

It had been signed by all the Maple Leafs Legends and the Flying Fathers!

So that was it, Travis thought. Muck didn't want a souvenir for himself. He wanted something special for Data, something other than money that would remind him of his special day.

Travis wondered if Muck had signed it too. He hoped so. Muck had belonged with the Legends – this day, anyway.

Data took the stick and waved it at the crowd. Everyone cheered.

With Muck's help, Data turned the stick over so he could hold the blade, and he then – very slowly, with some difficulty – lifted the stick so the handle was pointing directly at his team.

It was Data's salute to the Screech Owls, *his* team forever.

THE END

Roy MacGregor has been involved in hockey all his life. Growing up in Huntsville, Ontario, he competed for several years against a kid named Bobby Orr, who was playing in nearby Parry Sound. He later returned to the game when he and his family settled in Ottawa, where he worked for the *Ottawa Citizen* and became the Southam National Sports Columnist. He still plays old-timers hockey and was a minor-hockey coach for more than a decade.

Roy MacGregor is the author of several classics in the literature of hockey. *Home Game* (written with Ken Dryden) and *The Home Team* (nominated for the Governor General's Award for Non-fiction) were both No. 1 national bestsellers. He has also written the game's best-known novel, *The Last Season*. His most recent non-fiction hockey book is *A Loonie for Luck*, the true story of the famous good-luck charm that inspired Canada's men and women to win hockey gold at the Salt Lake City Winter Olympics. His other books include *Road Games*, *The Seven A.M. Practice*, *A Life in the Bush*, and *Escape*.

Roy MacGregor is currently a columnist for the *Globe and Mail*. He lives in Kanata, Ontario, with his wife, Ellen. They have four children, Kerry, Christine, Jocelyn, and Gordon.

You can talk to Roy MacGregor at **www.screechowls.com**